C000164498

THE DARK SHAH

A Jayne Robinson Thriller, Book 2

ANDREW TURPIN

The Write Direction Publishing

First published in the UK in 2021 by The Write Direction Publishing, St. Albans, UK.

The Dark Shah paperback edition

ISBN: 9781788750240

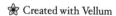 Created with Vellum

WELCOME TO THE JAYNE ROBINSON SERIES!

Thank you for purchasing *The Dark Shah* — I hope you enjoy it!

This is the second in the series of thrillers that features **Jayne Robinson**, formerly of the British Secret Intelligence Service (the SIS, or as it is often known, MI6) and now an independent investigator. She has strong connections with both the CIA and MI6 and finds herself conducting deniable operations on behalf of both services.

The **Jayne Robinson** thriller series is my second series and so far comprises the following:

1. The Kremlin's Vote
2. The Dark Shah
3. The Confessor
4. The Queen's Pawn (due to be published late 2022)

My first series, in which Jayne also appears regularly, features **Joe Johnson**, a former CIA officer and war crimes investigator. The Joe Johnson books so far comprise:

0. Prequel: *The Afghan*
1. The Last Nazi
2. The Old Bridge
3. Bandit Country
4. Stalin's Final Sting
5. The Nazi's Son
6. The Black Sea

If you enjoy this book, I would like to keep in touch. This is not always easy, as I usually only publish a couple of books a year and there are many authors and books out there. So the best way is for you to be on my Readers Group email list. I can then send you updates on the next book, plus occasional special offers.

If you would like to join my Readers Group and receive the email updates, I will send you, **FREE** of charge, the ebook version of *The Afghan*. It forms a prequel to this series and to the Joe Johnson series, and normally sells at $4.99/£3.99 (paperback $11.99/£9.99).

The Afghan is set in 1988 when Jayne was still with MI6 and Joe Johnson was still a CIA officer. Most of the action takes place in Pakistan, Afghanistan and Washington, DC.

To sign up for the Readers Group and get your free copy of *The Afghan*, go to the following web page:

https://bookhip.com/RJGFPAW

If you only like paperbacks, you can still just sign up for the email list at the above link to get news of my books and forthcoming new releases. A paperback version of *The Afghan* and all my books is for sale at my website, where you will find large discounts on bundles of my books. I can currently ship to the US and UK:

https://www.andrewturpin.com/shop/

Or if you live outside the US and UK you can buy them at Amazon.

Andrew Turpin, St. Albans, UK.

DEDICATION

For my brother, Adrian—thanks for all the encouragement!

"Iran doesn't need one centrifuge. Canada has nuclear energy. Spain has nuclear energy. Switzerland has nuclear energy, and they don't enrich uranium. You don't need to enrich uranium in order to use nuclear energy. You enrich uranium in order to produce a bomb."

Naftali Bennett, Israeli politician and current prime minister.

PROLOGUE

Monday, April 4, 2016
Samar gas platform, offshore from Tel Aviv, Israel

The US secretary of state, Paul Farrar, pushed his plastic protective glasses up his nose and climbed up onto the long speaker's soapbox that stood on the metal deck of the gas production platform, high above the sea.

He squinted a little in the bright sunshine, tugged his white safety helmet farther down over his eyes to ward off the glare, and glanced toward the Israeli coast, located seventeen miles to the east across the inky Mediterranean Sea.

A huge blue and white Star of David flag flapped gently in the sea breeze from its moorings on the tangled steel pipework behind him.

An even bigger flag had been stretched out across the helicopter landing pad as part of the welcome he and the Israeli foreign minister, Moshe Cohen, had received when they touched down.

Farrar waited until Cohen and Alexander Lowman, the

chief executive of the US-Israeli company Frontier Energy, which owned the platform, had joined him on the soapbox. All of them wore the obligatory personal protective gear required on the gas platform, as did the crowd of gas company executives, engineers, and managers in front of him. There were safety helmets and ubiquitous orange or navy-blue protective coveralls everywhere he looked.

A few yards to Farrar's right stood two of his dark-suited Diplomatic Security Service officers. Another officer was behind the assembled gathering, while Cohen's bodyguard stood to the left.

Two TV cameramen, using handheld units, and two photographers stood near the security officers to the right, recording the proceedings. Behind them a small phalanx of selected journalists scribbled in their notebooks and tapped away on their phones.

Tucked away at the rear were two men who wore dark glasses and were doing their best to melt into the background. Farrar and Cohen knew who they were, but few others did. One was Eli Elazar, the director, or *ramsad*, of the Mossad, Israel's foreign intelligence service. The other was Elazar's guest, Mark Nicklin-Donovan, director of operations and deputy chief at Britain's Secret Intelligence Service, otherwise known as MI6, who was in Israel for a series of meetings.

The visit to Israel and the Samar gas platform was of great significance for Farrar. After all, Frontier Energy was a US-controlled business that deserved some recognition from the government for its achievement in building one of the largest symbols of American enterprise and investment in the region. The enormous structure on which he now stood, which soared 180 feet above the sea, had been largely built in Texas, then floated across the Atlantic on a huge barge.

This trip, postponed on several occasions, had been in

Farrar's calendar for several months without ever being confirmed.

But then in December, Israel's near neighbor and archenemy, Iran, had at last signed an international deal to halt work to build nuclear weapons. Under the deal, Iran had committed to ensuring its nuclear development program was focused only on electricity production—not on nuclear weapons. It promised to produce only low-grade uranium of around 4 percent purity in its enrichment program, not the 90 percent or more required for nuclear weapons.

Only at that point was it perceived that the threat to Israel from Iran and its proxy militant arm, Hezbollah, had diminished sufficiently to give the trip the green light.

High overhead, two Israeli Air Force fighter aircraft circled the platform at a distance that ensured the gathering wouldn't be disrupted by the noise from their jet engines. Three navy patrol boats were also carrying out what was a clearly choreographed set of maneuvers in the surrounding waters. The Israelis, hit hard and often during their ongoing conflicts with neighboring states, were taking no chances, despite the agreement with Iran.

Apart from the gas platform trip, Farrar had more formal meetings with Cohen scheduled for later that day once they had returned to Tel Aviv, followed by a dinner in Jerusalem in the evening.

Cohen, a slim, wiry man in his fifties, whose hooked nose and gimlet eyes were just as hawkish as his political views toward Israel's enemies, stepped to a microphone on the platform, and the crowd in front of him became silent.

"This is a historic day, and I'm very pleased to be here to meet you all," Cohen said, his voice booming from loudspeakers. "As an Israeli, I had always felt that Moses did a poor job when he dragged our ancestors for forty years through the desert, only to bring us to the one place in the Middle East that had no oil or gas. Or so we—"

He stopped because his joke was greeted with loud laughter and applause by the engineers standing in front of him. Farrar joined in, although it certainly wasn't a quip he would have dared to make as an outsider.

"Or so we thought," Cohen continued. "No gas, that is, until Frontier Energy arrived on the scene. We have watched Frontier develop its plans, carry out exploratory drilling work, strike gas in rock and sand at an incredible five thousand meters below sea level, and then build this highly complex production platform to deliver that gas to the people of Israel. I'm proud that the fuel is now flowing through these pipes behind me, and as you know, it will power our homes and businesses for decades to come. I would like to congratulate Alexander and all of you for your monumental achievement."

Cohen went on to talk about the political, technical, and financial challenges that had been overcome and then invited Farrar to say a few words.

"Yours must be the most closely guarded gas molecules in the world," Farrar began, indicating upward to the fighter aircraft. To his relief, the audience laughed again, breaking the ice and allowing him to relax. Despite years of making speeches and presentations, he always felt slightly tense at the beginning.

"I am proud that the United States can stand alongside its long-term ally Israel and help achieve something quite remarkable. The story of gas production here is one of perseverance and persistence over many years in the face of seemingly insurmountable problems—a bit like the story of Moses." There was more applause and laughter from the audience.

"The people of Israel know what it means to be a free

people—just as we do in the United States—and self-reliance in terms of energy supplies is an important part of that."

Farrar wound up his short talk with a few more serious comments about his hopes for peace in the Middle East and the importance of the nuclear deal with Iran. Although those issues were not directly related to the gas platform development, he felt it was important to make his point about the wider political context while the television cameras were on him and journalists were paying attention.

"We all know that in the past, Iran has sworn to wipe both Israel and the United States from the face of the earth," Farrar said. "Let's hope that attitude is now something that remains firmly in the past."

He gave way to Lowman, who made a short speech thanking his colleagues for their hard work and the government of Israel for its support and help before surrendering the stage back to Cohen to conclude the event.

Twenty minutes later, waiters began to serve glasses of chilled orange juice, because the platform was an alcohol-free environment on the platform, and everyone began to relax. A number of the engineers came up to shake Farrar's hand, some of them commenting that it was a rare opportunity for them to speak to such a senior US cabinet member.

At the back, the two intelligence chiefs, Elazar and Nicklin-Donovan, were engaged in an intense discussion. Neither had taken a drink from the waiters.

Farrar noticed the head of his security detail talking animatedly into his cell phone. One of his colleagues was also in a vigorous discussion with Cohen's bodyguard. Farrar's attention sharpened.

Seconds later, Farrar heard the sound of running footsteps behind him on the metal platform. He turned to see four of the gas company's security guards bearing down on the platform where he, Cohen, and Lowman still stood.

At the same time, Farrar noticed that one of the Israeli fighter aircraft, which had been circling high above them, had gone into a steep dive and was approaching the platform at a much lower altitude.

What the hell is going on? Farrar thought.

The guards arrived, the man in the lead clearly stressed. As he approached Lowman, a loud siren suddenly blasted out from nearby, causing Farrar to jump slightly. Then the unmistakable chatter of machine gun fire erupted from somewhere over on the western side of the platform.

Farrar caught sight of the fighter aircraft again, now flying horizontally and very low on that side of the platform.

A jolt ran through the secretary of state, flipping his stomach over.

"Sir," the guard said, raising his voice above the siren. "You all need to go inside to the security room. *Now*. Come this way, all of you, quick as you can."

The guard beckoned them toward a steel staircase between two sets of pipework that ran vertically through the platform.

Cohen and Lowman reacted first and Farrar followed immediately.

He had taken no more than two steps after them when there was a whooshing sound to his right on the western side of the platform, then a metallic bang, followed by an enormous explosion that threw him instantly onto his back.

Farrar's head hit the metal decking of the gas platform, and he felt a sharp pain in his right shoulder, where he had been struck hard by a fast-moving object.

After becoming vaguely aware of debris and bodies flying past him, accompanied by shouts and screams, he put his left hand to his right shoulder, where his suit and shirt were torn and from which the pain had now become unbearable. He raised his hand to see it was covered in blood.

A few feet to his left, Farrar saw the head of his security detail lying on his front, trying to raise his head, also clearly injured. Just beyond him, the prone figure of the Israeli defense minister lay next to a metal safety railing.

"Are you all right, sir?" the security guard gasped.

Black smoke was now billowing from the side of the gas platform, no more than twenty yards away.

Farrar attempted to raise himself a little on his uninjured left elbow but struggled to do so. He tried to speak in answer to his security chief's question but couldn't. He then tried to shake his head but again found it difficult to make his body do as he wished.

There came another enormous explosion from somewhere ahead of him that threw his raised head backward, and once again, it struck the metal walkway.

Somehow he managed to roll over onto his stomach, from where he raised himself into a crawling position, his damaged right shoulder screaming at him in agony.

Then Farrar blacked out.

PART ONE

CHAPTER ONE

Monday, April 4, 2016
  Jerusalem

The pine trees and the tall, shuttered houses built from large limestone blocks that stood on both sides of Negba Street in central Jerusalem reminded Jayne Robinson of the elegant Roman towns in southern France that she had often visited in her youth.

But as she gazed down the narrow lane from her vantage point beneath an awning on an expansive fourth-floor terrace, the differences between here and Provence were clear. Most notably, here metal bars covering triple-glazed, supposedly bomb-proof glass in most of the windows.

Her host, Avi Shiloah, who sat next to her, crushed the remains of his Camel cigarette in a terracotta ashtray that was full of stubs. Most of them had been smoked right down to the filter. He pushed his black-rimmed sunglasses up onto his slightly receding mat of neatly cropped, wiry, graying black hair.

"Coffee or a glass of wine?" Shiloah asked in his thickly accented English. "I can't drink, as I have to go back to the office. But feel free to have a glass."

"I'll have a coffee," Jayne said. "But tell me, what reds would you recommend? I'd like to buy a couple of bottles."

Shiloah spread his hands wide. "Jezreel Valley and Tabor are excellent. Try the Golan Heights Winery. Their cabernet sauvignon. I think it's called Yarden, if you can find a bottle."

He then picked up a cafetière, filled Jayne's cup with a thick, dark coffee, and pushed the pot across the table toward Jayne's partner, Joe Johnson, who sat on the other side of the table with the fourth person present, the shaven-headed David Zahavi, who was hiding impassively behind his shades.

"You two can serve yourselves," Shiloah said. "Unless you'd like wine, Joe?"

Joe shook his head. "I need some caffeine."

The temperature had climbed into the mid-seventies, and the sun was beating down from a cloudless spring sky. A pair of olive trees in large pots next to the awning provided additional shade.

"Good to see you two have gotten back together," Shiloah growled in a low baritone, glancing first at Joe, then at Jayne. "What took you so long? David and I thought it would happen—eventually. I remember thinking it during that operation in Buenos Aires. I believe it was 1996."

Jayne noticed he was looking her up and down, a faint smile on his face.

"I hadn't been there long," she said. "Joe turned up looking for some Nazi officer. There was nothing going on between us then—Joe was happily married."

She remembered the meeting well. At the time, Jayne had been in the Argentine capital at the start of a four-year posting for MI6. Meanwhile Joe, who had left the CIA and was working for the Office of Special Investigations—a Nazi-hunting unit within the US Department of Justice—had visited briefly on a work trip.

They had both met in Buenos Aires for a drink with Shiloah, who was then still a fairly junior officer with the Mossad, and his colleague Zahavi. It was something of a reunion for the four of them, who had first gotten to know each other in 1988 when they were all working in Islamabad for their respective intelligence agencies.

Jayne had last seen Shiloah just over five years earlier in London, by which stage he had clawed his way up the ladder to become the Mossad's head of operations.

Since then, he had gone even further. While keeping his role as head of operations, he had also been elevated to be one of two deputy directors of the entire service: joint number two to the *ramsad*. Zahavi was his right-hand man and deputy head of operations. It was a meteoric rise for both of them.

Meanwhile, both Jayne and Johnson were self-employed investigators who had worked together for the past several years. A couple of years earlier, and almost a decade after Joe's wife had died of cancer, they had become more than just work colleagues when they finally rekindled the affair they once briefly enjoyed in Islamabad in the late 1980s.

"I wish I had time to offer you lunch," Shiloah said, glancing at his watch, "but David and I have an Iran strategy group meeting this afternoon. We have just had the all clear from the PM for a couple of operations and the office is busy, partly because we have so many honored guests in town."

They had just been discussing the VIP list for a trip orga-nized by Israel's foreign ministry that was taking place on the flagship Samar offshore gas platform. The US secretary of state, Paul Farrar, was a guest of Moshe Cohen, the Israeli foreign minister. And none other than Jayne's former boss at Britain's MI6, Mark Nicklin-Donovan, had been invited for discussions about the Middle East security situation by the Mossad's director, Eli Elazar, who was Shiloah's boss.

"They'll all be back in the city this afternoon," Shiloah continued. "They've indicated they don't want any briefings from us, but I had better be in the office just in case they change their minds."

"Don't worry about lunch," Jayne said. "You're a busy man."

Shiloah had invited Jayne and Joe to his home in Jerusalem rather than the Mossad offices in Tel Aviv because he and Zahavi had been in the capital for a meeting with the Israeli prime minister, Yitzhak Katz. The PM's official residence, at Beit Aghion, on Smolenskin Street, was less than a mile away. He had carried out the daily intelligence briefing in place of Elazar, who was away on the gas platform.

Shiloah turned to Joe. "I will be raising a glass tonight to my father—he would have been ninety today. I will drink a toast to your mother as well. They were both heroes."

He and Joe had formed a bond in Islamabad after they had discovered that Shiloah's father and Joe's mother, a Polish Jew, had been incarcerated by Hitler's Nazis in the same concentration camp at Gross-Rosen during the Second World War. Both had somehow survived despite illness, severe malnutrition, and torture, and both had ended up living to a good age.

"I will do the same," Joe said.

"They somehow got through the first Holocaust, unlike many," Shiloah said. "It is our job to make sure there is not a second. On the surface, relations with Iran may seem to be a little better than they were. But underneath? Not so much. It's our main focus, make no mistake."

"I'm speaking about the Holocaust tonight," Joe said. He was due to give a lecture at the American embassy to an audience comprising academic researchers, which was the reason he and Jayne had come to Israel. The plan was to take a few days after the lecture to explore Jerusalem and then head north to the region around the Sea of Galilee.

"Perhaps the Iranians are finally accepting that blowing your country off the face of the earth with nukes might not be very productive," Joe continued.

Shiloah shook his head. "I doubt it. You can tell your audience not to sleep too comfortably in their beds. It will always be their goal to destroy us, no matter what deals they sign. My gut tells me they are still refining weapons-grade uranium at some hidden sites. Maybe it's going slower, but it's still happening. It's my job to find them."

There was a downbeat, weary note to his final sentence that caused Jayne to look across at him.

"I'm surprised you sleep comfortably in *your* bed," Jayne said.

Shiloah gave a thin smile. "Sleep is not something I have a problem with. It's a temporary escape from reality—from the threat of nuclear obliteration."

A tough reality, Jayne thought to herself. Israel was indeed a small country under serious threat from all sides.

Shiloah paused. "Anyway, I have peace of mind from knowing that we have right on our side."

Jayne decided that now was not the time to have a debate about the rights of Palestinians whose territories Israel had occupied in 1967 and had not relinquished.

"Aren't the nuclear inspectors getting better access now?" Jayne asked. The International Atomic Energy Agency, based in Vienna, had been allowed to regularly monitor all Iran's nuclear facilities under the deal signed in December.

"In theory, yes. But they are nuclear experts, not intelligence officers. We, in our circles, hear a different story. However, proving it is difficult. We need to keep at it—we can't rely on the IAEA inspectors."

Jayne sipped her coffee and looked over the red tiled rooftops, many of them with elevated balconies and decks like Shiloah's, invariably decorated with vines, creepers, and potted trees to provide shade. It seemed so idyllic and peaceful that she had to remind herself that Jerusalem's troubled Old City lay only a mile and a half away. Although beautiful and historic, a UNESCO World Heritage Site, it also remained the focus of intense religious, political, and military conflict between Israel and its neighbors.

Shiloah drained his coffee and picked up his cigarette lighter and pack of Camels from the table, then stood and put on a black leather jacket. "David, ready?"

His phone pinged loudly as a message arrived, and he removed it from his pocket to study the screen.

"*Shit*," Shiloah hissed. His genial expression had vanished.

He froze, staring at his phone, then burst into rapid Hebrew that was too fast for Jayne to understand. Zahavi replied, also in Hebrew, at a similar machine gun pace.

It was obvious that something serious had happened.

"What?" Jayne asked.

"The gas platform," Shiloah replied, switching back to English, his head shaking slowly. "Drone attack. They've blown the thing up. With all of them on it."

Jayne felt her stomach turn over. "Bloody hell. Who?"

"Most likely Hezbollah," Zahavi said. "How the hell did they get a drone through? There were extra air and sea patrols out there today. Anti-missile systems were all fully operational. It's a hell of a long flight there from the Lebanon border and even farther from Iran."

"Casualties?" Joe asked.

"Sounds like a lot, yes." Shiloah tipped his head back and closed his eyes momentarily. "My office is trying to get details."

Shiloah's phone pinged again, twice in succession. Zahavi was tapping on his phone, which had also pinged a couple of times.

Zahavi tapped at the screen. There was a pause as he frantically scrolled down the messages he had just received, shaking his head.

"Holy *shit*. Moshe Cohen's dead. So is Eli. My *God*."

Jayne felt a jolt run right up her spine and her scalp tighten.

Mark?

It was as if Shiloah had read her mind. He glanced up at Jayne. "Your guy, Mark. He's badly injured. So is Paul Farrar. They're helicoptering them to Tel Aviv."

Shiloah tapped rapidly on his screen, dialing a number, then placed the device to his ear as he strode rapidly across the terrace toward the stairs, Zahavi a couple of paces behind him.

"Get me the prime minister's office," he snapped when the call was answered.

* * *

Monday, April 4, 2016
El Arish, Sinai Peninsula, Egypt

The Toyota truck left a trail of dust flying high into the air as it rounded a group of trees and bounced down the steep hillside track toward a group of flat-roofed concrete warehouses at the rear of an industrial unit. From the back of the truck, which was covered by a taut waterproof canvas, came the persistent sound of metal poles rattling and clanging.

The bearded driver, Emad Madani, rubbed his hand across the top of his shaven head. He could hear cursing from the three men sitting in the back as they tried in vain to stop the poles from making such a noise.

Eventually, he reached the bottom of the hill and accelerated toward the farthest building. On arrival, he clicked a remote-control button in his cab that opened a heavy steel shutter door. Once the door had clanked open, he steered the truck inside, pulled up the handbrake, and turned off the engine.

"You can come out now," Emad called as he pressed the button on the remote control again, causing the shutter door to begin sliding down. He jumped out of the cab onto the cement floor of the warehouse, landing athletically on the balls of his feet. Once the door had closed again, he fastened two large padlocks to its base, one on each side, just to be sure.

The men in the back unzipped the cover and jumped to the ground.

"Get that launcher kit out and let's get it back in the cache," Emad said. He was slightly concerned that although the Egyptian security forces based in the area were chaotically organized and generally ineffective, they were unfortunately improving. It was possible they might turn up and carry out a random search of the buildings if he was extremely unlucky. They were highly unlikely to find his cache, though.

The three men began to carry what looked at first glance like a bunch of scaffolding poles from the back of the truck. They placed them at the rear of the building next to a rectangular metal drain cover that hid a concealed underground dugout.

They weren't scaffolding poles but rather the components of a launcher frame for Ababil drones, one of which he and his men had dispatched from the northern Sinai coast in the direction of the Samar gas platform an hour or so earlier.

They had launched it from a deserted piece of ground just west of the coastal city of El Arish. It had then flown ninety kilometers across the southeastern corner of the Mediterranean to the Samar gas platform, offshore from the Israeli coast.

Easy to assemble and take apart, the frame was about three meters long, similar to the drone itself. Emad had propelled it into the air using a simple single-use booster rocket that fell to earth once its fuel was used up. Once the drone was airborne, its own piston engine and twin-bladed rear propeller had taken it onward at about 270 kilometers an hour to its target, guided flawlessly by a GPS system.

Half an hour earlier, Emad had received a one-word text message from a burner cell phone inside Israel that confirmed the drone had successfully completed its journey.

Online news reports that Emad read on his cell phone told him the same. The explosion appeared to have caused huge damage and multiple casualties, although no more details were available yet.

The only disappointment was that the impact had apparently not caused the entire platform to explode as he had hoped. It must somehow have failed to fracture the gas supply pipelines that ran through it.

Never mind—the operation had largely succeeded. His fear had been that Israeli radar and missile detection systems would have spotted the drone and shot it down. That hadn't happened. With any luck, the Israeli foreign minister and the US secretary of state, who were both visiting the platform, would not have survived. That should soon become clear.

The payment that would now arrive in his bank account

was the equivalent of several years' salary for most of his countrymen.

The operation had been made easier to execute by the state of chaos that existed on the Sinai Peninsula. After the Egyptian coup of 2011, in which President Hosni Mubarak had been overthrown, security on the peninsula had been appalling for some considerable time. The intelligence services had been driven out, and the Egyptian military units stationed there were often unenthusiastic. As a result, Islamic militants, including al-Qaeda and Hamas terrorists, who entered Sinai via tunnels from the Gaza Strip, had used the territory as a base from which to launch attacks on neighboring Israel, particularly the Red Sea holiday resorts around Eilat.

Although in recent times there had been a lot more cooperation between Israeli intelligence and security forces and their Egyptian counterparts, there remained little serious threat to Emad and his men. They were not militants like the others but rather professional assassins, paid by the job rather than driven by ideology or politics. They had added an expertise with drones to their list of options for potential employers in the past couple of years—and they were very careful not to be compromised. Security was tight.

As soon as they had finished here, the four of them would travel back to Cairo, their main base. If they needed to leave the country, it would be done using scheduled airline flights and fake Egyptian passports.

They would likely be back for another operation within weeks, Emad guessed. He had three more drones hidden in a larger underground cellar in the neighboring building. It was a perfect base for strikes at Israel, and they had the option of moving into the Gaza Strip to carry them out, as the border and the tunnels into Gaza were less than forty-five kilometers away.

He took out his burner phone and tapped in a single short message in English: *Job completed. Leaving soon.*

Then he dispatched the message, removed the SIM card and battery from the phone, and put them in his backpack. It was time to leave as quickly as possible.

CHAPTER TWO

Monday, April 4, 2016
Tel Aviv

Six hours after she and Joe had left Avi Shiloah's house, the full extent of the disaster caused by the attack on the Samar offshore gas platform had become clear to Jayne.

When the news initially hit, Shiloah and Zahavi had driven off at speed, headed back to Mossad headquarters. Meanwhile Jayne and Joe had taken a cab from Jerusalem to their hotel, the Sheraton in Tel Aviv, where they had a seventh-floor room overlooking the beach across the street.

Looking out to sea to the west, Jayne could make out a long plume of black smoke on the horizon where the gas platform continued to burn.

She watched as a stream of military helicopters clattered overhead to and from the stricken facility. A gaggle of television news crews, presenters, and cameramen had congregated along the beach and were using the distant trail of smoke as a backdrop for their reports.

Police and security patrols now seemed to be on every street corner.

Israel was once again back to its default state of red alert.

Joe's lecture at the US embassy, a seven-minute walk farther south along the seafront, had been predictably cancelled. Staff there had gone into meltdown following the injuries to Paul Farrar. It represented another big blow for the secretary of state, whose wife, Eileen, and two teenage children had been killed when a Malaysia Airlines passenger jet on which they were traveling was shot down over Ukraine by the Russians two years earlier.

At the British embassy in Hayarkon Street, also on Tel Aviv's seafront and a short walk north of the Sheraton, it was a similar story. Jayne tried several times to call the MI6 station there to get an update on Nicklin-Donovan's condition, but without success.

She and Nicklin-Donovan went back a long way. She had first worked closely with him in the early 2000s when they were both based in the Balkans for MI6. Their task was to collect information to prosecute war criminals across the former Yugoslavia. It had come to an end when both of their covers had been blown by a leak to local media in 2004.

Jayne and Nicklin-Donovan had exchanged a couple of messages over recent days after they both realized they would be in Israel at the same time, but her former boss's schedule was too busy for him to find time to meet up.

Both Jayne and Joe felt reluctant to call Shiloah or Zahavi at the Mossad, knowing the likely chaotic scenario there, given that the spy agency's director, Eli Elazar, was dead. They were therefore left temporarily reliant on news reports.

After the Israeli Air Force had managed to land a helicopter on the platform's helipad, which had suffered only minor damage, it had emerged that there were at least twenty-seven dead and around thirty people injured.

TV news reports stated that Secretary of State Farrar had been seriously injured after being hit by a piece of flying metal and was in critical condition in a Tel Aviv hospital.

Moshe Cohen had been thrown against a steel railing and died minutes after emergency crews reached him.

There was no specific news about Elazar and nothing about Nicklin-Donovan, although Jayne had not expected there to be, given the secretive nature of their roles.

The gas company chief executive, Alexander Lowman, had also survived and was also in the hospital. The dead included some of the guests and three journalists.

According to the TV reports, the death toll would have been much higher had the drone, laden with explosives, directly struck any of the pipes or vessels that contained gas. Rather, it had hit the living quarters, which accommodated up to fifty workers but were largely empty because most employees were out on the decks taking part in the ceremony.

Miraculously, the impact and explosion had not ignited any of the gas that was flowing through the platform via pipe-lines from five subsea wells located about ninety miles farther north, offshore from the Port of Haifa. The gas flows had also shut down automatically after the incident, which had helped reduce the likelihood of any further explosions. Otherwise, it was almost certain that the platform would have been completely destroyed.

All in all, it was one of the worst massacres suffered by Israel since the country was founded in 1948 following the separation of Palestine into Arab and Jewish territories. The most comparable previous incident was the Passover massacre of 2002, in which Hamas killed 30 and injured 140.

"Do you think it was Hezbollah, as David suggested?" Jayne asked, as she sat on the sofa in their hotel room. There had been speculation from commentators on TV, but no organization had claimed responsibility.

"Most likely," Joe said. "Got to be the Iranians or their proxies."

"I do recall Hezbollah previously claimed that those gas fields belong to Lebanon," Jayne said. She ran a hand through her short dark hair. "They've threatened several times to attack them. But Hezbollah is usually quick to claim responsibility if they've done something like this."

She got to her feet again and strode to the window. The sun had descended rapidly toward the western horizon, casting a broad strip of gold over the sea. A few people were still lying on the beach, ignoring the TV crews behind them.

"Hezbollah will likely get the blame whether they've done it or not," Joe said. "The Israelis will say it's them—with the Iranians pulling the strings. You heard what Avi said."

"They're already going ballistic," Jayne said. She turned and indicated toward the TV, where the Israeli defense minister was being interviewed outside his high-rise ministry headquarters building in Tel Aviv. He was gesticulating vigorously. "I wouldn't be surprised if they end up bombing the shit out of Hezbollah areas of Lebanon, maybe even Iran."

"They'll need to be careful," Joe said. "The Iranians are likely still developing nuclear weapons, despite that deal. I wouldn't like to be in Avi's shoes. The Mossad's going to get the blame for not knowing this was coming."

Jayne leaned back against the window ledge, arms folded. "Langley's also going to be in the firing line. They gave this trip the green light. Vic is going to be tearing his hair out—the White House and State Department will be on the warpath. They'll want to blame someone."

"I told Vic we were here. I'd like to call and ask how he's doing," Joe said. "But I'd never get through. He and Veltman are going to be crazy busy."

Vic Walter was director of the Central Intelligence Agency's National Clandestine Service, generally known as the Directorate of Operations. He was also number two in the organization, based in Langley, Virginia, just outside Washington, DC, and was a firm ally of the overall CIA director, Arthur Veltman. Vic was one of Joe's longest-standing friends, having been based with him in the same Islamabad CIA station in the late 1980s.

Like Jayne for the SIS and Shiloah for the Mossad, Vic and Joe had at that time been focused on arming the Afghan mujahideen in their battles with the occupying Soviets. Their shared experiences had created a lifelong bond.

Over the past few years, Vic had increasingly used Joe and Jayne on an informal, deniable basis to carry out various investigations and operations on behalf of the Agency. He trusted them like few others.

Jayne sat next to Joe on the sofa and took out her phone. "I don't want to call Avi, but I'll message him and ask if there is news of Paul Farrar and Mark."

"Securely?" Joe asked, glancing sideways at her.

"Of course. We have each other's keys."

Joe raised an eyebrow. "Since when?"

"Since about five years ago. He was visiting London when I was still at MI6."

She tapped out a short message, which she sent using the secure link she still had for Shiloah.

A few minutes later a reply came back.

Farrar and Mark N-D both in ICU at Sourasky Medical Center. Don't know much more yet. Need to talk to you both. 22:30. My house in Jerusalem. Get a cab. You can both stay overnight.

Jayne read out the message. "I'd like to go visit Mark."

Joe nodded. "Let's ask Avi tonight. Security will be tight at the hospital. We can't just turn up."

Sourasky Medical Center was Tel Aviv's main hospital,

located a mile and a half east of the Sheraton. Jayne had earlier seen rescue helicopters from the gas platform flying to and from the landing pad on its roof.

Jayne replied to Shiloah to confirm the arrangement.

As she hit the send button, the anchor on the i24 News channel they were watching interrupted an interview to say the Israeli government had announced that fragments of the drone that struck the gas platform had been recovered and would be analyzed overnight. It was hoped they would show the source of the attack.

Jayne grimaced. "If it's Iran, we could be sitting in the middle of a war zone by this time tomorrow."

"Probably right," Joe said. He placed his hand on Jayne's thigh and squeezed gently.

She draped her left arm around Joe's shoulder and lightly stroked his neck with her forefinger. "We've got an hour before dinner, and two hours before we need to get a cab," she said, lowering her voice to a murmur. "Better to make love, not war, don't you agree?"

Joe grinned and slid his hand slowly farther up her thigh. "I've heard worse ideas."

"I do need some exercise. So it's either bed or I go for a run. You choose."

Joe leaned over and began to kiss her.

* * *

Monday, April 4, 2016
    Jerusalem

"The good news is, I've arranged for you both to go see Mark at the hospital tomorrow morning," Shiloah said, clasping a tumbler of whisky between his plate-size hands. "But I have to warn you, like Paul Farrar, he's not conscious, and not in a good way."

He sat on the edge of his armchair, still wearing his trademark black leather jacket over his open-necked blue work shirt. Jayne, who had opted for shiraz rather than Scotch, took a sip from her glass and glanced around Shiloah's wood-paneled lounge. A floor lamp cast half of the Israeli spy chief's face in a dark shadow.

"Thank you," Jayne said. "What's the outlook for him and Farrar?"

Shiloah shook his head. "The doctors are planning surgery for each of them. You can ask the details when you get there. The ICU is heavily guarded, so my secretary will email you the visitors security clearances."

On the sofa beside her, Joe leaned forward. "What did the PM say?" he asked. Shiloah had come directly from a meeting at the prime minister's residence.

"He wants to put us on a war footing. He's fuming. He wants to hit Tehran."

"You don't have any proof that the Iranians did this," Joe said.

Shiloah reached for his black briefcase, from which he withdrew a slim folder. He removed four A4-size photographs and spread them on the coffee table between him and the sofa where Jayne and Joe were sitting.

"I shouldn't be showing these to you," Shiloah said. "They came from the gas platform this afternoon."

Jayne peered at the photos. They showed what appeared to be the broken fragments of a missile, including a gray-painted nose cone and tail unit. However, the shape of the tail fragments told her this wasn't just a missile.

"Drone casings?" Jayne asked.

"Correct. It's from an Ababil-3 drone. That's Iranian.

Probably had a forty- or fifty-kilogram warhead, conventional explosives."

"Any markings on the casing to identify it?" Joe asked.

"They don't leave signatures. But computer modeling has given us the shape. It's fairly unique. A twin-tail variant. It's a basic drone—cheap but effective."

"So that's what's convinced the PM the Iranians carried out the attack?" Jayne said.

"Yes."

She thought about that for a moment. "It may be an Iranian drone, but that doesn't mean they fired it."

"True," Shiloah said. "But on balance of probability, it was them."

Jayne pursed her lips. "And when you say he wants to hit Tehran, what with?"

"Rockets. And he also wants to launch strikes at Hezbollah bases in Lebanon."

This was serious. Jayne knew that apart from a few minor skirmishes, the last serious conflict between Israel and Hezbollah had been in 2006. She had been involved in endless meetings about it at MI6. About 1,200 Lebanese and 160 Israelis had died in the fighting.

"What was your advice to him?" she asked.

Shiloah gave a short, sardonic laugh. "Not to do it. We should let the dust settle and wait until we're sure it's them. And make sure any revenge is carried out when and where they are least expecting it. I can't get this wrong. I'd get the blame now."

"You'd get the blame?" Jayne asked.

"Yes. He's just appointed me acting *ramsad*."

"You're the new boss?" Joe asked.

"Acting boss," Shiloah said. "Only until he can decide on what to do."

Jayne nodded. "Well, congratulations."

"It's hardly the situation to celebrate. I was close to Eli for a long time. It hurts like hell."

"I'm sure it does," Jayne said. "But I think your advice to the PM was correct. As you say, revenge is a dish best served cold."

"The PM thinks differently. He's calling a meeting of the Security Cabinet for tomorrow morning to discuss next steps. He wants me to attend."

This information was dynamite. The State Security Cabinet was a small group of senior ministers within the wider cabinet that determined and implemented Israel's foreign and defense policy. They called in other relevant officials as required.

One thing was certain: the Israeli PM's stance wouldn't go down well with US president Stephen Ferguson, despite the injuries sustained by his secretary of state, nor with the British prime minister, Daniel Parker, and his cabinet in London.

"But you've said it yourself: Iran could be near to having nuclear weapons, despite that agreement," Jayne said. "You know they've probably continued development work, somewhere deep underground, hidden underneath an aircraft hangar or an industrial factory, or in tunnels beneath a mountain. Attacking them could lead to real trouble."

Although Iran had signed the international Nuclear Non-Proliferation Treaty in 1970, barring it from developing nuclear weapons, it hadn't stopped work. Almost ever since, it had a long track record of deception and underhandedness about the extent to which enrichment of uranium to levels above 90 percent had been carried out, which would enable it to develop nuclear warheads.

Nor had Iran been honest about the number and quality of centrifuges it possessed—the key piece of equipment necessary to facilitate enrichment—and the technology it had to develop more.

It seemed unlikely the new deal would guarantee a change in behavior.

Shiloah spread his hands wide. "I've told him they could retaliate hard."

"That could end up wiping your country off the face of the earth. Even if it didn't, it would cause political and economic chaos. Oil prices would rocket. They're already up sharply."

It was true. TV news had reported that oil prices had risen from $48 a barrel to $60 after the attack.

"Yes," Shiloah said. "But remember, our late foreign minister was one of the PM's longest-standing friends. The gas platform is now out of action, and it supplies a large chunk of Israel's energy. He's not going to let this lie."

Jayne refrained from rolling her eyes in dismay. "There is, of course, the question of how the Iranians knew your foreign minister and the secretary of state would be on the platform."

"A good question," Shiloah said. "It was kept extremely tight. Nobody knew, apart from a compartmented group in the CIA and the Mossad. Not even the gas platform engineering team knew until the chopper landed. The journalists thought they'd been invited to a briefing onshore."

"Do you have a mole?"

"If we do, we'll find out who it is," Shiloah said, his tone grim.

Jayne paused, feeling slightly hesitant to be poking her nose into Mossad business, but then decided she needed to at least offer assistance. After all, she had known Shiloah for a long time.

"Can we be of help?" she offered.

Shiloah stroked his chin with his left hand. "Possibly. There is something I wanted to discuss with you. The physical evidence, the type of drone, the target, the timing—all points to Hezbollah operating on behalf of the Iranians."

"But?"

Shiloah finally leaned back in his chair, his right elbow propped on the armrest, his whisky held in midair. "But there is the issue of where this drone originated. It didn't come from the east or the north, which is why our radar batteries, our Iron Dome, our missile detection systems, our air force and naval patrols, didn't pick it up until too late in its flight. It wasn't coming from Lebanon or from Iran itself. No. It came across the sea from the southwest at low altitude."

"From a ship?"

"We think from Egypt, the Sinai Peninsula."

Jayne let out a short whistle. "Could the Iranians have run a covert operation from the Sinai?"

"Our sources say that's a possibility, yes," Shiloah said. "As you know, Hezbollah can strike at us from anywhere. There have been rumors of a planned hit from the sea for some time, for example. Remember that Egypt has been in shambles ever since Mubarak was overthrown five years ago. Their security is poor, but Sinai is particularly bad, despite our efforts to help the Egyptians. All kinds of militants operate there, including Hezbollah."

"So if Hezbollah wanted to lay a smoke screen and create doubt about who did it for whatever reason, launching a drone from there would be a smart move," Joe said.

"It's possible. That is what we need to check out," Shiloah said. "I don't have long. The PM is not a patient man. And for us, poking our nose into Iran to do some checking would be difficult right now." He glanced at Joe. "For you Americans too, it is difficult, given the enmity between your countries."

Joe nodded. "I'm sure you know already that Vic finds it very difficult to get accurate information out of Iran."

That's for sure, Jayne thought.

It was the tough sanctions regimen, driven by Washington, that had caused considerable isolation and deprivation among the Iranian population, had triggered protests and unrest, and had pushed Iran's Supreme Leader, Ali Hashemi, into signing the nuclear deal. There was no diplomatic relationship between Iran and either Israel or the US.

"How is Vic?" asked Shiloah. "I saw him last year, but we haven't spoken much since."

Vic Walter and Shiloah, counterparts at the top of their respective intelligence services, also knew each other from 1980s Islamabad. They had gotten along well, although Jayne knew their respective countries' differences on many international issues challenged their relationship—as did their surveillance of each other's operatives.

"I told him we planned to see you," Joe said. "He sends his regards. Today's events won't help his peace of mind."

"We have that in common, Vic and I," Shiloah said.

The Mossad chief turned and fixed his gaze on Jayne. "However, what I wanted to move on to was the fact that relations between Iran and the British are a little better. You are soon to reopen your embassy in Tehran, and they to reopen theirs in London. And you speak Persian, as I recall?"

Jayne immediately shook her head. She did speak Persian, or Farsi as it was often known, which was Iran's most common language, but she could now see where Shiloah was trying to take this conversation. It took her by surprise.

"Let me stop you there, Avi," she said. "I'd like to help you here informally if I can, but I do mean here. I'm not getting involved in an operation inside Iran—it's too dangerous right now. In any case, I'm already doing work for Vic and for MI6. It would be tricky to serve three masters."

Shiloah's face remained expressionless. "I hear what you're saying." He took a sip of his whisky. "That's a pity because I could use some help, Jayne. At least think about it."

CHAPTER THREE

Tuesday, April 5, 2016
  Washington, DC

"I've just had Katz on the phone," President Ferguson said. "Given what's happened, he wants me to support an Israeli strike on the Iranians and Hezbollah. A hit on Tehran. A strike on Lebanon. My God."

Ferguson rose from his seat behind the historic carved wooden *Resolute* desk, named for HMS *Resolute*, a nineteenth-century British frigate from whose timbers it had been made.

He clasped his arms somewhat theatrically behind his back and made his way across the presidential seal woven into the carpet to the twin sand-colored sofas in the center of the Oval Office.

Vic Walter and Arthur Veltman were sitting on one of the sofas, while on the other sofa were Mike Hill, head of the Near East Division in the CIA's Department of Operations, and Jodie Geary, head of the Israel desk in the Department of Analysis. It was very rare for Veltman and Vic to take others from Langley to join a meeting with the president, who preferred small gatherings, but these were exceptional circumstances.

The gravity of the situation had been underlined when Ferguson summoned them to the Oval Office rather than to their usual spot in the Situation Room in the basement of the West Wing.

The only other person present was Ferguson's chief aide, the bespectacled Charles Deacon. He was perched somewhat uncomfortably on a chair next to the *Resolute* desk at the southern end of the office.

A TV, with the sound muted but the closed captioning on so Ferguson could see what was being said, was tuned to CNN. The station was interviewing the Israeli ambassador to the US, Yosef Zeevi, about the gas platform attack. He was making clear his disgust.

"Katz says he's got proof the Iranians did it, fragments of an Iranian drone casing," Ferguson said as he sat in an armchair facing his guests. "It's outrageous, this attack—I'm trying to keep my personal feelings out of this, but I go back a long way with both Moshe and Paul, you know. Moshe and I were close from our work on the Middle East accords—a good friend. And Paul, well, we're like brothers. It's difficult to stay objective about this. What do you guys think about the prime minister's request?"

There was silence for several seconds. There was no way Vic was going to speak ahead of his boss.

"It's a big call," Veltman said eventually, running a hand through his neatly groomed graying hair. "We've got, what, thirty-something thousand troops across the Middle East? I'm sure you don't want to put them at risk. If it's the Iranians who did it, then the bastards deserve a punch in return. But just because they've found an Iranian-made drone, it doesn't prove the Iranians fired it." He characteristically stuck out his barrel chest as he spoke.

"Of course, you know what's giving me pause, don't you?" the president asked.

"The nuclear deal, I assume," Veltman said.

"Yes. I signed it. I want it to work. I don't want to be responsible for unnecessarily triggering a war in the Middle East. Not least because of the election coming up in November."

"I agree, although let's be honest, it would be Tehran who's responsible, not you, Mr. President," Vic finally said.

"Yes, Tehran would be to blame," Geary said. She smoothed her mane of curly graying hair. "And we're certain they don't yet have nuclear warheads they could actually use in retaliation if we carried out a strike. We know they're continuing with development work, but that's a different matter."

Ferguson frowned. "Be that as it may, we all know my political opponents would spin it against me."

There was no doubt that if the US was sucked into a large-scale conflict in the Middle East that required the commitment of large numbers of American armed forces—in addition to those already based in the region—it would count very heavily against Ferguson in the presidential election. The military cost would be enormous, and the US economy, after belatedly recovering from a deep recession, had recently seen another dip in growth.

Ferguson's rival for the presidency, Republican Nicholas McAllister, the governor of Maryland, was known to have amassed huge funds to fight the election. He and his backers had opposed the nuclear deal with Iran and instead had argued for tough sanctions that would deny the country most Western imports and business investments. Any cracks in the deal would be ammunition with which to attack Ferguson.

Ferguson glanced back toward the three floor-to-ceiling french windows behind his desk. The terracotta-colored curtains were still open, although it was getting dark outside.

On the TV, CNN was now interviewing a string of businessmen about Iran. The first one, Ian Nettles, the silver-haired owner of the Nettles Food Group, was arguing that tough sanctions would work better than the nuclear deal. Another, Richard Moffle, whose company made car components, made similar points, as did a third, Leslie Crowther, owner of a software company.

"We believe sanctions would badly damage the Iranian economy," Moffle said. "In turn, this would persuade the population to oust Supreme Leader Ali Hashemi and bring in a more democratic regime."

It was almost identical phrasing to that used by McAllister in many of his recent speeches.

"This is a joke," Ferguson said. "These are rent-a-quote supporters of McAllister. None of them sell anything to Iran. That's why they can afford to argue for sanctions. It would be a different story if they actually did business there. McAllister's put them up to this—they all bankroll his campaign. They'll say what he tells them to. It's already begun."

Vic agreed. He knew exactly where Ferguson was coming from, and they were, without a doubt, hitting the president hard.

But Vic took the view that it wasn't his job to get involved in politics. He was meant to be impartial and serve whoever happened to be sitting in the White House, no matter what party they belonged to. So he didn't comment and instead focused on the decision at hand.

It seemed to Vic that the president didn't really know what to do. One minute he was saying he was of mind to stand alongside the Israeli prime minister, the next he didn't want to start a war.

"Sir, I understand your difficulty," Vic said. "My feeling is that we need some solid evidence that the Iranians, or Hezbollah, actually did this before we make a decision."

"I did say that to Katz," Ferguson said. "But he has a lot of hawkish colleagues in his cabinet, and he was talking about a rocket strike tomorrow. I think I managed to dismount him from that particular horse."

"Thank God for that," Veltman said.

Ferguson eyeballed Vic. "Your point is right on the money, Vic. If Tehran has done this, I agree with Katz that we should hit them hard. But evidence is what we need first. Can you get it?"

Vic had anticipated this, and so had Veltman, Geary, and Hill. Indeed, they had discussed the possibility of the president asking that very question as they drove the nine miles along the Potomac River from Langley to the White House. Unfortunately, they had not come up with a clear response.

One issue was the somewhat strained relations between the CIA and the Mossad. Although Vic knew Avi Shiloah from the 1980s and got along reasonably well with him on a personal level, the rivalry between the two organizations often overshadowed that.

Quite recently, the CIA's Tel Aviv chief of station, Garfield Wattley, had arrived home one evening to find that the securely locked case containing his communications equipment had been tampered with. It was likely an attempt to install a bug. There was no doubt who had done it. Little could be said, though, because the CIA, from its two-story station within the sprawling US embassy complex, made extensive efforts to bug and monitor officials at the Mossad and within the Israeli government, including the prime minister.

Vic leaned forward. "As you know, sir, our ability to extract good intelligence from Iran is limited, and—"

"I'm looking for solutions, not problems," the president interrupted. It was one of his catchphrases.

"The Mossad are better placed," Vic said. "However, we still have issues with them." He turned to Hill. "I think that's a fair assessment, don't you, Mike?"

"Unfortunately that's the case," Hill said. "They don't always play the game according to conventional rules."

Ferguson slapped the cushion on which he was sitting with the flat of his hand. It wasn't a good sign.

"I'm going to say this only one more time," he said. "Get me some reliable information. If we don't make the effort to get it and then make the wrong decision, the media will put me on a spit and roast me in front of that fire."

He indicated with his hand toward the ornate white marble fireplace at the northern end of his office, topped with potted ivy on the mantelpiece and a portrait of President George Washington on the wall above it.

"You've got good people," the president added, eyeing first Veltman, then Vic from beneath his spiky eyebrows. "Now use them."

Vic exchanged glances with Veltman. He did have a couple of ideas, but now wasn't the time to discuss them in front of the president.

"Sir, we have a few options," Veltman said.

"Good," Ferguson said. "Katz said that there will be a state funeral for Moshe Cohen in Jerusalem on Thursday, April 28th—a much longer delay than they hoped—and a private memorial ceremony afterward, and he's invited me. I suggested we have an in-depth meeting at that time to make decisions and that he hold off until then, which he agreed to."

Out of the corner of his eye, Vic could see Charles Deacon nodding in agreement, his black-rimmed glasses and dark eyebrows moving up and down in unison.

"Of course, sir," Veltman said.

"I think that would be an excellent idea, Mr. President," Geary said.

"Good. I'm glad you agree," Ferguson said. "So I want results by the time of the funeral. You've got three and a half weeks. Understood?"

"Yes, sir," Veltman said.

Vic knew that the Israelis liked to bury their dead as quickly as possible, usually within a few days at most. It was their custom. But the long delay, reflecting the complexity of the situation, would give the CIA a little breathing room to get the information the president wanted.

The president glanced at the grandfather clock next to the northeast door, which led to his secretary's office, and rose. "I need to go. I'm joining Yosef Zeevi for a meeting with Paul Farrar's sister. I'm not looking forward to it, and I know the ambassador isn't either. We need to express our sympathies, tell her we're doing what we can. I just pray to God that he pulls through. She's flying to Tel Aviv tomorrow morning."

Ferguson nodded at the CIA contingent, signifying the meeting was over, and turned to Deacon. "See these people out, please, Charles," he said.

* * *

Tuesday, April 5, 2016
   Washington, DC

The key to the plan was going to be the garbage truck collection schedule.

After a long period of careful and unobtrusive surveillance, it had become clear that the timetable was regular and unvaried, as was the routine observed by the truck driver and his colleague.

Every Monday morning at just before quarter to eight, a large green garbage truck from DC Business Waste rolled along Van Ness Street NW, a broad tree-lined avenue in the small Van Ness neighborhood of northwest Washington.

Cyrus Saba knew this because he had watched it happen every Monday morning over the previous four weeks, most recently the previous day.

The truck then turned left and up International Drive NW, a campus-style enclave of office buildings built on a slight hill that housed a series of foreign embassies, mainly from the Middle East and Africa.

Elegant and unobtrusive in design, the embassies were differentiated by architectural features that reflected the cultural heritage of their respective countries. But they all had one specific feature in common: they sat behind deceptively strong steel fences and had high-tech security systems in place.

The DC Business Waste crew's first port of call was the embassy of Jordan, where they spent a few minutes emptying the dumpsters using a hydraulic system that tipped their contents into a huge steel container on the back of the truck.

The driver then exited the embassy grounds and parked in a spot across the street outside a leafy park, populated with trees, paths, and benches. He and his colleague got out of their cab, sat on a bench, and poured themselves coffee from a flask. Usually they also ate a snack and smoked a cigarette.

After several more minutes, at about quarter past eight, they climbed back into the truck and continued on around the corner and down the slope to the Israeli embassy, the last building on the street at the intersection with Van Ness Street NW.

The embassy, built from buff-colored brick, was four

stories high and stood well back from the street behind a blue steel fence and a security building at the main entrance. The top-floor windows, deeply recessed into the brickwork, were built in a striking arch shape.

On arrival, the garbage collectors turned into the entrance and paused outside the blue heavy steel sliding security gate to show their credentials to a security guard. After signing in, they were then allowed to proceed to collect the waste from dumpsters stored at the rear of the building.

At about twenty minutes past eight each weekday, the Israeli ambassador, Yosef Zeevi, arrived in his chauffeur-driven black Mercedes S55 AMG sedan and entered the premises. Usually there was a man in a dark suit sitting next to him in the rear seat, whom Saba knew to be a bodyguard.

Across the street and some distance farther up the hill, Saba sat in the driver's seat of his Ford Ranger pickup, scrutinizing the building one final time.

He knew from a previous covert visit to the embassy a couple of years earlier, under the pretext of inquiring about an Israeli visa, that all the floors faced inward into an airy brick entrance atrium.

However, although the building was designed to create the impression of light and space, security inside the complex was predictably tight.

Too tight to carry out his first choice of operation.

However, for the alternative plan that Saba had devised, that didn't matter.

CHAPTER FOUR

Tuesday, April 5, 2016
    Tel Aviv

The silver steel elevator doors opened at the third floor of the Sourasky Medical Center's main building, and Jayne, closely followed by Joe, stepped out into the reception area for the intensive care unit to find herself confronted by three security guards with holstered pistols at their hips.

"Good morning, can I help you?" one of the guards said as he stepped forward and stood firmly in her path, arms folded and legs apart.

After explaining the reason for their visit, they showed their ID and the security clearance email from Avi Shiloah's office. The guards gave Jayne and Joe a thorough search before handing them over to the head nurse at the reception desk, who introduced herself as Nina Raslan.

Nina, dressed in a pale green uniform, made them sign a visitor's register, then turned to Jayne. "I have to warn you,

Mr. Nicklin-Donovan is still unconscious and you may be shocked by his appearance."

"How is he doing?" Jayne asked. "What are his injuries?"

She hesitated. "He is not good at all. He had a heavy blow to the rear of his skull that has caused some internal bleeding, which we are monitoring. We're temporarily keeping him in an induced coma to help reduce the pressure until we can determine the best next step. We are likely going to operate to relieve that pressure. He also has two fractures in his right leg and three broken ribs. We've reset those already and they'll mend in time. We also had to stitch up a few deep cuts."

"And his chances of recovery?" Jayne asked.

Nina looked at the floor. "I don't know. We don't usually give that type of opinion. But I'm sure he's a fighter."

Jayne felt her stomach sink as if a heavy weight had suddenly been dropped into it.

"Dear God," she murmured. "But you're right. He is a fighter."

Nina glanced at her. "It can be something of a shock to see someone like this."

"Has he had any other visitors?" Jayne asked.

"Not yet. I believe his wife is flying here from the UK. Come this way. You can see him very briefly."

She led the way past a brightly lit reception desk to a cream-painted corridor, at the end of which was a set of automatic sliding glass doors where two more armed security guards were stationed. After they passed through, she stopped at a wooden door and peered through the glass viewing panel before opening it.

"You can come in. It's okay to approach him. Just be careful of the tubes," Nina said.

The room, with a white tiled floor, contained a hospital

bed with an array of equipment behind it, including a large monitor screen.

On the bed, motionless, lay Mark Nicklin-Donovan, although he didn't look at all like the Mark that Jayne knew.

His eyes were closed, and his face was swollen and ashen behind a clear plastic ventilator mask through which he was breathing. His gray hair, normally neatly combed forward in a fringe, was messy and lank, and he had a large square bandage on his right cheek that had a bloodstain in the center.

A plastic tube ran from a drip in a pouch on a stand next to his bed to a cannula fixed to his wrist. The monitor screen displayed five of his vital signs in differently colored digits along with moving waveforms that constantly updated. The top set of digits, showing his heartbeat in green, looked steady at seventy-two per minute.

This was a man with whom she had worked hand in glove for years. After Yugoslavia, their paths had crossed frequently. His star had risen at MI6's Vauxhall Cross headquarters and he later became head of the UK controllerate and her manager. She had always gotten along very well with him, and there was a great deal of mutual respect. Since she had left the service in 2012 to go freelance, he had often pushed work her way.

He had recently been promoted again to director of operations and deputy to the overall chief, Richard Durman, universally known simply as C, as all directors of the service had been dubbed.

The sight of her old boss like this suddenly sent another image flashing across Jayne's mind, and a wave of despondency flowed through her.

Dad.

It was a vivid flashback to her father, Ken, a detective inspector with the anti-terrorist branch of London's Metropolitan Police, who died after being caught in a bomb attack on the Israeli embassy in 1994 at the age of only fifty-nine.

She missed him. There were the games of chess, which he had taught her to such a good standard that she made the county girls team when she was young and was able to compete strongly with a boy she was friendly with who went on to become a grandmaster.

Jayne and her father continued to play chess competitively together in later years and also bonded tightly during long walks together along coastal paths and in the mountains and on occasional runs in the countryside.

He spent two months in a London hospital bed very similar to the one Nicklin-Donovan was now in. Jayne still had occasional dark dreams about a friend of her father's, a Roman Catholic priest, giving him the last rites not long before he passed away.

It was initially thought that Hezbollah had been behind the embassy attack, which injured eighteen other people, but it was never proven. Although two Palestinians were subsequently convicted of conspiring to cause the bombing and imprisoned, there was widespread doubt about the convictions. Jayne and many others felt strongly that the wrong people were jailed and the real culprits remained free.

The thought of her father made Jayne suddenly wonder how Nicklin-Donovan's wife, Shirley, and their two grown-up children, Eric and Ria, were coping with this. Very badly, she assumed. They hadn't even seen him yet. Jayne cast a quick glance at Nina, then took a couple of steps forward toward Nicklin-Donovan's bed.

"Mark, if you can hear me, I want you to hang in there," she said in a low voice. "Keep going, we're all with you. And I'm going to track down and find whoever did this."

Jayne paused, then added, "Mark, keep fighting. You can

do it. Shirley will be here soon to see you. She's flying here right now." She took a few steps back again.

"Maybe he can hear what I'm saying to him," Jayne said to Nina.

"Maybe," she said. "It could make a difference. Sometimes a familiar voice does that."

"Do you have Paul Farrar in this section of the ICU too?" Joe asked.

Nina threw a sharp glance in Joe's direction. "I am not allowed to say where Mr. Farrar is."

"Of course," Joe said. "You must have had a very difficult time, with so many coming in here from the gas platform."

Nina shook her head. "Horrendous. Some of the injuries are terrible. I hope you people can track down who did this."

"We hope so too," Jayne said. "Can I give you my phone number? Maybe you could keep it and just get someone to let me know if Mark's condition changes significantly?"

Nina frowned. "We're very busy here, as you can imagine. But give me the number. I will put it in Mr. Nicklin-Donovan's notes and we will do what we can."

Jayne thanked her and gave the number, which she wrote down on a notepad.

"I'm sorry, I can't let you stay here," Nina said. "Take another minute, then I'll have to show you out."

Jayne nodded and they stood in silence for a short time, gazing at Nicklin-Donovan. His chest was rising and falling steadily, and he was wheezing slightly.

As they watched, a raucous, continuous beeping noise began from the vital signs monitor, which made Jayne jump.

She looked at the screen.

The top set of data, in green digits, showed that Nicklin-Donovan's heart rate had dropped to thirty-nine, and the waveform, instead of displaying a steady rhythmic pattern as previously, now appeared haphazard to Jayne.

Nina acted instantaneously. She stepped rapidly to a bank of controls behind Nicklin-Donovan and pushed a red button. A Klaxon began to sound.

Then she ran to the door and flung it open.

"Can I have some help, please," she shouted down the corridor. "Get the resuscitation team in here. He's going."

The heart rate monitor was now showing twenty-seven.

Nina stepped briskly over to Nicklin-Donovan, placed both hands one on top of the other on his chest, and began pumping down rhythmically.

A few seconds later another nurse came running in.

"Sorry, but you'll both need to get out of here," she said as she picked up a phone from a cradle on the wall. "It's his heart. Go, please."

Jayne, so stunned by what had just happened, stood rooted.

Joe grabbed her arm. "Come on, Jayne. We need to go. Let them deal with this. We're in the way."

She turned and followed Joe out the door.

As they exited, a group of three nurses and two doctors in white coats ran along the corridor and into the room they had just left.

"He's going to die," Jayne said, her voice level and matter-of-fact as they walked toward the elevators. "His heart's going."

Her voice sounded disembodied to her.

It somehow felt as though someone else was speaking.

Her mind flashed back to the countless operations she and Mark had worked on together in some of the darkest corners of Europe and beyond.

They had held clandestine meetings with everyone from Bosnian warlords to Serbian hitmen and Russian spies—men and women who were risking their lives to convey secrets from their governments that were vital to the West.

As the elevator car headed down, she thought of dingy safe houses, dubious bars, and the midnight oil burned during late nights spent planning operations together at the SIS offices in London.

All that shared history was over, thanks to some anonymous Iranian drone operator.

* * *

Tuesday, April 5, 2016
Tel Aviv

The twenty-five-minute walk through western Tel Aviv passed in near silence. As they made their way through the broad concrete expanse of Rabin Square, lined with palm trees and office blocks, and along Frishman Street to the Sheraton, Jayne's mind felt tangled and jumbled inside.

She certainly didn't feel like talking, and neither, it seemed, did Joe. The image of Nicklin-Donovan in his ICU bed, the vital signs alarm squawking, and Nina shouting loomed large inside her head.

Twice she tried to call the ICU unit.

The first time a nurse brusquely told her there was no news and she should call back later.

The second time the call rang and nobody answered.

She told herself that Mark was gone, there was nothing she could do, and until she heard a confirmation or an update she should try and focus on the decisions that were now needed, following Avi Shiloah's proposition.

She said as much to Joe, who agreed.

But rather than discuss it in their hotel room, they decided instead to take a further stroll on the beach. Based on past experience with the Mossad and despite their long-standing friendship with Avi Shiloah, Jayne couldn't rule out the possibility that the en suite bedroom he had provided on the top floor of his home on Negba Street was bugged, and the same applied to their hotel room.

To avoid any indiscretions at Shiloah's house last night, she had called a halt after two generous glasses of shiraz, pleading a headache. Joe had continued to drink Scotch with their host, whose legendary capacity to absorb alcohol clearly hadn't diminished. That was despite his daily 5:30 a.m. wake-up alarm to enable him to beat the commuter traffic on his one-hour journey into the office. As a result, Joe was a little worse for wear today but was holding up.

While they were walking, Jayne received a short message from Shiloah.

Katz and Ferguson have agreed no retaliation until after Cohen funeral. They will discuss next steps then. Thought you would want to know. My proposal still stands.

Well, that was some sort of temporary relief.

Jayne glanced out to sea. The sunshine of the previous day had disappeared, as had the trail of smoke on the horizon from the gas platform. The blaze had been fully extinguished, according to Israeli radio.

Despite their location, near the sea and well away from anyone else, Jayne still carried out a precautionary check for any surveillance. There seemed to be none.

A stiff breeze was blowing from the south, causing her blouse to flatten against her breasts, and throwing them into sharp relief. She couldn't help noticing Joe's gaze was following them, which caused her to smile for the first time that day.

"Avi is more desperate than I imagined," Jayne said. "I don't quite get it. His team has, in the past, carried out surgical strikes at Iran's nuclear sites. But now he's saying he wants me to do his investigative work for him."

She jumped nimbly over a pool of seawater. At the age of fifty-four, Jayne remained roughly the same weight she had been at twenty-four and prided herself on her level of fitness.

"He's just trying to distance himself," Joe said. "If he can get some Brit to poke their nose in and ask his questions for him, then he's removing himself from finger-pointing by the Iranians."

"So what do you think we should do?" Jayne asked.

"I'd like to do something for Mark's sake and Paul Farrar's. But I can't afford to get caught in a conflict. Peter's exams start in a couple of weeks. He's in a bunch of APs as a senior —hoping for that early college credit. I can't have him worrying about me and getting distracted right now."

Joe's younger sister, Amy Wilde, had moved into the home he now shared with Jayne in Portland, Maine, to look after Peter while they were away. Not that he needed much looking after these days now that he was approaching his eighteenth birthday.

Meanwhile, Joe's daughter, Carrie, who was nineteen, was away preparing for exams at the end of her first year of college. She was studying political science at Boston University, where Joe had studied history in the late 1970s.

Jayne had moved from her apartment near Tower Bridge in London to Portland to join Joe a couple of years earlier to give their relationship a real go. It had gone so well that she had stayed. Adjusting to being a kind of stepmother to his children had taken some time, as she had never had children of her own. But both Carrie and Peter had for the most part been welcoming, and that had made it easier.

She noticed Joe looking at her.

"What were you thinking in that hospital room?" Joe asked.

She looked at the ground. "It brought back memories of my dad, in another hospital bed in London."

"Thought so," Joe said.

"His priest giving him the last rites. I can't forget that," she said.

Joe nodded. "Not surprised. Who was the priest?"

"Old school buddy of his, Michael Gray, though they seemed like chalk and cheese. A Catholic. Ended up as archbishop of Westminster. Works in the Vatican now too. He's a cardinal. I still hear from him occasionally."

"That sounds like a meteoric rise."

"It took him years. And he's as down-to-earth as they come," Jayne said. "Anyway, what are you going to do now? You want to head home? Back to Portland?"

"There's a flight available tomorrow morning," Joe said.

"I was looking forward to seeing the Galilee area," Jayne said. She had never visited that northern part of Israel previously. "But I don't think we should go there right now if things might really heat up. I do want to try and do something to track down whoever did this to Mark, though, but I'm not sure what."

Joe nodded. "Why don't you brief Vic on the conversation with Avi. I told him we were here. He's bound to be working on this, given what happened to Farrar. He might have some ideas about how you could help. Message him and see what he says."

"All right. I'll dangle the carrot with Vic and hint that we've seen Avi. He'll call if he wants more info."

She took out her phone and typed a short message.

Just been to see Mark in ICU. In a bad state, unconscious with brain bleeding in same hospital as PF. Had cardiac arrest while we were there. Don't know outcome yet. Hoping for best, fearing worst. Joe and I picked up details re gas platform incident you might find useful. Call if you want a briefing.

She dispatched the message via the secure link she

normally used with Vic and checked her emails. There was only the weekly issues update that came from Nicklin-Donovan's office, compiled this time by his deputy. The update never contained classified information, but it was a useful backgrounder into the key global and UK issues concerning SIS.

This week's update didn't mention Nicklin-Donovan's situation but was more of a general commentary. It covered concerns about oil prices following the Samar attack and also mentioned the heightened risk of nuclear conflict.

Jayne scrolled down the email. Farther down there was a paragraph about a conference on nuclear security in Vienna that was due to start soon. It stated blandly that work at MI6 was underway to arrange meetings with some of the 1,500 delegates.

They continued along the beach until they reached a café with outdoor seating, where they decided to stop for a coffee. A few people were lying on loungers near the lifeguard's station, despite the lack of sunshine.

As Jayne took a sip from her drink, her phone rang. It was Vic, calling on his encrypted line.

"I just saw your message," Vic said, typically without preamble or greeting. "Sorry to hear about Mark. Any updates? And I'm here with Neal on the conference phone, by the way."

Neal Scales was Vic's deputy and closest colleague in the Directorate of Operations and a man whom Jayne had first gotten to know in Islamabad in the late 1980s, along with Vic and Joe. After Vic had been elevated into his current role, almost his first act had been to also promote his trusted friend. Neal was someone who preferred to be active in the field rather than stuck at headquarters, although that was usually his fate these days.

"We don't know anything more right now," Jayne said. "I

can't get anything from the ICU about Mark. But his chances seem low."

"That's terrible. Let me know when you hear more."

"Will do," Jayne said. "Now, do you want to hear more about what Avi said?" She knew that Vic would have surmised from her cryptic message that Shiloah was the source of her information.

"That would be helpful."

Jayne glanced around her before replying. There was nobody nearby, and the waitress had gone back inside the café.

"I don't know if you've heard, but Avi is now the acting *ramsad*. The PM appointed him."

"Really? It's well deserved," Vic said.

"Yes, I agree. And based on what he's saying, it seems obvious this drone attack happened because there was a leak about the gas platform visit. A mole told the Iranians, it seems."

"It seems so. We thought it was kept watertight," Vic said. "Completely compartmented at our end. I had hoped like-wise at the Mossad end."

"Well, someone told Tehran. They found fragments of an Ababil drone on the gas platform," she said, and went on to recount the conversation from the previous evening.

"Yes," Vic said. "The president said that Katz told him about the fragments."

"The only problem is, the drone didn't actually come from Iran," Jayne said. "They might have dispatched it, most likely, but it didn't fly from their territory, nor from southern Lebanon. That's why the Israeli missile-defense systems and radar didn't pick it up. They think it came from the south-west, most likely the Sinai."

"The president didn't mention Sinai," Vic said. "Interest-ing. It's possible someone else fired it, then."

"Possibly. Difficult to say."

"Well, you might be pleased to know Ferguson's talked Katz out of an instant retaliation. We've got a bit of breathing room to figure this out."

"Yes, I just heard from Avi," Jayne said. "At least until Moshe Cohen's funeral and memorial service on the twenty-eighth, correct?"

"Yes, precisely," Vic said. "Ferguson is attending and has a summit meeting with Katz scheduled. He wants us to get evidence by then of who launched the drone. So we've got three and a half weeks."

"It's not long," Jayne said. "Avi's been so desperate that he's hinting he wants to send me into Iran. He thinks it would be easier for a Brit to get in and out."

There came a muffled snort down the line from Vic. "What was your response to this invitation?"

"I said no."

"Glad to hear that because I do have a potential proposition for you. What about—"

"Vic, I am *not* going into Iran. Period."

"Okay, okay, I wasn't necessarily going to ask you to," Vic said, his voice taking on a defensive note.

Yes, you were.

"But if you've built a link with Avi again there," Vic continued, "I would appreciate it if you're able to feed back to me anything you're picking up. Apart from any proof of who dispatched the drone, we also need to know how close Iran really is to producing nukes. And I need to be completely on top of what the thinking is in Tel Aviv about all of the above so I can properly brief Ferguson. So if you hitch your wagon to Avi temporarily, and work on all that, it would help me."

"Can't you talk to Avi directly?"

"I get on reasonably well with him, but at an institutional level it's not easy," Vic said.

"What about Garfield Wattley? Doesn't he have a route into Avi?" Jayne couldn't help thinking that although the CIA's chief of station in Tel Aviv was well regarded within the Agency, he should at least have been trying to forge a relationship with Shiloah already. If not, he wasn't doing his job properly.

"Garfield has his work cut out for him right now. They tried to bug his comms gear recently. It caused a lot of bad blood. Relationships between him and the Israelis aren't the best. But he's very good, and just between you and me, I'm thinking of moving him to Paris for that reason. Bigger station. It would be a promotion."

"Who's going to replace him?"

"I'm considering the options with Neal and Mike Hill. Maybe we'll send Jodie Geary. Heads up the Israel desk."

"Yes, she's the front-runner," Neal chipped in. "She's tough enough."

Jayne knew of Geary, who like Wattley was a long-standing colleague of Vic. She couldn't resist a smile. Not because she thought it was amusing, but because Vic and Neal could only have shared such confidential, sensitive information with someone they had known for decades and trusted implicitly. She took it as a compliment.

"So what do you say?" Vic asked.

Jayne glanced at Joe. "We were just discussing what to do," she said into the phone. "Joe's thinking of heading home tomorrow morning. Peter's got his senior-year finals and APs starting very soon."

Since moving to Portland, Jayne had quickly got to grips with the US high school and college system, given that Joe's children were embedded in it. The Advanced Placement, or AP, program for high school students could give them advance credits prior to starting their college or university courses.

There was a pause at the other end of the line.

"Right. I understand that," Vic said. "But could you stay on there by yourself and help me out?"

There was a distinct note of anxiety in Vic's voice.

Not so different from Avi.

"I'll have a think about it," Jayne said. "I'd like to do something, not least because of what's happened to Mark."

"Good. Let me know. Talk soon," Vic said. He ended the call.

Jayne put her phone back in her pocket and turned to Joe. "Maybe I should stay on. I did quietly promise Mark in the hospital that we'd find whoever did it. Perhaps it might also dilute a little of the bad blood between Langley and our friends at Glilot Interchange."

Glilot Interchange was the complex highway junction next to the Mossad's headquarters, about eight kilometers north of where Jayne and Joe were sitting.

"Nice to be in demand. Is it okay if I book for tomorrow morning's flight, then?" Joe asked.

"Yes. You go look after Peter."

After a previous incident during an operation that had put both of Joe's children's lives at risk, his priorities had reoriented. While his children still needed him around, he was trying to be more careful and avoid high-risk jobs. She guessed that in the future that was likely to change again.

Jayne's phone beeped as another message arrived.

Hello Ms. Robinson, Nina here from Sourasky to let you know we have stabilized Mr. Nicklin-Donovan's condition for now. If you call tomorrow we can provide an update. Thanks.

She read it out to Joe.

"Thank God for that," he said. "He's a fighter."

Jayne nodded and stared out to sea while Joe completed his flight booking.

Mark was a fighter, but his battle had a long way to run yet—she knew that. And in accepting the challenge now being dangled in front of her, so did hers.

From an intelligence point of view, the task facing her seemed clear. Both the Mossad and the CIA needed to somehow get hold of the same information, which was going to be far from easy to obtain.

But Jayne meant what she had said. She didn't want to go into Iran.

True, she spoke fairly fluent Persian and had been to Tehran a handful of times while at the SIS prior to 2011, when the embassy was attacked and the ambassador expelled. Diplomatic relations had been broken off at that point.

However, despite the recent slight thawing in relations, the risks had multiplied as of late. To make real headway there, it would help to be Persian.

Then she was struck by an idea.

Perhaps there was another way of doing this.

CHAPTER FIVE

Wednesday, April 6, 2016
   Tel Aviv

"Where did you get this list?" Avi Shiloah asked, scanning down the list of names in a spreadsheet displayed on Jayne's iPad.

Jayne stifled a grin. "It's what's known in the trade as open-source intelligence," she said.

A fleeting look of annoyance crossed the acting *ramsad*'s face. "Don't patronize me. You mean you did a Google search?"

"There was a bit more to it than that. The IAEA website had a roster of attendees buried in one of its pages. It's unpublished, ready to go live once the conference has begun, but I managed to get to it."

Shiloah stared at Jayne from behind the steel-and-glass desk in the second-floor office allocated to the *ramsad*, which he was now using. His eyes narrowed.

"You hacked their website?" David Zahavi asked. He was

standing next to the window behind Shiloah. His bald head glinted in the sunlight that streamed through the open blinds.

Jayne said nothing. Getting into the International Atomic Energy Agency website had been more straightforward than she had expected. The lessons she had learned from the technical department at Vauxhall Cross, the SIS's headquarters building overlooking the River Thames in London, had proved to be very useful yet again.

However, it was the only section of the site that was dedicated to the forthcoming International Conference on Nuclear Security, due to start the following Monday in Vienna, that proved so easily accessible. The rest was more secure.

"All right, I'll take that as a yes," Shiloah said. He glanced at the iPad again. "What's the significance of this?"

"If you scroll down, you'll see the list of fifteen attendees scheduled to be there from Iran. As for their significance, I was hoping you and your team might be able to help with that."

Jayne waited as Shiloah flicked down the screen. She was working alone now, as Joe had departed in a cab for Ben Gurion International Airport earlier that morning. In his bag were two bottles of the wine that Shiloah had previously recommended, Yarden cabernet sauvignon from the Golan Heights Winery, north of the Sea of Galilee. They cost more than forty dollars a bottle from a store near the hotel. "Don't drink them—we'll have them when I'm back," Jayne had instructed as he climbed into the cab.

After he'd gone, she got down to work. Once she had finally located what she wanted, she had called Shiloah's secretary and requested a meeting.

She had then gone by cab to the expansive Mossad complex, which was situated next to a Cinema City outlet and stood in carefully manicured gardens containing sculptures by well-known Israeli artists.

The complex housed about six thousand employees and was certainly well equipped, including a fitness center, a gymnasium with a basketball court, and an indoor shooting range, as well as separate meat and dairy restaurants to ensure food remained kosher. Nearly all the signs were in Hebrew.

Shiloah placed both elbows on his desk as he scrutinized the list. "I recognize some names. This one, Amir Rad, is the head of the Atomic Energy Organization of Iran, the government's main nuclear energy agency. We actually tried recruiting him a few years ago—but no chance. He's loyal. And this one, Jafar Farsad, is his deputy director, although we think he's also got another, much more secret role in practice. He's the nuclear physics expert who's been running the weapons development program for Rad, organizing Iran's uranium enrichment program and heading research into the warheads. He's supposedly been sidelined by the nuclear deal. Interesting that he's attending the conference."

He turned and held the iPad out to Zahavi. "Recognize any of the other names?"

Mossad's deputy head of operations took the device and sat in a chair next to Jayne. "Yes, I know a few of the others. People we've been keeping a watch on these past few years. Some went to the last IAEA conference a couple of years ago."

He handed the iPad back to Jayne. "What is your thinking here?"

Jayne placed both hands behind her head. "Well, it's difficult to get into Iran and to get close to these people. But this seems to be an unusual occasion when they are coming to us instead. Maybe it's an opportunity to try and get answers to two questions: were the Iranians behind the gas platform attack, as seems overwhelmingly likely, and what is the current state of their nuclear weapons program."

The two Mossad leaders exchanged glances.

"I see what you're saying," Shiloah said. He fiddled with the ashtray on his desk, which was full of Camel stubs, despite the no-smoking policy in the building.

"How close are these men to the leadership, the Supreme Leader and the president?" Jayne asked.

"Very close," Zahavi said. "Both are trusted personal advisers to Hashemi and have a lot of influence."

"So with the drone attack on Samar, would Hashemi have consulted these nuclear experts before giving it the green light?" Jayne asked.

"Almost certainly," Shiloah said.

"It might be a rare chance to see if one of them cracks, if we do a dangle," Jayne said.

Zahavi nodded. "We could try Farsad. It's not worth bothering with Rad. But you're right, they hardly ever get out of their laboratories, let alone out of Iran. If Farsad is open to an opportunity, this will be it."

"That's exactly what I had in mind," Jayne said. "There's nothing to lose. Do you know much about their backgrounds?"

"We have files on them," Zahavi said. "I recall both studied at universities in the UK—nuclear physics, I believe."

"Which universities?" Jayne asked.

"It will be in the files."

There was a pause of several seconds before Shiloah asked, "So you're going to work with us?"

Jayne nodded. "It seems so."

"What changed your mind?"

"The sight of Mark in the ICU with life-threatening injuries was part of it."

"And what about not serving three masters?"

Jayne pursed her lips. "I discussed it with Vic, and he thought that given the tense environment, it might benefit all parties if we got to the bottom of the issue soon. So he said it's fine to work with you as long as I keep him updated. I assume if we do work together, we'll be tightly compartmented anyway, so there's no risk of it going any further."

Shiloah nodded. "Strict compartmentation is how we operate here, as you'd expect. It should be manageable. Just make sure you don't step out of line, though. Nothing more than this specific operation. Our counterintelligence people watch everyone like hawks, especially outsiders."

Jayne nodded. She was used to that.

"Listen," Shiloah said. "There's a couple of people you'll need to meet if we're going to run an operation in Vienna. Come this way."

It's that simple. He's made a decision, Jayne thought.

Shiloah stood and led the way out of his office into an anteroom, furnished with a leather sofa, a bookcase filled with volumes in both English and Hebrew, and a variety of memorabilia from various operations and triumphs during his long career.

Jayne noted a gilded wooden plaque on a plinth in one corner with several small brass plates attached to it bearing the names of past directors of the Mossad.

"That's always been in the director's office," Shiloah said as he followed her gaze. "There's ten names on it. Four have died."

Jayne nodded. These were the names of men who had overseen some of the most legendary operations in the history of global intelligence services.

Their deeds included Operation Garibaldi in 1960 to locate, kidnap, and remove to Israel the German Nazi architect of the Holocaust, the fugitive Adolf Eichmann, who was hiding out in Buenos Aires. He was hanged in Jerusalem two years later after being found guilty of war crimes.

Jayne also recalled Operation Wrath of God in the 1970s to wreak revenge against members of the Palestinian terrorist group Black September, who killed eleven Israeli athletes, coaches, and officials at the 1972 Olympics in Munich.

In 1995 there had been the assassination of Fathi Shaqaqi, leader of the Islamic Jihad organization.

And then there was, more recently, a series of assassinations of Iranian nuclear weapons scientists—the men who were working on the warheads that would be used to destroy Israel.

These were not men to get on the wrong side of.

"Wait here," Shiloah said. "I'm just going to fetch Odeya and Rafael, whom I'd like you to meet."

He indicated that she should sit on the sofa, then nodded at Zahavi. "Keep her company, David."

Jayne's glance returned to the wooden plaque. At the bottom was another small brass plate with an inscription in Hebrew. Her knowledge of the language was decent, and she realized that this was the Mossad motto, with its origins in a biblical verse.

By way of deception you shall make war.

She turned to find Zahavi studying her from the sofa.

"You know that?" he asked.

She nodded. "From Proverbs. Avi was the one who told me about it first, in Islamabad. It's appropriate."

She took a seat next to Zahavi and they waited, as instructed.

"Odeya and Rafael," Jayne said. "Who are they?"

"Rafael Levy and Odeya Leibovitch. I've been running an operation with them in Zürich against the Russians. It finished recently. Very good. Deep cover specialists. Fluent in German, which you'd need in Vienna," Zahavi said.

He explained that Rafael and Odeya were two of very few *katsas*, or case officers, who now operated out of the head office after spending years in the field, mainly in Europe. Most *katsas* rarely, if ever, came to headquarters.

"You speak German, don't you?" he asked.

Jayne nodded. It was one of several languages in which she was fluent, including Spanish, Russian, and French. She didn't ask what the operation was against the Russians, as she knew she wouldn't get an answer.

"I learned my first German words from my mother, who picked them up from her concentration camp guards during the war," Zahavi said.

Jayne looked at him. She recalled Zahavi telling her many years ago that his mother, Astrid, had survived the camps.

"Bergen-Belsen, wasn't it, I seem to remember?" Jayne asked. "She was Dutch and knew Anne Frank and her sister, Margot, I think you told me?"

"You've got a good memory," Zahavi said. "She was very fortunate. She was very ill, days from death, when the camp was liberated by the British in April 1945. She knew Anne and Margot from Amsterdam, where they all grew up."

Anne Frank, who later became posthumously famous for her diaries, died in the same camp a month or two earlier, Zahavi said.

"That was the twist of fate—Anne and Margot died, and my mother survived and eventually made it back home. But the rest of her family were all murdered by the Nazis. Then she came to Tel Aviv ten years later and met my father. Anyway, enough of that. I'll tell you more another time."

A minute later, Shiloah returned, accompanied by a man and a woman. Both appeared to be in their forties and looked physically fit.

He first introduced Odeya, a slim, striking woman of similar height to Jayne, with olive skin and short dark hair was brushed back in a style that was also like hers. Then came Rafael, with receding short salt-and-pepper hair. Both had specialized in Continental Europe for much of their twenty-year careers.

Jayne shook hands with both of them as Shiloah closed the door. She stared at Rafael. The name rang a bell with her, but she didn't recognize the face. "You're not the runner, are you?" she asked.

Rafael looked surprised. "Do you follow athletics?"

"I do."

It turned out that he was indeed the same Rafael Levy she recalled who had run in the 5,000 meters for Israel in the 1992 Olympics in Barcelona and in the 1996 Olympics in Atlanta.

"I missed a bronze in Barcelona by a quarter of a second and in Atlanta finished fifth. That was the end of my high-level career," he said, with a grin. "Work got in the way of training. I run occasional marathons these days."

He modestly admitted that his current marathon times were usually around two hours forty minutes, putting him very high up the rankings for his age group.

"Don't you ever get recognized?" Jayne asked. "Does it cause issues?"

"Never. I'm yesterday's man. Only athletics followers of a certain age like you would recognize the name—which I never use anyway. I have multiple identities. And the disguise department is very good. Running is actually a good cover story, I find. Races are held everywhere, all the time. It's a good excuse to travel."

Shiloah rubbed his hands together. "That's enough sports talk. We need to discuss running an operation, not a marathon. Shall we make a start?"

CHAPTER SIX

Sunday, April 10, 2016
  Vienna

It seemed somewhat ironic to Jayne that the Iranian delegation had chosen the magnificent Hotel Imperial that once employed Adolf Hitler as a teenage casual laborer, given that they themselves were seemingly intent on facilitating a second Holocaust.

But ironic or not, they were certainly staying in style. The Imperial, which dated back to 1863 and was originally the home of the prince of Württemberg, was located a short distance along the tree-lined Kärntner Ring from the Vienna State Opera. Most of the delegation to the International Conference on Nuclear Security were in rooms costing about three hundred euros per night.

The more lavish junior executive suite reserved for the deputy director of the Atomic Energy Organization of Iran, Jafar Farsad, cost even more at five hundred euros for each of the six nights the delegation was booked for.

Clearly the Iranians were making up for their somewhat more spartan existence at home, where most of them worked at the Natanz nuclear facility, in the center of the country.

The nuclear facility, a twenty-minute car journey north of the small, dusty town of Natanz and a good two hundred kilometers south of Tehran, was at the foot of the soaring Karkas mountain chain. It was there that Iran was suspected of secretly building underground nuclear warhead development facilities. Jayne knew it was a barren, almost treeless region, and there would be few luxuries available to nuclear scientists.

It had taken a few hours of work by the technical team at the Mossad headquarters building to find the Iranian delegation's hotel booking. But once they had, Zahavi, Jayne, Odeya, and Rafael were checked into the five-star Imperial, and Zahavi made sure to obtain a generous expenses clearance from Avi Shiloah.

All were traveling under false identities. In Jayne's case, she used her favorite legend of Carolina Blanco, born in Buenos Aires of British parents. She possessed a full set of identity documents for Blanco, including a British passport, a driver's license, and a working credit card, as well as a full backstory that would stand up to scrutiny. She had recently acquired another false British identity, Ashima Caire, to add to her other backup of Siobhan Delks, but decided to save that for another occasion.

Just after they checked in, a brief update came through from Shiloah's office in Tel Aviv. The condition of Paul Farrar and Mark Nicklin-Donovan was unchanged. Both remained unconscious.

The five-day nuclear security conference, scheduled to run from Monday to Friday, was to be held at the International Atomic Energy Agency's building, part of the enormous United Nations complex on the north bank of the River Danube.

A visit by a specialist Mossad surveillance team to the IAEA building confirmed Jayne's thought that security at the conference would be tight.

Nonetheless, the Mossad was in the process of securing passes to the event for both Odeya and Rafael, positioning them as members of the real Israeli nuclear energy delegation that was attending, but under their false names. Israel had research reactors and was considering building full-scale nuclear power plants. Jayne didn't ask how they had managed to obtain the passes.

However, the main focus in terms of surveillance was the seven-story Hotel Imperial.

The technical team in Tel Aviv had hacked into the hotel's computer system and obtained room numbers for the Iranian delegation. It turned out that Amir Rad had not traveled to Vienna and presumably wasn't attending the conference. Otherwise, all were on the second floor apart from Farsad, whose suite, with a balcony, was on the top floor, helpfully well away from the others.

Jayne's team was on the third floor, in similar rooms to the Iranians.

She was impressed with the speed at which Odeya and Rafael worked. Within two hours of checking in, they had made contact with a *sayan,* one of the Mossad's secret army of unofficial and usually unpaid helpers scattered across the Jewish diaspora.

The woman, who worked in the hotel's administration team, helped them to gain access to the staff quarters. There they obtained two butler's uniforms, complete with white bow ties and waistcoats, black jackets, and white gloves, used by the men who provided service to the hotel's premium rooms. They also produced two maid's uniforms and a room service waitress's costume, along with staff passkeys the *sayan* had sourced for all the Iranians' rooms.

The intention was to use the uniforms as cover to mount a surveillance operation on Farsad.

Odeya handed Jayne a briefing note on Farsad, which she read quickly, together with a photograph. He was fifty years old and had been married in 1992, and his photograph showed him with a neatly clipped short gray beard, a full head of similarly gray hair, and modern frameless glasses.

He and his wife had four children, the eldest of which was now twenty-two and the youngest thirteen. He had spent his entire working career with the Atomic Energy Agency of Iran, having studied nuclear physics at Manchester University in the UK in the 1980s.

"Can we put cameras in Farsad's suite?" Jayne asked. "And the others too? And also in the corridors outside their rooms?"

Odeya nodded. She reached into her jacket pocket and removed two lightbulbs of different sizes. "There is a camera built into the neck of the bulbs, and of course, they are recharged whenever the bulb is switched on."

"Neat," Jayne said. "What's the operating life?"

"We'll easily get five days out of these, even if the bulbs aren't recharged. The transmitter range is good too. We get up to three hundred meters, even with walls and windows between. We can record the footage onto the laptop—all high definition. We can upload it to Tel Aviv and view it on a phone app too. We can also grab still images from the video. No problem."

Jayne nodded. The candle-bulb cameras matched almost exactly the hotel's existing bulbs that were fitted in wall lights and chandeliers.

Zahavi handed out thin flesh-colored rubber gloves to all of them. "Wear these when needed. No fingerprints."

He also produced a plastic bag containing a variety of wigs of different hair colors and also glasses with plain lenses.

"These are compulsory," Zahavi said. "I suggest you pick a color different to your natural shade, and make sure it covers everything up. We'll wear these for the operation only."

Jayne chose a neat shoulder-length blonde wig, put it on, and checked in the mirror. She had to admit, it was of exceptionally high quality. It was impossible to tell that it was a wig. The Mossad's disguise department knew their business. She also picked a pair of black-framed designer glasses.

The first step was to install the camera bulbs in a light fixture in the corridor opposite the door to Farsad's room. This was made easier once Rafael had established that there were no hotel security cameras in that particular section of corridor. The feed from the microcamera could then be accessed from Zahavi's laptop computer.

Once completed, Odeya and Rafael repeated the exercise in the second-floor corridor where the other Iranians were staying.

Once the cameras were in place, the four of them gathered in Zahavi's room to check the outputs and to formulate a plan to install more bulbs in the Iranians' rooms.

They agreed that the earliest opportunity to do this would be when the delegation left the Imperial the following morning to head to the IAEA buildings, about four and a half kilometers northeast across the other side of the Danube.

"What about weapons?" Jayne asked. "Handguns?"

Zahavi nodded. "They're being taken care of. Our embassy has its uses."

At about half past ten that evening, Jayne was back in her room, thinking about taking a shower, when there was a knock at the door. It was Zahavi, carrying his laptop.

"We have a problem," he said after she had let him in. "The corridor cameras have picked up some activity. We probably shouldn't be surprised at this, but our Iranian guests have company. Two men. We think they were actually already installed in the hotel when Farsad and the others arrived. One is in the suite to the right of Farsad's. The other is in a room on the second-floor corridor with the other guys."

Jayne grimaced. "You mean bodyguards?"

"More than bodyguards. I sent images of them back to Tel Aviv, and they've run them through the facial recognition system. Both men are known to us. They're Quds."

"Ah."

The Quds Force was part of Iran's notorious Islamic Revolutionary Guard Corps, the IRGC, and specialized in military intelligence and special operations, including assassinations and terrorist-style activities overseas.

"Look at them," Zahavi said. He opened his laptop. On the screen, the video in pause mode, was an image of two heavily muscled men dressed in dark clothing standing in the corridor on the second floor. Despite the slightly blurred image, Jayne could see that both men looked to be in their thirties, with cropped hair.

"This complicates things," Zahavi said. "I'm hoping they are just here in a protection role and that they'll go to the conference with Farsad and his colleagues."

"How senior are these guys?" Jayne asked. The presence of guards was to be expected, given the Mossad's track record in eliminating Iranian nuclear scientists in the past, but she wanted to gauge their likely capability.

"High level. We think they are the same two who tried to assassinate the Saudi Arabian ambassador in Washington a couple of years ago."

Jayne cursed out loud. She well remembered the failed hit

on the Saudi ambassador, not least because Vic had gone into a tailspin at the time and still sometimes talked about it. It was the latest strike in the age-old Iran-Saudi power struggle and was seen as the Iranians' way of making a point about the close relationship between the Saudis and the US.

"What's their routine?" Jayne asked.

"They seem to be checking the corridors every half hour or so."

"We'll just have to work around them," Jayne said.

Zahavi nodded. "I've already got Unit 8200 involved. They've managed to get a tap on Farsad's phones. He's already made one interesting call—not using his official phone, but one with a locally bought SIM card."

Unit 8200, also based near Glilot Interchange, was the Mossad's equivalent of the National Security Agency in the US or Government Communications Headquarters, GCHQ, in the UK. It specialized in the collection of all kinds of signals intelligence by tapping into phones, computers, emails, and other electronic communications globally.

Jayne folded her arms. "Who to?"

"A woman."

"Not his wife, I assume?" Jayne asked.

"Correct. It was to a British cell phone, but the person he called was here in Vienna."

"Really? What did they talk about?"

"It was a very short call. He simply said he was at this hotel and would be here until Saturday morning. She said okay and hung up. They spoke in English."

"An affair?" Jayne asked, her tone giving away her surprise.

Iranians, particularly those in leadership positions, were generally conservative in moral matters. Iranian law was strict, and if this was an adulterous liaison that Farsad was arranging, he would almost certainly face punishment at home if discovered, potentially a hundred lashes. But maybe it wasn't what it seemed.

Zahavi shrugged. "Let's find out."

"We need to put him under round-the-clock surveillance, then, including the conference," Jayne said. "It might well be an opportunity."

CHAPTER SEVEN

Monday, April 11, 2016
  Vienna

Odeya returned to the hotel that evening to report that she had seen nothing from Farsad at the IAEA conference that aroused interest.

The Iranian nuclear chief had attended plenary sessions for all guests in the main conference hall during the morning and afternoon, Odeya said, and also a couple of side events on the fringes of the conference about reactor safety. But he didn't speak in public or ask any questions and made only a few cursory notes during the presentations.

To Jayne and Zahavi's relief, the two Quds Force guards accompanied the Iranian delegation to the IAEA, which left the way clear for Rafael to enter Farsad's and the others' rooms and install the bulb cameras. In most rooms they had been able to place two bulbs.

So far, the video surveillance had not revealed much of note either.

Apart from eating a simple dinner of grilled fish and vegetables in the hotel's restaurant, Farsad didn't move from his room that evening. He didn't change out of the collarless white long-sleeve shirt and black jacket he had been wearing all day.

The two cameras in his room showed him sitting at his desk to work on his laptop, saying prayers, reading a magazine, and then watching a news program on the TV as he lay on his bed.

Farsad made only one short phone call, to his wife in Natanz, and received no calls.

At one point, he opened the door that led to his balcony and stood outside looking down at the scenes on Kärntner Ring far below him. The grand old boulevard, with its trams, bars, and cafés, served as a kind of ring road for the historic Inner City district of Vienna. It formed part of the area of the city that UNESCO had designated as a World Heritage Site. There was plenty to watch.

It was only at just after eleven o'clock, when Jayne, Zahavi, Odeya, and Rafael were having a final meeting to decide on a plan for the next day, that the activity began.

Zahavi had six video feeds from different cameras running permanently in a grid pattern on his laptop screen, showing the two corridors and Farsad's room. He kept a close eye on them as the team chatted. The two Quds officers maintained a routine of patrolling the corridors past all the Iranians' rooms every thirty minutes or so.

Jayne, sitting on the opposite side of his desk, noticed Zahavi yawn, then stiffen and focus on the laptop. He hunched over the screen.

"Seeing something?" she asked.

He nodded. "Our guy may have a visitor."

Jayne jumped from her chair and went to look at the screen. On the top right feed, coming from Farsad's room, the video showed him standing next to the door, peering out through the fish-eye peephole.

"I think he's looking out for someone," Zahavi said, his arms folded.

Jayne kept switching her attention between the feed from Farsad's room and the one from the corridor camera, in the top left box on the screen.

The corridor remained empty.

But after a couple of minutes, a hotel room service waitress, wearing the usual black waistcoat and white blouse, appeared around the corner from the direction of the elevators, carrying a tray with a plate of cookies and a white mug.

She was glancing at the room numbers and stopped outside Farsad's. As she did so, the door opened and the Iranian stood on the threshold, holding the door open to allow her to enter.

The microphone picked up audio from the corridor. "Mr. Farsad?" the waitress asked.

"Yes, please come in," Farsad could be heard saying.

Zahavi's shoulders sank and he relaxed back into his chair. "Late-night hot chocolate."

The door closed behind the waitress, who was slim, with black hair pulled back into a bun. The room camera showed her walking to a coffee table next to the long sofa near the window and placing the tray on it.

Zahavi turned and faced Odeya and Rafael. "So, tomorrow, I think we'll need to have a virtual repeat of today, so I suggest that—"

"Wait," Jayne interrupted. "Look."

She pointed at the laptop screen.

The waitress was embracing Farsad, and then they began to kiss—long and deep. His hands were spread across her back, drawing her closer.

"Unbelievable," Zahavi said. He returned to his hunched position over his computer.

The conversation between the two of them was now clearly audible. They were asking each other how they had been and giggling a little. These were clearly two people who had known each other for a long time.

The woman, it quickly became obvious from her accent, was British.

"Bloody hell," Jayne said.

"Obviously the woman he spoke to on the phone," Zahavi said. "But who the hell is she?"

"I don't know, but she's getting her clothes off," Jayne said. The woman had removed her waistcoat, kicked off her black shoes, and was loosening her skirt. Within another ten seconds, she was standing in her underwear, revealing a shapely pair of thighs, and was unbuttoning Farsad's shirt.

The Iranian, somewhat to Jayne's surprise, had a well-muscled torso covered with a layer of graying hairs rather than the flab she had been expecting. It looked as though he had been doing gym workouts for some time.

"Right, what are we going to do?" Zahavi said.

"You're sure it's recording?" Jayne asked.

Zahavi pointed to the red dot at the top of the grid on his laptop. "Of course."

"This is gold dust," Jayne said. "I think we need to take a Russian approach to this."

"Yes, blackmail the bastard," Odeya said, a half smile on her face. "He deserves it."

Jayne nodded. "My thinking exactly. But get the video to your HQ and find out who the woman is first. How they know each other. How long this has been going on for."

"It's going through in real time," Rafael said. "They're seeing it live. But it's more a question of what we do now. Do we bust in there and catch them in the act?"

"They're basically in the act now," Jayne said. Indeed, the pair of them were now lying on the bed, naked apart from their underwear, continuing to kiss and fondle each other. "I'm sure your office in Tel Aviv will love this."

Jayne paused for a few seconds, thinking. "If we go in there now, the woman will probably scream or something, or tell someone later. And if she screams, he'll go down in flames because all hell will break loose. Those two Quds Force guys will be in there next. Maybe we just tackle him later, after she's gone. As long as we've got the video, we've got the proof. That will be enough to frighten the shit out of him. He won't want the video to reach Tehran. Perhaps we can even spin this out over a long period—milk him for all the information we can get out of him."

"Is it enough to make him talk?" Zahavi asked.

"A hundred lashes? Maybe much worse?"

By now, the woman's bra had come off and so had Farsad's boxer shorts, swiftly followed by her underwear.

"I'm not going to watch this," Jayne said. "Tell me when they've finished." She walked around the other side of the desk and sat in her original chair.

Zahavi grinned. "They're not exactly porn stars, are they."

"Not bad for a couple in their fifties."

"Like you, then," Zahavi said, winking at Jayne.

Jayne rolled her eyes. "Thanks for the compliment, but I suggest you concentrate on the task in hand."

Zahavi's phone rang. He answered it, then a few seconds later mouthed "HQ" at Jayne.

"You've got it? Good," Zahavi said into his phone. "Can you get some stills of her for facial recognition? We need an ID."

He ended the call, then glanced back at the laptop screen. "The show seems to be over. Farsad didn't last long."

Zahavi glanced at Rafael. "Can you get on the woman's tail when she leaves? We need to know where she's staying."

Rafael put on his jacket and laced his shoes. "I'll wait in the lobby and pick her up there. Let me know when she leaves the room." He headed for the door.

For the following fifteen minutes, Farsad and the woman chatted about people they knew, the references implying they were all in the UK. It was all inconsequential gossip, punctuated with reminiscing about previous encounters between the two of them in other cities.

This was primarily about lust, then—not much substance. It was obvious to Jayne too that their relationship must have dated back many years and must, out of necessity, have been very sporadic in nature.

It seemed impossible that the affair could have been conducted in Iran and therefore presumably depended on Farsad's occasional trips overseas for work reasons.

Fifteen minutes later, the woman got dressed and kissed Farsad. "I will see you on Wednesday night," she said. "Are you sure you can't see me tomorrow?"

"No, I'm sorry," Farsad said. "Tomorrow night I have a visitor." He looked and sounded genuinely peeved.

She put her hands on her hips in a mock show of disappointment.

Farsad walked to the door, opened it, and looked out.

"Checking for Quds," Jayne murmured. There was no sign of the guards.

"Okay, you can go," Farsad said, and the woman headed out the door after a final kiss.

Zahavi immediately sent a message to Rafael, down in the lobby, then turned to Jayne.

"So she's coming back for more later in the week," Zahavi said.

Jayne nodded. "Yes, so whenever he's finished his meeting tomorrow night, that might be the best time for us to strike. It'll give us time to get the information we need. Maybe the visitor tomorrow might give us more ammunition too."

"I agree with you," Zahavi said. "Tomorrow night."

CHAPTER EIGHT

Tuesday, April 12, 2016
    Vienna

The Mossad's combined resources worked quickly overnight.
By breakfast time, they had produced some of the information needed for the approach to Farsad.

Rafael's surveillance of Farsad's lover revealed that she was
staying on the fourth floor of a significantly less luxurious
hotel than the Imperial, about a kilometer away toward the
Danube.

With that information, Unit 8200 then hacked the hotel's
computer system and discovered only one single woman in
the reservations for that floor, named Yassamine Tabrizi.

The research department picked up the case and found
that she had been born in the UK of British-Iranian parents.
Her connection to Farsad stemmed from Manchester University in northern England, where they had both studied
nuclear physics in the 1980s.

There was no confirmation, but Jayne assumed that their

affair had either started at university or they had developed a close friendship there and it had later turned into something more intimate.

Yassamine, it turned out, was also attending the IAEA conference in Vienna because she now worked for Sellafield, a large nuclear fuel reprocessing business in Cumbria, northern England.

However, the two clearly hadn't taken the risk of speaking to each other at the conference, as confirmed by Odeya, who continued to keep a very close eye on Farsad each day.

It emerged that Yassamine, like Farsad, was married. She had two teenage children, one of whom had recently started at university in London, and the other was still at school in the town of Whitehaven, near the Sellafield site, where the family lived. Her husband, who was English, was an engineer who worked on offshore wind farm construction projects.

Unit 8200 also unearthed a handful of very short text messages between the unofficial cell phone that Farsad was using and Yassamine's device, confirming what they'd said during their liaison: their next meeting was set for late Wednesday evening in Farsad's hotel room.

Jayne and Rafael had gathered in Zahavi's room to begin planning work for the operation against Farsad when a very brief medical update came through from Shiloah's office in Tel Aviv. Paul Farrar had regained consciousness but still required surgery to repair unspecified internal organs that had been damaged in the blast. Mark Nicklin-Donovan remained unconscious despite an operation to relieve the pressure on his brain from bleeding.

Jayne sighed as Zahavi read out the update. At least Mark was still alive. She would have to just keep on hoping and praying. They turned their attention back to planning details for the operation.

There was broad agreement that Zahavi and Jayne would

go to Farsad's room, while Rafael and Odeya would act as backups, wearing their hotel uniforms as cover while waiting in the corridors nearby.

Zahavi took a small backpack from the safe at the back of his wardrobe and from it removed three Beretta 71 pistols and a heavier duty Walther PPK, the .32-caliber variant, together with a spare magazine and a silencer for each gun. These were the weapons that the Israeli embassy had provided at the team's request.

He handed Berettas to Rafael and Odeya, took the third for himself, and gave the Walther to Jayne.

Jayne was interested to see the Israelis had chosen the Berettas, along with .22 Long Rifle rounds. They definitely had less stopping power than the Walther Jayne had asked for, but Rafael explained that they all liked the 71s because they were light and quick, as well as reliable and relatively quiet.

"Provided we shoot accurately, they're superb," Rafael said.

"Let's hope we don't need them," Zahavi said.

"Probably not unless the Quds get involved," Jayne said.

Zahavi looked at her for a second before answering. "I wasn't going to say that."

Rafael had sent a copy of the video from Farsad's hotel room the previous evening to all their phones. He had also obtained from Mossad's research department phone numbers for Farsad's wife, Rana, in case they were needed while persuading him to talk.

Finally, Zahavi handed out a bunch of long plastic cable ties to each of them, in case they needed to restrain Farsad, together with a soft rubber ball that could be used as a gag and a small reel of duct tape to secure it.

Zahavi pulled a plan of the hotel from a folder and picked up a pen.

"This is what I think we should do," he said as he began to draw on the map.

* * *

Tuesday, April 12, 2016
Vienna

It turned out that Farsad hadn't been lying when he told his British girlfriend that he couldn't see her that evening because he had a visitor, Rafael noted with some surprise.

Soon after the Iranian nuclear scientist arrived back at the Hotel Imperial from the IAEA conference, he headed down to the restaurant, where an elderly man joined him for dinner.

Rafael, who had carefully positioned himself ten meters away at a table by himself, used his phone to surreptitiously take a photograph of the man, which he dispatched to Tel Aviv for identification.

Some rapid research at Mossad's head office determined that he was a retired Iranian nuclear engineer who had acted as Farsad's mentor in the early years of his career. A resident of Tehran, he was now attending the Vienna conference in a private capacity, perhaps as a hobby.

The two men enjoyed what appeared to be a convivial evening. Indeed, after finishing their meal, they moved to the lounge, took seats next to a blazing log fire, and ordered coffee.

Rafael followed a few minutes later, also ordered a coffee, and took a seat across the room that gave him a good view of Farsad.

He glanced around the lounge. There were a lot of well-heeled elderly people there. It made him think of his grandmother, who had grown up and lived in Vienna.

Years earlier, he and his mother had visited her old house, only two kilometers from where he was now sitting. The memory of the pain etched on his mother's face made him feel momentarily teary, something that seldom happened, if ever.

His grandmother had been murdered at the Auschwitz concentration camp, where she was sent three years after the Nazi Anschluss, or annexation of Austria, in March 1938.

Like many of her fellow Austrian Jews, she had failed to obtain the necessary documents to permit her to leave Austria for somewhere safer. By some miracle, her daughter, who later became Rafael's mother, managed to flee from Vienna unscathed to the Netherlands and then the UK, thanks to the Kindertransport initiative to rescue Jewish children, organized by a Dutch woman, Geertruida Wijsmuller-Meijer. His mother later moved to the newly founded Israel in the 1950s.

His grandmother's fate had been one of the factors that had inspired Rafael to take up a career with the Mossad. He had always sworn to himself that he would do everything in his power to prevent such genocide from occurring again, and that included the threat from Iranian nuclear missiles.

The other inspiration had been the 1972 Munich Olympics massacre. Although Rafael had only been two years old at the time, the story of the murder of eleven Israeli team members and the ensuing Mossad mission to hunt down the killers from Black September—Operation Wrath of God— had been a major factor in his decisions to become an athlete and a *katsa*.

Farsad was still sipping his coffee and talking animatedly with his friend. Rafael sank back into his chair and pretended to read something on his phone.

This kind of surveillance work was very routine for him. He had joined the Mossad after the usual three-year period of compulsory service in the Israel Defense Forces, which he completed at age twenty-two, followed by a degree course in international relations at Loughborough University in the UK. He had chosen the university partly because of its reputation for sports and his running ability.

Part of his IDF service was spent with the Sayeret Matkal special forces unit, which was ostensibly involved in intelligence gathering and surveillance but in practice was a lot more hands-on in commando-type operations. The other part was with the Mista'arvim unit, an elite counterterrorism team, usually working undercover to either assassinate or capture terrorists intent on damaging Israel.

From there, after he left the IDF, it seemed a logical step to become a *katsa*—a case officer—with the Mossad. But his Mista'arvim experience meant he also worked as a *kidon*—one of the Mossad's team of assassins.

Now, at the age of forty-six, he was a seasoned professional who had taken part in some of the agency's highest-profile, and notorious, operations over the past couple of decades. Most of them had been on European soil, with the usual targets being individuals who were intent on damaging Israel in one way or another. The Iranians, Hezbollah, Hamas, and the Russians were usually near the top of the list.

Farsad and his friend remained in the lounge until just after ten, when Farsad rose, shook hands with his former colleague, and headed for the elevators.

At that point Rafael sent a message to Zahavi's phone on the third floor and walked toward the staircase.

The time was near to put another operation into action against the old enemy, although this time the intention was to extract information from the target, not end his life.

Rafael suspected that, depending on what was obtained from Farsad, the latter objective might follow. It was often the way of things.

* * *

Tuesday, April 12, 2016
    Vienna

While Jayne was waiting for Farsad to finish his dinner downstairs, she was summoned onto a conference call by Vic, who together with Veltman wanted a short briefing on the operation that was about to start.

Vic also patched in the head of his Near East Division, Mike Hill, and the analysis directorate's Israel desk chief, Jodie Geary, along with Garfield Wattley from the Tel Aviv station, all of whom had been heavily involved in the gas platform visit since the planning stage.

"How confident is the Mossad team that Farsad will have the information we need about the gas platform and the Iranian nuclear program?" Vic asked.

"He must know about the nuclear program," Jayne said. "Regarding the gas platform, we know he's a very trusted adviser to the Supreme Leader and the president. We're hopeful."

Jayne went on to briefly outline the operation that was planned for that evening, including details of Farsad's British girlfriend and the liaison that had been filmed.

"We had another meeting with Ferguson today," Veltman said. "He's getting increasingly anxious about his trip to Israel. The Israelis are planning for Moshe Cohen's funeral to take place at the Knesset, which is fine. Jerusalem can be secured for that. But then Cohen's family wants the memorial service and burial afterward to take place at their farm, a winery down in the south near Sderot."

"As you can imagine, that's more complicated," Geary

chipped in. "The winery's only a few kilometers from the Gaza Strip."

"And they want Ferguson to go there?" Jayne asked.

"Yes, that's the plan, along with everyone else," Geary said.

"I've spoken to Charles Deacon about this," Veltman said. "Quite apart from the personal connection the president has with Cohen, he felt that he should accept the invitation given everything that has been done for Farrar—he's had first-class medical treatment. He also wants to make a statement—he's not going to be cowed by terrorists."

Jayne paused for a few seconds to digest what Veltman was saying. She knew there had been ongoing rocket attacks on towns and villages in the Negev Desert area of southern Israel, all launched by Hamas from within Gaza.

"That sounds risky," Jayne said. There were any number of ways for Hamas or other terrorist groups to get their weapons into Gaza, and although the Israelis had their Iron Dome rocket protection system, it wasn't yet geared to stopping drones.

"Tell me about it. Anyway, Ferguson has had another call with Prime Minister Katz and thinks he's sounding increasingly trigger-happy. So no pressure, Jayne."

Jayne felt like telling Veltman what to do with his pressure but held herself back. "I'll report back to you all when we're done here," she said in a flat tone.

"Right," Veltman said. "And also make sure nothing happens tonight that might provoke the Iranians any further."

This time Jayne couldn't hold back a snort. "Of course. Look, I need to go. We're beginning this operation soon."

Without waiting for a reply, she ended the call.

CHAPTER NINE

Tuesday, April 12, 2016
　　Vienna

As was always the case before an operation, Jayne felt the butterflies fluttering in her stomach. She had learned over the years to view it as a good thing, as it meant all her senses were in overdrive and, if anything, made her sharper under pressure.

She and Zahavi, who had each changed into an Imperial Hotel maid's and butler's uniform respectively, planned to wait until the Quds officers had done their usual corridor check before they made their move.

As the clock ticked, the room became quiet in anticipation.

Each of them checked their pistols, attached the suppressors, and placed a spare magazine in their pockets. They also all put on their wigs, fake glasses, and skin-tight rubber gloves. Then they checked the feeds from the surveillance cameras on Zahavi's laptop once again.

The camera feed from Farsad's room showed him in an armchair reading something on an iPad.

At twenty minutes past ten, one of the Quds carried out his usual patrol along the corridor before returning to his room.

At that point, Rafael, also wearing a butler's uniform complete with white cotton gloves over his rubber ones, left to take up his position near the elevators on the seventh floor, around the corner from the corridor where Farsad's room was located.

Jayne checked the seventh-floor surveillance camera, which showed that the corridor outside Farsad's room was deserted.

Zahavi, who had an open line to Rafael, muttered into his phone, "Are we all clear?"

When the answer came in the affirmative, he turned to Jayne. "Let's go."

They left Zahavi's room, followed by Odeya, also in a maid's uniform. The three of them climbed the stairs to the seventh floor. They met nobody. At the top of the stairwell, Odeya took up a position near the door to the corridor, no more than twelve meters from Farsad's room.

Jayne and Zahavi continued through the door into the corridor, which remained clear, to Jayne's relief.

Zahavi, also wearing white butler's gloves, knocked gently on Farsad's door, while Jayne remained farther down the corridor, pressed against the wall.

There came an extended silence that lasted for what seemed like an eternity but was probably no longer than fifteen seconds. Jayne assumed that Farsad was looking through the peephole at his visitor. Then the door finally clicked open.

"Good evening, Mr. Farsad, I apologize for disturbing you late in the evening," Zahavi said in English. He gave a short bow in Farsad's direction. "Our monitoring system is showing an error with your television, unfortunately. It's the wake-up alarm function. We need to change a setting manually to correct it. It won't take more than a minute. I am sorry for the disturbance. May I come in?"

There was a pause. "Can it wait until the morning?" Farsad said. "I have no plans to use the alarm."

From her position against the wall, Jayne couldn't see the Iranian but she could hear him.

"Regretfully not," Zahavi said. "If we don't change the setting, the alarm could turn the TV on automatically during the night, which I'm certain you don't want."

Another pause. "This is very annoying. I was about to go to bed. All right. Come in. As long as you are quick."

"Thank you, sir. Once again, apologies for the disturbance."

Zahavi stepped into the doorway, and Jayne moved smartly to follow him into the room. She closed the door behind her.

"Where did she come from?" Farsad demanded when he saw Jayne. "Why does a maid need to come too?"

"She's my assistant," Zahavi said. "I hope you don't mind."

Jayne saw Zahavi slip his Beretta from his jacket while Farsad's attention was diverted toward her.

"I'm afraid we also need to ask you a few questions," Zahavi continued. He neatly flicked off the safety on his pistol, raised it, and pointed it directly at Farsad's head. "Don't say a word until I tell you. Raise your hands."

"*What?*" the Iranian spat. "Who are you?"

"I said raise your hands and don't speak until you're told," Zahavi said.

"Shut up, else we will gag you," Jayne added in Farsi. "Keep your voice down and you won't get hurt. We need to talk."

Farsad slowly raised his hands.

Jayne took her Walther from her pocket, turned off the safety, and leveled the gun at Farsad. "Do you want to search him while I cover you?" she asked Zahavi, reverting to English.

Zahavi removed a wallet and two phones from Farsad's pockets, which he placed on a table near the door that led to the balcony, out of the Iranian's reach.

"Now sit in the chair," Zahavi said, indicating the armchair behind Farsad. He removed his phone from his pocket.

The Iranian sat while Jayne covered him with the Walther.

"I just want to play you a short video. Watch this," Zahavi said as he tapped the screen of his phone.

The film began playing at the point where Farsad and Yassamine were lying on the bed, wearing only their underwear.

"You bastards," Farsad said, his voice low as he watched the screen.

"Would you like us to send this to Tehran?" Zahavi asked.

Farsad's face stiffened, his eyes flicking between Zahavi and Jayne. "No, don't do that."

"If you answer our questions, we won't," Zahavi said.

Farsad's face visibly drained of color. "What questions?"

Zahavi turned off the video and instead switched on his video-recording app. He tapped the record button and pointed the lens at Farsad.

"First, we would like to know about your nuclear weapons program. Last year, your country signed a deal with six other countries under which you agreed not to enrich uranium beyond 3.6 percent purity, restricting it to use for power generation only. And enrichment must be carried out only at Natanz. Have you stuck to that agreement? Or do you have other secret sites where enrichment is taking place? Are you developing nuclear warheads?"

Farsad bowed his head against his chest. "I cannot answer."

"All right," Zahavi said. "My understanding is that the punishment for what you have been doing in this hotel room is likely a hundred lashes in public. You will also lose your job and face disgrace. I have three email addresses here—for the office of your director, Amir Rad, for the office of the president, and for the Supreme Leader's assistant." He read out the addresses. "I will email clips from the video of you and Yassamine to them. Do you want me to do that?"

Farsad's eyes widened at the mention of Yassamine's name. He slowly shook his head.

"Then give me an answer. If you answer truthfully, this video will go nowhere. You can continue with your conference and return to Iran on Saturday as planned."

Farsad closed his eyes and lowered his head, visibly wilting as he realized he had been checkmated.

"There is work going on," Farsad said eventually, his voice faltering. "It's underground."

"Thank you," Zahavi said. "Where is this work happening?"

"Not at Natanz."

"Where then?"

"Military sites," Farsad said, his voice now barely audible. He was staring at the floor.

"Which ones?"

Farsad said nothing.

Jayne knew that Iran had refused all access to classified military sites by nuclear inspectors from the IAEA, which was responsible for monitoring nuclear activity by Iran. The IAEA had accepted that position. But there had been suspicion in many quarters that enrichment was continuing at military bases.

"I'm waiting," Zahavi said.

"Parchin and Bandar," Farsad muttered.

"Any others?"

"And Lavizan." Farsad's eyes were now closed.

"Lavizan. That's three. Any more?"

Farsad shook his head. "That is all, to my knowledge."

Jayne breathed out. These were all military sites that rang true with Jayne. This was a huge disclosure.

Game-changing.

"Okay, we will come back to that later," Zahavi said. "My next question relates to the recent drone attack on the offshore Samar gas platform, near Tel Aviv. Was your country responsible for that attack?"

At this, Farsad became visibly animated. He opened his eyes and stared at Zahavi, shaking his head vigorously. "No, Iran did not do it."

"Are you certain? Who was responsible, then?"

"It was not Iran," Farsad said. "We are not trying to provoke a war. I speak to very senior people in our government regularly. I know these things. The speculation is incorrect."

Zahavi continued to video Farsad's responses on his phone.

"So who was it?" Zahavi asked.

Farsad shook his head.

Jayne sensed that Farsad was holding back information. "You must have some idea," she said. "You insist it was not Iran. So who was it?"

There was another silence. Farsad glanced first at Jayne, then at Zahavi, before returning his gaze to the floor.

"Come on," Jayne said. "Who was it?"

"Follow the money," Farsad muttered, still staring at the floor. "That's what you British say, isn't it?"

"What do you mean, 'follow the money'?" Jayne asked. "You mean, who's benefiting from the attack?"

"No. Who would benefit if Iran was attacked and it retaliated and a war started. And if sanctions were reimposed on Iran. And if Iran truly started increasing its nuclear program once again in response," Farsad said. His head came up again and he looked Jayne in the eye.

She grasped what he was saying. "You mean the black market? The illegal nuclear supply chain?"

"Yes."

"Nuclear equipment suppliers?" Jayne asked.

"Yes."

"Give me some names."

Farsad tipped his head back and stared at the ceiling. "I can't. They'd kill me."

"If you don't, you're finished," Jayne said. "And they wouldn't know you had provided the names, anyway."

Farsad groaned. "Get the names from someone else."

"They wouldn't—"

"We want them from you, right now," Zahavi interrupted her. "And we want to know exactly who attacked the gas platform."

Now Jayne felt a spike of irritation at Zahavi disrupting her flow of questions.

"Like I said, follow the money. Follow the supply chain," Farsad muttered. "There's a retired IAEA official called Heinz. Talk to him."

"Right. Heinz who?" Jayne asked.

"I don't recall the last name. Just go and—"

But Farsad got no further.

He was interrupted by a knock at the door, followed by the rattle of the door handle.

Jayne turned and looked at it. The handle was being jerked up and down by someone out in the corridor who was trying to get in.

It stopped, and then came the multiple *thwack, thwack, thwack* of suppressed gunfire as rounds smashed into the door from outside the room.

Although the door was thick, holes were appearing in the wood around the lock and handle, sending splinters flying.

Jayne felt a wave of adrenaline shoot through her body. "Shit, let's get out of here."

"The balcony door," Zahavi said as he shoved his phone into his pocket. "Go. Take him with us. He's compromised."

"Yes," Jayne said. "Go left on the balcony. Room to the right is Quds."

Zahavi nodded at the reminder, moved to the balcony door, twisted the key that was in the lock, and opened it.

"Come on, quick," he barked as he led the way outside.

Farsad, his eyes popping and his fists clenched, had already jumped to his feet.

The sound of gunfire continued as more rounds splintered through the door.

Jayne grabbed Farsad by the elbow, but the Iranian needed no encouragement. He grabbed his two phones and his wallet as he passed the table where Zahavi had placed them.

"It's the Quds," he said.

"Yes," Jayne said. "And they'll be in here in a second. Go!"

She exited the room onto the balcony, Farsad right behind her.

The balconies, clearly a relatively new addition to the hotel, were formed from a long steel and glass structure that ran across the entire width of the top floor. Each balcony was separated from the one belonging to the neighboring room by a waist-high glass panel.

As Jayne exited the room, Zahavi was already vaulting

over the panel to the neighboring balcony on the left side. A young couple in evening dress, both holding glasses of champagne, stood against the railing. The woman let out a scream as the action erupted around them and dropped her glass on the floor.

From behind her, Jayne heard a loud smash as the door to the hotel room finally gave in, and the sound of gunfire became far louder.

She jumped over the glass panel, following Zahavi, and turned to give Farsad a hand over the barrier.

But as she reached out, Farsad tripped and, instead of jumping the barrier, fell headlong against it, using his arms to break his fall.

A couple of stray bullets flew out of the open door behind him and smashed into the front safety railings of the balcony.

* * *

Tuesday, April 12, 2016
Vienna

Thwack, thwack, thwack.

As soon as Rafael heard the first muffled gunshots, he guessed what was happening.

He pulled his Beretta 71 with its silencer attached from his jacket pocket, turned off the safety, and moved along the corridor wall until he could sneak a glance around the corner through a narrow gap between the wall and a fire extinguisher.

Outside Farsad's room were the two Quds Force officers. Both were holding guns and one was shooting steadily at the lock.

The other was covering him, sweeping the corridor in

both directions. He had thankfully been looking the other way when Rafael poked his nose around the corner, and Rafael pulled back unseen.

Rafael knew if he didn't act, the Quds would be in the room in moments and would then kill Zahavi, Jayne, and Farsad in seconds.

He couldn't get a shot off without breaking cover, and in a corridor like this, with two men potentially firing at him, he would be a certain goner.

Rafael paused for a couple of seconds, calculating.

Then he had an idea.

He retreated along the corridor toward the elevators, took out his phone, and dialed Odeya, who sensibly had not emerged from where she was stationed in the stairwell on the other side of the gunmen.

"Rafael," she whispered when she answered. "You okay? What the hell—"

"Listen," Rafael murmured into his phone. "I need you to cause a diversion. There's one guy shooting the shit out of Farsad's door; the other's covering him and I need you to distract him. Just slam the stairwell door hard so he hears it and looks. When I hear the door slam, I'm going to take him out. Okay?"

"Got it."

"Go. Count to ten, then do it."

Rafael ended the call and inched his way back along the wall until he was almost level with the corner.

This would require precision shooting. He estimated there was a distance of roughly fifteen meters from the corner to Farsad's room door. There was no margin for error over that distance with a .22 pistol. He would need a head or heart shot to be sure of taking the guy down, but he knew he could do that.

A few seconds later, above the sound of the suppressed

gunshots, he heard the sharp clang of the stairwell door slamming shut.

Immediately, Rafael emerged into the corridor, just in time to see the first Quds officer disappear inside Farsad's room.

Shit. Too late.

Rafael acquired a flash sight picture and fired directly at the Quds operative still in the corridor, who, as he had hoped, was staring away from him toward the stairwell door, his gun raised.

His first shot missed fractionally to the right, but the second struck the Quds officer somewhere on the head, causing him to stagger forward.

Rafael fired again, this time striking the man on the upper body. Then he began to run toward the room.

The man he had hit was now on the floor and was trying to flip himself over to return fire. Rafael swore, realizing his first headshot must have been a glancing blow. He fired again, this time on the run, and again hit the guy in the head.

He continued running until he reached the room door. There he put another bullet into the head of the man on the floor, just to be certain, and peered cautiously around the threshold.

He was just in time to see the other Quds officer disappear out the door onto the balcony, firing rounds as he went.

There was no sign of Jayne, Zahavi, or Farsad.

* * *

"Quick, get up," Jayne urged Farsad.

Farsad hauled himself to his feet, but as he did so, a figure in black emerged from the hotel room onto the balcony, a gun in hand.

Jayne's sense of self-preservation immediately took over,

and she dived for the safety of the neighboring room's balcony door.

Behind her the muffled sound of semiautomatic gunfire erupted, accompanied by loud screams from the young couple who were still standing outside.

Jayne bashed her knee on the doorframe as she rolled inside the room, just as a couple of rounds shattered the glass door a few inches to her right.

She jumped to her feet, ignoring the pain shooting up from her knee, and saw Zahavi ahead of her, opening the door into the corridor.

Farsad had not appeared through the balcony door behind her.

Just then, more gunfire sounded from outside.

He's a goner.

She sprinted as fast as she could after Zahavi and out the room door.

As she emerged into the corridor, she caught sight of Rafael entering Farsad's room next door, the same one they had just escaped from.

On the floor of the corridor lay the dead body of another black-clad man, recognizably one of the Quds, a gun in his hand. A pool of blood from his head was spreading out across the marble floor.

CHAPTER TEN

Tuesday, April 12, 2016
   Vienna

Rafael sprinted into Farsad's hotel room and took cover behind an alcove that housed the minibar and coffee machine.

As he did so, he heard multiple gunshots from outside and a piercing, bloodcurdling scream from a woman. He prayed it wasn't Jayne.

Rafael edged forward until he could see around the side of the alcove, which gave him a view of the balcony door.

Seconds later, the Quds officer reappeared, gun in hand. He was moving fast, but before he could react, Rafael moved out enough to fire two shots in rapid succession. The first struck the Quds guy in the head, the second in the chest.

He hit the floor and lay still.

Rafael ran to him, put a third bullet into his head, and continued to the balcony.

On the balcony to the left there was a young couple. The

woman was crying hysterically and the man was trying to get her inside their room.

They didn't notice him immediately and he tucked his gun behind him.

"Are you all right?" Rafael asked. "What happened?"

The man turned, clutched the woman to him, and shook his head. "We're not all right. A man in black just came out firing his gun, and the other guy jumped straight off the balcony down into the street."

Rafael swore and peered over the edge of the balcony.

There on the sidewalk seven floors down lay a man's body, spreadeagled, with a large pool of blood visible around his head and torso. There was a small crowd gathered around him and more people were running toward him. Some were looking up.

Rafael knew it was Farsad.

On the balcony floor was a cell phone, which Rafael picked up and pocketed.

Before long, the entire hotel was going to be lit up with blue and red police car lights, and the building would be shut down.

"Did you see anyone else?" Rafael asked.

"Other people ran through our room," the man said. "I think they were trying to get away from the guy in black."

Rafael turned and went back into Farsad's room to find Jayne and Zahavi standing in the doorway.

"Thank God. You all right?" Rafael asked. "Farsad's gone. He apparently jumped off the balcony. This bastard was after him." He indicated toward the Quds officer on the floor.

Jayne grimaced. "Jumped? Oh *shit*. That's our fault."

"Don't know," Zahavi said. "But let's get the hell out of here."

He and Jayne turned and moved toward the stairwell where Odeya was stationed, Rafael close behind them. Zahavi shouted through the door to warn Odeya it was them before opening it.

"Grab your laptops and gear from the rooms," Zahavi said as the four of them hustled down the stairs. "We need a way out of here."

"We can get out the rear," Rafael said. "Down the back stairs and into the street. I've already worked out a route."

Outside he could hear sirens wailing.

This is a complete screwup, Rafael thought as they reached the third floor and ran through the stairwell door toward their rooms.

It was obvious the Quds knew something was wrong inside Farsad's room.

Perhaps they too had bugged it, or perhaps Farsad had pressed a hidden alarm button.

Or perhaps they had received a tip-off.

* * *

Tuesday, April 12, 2016
Vienna

Less than five minutes after they had left their rooms with all their belongings, Jayne found herself sitting in the back of a cab next to Odeya and Rafael, heading eastward around the Vienna ring road.

Zahavi was in the front seat, directing the driver to a street near the River Danube where a silver BMW sedan had been left by someone at the Mossad's Vienna station in case of emergency.

The plan now was to use the BMW to drive out of Vienna, and out of Austria, over the border into Germany. It was about a four-hour drive to Munich, where Zahavi had reserved a safe house near the Israeli consulate. They could then fly from Munich if needed. It seemed a much safer bet than the Vienna airport, where security would be on full alert.

They had been helped in their rapid exit from the Hotel Imperial by the state of chaos that had erupted following the shootings.

Rafael's escape route had worked perfectly. There had been no time to change out of their hotel uniforms, so the four of them had thrown on jackets, stuffed their belongings into their cases, and run down the rear stairs.

On the ground floor, hotel guests were running in all directions, calling on phones and yelling at hotel staff, who were trying in vain to control the disordered throng.

Still wearing wigs and fake glasses, they had passed through the ornate lobby, with its gilded balcony, chandeliers, and black, red, and gold marble floor. They all tried to match their movements and body language to the somewhat frenetic actions of those around them in order to avoid attracting attention.

By that stage, there were police and ambulance sirens wailing outside. Two uniformed officers were running toward the reception desk.

Rafael led the way through the rear exit into the street, Bösendorferstrasse, opposite a concert hall, where they quickly picked up the cab.

But now, Jayne had a sinking feeling in her stomach.

The operation had gone badly wrong.

But why?

On no other evening had the Quds Force officers entered Farsad's room.

The rooms and doors were well soundproofed, so although one Quds officer was occupying the room next door, he would not have heard their conversation with Farsad.

Rafael had checked the room thoroughly on both days, and there had been no evidence of a bug.

The truth was, they were lucky to be alive. It seemed clear to Jayne that the Quds officer would have killed her and Zahavi if he had been able. She doubted Farsad was the prime target, unless there was some internal Iranian plotting going on, although he would have met a grim fate as a traitor and an adulterer.

She suddenly felt a little nauseous as a wave of guilt shot through her. Farsad must have believed there was no alternative to jumping. The prospect of being caught by the Quds officers and likely hauled back to Tehran must have been too much.

Zahavi turned around from his position in the front seat of the cab and caught Jayne's eye.

He grimaced, without saying anything. He didn't need to.

"The Quds knew," Jayne said.

"Yes. They knew."

PART TWO

CHAPTER ELEVEN

Wednesday, April 13, 2016
Munich

The Mossad safe house, a three-bedroom apartment above a women's fashion store in Augustenstrasse, two blocks west of the Israeli consulate building in Barer Strasse, was sparsely furnished, and to Jayne's dismay, the fridge was almost empty.

The inquest into the debacle in Vienna therefore began over a makeshift breakfast of plain croissants purchased from a bakery just along the street and black coffee.

All their phones had been pinging and ringing ever since news broke of the killings at the Hotel Imperial in Vienna.

Austrian and international media were all leading with news of the deaths of one of Iran's leading nuclear scientists and two unnamed military men who were believed by Austrian police to work for the Quds Force, part of Iran's notorious IRGC—the Islamic Revolutionary Guard Corps.

Zahavi turned on the television in the living room and switched to Germany's ZDF channel.

A news interview was underway outside the hotel with the woman and her fiancé who had been on the balcony. She tearfully told of the gun battle and how a man had jumped off the balcony while being pursued by another man dressed in black who was firing a pistol.

Jayne was surprised that the couple was being permitted to give TV interviews, guessing that they must surely become key witnesses as police investigated the death of Farsad. Maybe officers simply hadn't gotten that far with their investigation. It seemed quite sloppy, if so.

She gave silent thanks that they hadn't become collateral casualties in the battle, and also felt grateful for the effectiveness of the disguises she and the Mossad team had used.

It seemed from the TV coverage that neither the police nor Austria's domestic intelligence and security agency, the BVT, were able to shed any light on why the Quds Force were in the hotel or why the nuclear scientist had seemingly jumped to his death, or who in turn had shot the Quds officers dead. No useful evidence had yet been found, according to journalists.

However, commentators had already begun pointing to the long history of Israel's intelligence agency, the Mossad, in carrying out bold executions of Iranians and their proxies on European soil. They were suggesting there was a strong possibility it could have been some kind of retaliation for the attack on the offshore gas platform and the deaths of Israel's foreign minister and the head of the Mossad.

"This is a mess," Zahavi said, looking round at Jayne, Rafael, and Odeya. "If it hadn't been for Rafael's quick thinking, we'd all have been history."

He nodded at Rafael. "You did a great job, my friend. I'm going to tell Avi Shiloah that if he criticizes me this weekend."

Shiloah had instructed Zahavi to return briefly to Tel Aviv

on Saturday, first so he could attend Eli Elazar's funeral on Sunday in Jerusalem and also to take part in a crisis meeting for the Mossad's senior team on Sunday evening and Monday.

Zahavi, however, was worried that the meeting might turn into a blow-by-blow inquiry into what had just happened in Vienna.

Rafael inclined his head in acknowledgment of the praise but said nothing.

Typical *kidon*, Jayne thought to herself. Long on action, short on words.

Privately, she agreed that it had been a mess in Vienna, and the truth was that they had Farsad's blood on their hands to some degree. She had been here many times before. The pursuit of critical intelligence had too often resulted in collateral damage to the wrong people. The shadow of guilt loomed large over all of them.

But she was worried that it could yet turn even messier. No doubt at some point police or hotel staff would find the lightbulb cameras in the Iranians' rooms and in the corridors.

It was clear that if the operation did create an impression internationally that the Mossad had struck a retaliatory blow against the Quds Force officers, that would only stoke the fires even further in the Middle East generally.

What if it provoked another Iranian counterattack on Israel?

If so, it certainly wouldn't go down well in Washington or London.

And had they inadvertently left anything in the hotel that would point to their true identities and roles? She was confident that was not the case, given the extensive precautions taken by the Mossad team, but they had left in a complete rush, so only time would tell.

"Much will depend on how deeply and thoroughly the Austrians want to get into investigating this," Zahavi said.

"Everyone hates the Quds and knows their reputation. We'll have to hope the BVT view it as some kind of internal Iranian conflict that went wrong and don't put too much effort into it."

"Yes, but the question for us now is how did the Quds know we were interrogating Farsad in that room?" Jayne asked. "They clearly must have. And they wanted to kill us, and presumably capture him, before he spilled the beans."

"There's only one conclusion," Zahavi said.

Jayne looked at him.

She could only think of one conclusion too.

"I was thinking that after Samar. Now I'm certain. There are too many people who knew about the secretary of state's visit to the platform and about our operation in Vienna. It seems likely to me, though, that our mole has to be either in your headquarters in Tel Aviv or—"

"Or your headquarters at Langley," Zahavi interrupted, pointedly.

"It's not my headquarters," Jayne said. "I'm not a CIA employee."

"You might as well be."

Jayne frowned. She still viewed herself as more aligned with MI6 than anything. That was where she had worked nearly all of her career. It just happened that she had more recently found herself working for the CIA thanks to her relationship with Joe.

"I might consider myself a Mossad employee right now," she retorted. "Anyway, I'll talk to Vic, and you talk to Avi Shiloah, and let's see if we can get investigations underway before any more damage is done."

"Agreed," Zahavi said.

Jayne glanced at Odeya and Rafael, who had sat listening in silence. "I think we need to give Vic and Avi some good news along with the bad. Shall we go through what we've got?"

The sound of a cell phone ringing from one of the bedrooms made them all stop. Whose was it? Rafael jumped up and walked through to go and fetch it.

The truth was, in the short time they had with Farsad, before it came to such a horrific conclusion, he had at least disclosed some massively useful information.

"He's given us some targets," Zahavi said. "Parchin, Bandar, and Lavizan. Tough to get to, as they're military, but we might be able to find a way, once the dust settles in a few months. That's if the IAEA can't get to them first."

Jayne nodded. "But what about the attack on the gas platform? I have the feeling Farsad was about to cough up some useful info. And do we believe him when he said Iran didn't do it?"

Zahavi folded his arms. "He denied it immediately. He seemed almost angry we were accusing Iran of doing it. My guess is he was telling the truth as far as he knows it."

Jayne was inclined to agree with him, although she was going to reserve judgment. "But if not Iran, then who?"

"Follow the money," Zahavi said. "That was his advice. The black market nuclear equipment supply chain."

"But where do we start?"

Rafael reappeared holding a cell phone, sat down, and began tapping at the screen.

Zahavi leaned back in his chair. "Farsad mentioned one name, didn't he? Heinz. He didn't recall the last name."

"Yes, a retired IAEA official," Jayne said. "The name Heinz is all we've got. Can you send that over to Glilot Interchange so they can track him down?"

Rafael interrupted. "Don't bother," he said, holding up the cell phone.

"What?" Jayne asked.

"It's Farsad's phone. There's a Heinz in the directory," Rafael said. "Heinz Müller. It's a German number."

"You got Farsad's phone?" Zahavi asked. "How?"

"I saw Farsad pick it up when we ran out the room," Jayne said. "He took it. I thought it went over the hotel balcony with him."

"Yes, and I picked it up on the balcony," Rafael said, a faint grin on his face. "He must have dropped it."

CHAPTER TWELVE

Wednesday, April 13, 2016
Tehran

"Given that you supposedly allocated your two best operatives to this task and had the advantage of surprise, I am stunned and greatly disappointed that you failed me," the Supreme Leader, Ayatollah Hashemi, said. His voice remained level and menacing.

Despite his external reputation for ruthlessness, the head of Iran's Quds Force special operations group, Nasser Khan, felt his stomach turn over. It wasn't generally a good idea to upset Ali Hashemi.

Khan glanced around the small meeting room at the Office of the Supreme Leader—also known as the House of Leadership—where he and the minister of intelligence and security, Abbas Taeb, had been summoned.

Unlike most of the grand, ornate meeting rooms within the complex of buildings off Azarbayejan Street in District 11, this one was no more than ten meters square, blandly decorated in beige, and with no adornments other than a small portrait of the Supreme Leader that hung on a wall.

In the past, Khan had been to the House of Leadership several times. It wasn't a house but rather a group of historic buildings that served as Hashemi's official residence, his place of work, and a base from where his administrative staff could operate. The complex also included the Imam Khomeini Hussainia, an enormous Shia Muslim congregation hall.

Now this could be the last visit, Khan felt.

He shifted on the low-backed sofa, also covered in beige, and felt a bead of sweat form on his brow. Next to him, Taeb, only a few months into his role, remained motionless.

"Explain, please," Hashemi said, from his seat four meters away. He remained perfectly still. The only part of him to move was his mouth. It was unnerving.

"Sir, I can tell you the operation was carefully planned," Khan said. "As you said, both men are, or rather were, our best operatives. They had the element of surprise. It is quite possible that we will never know exactly how it went wrong. There is nobody we can ask."

Hashemi stroked his long gray and white beard, which was as neatly clipped as ever. "My instructions were clear. We had intelligence that foreign agents were targeting Farsad in that hotel. I wanted the foreign agents eliminated, and I wanted Farsad secured and brought back here for interrogation."

"Yes, sir, they were clear. And those were the instructions given to our men, who—"

"But instead you have lost three of our best men," Hashemi interrupted. He paused, his right hand fingering the checkered black and white Palestinian kaffiyeh that was draped around his shoulders beneath his black robes.

"You have lost our head of nuclear weapons development plus two of our Quds Force, and the foreigners got away untouched," Hashemi continued. "For all we know, Farsad told them everything. *Everything*. Most of all, I fail to understand how he threw himself off a balcony." He stared at Khan. "Could your men do nothing to prevent him?"

Khan bowed his head until his chin touched his chest. "Sir, I am deeply sorry. Our men were instructed to bring him back. That is all I can say. I am certain they would have tried their utmost to do that. None of us suspected that Farsad might commit suicide in that manner."

"Not good enough."

"I suspect the issue may have been one of timing," Khan said. "We received the information from our source quite late, and we acted as soon as we had it."

"We needed to know why Farsad was talking to those foreign agents," the Supreme Leader said in the same level tone, devoid of emotion. "We needed to know whether he had been compromised, and if so, how. We needed to find out what information the agents sought from him. And whether that means a threat to our weapons program—we might be going much more slowly with it right now, given the nuclear pact, but that could change in a flash. It is something we need to protect like a casket of gold."

Khan's chest tightened. He was surely facing jail and torture for this.

Of all the projects under the Supreme Leader's control, the one to develop nuclear weapons that could be used to target the Small Satan—Israel—and eventually the Great Satan—the United States—was the one closest to his heart, despite the current slowdown. The loss of the deputy director of the Atomic Energy Organization of Iran and the head of their nuclear weapons development was therefore a severe blow.

The Supreme Leader turned his gaze to Taeb. "From you,

Abbas, I would like to know who those foreign agents were in the hotel. Have you been able to find out?"

Taeb nodded. "We have, sir. We understand that one of the agents in the hotel room was Israeli, David Zahavi, who is head of operations at the Mossad. That tells you the importance the Israelis attached to this meeting with Farsad."

"And the other?"

"The other was a British agent, a contractor, named Jayne Robinson, formerly of the British Secret Intelligence Service. We believe she is also aligned with the CIA and so may quite likely have been there under their direction. There were also two other Israelis in the building, a man and a woman, both also Mossad people."

"What is your source for this information?" the Supreme Leader asked.

"Our source is a Westerner, someone whom we have code-named SOHRAB. The information came from SOHRAB via another source, ROSTAM, sir."

"Do we know which of the four killed Nasser's Quds officers?"

"No, we do not, sir," Taeb said. "We hope to find out."

Hashemi nodded and pushed his lightly tinted glasses up his nose.

In all of Khan's thirty-one years as a Quds Force officer, including twenty-two years in the field carrying out lethal operations against Iran's enemies and four years spent leading the organization, he had never seen eyes as hard and as unyielding as Hashemi's. There seemed to be so little emotion behind them they might as well be made from glass.

And yet as soon as Hashemi stepped onto a speaker's platform or in front of the television cameras, with a microphone in his hand, he somehow metamorphosed into a charismatic leader who enraptured his audience. Khan had once read about Jekyll and Hyde, and that summed up the Supreme Leader.

There was silence for several seconds as Hashemi stared at the far wall of the small room.

Eventually he turned back and looked first at Taeb, then at Khan. "What could those foreign agents have gotten from Farsad?" Hashemi asked. "What might they have been seeking?"

Taeb leaned forward. "Probably the obvious things, sir. The two key things Farsad was in charge of were the domestic weapons development program and the suppliers from whom he could procure the equipment, the know-how, and the technology to build those weapons."

Hashemi nodded. "The manufacturing operation is contained in Iran. It is secret and secure. I am not concerned about that. But the suppliers are out there across the globe. They are accessible, yes? The same applies to the financiers, our Swiss bankers."

Both Taeb and Khan nodded.

"So if Farsad gave anything away about those suppliers or the bankers, we can assume the Western agents will now be targeting them?"

"It is quite possible, sir," Taeb said.

Hashemi pressed his lips together. "I am worried. We have very little control over either suppliers or bankers. If they are compromised, we are in potentially significant trouble."

Khan could understand his leader's concerns, but he wasn't quite as worried.

"Sir, I agree there is a risk," Khan said, "but they are very resourceful, intelligent people and have often been targeted before. I will ensure they are warned to be on their guard. They're all used to dealing with scrutiny and surveillance."

"Maybe, but the bankers are a particular concern. They sit

there in Zürich, even farther out of our orbit than the suppliers are, and we have no direct relationship with them. We never see them. We don't know what they do or who they talk to."

"Sir, with respect, the bankers have never let us down in all the years, the decades, they have worked for us. They are models of discretion and their entire ethos is one of secrecy —their entire business depends on that. I think we can rely on them one hundred percent, sir, even if they are interrogated."

Khan felt complete confidence in what he was saying, despite the pressure he was feeling. He knew that if Western intelligence agencies had the ability to trace payments made by the Swiss bankers to Iran's black market equipment suppliers, they would have done it years ago, and the entire nuclear weapons program would have been completely busted.

The Supreme Leader inclined his head to one side, then the other. Khan could see he didn't entirely concur, but he made no further comment.

"Let's leave that issue for now. Now listen, this is what I want," Hashemi said eventually. He fixed Khan with a stare. "I am going to give you one more chance. I want the people who were in that Vienna hotel eliminated—the Israelis and the British woman. I want it done before they can even get to our suppliers and bankers, let alone talk to them. It is your responsibility to do that."

He pointed a finger in Khan's direction, then continued, "I expect you to work closely with Taeb, whom I expect to provide you with whatever intelligence you require."

Khan exhaled involuntarily as a deep surge of relief passed through him. "Yes, sir, thank you."

Hashemi turned to Taeb. "You obviously have some useful Western sources, and I expect you to use them further, as appropriate. Is that understood?"

"Of course, sir," Taeb said.

The Supreme Leader's gaze returned to Khan. "You can use Hezbollah to do this if you need to. I don't care how you do it, but just get it done."

"Yes, sir, understood." Khan had a strong set of senior-level connections in Hezbollah, whom he frequently drew on when required and who arranged operations on Iran's behalf in Europe and beyond. But he also had his own small set of operatives.

"But when you do eliminate them," Hashemi continued, "you must leave no fingerprints. No sign it was an Iranian operation. They will guess it is us, of course, but I do not want them to know for sure. I do not want them to be able to justify an attack on us."

"We will be sure to deliver your instructions," Khan said. "I am thankful for the opportunity to serve you further."

This was going to be a task for Unit 910, he thought, and specifically JAFFA, who in Europe at least was probably the person best equipped for this task.

"Good," the Supreme Leader said. He ran his right hand across his black turban, a symbol of his claim to be a descendant of the Prophet Muhammad—a group known as the family of Sayyids.

Hashemi turned to Taeb again. "The second thing is, Taeb, as you well know, my ambition remains to wipe the Small Satan and the Great Satan off the planet. It's Allah's will. But I want to stress something—now is not the time to be provoking Israel or the United States into striking at us. Not before we are properly ready with our nuclear arsenal in place. That time will come soon, but not yet. Neither do I want them to reimpose sanctions. They are hugely disruptive for us and will cause a lot of unrest among our people. I want calm. I don't want to cause unnecessary political opposition inside Iran. That's why I signed the nuclear deal with the West—to get the sanctions lifted. Understood?"

"Yes, sir," Taeb said.

"Now, I can't pretend I was sorry to see Cohen and Elazar killed and Farrar badly injured," Hashemi continued. "They're leaders of the infidels. But I do not like the trouble it has stirred up, so I have a task for you."

Taeb leaned forward, his palms pressed against each other, as if in prayer. "What would you like me to do?"

The Supreme Leader's eyes bored into him. "I want to know who *did* blow up that gas platform. Who ordered it. And why."

Taeb visibly tensed up. Khan could see it.

"Yes, sir. I will do my best to find out," Taeb said.

* * *

Wednesday, April 13, 2016
Washington, DC

The Fox News anchor listened impassively as Nicholas McAllister, the Republican nominee for the presidential election, forcefully explained why, in his view, the bloody deaths in a shootout in a Vienna hotel were a good reason why sanctions should be reimposed on Iran and the nuclear deal scrapped.

Cyrus Saba, who sat watching the news program in his rented apartment in the Mount Pleasant neighborhood of Washington, DC, nodded silently in agreement as he sipped his black coffee.

The story of the deaths during a nuclear safety conference being held in Vienna by the International Atomic Energy Agency had reverberated through the US. It had generated huge coverage, especially given the American secretary of state was still in the intensive care unit of a Tel Aviv hospital after the Samar attack.

"These men were hostile Quds Force officers who happen to have met their match in this incident," McAllister was saying. "They were in the hotel, armed to the teeth, and appear to have forced one of their own top nuclear scientists to jump to his death. They were on a lethal mission in a civilized European hotel. They're dangerous—we can't allow Iran to do this kind of thing. It's a perfect illustration of why we should be pushing for sanctions in order to force a regime change in Iran."

The news anchor then interviewed a couple of political commentators, who spoke about the rapidly rising risks to peace in the Middle East.

Saba gave a short grin when he heard that.

They had no idea. He hadn't been studying garbage truck routes and timetables for weeks for nothing.

It seemed to him that the bandwagon was now rolling along nicely—and he was sure his main paymaster would agree with that.

But there was a lot more work to be done before it reached top speed.

CHAPTER THIRTEEN

Friday, April 15, 2016
   Gundremmingen, Bavaria, Germany

The neat two-story house with its daffodils and rose bushes in a well-maintained garden lay down the street from the red-roofed parish church of St. Martin in the village of Gundremmingen and less than a mile from the River Danube to the west.

As Rafael parked their silver BMW unobtrusively a couple of hundred meters down the street next to two similar vehicles, Jayne couldn't help feeling that the chocolate box scene was spoiled by what lay beyond. The skyline was dominated by the twin 160-meter concrete cooling towers of the Gundremmingen nuclear power plant.

A quick piece of work by the Mossad's research team had informed Zahavi and Jayne that the power plant had been Heinz Müller's workplace for two decades before he had joined the International Atomic Energy Agency in Vienna in his early fifties.

Although he had worked on projects involving several countries, Iran had taken most of his time. From 2004 onward he had acted as a nuclear safeguards expert and inspector in the country.

Now aged sixty-five and retired, he and his wife had rented out the apartment he had bought in Vienna upon taking up the IAEA role, and they had returned to their original home in the village where his children had grown up.

It had taken a couple of hours and several phone calls the previous day from the Munich safe house to set up the meeting.

Jayne had introduced herself to Müller using her second British false identity of Siobhan Delks to distance herself further from events at the Hotel Imperial. She explained in fluent German that she was a member of a discreet international government investigative unit, led by the US and Israel and quite separate from the IAEA. The unit was trying to pinpoint black market suppliers of equipment that could be used for nuclear weapons production and was writing a report that would be used to determine future policy on sanctions toward Iran. In particular, it was interested in centrifuges for uranium enrichment.

"Iran?" Müller asked, coming straight to the point. "The nuclear con artists?"

"Precisely," Jayne said. "We were given your name as someone who has a deep knowledge of Iran's nuclear program and equipment suppliers from your work at the IAEA."

Anticipating that Müller would want to check out her story, Jayne had supplied a number at the team's supposed headquarters in London that in reality was a Mossad line that diverted to Rafael's cell phone.

When Müller made his check call, Rafael, who spoke English with quite a British-sounding accent, proved a convincing "administrator" for the supposed investigative team. He eventually managed to reassure Müller that Jayne and her colleague Saul Hillel—Zahavi's backup false identity —were genuine.

Through her telephone conversations with Müller the previous day, Jayne had come to the view that he was feeling pleased to be consulted on a subject that he had been very close to. Perhaps, two years into retirement, he was missing the cut and thrust of his working life, she thought.

But she was wrong, it seemed.

Now on the doorstep, as he stared at Jayne from beneath sprawling dark eyebrows that stood in contrast to his white curly hair, Müller looked uncertain and asked to see their identification. Both took out their false passports and a letter of introduction produced by the forgery department in Tel Aviv, which he scrutinized.

"I obviously do know Iran, and I do have knowledge of the supply chain," Müller said as he led them into his living room. "But I have been retired for two years, and there are people at the IAEA currently I suggest you see, as they'll be more up to date."

Müller seated them on a black leather sofa, then perched on an armchair facing them. He poured coffee and handed cups to Jayne and Zahavi, sizing them up with a pair of small, dark eyes.

"We fully intend to speak to other IAEA people," Jayne lied. "But we were told you were the foremost authority on Iran's nuclear program and that we would be wise to see you first. We are trying to build up a list of possible suppliers."

Müller remained silent for a few seconds. "You say you're government. Are you intelligence agency people? CIA, Mossad?"

Clearly he's no fool.

"No," Jayne said. "I'm a consultant, working for the State

Department, and Saul is with Israel's Ministry of Foreign Affairs."

"Do you know what you're getting into?" There was no mistaking the skeptical tone.

Jayne shrugged. "We're talking about a black market. And huge amounts of money at stake. It's not a riverside picnic."

"These people don't take prisoners," Müller said. He stood and walked to his window, looking out across a lawn and a low stone boundary wall toward a tennis club across the street.

"Did you ever meet any of the suppliers?" Jayne asked.

Müller gave a brief, sardonic laugh. "It would be easier to get our German chancellor around here for dinner."

He turned and sat on the window ledge, now facing Jayne. "Who sent you to me?"

"As I said on the phone, it was a source within Iran's nuclear industry." He had actually asked twice, and she had given the same answer.

"A dead one?"

"I can't say."

Another long pause. "Jafar Farsad, by any chance?"

Jayne remained silent, as did Zahavi.

Müller raised both eyebrows. "I'll take that as a yes, then. If it was, then you know very well what you're getting into. Did your source say why they sent you here?"

"The source simply said to follow the money and to talk to you," Jayne replied.

"Follow the money?"

Jayne nodded.

"Good advice." Müller said. He sipped his coffee delicately. "At the IAEA we tried to get into Iran's illicit nuclear supply network. I interviewed a number of people and tried to get details of where the centrifuges and other equipment were coming from. It was part of our job, along with monitoring Iran's compliance with its voluntary commitments to suspend uranium enrichment and reprocessing activities. We needed to know what Iran had and what it was doing with it."

"How much progress did you make?" Jayne asked.

Müller slowly shook his head. "It was like trying to find a black cat in a dark room."

"Nothing at all?"

"I talked to a lot of people, both officially and unofficially. From the latter I picked up information that I couldn't always put into my reports."

"Such as?"

Müller paused, as if evaluating how much to disclose.

"Our information was that the main black market suppliers consisted of what we named the Ring of Five, although we were never able to nail down precisely who they were with proof."

"The Ring of Five?" Zahavi asked.

"Five main suppliers."

Jayne leaned forward on the sofa, her chin cupped in her hands. "Who were your suspects for this Ring of Five?"

"I was only fairly certain of one, and that was the alpha male of the pack, the AQ Khan network, which you may know of. The Pakistani group."

Jayne did know of AQ Khan—Abdul Qadeer Khan. He was a Pakistani nuclear physicist who played an important role in his country's development of nuclear weapons, particularly in the use of centrifuges for uranium enrichment. But from the 1980s onward, he also secretly helped Iran to obtain centrifuges, along with designs and construction technology to help the Tehran regime develop its own equipment.

"And your other suspects, however uncertain?" Jayne asked.

"I was told there were German and Swiss companies, but we found little proof," Müller said. He rattled off a list of company names on the suspects list, only one of which Jayne had heard of. She made him slow down and repeat the names, which she noted in her phone.

"If it was any of them, they operated so far under the radar they were subterranean," Müller continued. "We spoke to governments about them, but neither we nor they ever managed to pin down enough evidence."

"It certainly sounds difficult," Jayne said.

"Yes, it was," Müller said. "The main problem is that this black market equipment is usually supplied indirectly through incredibly complex routes across multiple continents and countries—Europe, South America, China. It is always repackaged several times and improperly documented for freight purposes. Almost impossible to trace. And even if we did trace equipment, it was usually designed to be dual-purpose—potentially for use on both military and civilian products. They could say the equipment was for innocent purposes."

Jayne was well aware from projects she had worked on at MI6 that German and Swiss companies had indeed been suspected of illicitly supplying equipment to Iran for use in its nuclear weapons development program. What Müller was saying made complete sense.

"So now that the Iran nuclear deal is in place, the money these companies and others were making has stopped, right?" Jayne asked.

Müller stroked his chin. "Slowed sharply, yes, definitely. Maybe stopped altogether, though I doubt it. We don't know for sure. But the slowdown from the nuclear deal will be costing them massive amounts. Hundreds of millions of dollars. Billions, maybe. They will be spitting blood about the deal. A good thing, in my view."

Jayne leaned back and sank into the sofa, clutching the remains of her coffee, which had now gone cold. What

Müller was saying could easily explain why those companies were keen to see the nuclear deal scrapped and Iran resuming its illicit black market work toward building a nuclear weapon.

Without the need to appear clean to comply with the deal and the IAEA inspections that went with it, Iran could go back to a full-speed undercover program supplied by black marketeers—who would all make a killing again.

Could this provide the key to who had blown up the gas platform, killed the Israeli foreign minister and Mossad chief, and put Paul Farrar and Mark Nicklin-Donovan in intensive care?

"So how do we prove the connections, that these companies actually were supplying Iran?" Jayne asked

Müller grimaced and exhaled slowly. "It goes back to your contact's advice. Follow the money. It certainly sounds like something Jafar Farsad would say."

Jayne didn't take the bait. "Yes, but how do we follow the money? Where is it?"

Müller put his coffee cup down on the table and pressed his palms together.

"Where is the money?" he said. "It's where money always goes to and from."

There was silence for several seconds.

"Bankers. In Switzerland?" Jayne asked. It seemed the obvious answer.

"Right the first time."

Jayne shook her head. "Of course, it would have to be," she muttered, half to herself.

She looked back at Müller. "So a Swiss bank is handling all the transactions on behalf of the Iranians?"

"Correct."

"Which bank?" Jayne asked.

"Zeller and Steiner Bank, in Zürich. It's run by Martin

Zeller and Carl Steiner. A private, family-owned bank. Zeller is the current chairman and Steiner the chief executive. They will have a complete list of suppliers because they have to pay them. And if you can crack those two open, you're a better operator than I am." He pressed his lips together. "I tried for years. But they hide behind Swiss banking secrecy laws. Horrible men, real Nazi lovers."

"Nazi lovers?"

"Yes. They built their fortunes on the Nazis, or more accurately, their fathers did, who were running the bank at the time. The gold and jewelry that was ripped from the mouths, necks, and hands of Jews on their way to Auschwitz and the other camps during the Second World War. Artwork looted by the SS from all over Europe. All of it massively valuable, worth maybe a billion. They probably still have some of it stashed away in their vaults. They feasted on the bones of those killed in the Holocaust. Hitler, Eichmann, and the rest made me ashamed to be a German, but what the likes of Zeller and Steiner did was just as bad in a different way."

Jayne sat still for a moment. She knew that many Swiss banks had profited hugely from the Holocaust in exactly the way Müller had described. But the idea that such immorality and corruption was being passed down a generation or two probably also rang true.

"So having financed and profited from one Holocaust, they're now financing the attempt to deliver another," Jayne said.

Müller nodded.

It crossed Jayne's mind that if the bank had been involved in financing Nazi activity during the war, or acted as a banker for war criminals, there might be a file on them somewhere. She made a mental note to check.

"Did you meet these two men, Zeller and Steiner?"

"Yes, I met them."

"What exactly were you trying to get from them?" Jayne asked.

"It was a short and unproductive meeting. I wanted to run my list of suspects for the Ring of Five past them. But I also wanted to check an unsubstantiated report I had from one source about a sixth supplier, not a company but a supposed middleman who was a central contact for a number of illegal equipment providers. They refused point-blank to help."

"A sixth one?" Jayne asked.

"Yes, a sixth."

"Do you have a name?"

Müller shook his head slowly. "My source had only a nickname, or maybe it was a code name."

"What was that?"

"The Dark Shah."

Jayne glanced at Zahavi, who shook his head. "I've never heard that name."

"The *Dark Shah*? Is that all you know?" Jayne asked Müller.

"Yes, that's all. It was a new name to me also. You will have to do your own digging, I am afraid."

CHAPTER FOURTEEN

Friday, April 15, 2016
  Paris

The man known to his customers as Charles Simenon glanced at his watch and walked to the door of his tailor shop. There he stood for a few moments, looking each way up and down Rue de Saint-Simon through the unusually thick bulletproof glass in his shop window and door.

The building stood a few hundred meters south of the River Seine and the Musée d'Orsay in the Seventh Arrondissement.

Across the street, the entrance to the Hôtel Duc de Saint-Simon was deserted. One of the wide green entrance doors was open, and through it the shop owner could see a lone waiter in the hotel's courtyard setting one of the outdoor tables.

There was nobody else in the street, which had become unseasonably warm in the afternoon sunshine. The tables outside the L'Affable bistro farther down the street were unoccupied. And some of the elegant five-story apartment buildings, with their wrought-iron balconies, even had shutters pulled across their windows.

The tailor, a tall, muscular man with a short, stubbly beard, scratched his bald head, bordered by a steel-gray semicircle of close-cropped hair, and checked his watch.

It was almost five thirty, so he reached out and turned the Ouvert sign that hung in his doorway around so that it read Fermé. He then pressed a button, and a mechanical green metal roller shutter clanked its way down until it covered the entire shop window and door.

He took a key from his pocket, inserted it into the lock, and turned it. The five-point security locks clunked shut. Business was over for another day.

The shop produced high-quality custom-made men's suits for a select list of clients across Paris. Many of the clientele said the price tags were extortionate, but they kept returning. The business also had a smaller but lucrative sideline producing clerical gowns, cassocks, hats, and other garments for the Catholic Church. Most of the customers were in France and Italy, and indeed, the business had a connection to a similar but larger business in Rome, to which it acted as a supplier when required.

The owner turned and walked back to his shop counter, where he resumed checking the spreadsheet on his laptop. He used it to record his business activity each day that he was open, which was not always.

Although his customers knew him as Charles Simenon, that wasn't his real name. His real identity was Henri Fekkai, and his code name was JAFFA.

Henri, born in Marseille fifty-two years earlier as one of twin brothers of Iranian-Lebanese parents, was one of an estimated three hundred thousand people with Lebanese roots living in France. But only a tiny handful of them knew him well, and most of those were also members of Hezbollah's Unit 910, also known as the External Security Organization.

His twin, whose real name was Pierre, was also a tailor, known locally as Philippe. He was also a member of Unit 910, code-named VALENCIA, and the two of them had worked together for a long time. That was reflected in the names displayed in gold lettering on the green-painted frontage of Henri's shop: Charles & Philippe Simenon.

But these days, Pierre lived in the Westwood neighborhood of Los Angeles, where there was such a large Persian population that the area was known colloquially as Tehrangeles. He had moved there after falling in love with an American-Iranian woman, and when the marriage foundered, decided to stay.

Henri finished entering that day's takings into his spreadsheet, closed the application, and turned off the laptop. He then pulled shut the sliding door of a long cupboard behind him, where a rail full of new and repaired suits hanging in plastic protective covers were awaiting collection.

Henri picked up the laptop and was heading toward the rear door of the shop when his cell phone rang. He glanced at the screen, tapped in his private key to allow access to the encrypted call, and answered it.

"Hello."

"Hello, my friend. The market price of Super 180's twelve-ounce, superfine cloth is rising. I was wondering if you might need another order?"

He gave the required response to indicate that he really was Henri and was not busy on assignment right now and was therefore able to accept one. "Customer demand for that particular type of cloth right now is nonexistent, you will be pleased to hear."

"Good. Now, I do not have much time," came the voice

down the line from Beirut. "So listen carefully. I am going to give you the names of four targets."

"Spell them out for me, please."

Henri, as always, didn't need to write down the names or any other details about his targets. He had an almost flawless memory for such things.

"There are two men, both Israelis, David Zahavi and Rafael Levy." The caller, Talal Hassan, leader of Unit 910, spelled out the names as requested.

"Got that," Henri said.

"And two women. Odeya Leibovitch and Jayne Robinson." Again the names were spelled out. "The first one is Israeli, the second British."

"*British?*" This was unusual.

"Yes, correct. You heard me, Israeli and British," Hassan said.

"Photos?" Henri asked.

"I'll put pictures in the secure drive." They had a folder in an online password-protected account that they both used for such purposes.

"Location?"

"All four of them are currently based in Munich in a safe house," Hassan said. He gave the address of an apartment on Augustenstrasse, near the city center.

"Got that too," Henri said. "Can I ask, how quickly do you need me to do this?"

"As quickly as possible," Hassan said. "If the location changes, I will let you know. We will pay more if you are able to do this swiftly."

"All right. My usual plus fifty percent. And half the fee to be paid in my normal account by the end of today."

"I accept that. We can wire it," Hassan said.

"And I will need access to a lot of information," Henri continued. "Specifically from our people who have access to the usual systems." The caller would know what he meant—they included police and security services databases and immigration and passport control information.

"That is not a problem. You can use the usual channel to obtain the information you require."

That was reassuring. In fact, the ability to extract intelligence and information from government and security systems all over Europe was one of the key factors that facilitated Henri's role. There were a lot of well-placed people connected to Unit 910, which was the Hezbollah special forces team that carried out external operations all over the world against the many enemies of Iran, particularly in Europe. The targets were usually either Israeli or American, but occasionally they were Arab.

The unit also encompassed a business affairs component, responsible for fundraising, drug smuggling, and money laundering through a complex network of companies and organizations. Henri and Pierre had been involved in that side of the operation too.

Henri knew better than to ask Hassan the reason for the requested killings—it would be a good one.

Hassan, a tall, bearded man, held legendary status within Hezbollah's military arm for his long track record of personally carrying out such operations in earlier years as well as directing them more recently as he gained seniority. His successful initial operations included a series of attacks against US Marines based in Lebanon in the 1980s and a truck bomb attack at a Jewish community building in Buenos Aires in 1992 that killed twenty-eight people and injured more than two hundred others.

Henri and Pierre's careers with Unit 910 had started only slightly later than Hassan's, in the early 1990s, with a series of successful and devastating operations in London, Paris,

Berlin, and other cities, most of them masterminded by Hassan. He proved a highly capable mentor.

But Henri and Pierre had chosen to stay operational, out in the field, and to remain based in their beloved Paris rather than move to Beirut for a management role like Hassan's. The partnership was only broken after Pierre's move to Los Angeles in 2006.

Henri knew that one of Pierre's few regrets about moving to the US was the lack of operational opportunities. Hezbollah simply wasn't as active there as in Europe, although a lot of work was going on underground to ensure it could quickly become so. Pierre had been focused more on fundraising for Hezbollah through setting up a variety of illegal businesses, including drug dealing, and laundering the proceeds, mainly via Europe. He had been itching to get himself back into action for a long time, and Henri sometimes sensed that Hassan had a similar itch.

"One final point," Hassan said. "These four people are difficult. We ran an operation against them in a hotel in Vienna recently. It didn't go well. Do you understand?"

"I'm aware of what happened," Henri said. He immediately knew the incident to which Hassan was referring. He couldn't have missed it because it had been all over the television news. This was the group that had killed the Quds officers.

"Are they all intelligence services?" Henri asked.

"All of them."

Henri ended the call and replaced the phone in his pocket, then paused, collecting his thoughts. Operations against intelligence services personnel were often far from straightforward. He assumed in this case they were Mossad and Secret Intelligence Service targets, based on their nationalities.

The call had changed things. His plans for a quiet

weekend resting at his apartment near the Sorbonne would have to be abandoned. But that was the nature of his work. These jobs often came up on short notice. His shop would remain closed for a week or so. Regular customers understood the explanations he gave them for his frequent absences, especially the need to travel overseas to buy cloth of the required quality to meet their demands.

Henri and Pierre had been brought up by their parents as devotees of Shia Islam and had gradually become motivated by Ayatollah Ruhollah Khomeini's revolution in Iran after 1979. They looked for ways to support the regime from afar. At first, this was no more than a low-key ambition, restricted to handing out pamphlets highlighting the benefits that Khomeini had brought to Iran and the wickedness of the West.

But that all changed in April 1996 when Israel launched Operation Grapes of Wrath, a massive sixteen-day bombing campaign against southern Lebanon to try and stop Hezbollah rocket attacks on towns near Galilee in northern Israel.

Among the estimated 170 civilians who were killed during the Israeli air raids was Henri and Pierre's aunt Nadine, their father's sister. Prior to settling in Lebanon, their family had originally been Palestinian refugees from the town of Ramla, about halfway between Tel Aviv and Jerusalem. They had been forced out by the Israelis during the 1948 Arab-Israeli War and were slowly getting back on their feet in a new home. But Nadine had her legs blown off by an Israeli bomb and died an agonizing death from blood loss and shock. His father was overcome with grief and made both of his boys promise they would do all they could to avenge the killing.

After that, it seemed to the twins that joining Hezbollah was the only way forward if, as French citizens, they were to devote themselves to defending Iran. They signed up and gradually increased their involvement, taking part in a series of assassinations starting in 1990 with an Iranian opposition spokesman in Geneva. Both he and Pierre failed to see how Israel had any right to exist and take over land that belonged to the Palestinians.

There was a house and a piece of land in Ramla that as far as Henri was concerned still belonged to his family, who had never received any compensation for their loss all those years ago. Many other families had suffered a similar fate, and the town had been largely wiped clean of its Arab population.

Henri walked through to the room at the rear of his shop, closed the door, and unlocked another door that led down a short flight of stairs to his cellar.

He flicked on a single lightbulb as he descended. In a corner of the cellar just above floor level behind three crates of wine bottles was a large, square, rusty black metal grate that appeared at first glance to be simply for ventilation purposes.

Henri shifted the wine crates to one side, undid two loose screws, removed the grate, reached inside the cavity behind it, and tugged out a plastic container filled with yellow-colored home heating oil, a burlap bag containing two cell phones, and two large boxes.

Inside each box were about a hundred plastic pouches, all of which were labeled as disposable single-use cold packs for use in treating sprains and other sporting injuries.

However, for Henri, the packs had another use.

Each plastic pack had two adjoining sections, one containing water, the other about fifty grams of dry ammonium nitrate granules. In normal use, when the pack was squeezed hard, the plastic divider separating the two components split, allowing the water to mix with the ammonium nitrate. The ensuing chemical reaction lowered the temperature of the water to almost freezing.

However, Henri didn't want the water. He just wanted the ammonium nitrate—the explosive.

To get it would require an hour or so of laborious work with a razor blade to carefully slice the packs open. When he had removed the granules from all two hundred packs, he would have around ten kilograms of explosive.

That would then be repackaged in a far more deadly form as an improvised explosive device: an IED.

He would mix the granules with a small amount of the heating oil and then arrange the concoction with a small nine-volt battery and a detonator fired by one of the cell phones. Or maybe he would split the granules into a few smaller packages, each with their own detonators, depending on his requirements.

Henri also had a variety of containers into which the explosive material and detonators could be packed for deployment. They included small black plastic holders with strong built-in magnets that could be attached to anything metallic, such as a vehicle chassis or body. He also had several rectangular cardboard boxes of the type used by mail-order companies and slim enough to fit through a mail slot.

Hezbollah had huge caches of such ammonium nitrate hidden all over Europe, which meant Henri was never short of stocks for the various operations he was tasked with. The caches included eight tonnes in Cyprus—well placed for attacks on nearby Israel if required—three tonnes in London, and a tonne or so at warehouses in southern Germany.

Pierre and his colleagues in Los Angeles were building a cache that so far consisted of about half a tonne, and there were other stocks farther afield, including in Thailand.

However, the biggest and most deadly stock of all, comprising around 2,750 tonnes of the explosive, stored in plastic bags that were supposedly destined for agricultural fertilizer purposes, lay in a dockside warehouse in the Port of

Beirut. Henri hoped that the Beirut stocks would never be accidentally triggered, as he knew the resultant explosion would blow half of Beirut away. He was glad he wasn't responsible for that particular cache.

Next, Henri reached into the cavity again and this time withdrew two bags made from heavy black canvas.

One bag was small and contained a Heckler & Koch P7 semiautomatic pistol. In fact, it was a variant of the standard P7. This one had a double-stack magazine that held thirteen rounds and was known as the P7M13SD. The gun, originally designed for German special forces, had a longer threaded barrel into which he could screw the silencer that was also in the bag.

The other canvas bag was larger and contained a special sniper rifle, the VSS Vintorez. Henri had come to favor the weapon, a Russian military favorite sometimes used by Spetsnaz special forces, after experimenting with a wide variety of alternatives.

Because it fired its 9x39mm SP5 rounds at subsonic speeds, there was none of the sonic boom associated with many weapons. The noise was further dampened by a long integral silencer that fit over the barrel like a slim tube.

It was ideal for covert operations of the type he was usually engaged for and that might now be needed in Munich.

Henri liked the fact that the gun could be rapidly dismantled into three parts and carried in a briefcase that was less than forty-five centimeters long and looked little different from those carried by businessmen. It made getaways after operations easier.

In fact, it was his and Pierre's expertise with the Vintorez that had earned them their code names, JAFFA and VALENCIA—both devised by Hassan.

They both had an unerring ability to hit an orange mounted on a pole from a distance of three hundred meters.

All Henri needed now was the right opportunity. And the instructions for that were likely to arrive very soon.

* * *

Friday, April 15, 2016
Munich

The discussion in the Munich safe house about the required approach to extract details of the Ring of Five—or possibly Six—from Martin Zeller and Carl Steiner was not an easy one.

None of the Mossad team had heard of a black market Iranian nuclear supplier code-named the Dark Shah, and initial inquiries with the Tel Aviv office also drew a blank. The overnight research team promised to dig into it but warned it would take time given they were starting from scratch.

Jayne, Zahavi, Rafael, and Odeya had brought back take-out pizzas in boxes and sat eating them and drinking coffee in the living room, debating a variety of options. They ranged from using the blunt instrument of forcing a disclosure at gunpoint to blackmail.

None seemed likely to result in a productive ending.

It was only at about half past two in the morning when Jayne finally came back to the disclosures that Heinz Müller had made earlier in the day about Zeller and Steiner Bank's role in financing the Holocaust.

"I think using force can wait. Better we get leverage against them," she said. "Surely, given their Holocaust role, there must be a file on them."

"The secrecy factor makes it damn hard to get leverage against Swiss bankers," Rafael said.

Maybe he was right, but Jayne immediately had an idea. "True, but my partner, Joe, has dealt with these situations before. He was a war crimes investigator. I'll give him a call and see if he's got any ideas."

Jayne disappeared into a bedroom and made the call to Joe, six hours behind, who had just finished eating dinner with his two children. She outlined the conversation they'd had with Müller.

"Have you ever heard of a black market nuclear equipment supplier code-named the Dark Shah?" she asked.

"No," Joe said. "Have you checked with Vic?"

"Not yet. What about a Swiss bank, Zeller and Steiner?"

"That's interesting," Joe said. "That does ring a bell from when I was at the OSI."

Joe had been a senior historian at the Office of Special Investigations, part of the Department of Justice, in Washington, DC, for many years after leaving the CIA. His role there was primarily that of a Nazi hunter, to track down and prosecute the many SS war criminals who—to subsequent widespread disgust—were given refuge in the United States after the World War II. In many cases, such refuge was given in return for information about the Soviet Union and its activities, something that the US was lacking in the postwar years.

"What bell does it ring, exactly?" Jayne asked.

"I'm not sure," Joe said. "Maybe it was something from an investigation I once did. I can check my files, but it will be a shot in the dark—there are better sources. First, get Vic to check his files. But also, I would go to Yad Vashem. I've got a couple of friends there, both top historians, good investigators."

Of course. Yad Vashem.

Why hadn't she thought of that? Yad Vashem had been on the short list of places to visit that she and Joe had drawn up prior to their trip to Israel. It was a memorial to the six million Jewish victims of the Holocaust, built on a sprawling forty-four acre site on Mount Herzl in western Jerusalem. However, it was also a world-leading Holocaust research center, with archives that included huge databases about those who survived and died during that period, complete with personal testimonies.

"You think they would have that kind of detail?" Jayne asked.

"There's a good chance. If these Swiss were bankers to German or Austrian Holocaust victims whose accounts were confiscated by Nazis who were later put on trial for war crimes, they may have files on them. A lot of assets belonging to Holocaust victims and survivors would have passed through their hands."

He gave the names and email addresses for his two friends at Yad Vashem: Dr. Leo Goldwasser, head of archives, and his deputy, Daniel Yoran. Both remained as consultants to the Office of Special Investigations, which had since been renamed the Human Rights and Special Prosecutions section of the Department of Justice—the HRSP. Jayne wrote down their details.

"Try Leo first," Joe said. "Make an appointment and brief him when you get there. They have a good filing system. He'll find what you need quite quickly, if they've got it." Given that Zahavi was in any case returning to Tel Aviv the next day for Eli Elazar's funeral on Sunday and to join Avi Shiloah's internal crisis strategy meeting, Jayne decided it would make sense to go with him and make a visit to Yad Vashem, as Joe had suggested.

"Thanks, Joe. This is why I love you."

"I have my uses. Stay safe, Jayne. Love you too."

Jayne ended the call, returned to the living room, and told the others of her plan, which met with broad agreement.

"I know both of those men at Yad Vashem," Zahavi said. "They've helped me a couple of times. I'll send an introductory email right now for you as well. It might help." He reached for his laptop.

It was decided that while she and Zahavi were in Tel Aviv, Rafael and Odeya would drive to Zürich and begin surveillance of the two Swiss bankers. Jayne and Zahavi would join them later.

The satellite TV was tuned to CNN, which was running an analysis special on the Iran nuclear deal and the increased risks of a conflict in the Middle East following the attack on the Samar gas platform.

The Republican nominee for president, Nicholas McAllister, was dominating a roundtable discussion with politicians and businessmen on the issue and was calling vigorously for the nuclear deal to be abandoned. He argued that Iran was continuing with its covert development of nuclear weapons while also benefiting from the lifting of international sanctions. Several of the business leaders agreed.

On balance Jayne thought they were wrong. Her view was that the IAEA and intelligence services combined could keep a check on Iran's nuclear capability.

On the other hand, sanctions that blocked sales of goods to Iran were massively punitive to millions of innocent Iranians and often made it hard for them to get food and other basic necessities. Sanctions hit the poorest the hardest. She knew for certain that they would not affect the Iranian leadership who, with their vast wealth, would always find ways to get what they wanted.

True, hitting the poorest might increase the likelihood of an internal uprising and the government being overthrown from within. But history had shown that Iran's military and security services, with all the perks they were given by the leadership, stayed loyal and viciously repressed any dissent.

Jayne turned her attention back to the task at hand.

First, she wrote a secure email to Vic, asking if the CIA had any files on either the Dark Shah or Zeller and Steiner.

Then she emailed Leo Goldwasser at Yad Vashem, outlining what she was seeking and asking if she could make a visit over the next two days. She mentioned Joe and Zahavi in the email.

Within thirty minutes, Jayne had replies back from both. Vic had not heard of the Dark Shah or Zeller and Steiner but would ask his team to get what they could from the files. And Goldwasser indicated that Jayne would be welcome anytime if she was a friend of Joe's and Zahavi's.

To her relief, it felt as though the wheels were moving. Now she just needed to keep on the move too.

Following the near miss at the Hotel Imperial, she felt anxious about remaining in one place for any length of time. The Iranians and their proxies, especially Hezbollah, had tentacles that spread all over Europe, where they had an extensive intelligence network.

It was dangerous to become a static target, especially if leaks were happening—and so far there had been no progress on tracking down the culprit.

CHAPTER FIFTEEN

Monday, April 18, 2016
  Jerusalem

Yad Vashem, set in the hills west of Jerusalem, reminded Jayne of a modern university, all curved concrete walkways and sculptures alongside low-rise buildings with floor-to-ceiling windows and landscaped gardens.

But Dr. Leo Goldwasser, despite his academic background and title and his brown corduroy jacket, had more the air of a driven campaigner about him than that of a professor. He was a man on a mission, as were many of his colleagues at this international monument to the six million Jews murdered by the Nazis in the Holocaust.

A hawkish, thin man with a mop of steel-wool curly hair, a sharp nose, and a pair of flickering brown eyes that oozed intelligence, Goldwasser met Jayne on the stone plaza outside the visitors' center.

He shook hands with a firm grip and said that he had been exchanging emails with both Joe Johnson and David

Zahavi. "Your reputation precedes you," he said, glancing at Jayne from beneath eyebrows that were as frizzy as his hair.

"Yours likewise," Jayne said. There was no harm in beginning with a little mutual flattery.

Goldwasser nodded with a faint smile. He turned and pointed toward the eleven white stone arches that formed the entrance to the complex from the parking lot, which was full of tourist buses and cars.

An inscription from Ezekiel 37:14, carved in large letters, ran across the top of the arches in English and Hebrew: "I will put my breath into you, and you shall live again, and I will set you upon your own soil."

Goldwasser glanced back at Jayne. "That sums up why Israel exists and why we're here. I always point it out to visitors."

He escorted Jayne up a sloping path to the northern side of the site, past the administration block and into the entrance lobby of the archives and library building.

Goldwasser led the way across a gleaming marble floor to the reception desk, where Jayne had to sign the visitor's register under the watchful eye of an olive-skinned woman wearing a green hijab. She issued Jayne with a visitor's security pass on a lanyard to hang around her neck.

They then passed through airport-style metal detectors and into a reading room furnished with bookshelves and rows of gray tables occupied by people who were scrutinizing documents and making notes.

"We'll find somewhere more private," he said, to Jayne's relief.

He took her through another long room full of shelves stacked with cardboard boxes that bore barcodes on the front, together with a letter and a number.

"We have millions of items filed here relating to those who died and those who survived," Goldwasser said.

Jayne knew that several years earlier Joe had sent a copy of a long memoir written by his mother, Helena, to Yad Vashem. It detailed her horrific experiences in the Gross-Rosen concentration camp at the hands of the Nazis during the Second World War. Helena, originally from southern Poland, survived only after being transferred in December 1944 to the Brünnlitz camp, which decades later was featured in the film *Schindler's List*.

Helena had eventually been liberated when the Red Army arrived in April 1945, just after her twentieth birthday. She later moved across the Atlantic to Portland, Maine, and married Joe's father, Bernard, who died in 1992 from cancer. Helena herself died in 2001. Jayne had read her long account of her life in the camps and indeed, a few years earlier, had helped Joe to trace the Nazi commander who tortured her, Erich Brenner, to his home in Buenos Aires. Brenner, then aged ninety-one, was eventually convicted and imprisoned in Germany for his war crimes.

Goldwasser took Jayne to a small meeting room that looked out over the valley stretching to the north, and they sat at a circular table.

"We're used to visitors from various intelligence services here," Goldwasser said. "But they are not usually British. What can I do for you?"

Jayne explained briefly how she came to be working along-side the CIA and the Mossad and why she was there, without specifically mentioning the IAEA official Heinz Müller.

"We were given the names Martin Zeller and Carl Steiner. Swiss bankers from Zeller and Steiner in Zürich," Jayne said. "Our understanding is that their bank, having helped fund the first Holocaust, is now trying to finance the second."

Goldwasser stared at her. "Iran? Nuclear weapons?"

Jayne nodded. "We'd like to find out a bit more about them before we try and talk to them."

Goldwasser creased his eyes and looked out the window. "Carl Steiner. That is a name I know, and I'm trying to think precisely why."

He turned back to Jayne. "You will need to give me some time to search through our files."

It occurred to Jayne that this was a good opportunity to look around the complex. "Of course. I can explore your site in the meantime. Can you call me when you're finished?"

"Yes, sure. It might take a couple of hours, though."

"That's fine."

Goldwasser escorted Jayne back to the lobby and pointed her in the direction of the Holocaust history museum. The spectacular white concrete building, 180 meters long but narrow and partly buried underground, ran across the width of the campus and split the hillside in two like some kind of white stone spike that had been driven horizontally through a ridge in the ground.

She spent the next two hours wandering through the museum, shaped inside like an inverted V and topped by a skylight. The structure was filled with the belongings—clothing, toys, books, poems, diaries, dolls, shoes—of countless victims of the horror that enveloped Europe in the 1940s. There were video testimonies of survivors playing on large screens and written accounts that told of sadistic torture, of innocent children shot in the head, men and women cremated alive, gassed in sealed "shower rooms," whipped into unconsciousness, and starved into submission.

All this happened at the hands of Hitler's SS officers, who systemically stole every item of value they could find from their victims, ranging from rings to watches and even gold tooth fillings that were pulled out before and after their owners were murdered. Homes and businesses owned by Jews all over Europe were plundered, as were the gold reserves of central banks. Gold and silverware was melted down and reshaped.

Much of the resultant wealth was deposited by those SS officers into Swiss bank vaults.

Finally, Jayne came to the Hall of Names, the large circular structure that served as a repository for more than four million individual folders bearing the names and personal details of most of the victims of the Holocaust. Most folders included pages of testimony that gave further background details about the victim, supplied by relatives or friends. Many also contained photographs.

The files were stacked in shelves around the walls of the structure. The volume of records, a museum assistant informed Jayne, was even now growing by the day as more evidence of victims' identities came to light, even so long after the event. There was room for files for all six million victims, and the ultimate objective was to ensure the record was complete.

All the testimonies had also been digitized and were available online, the assistant said.

Jayne stepped onto a walkway that was halfway up the building. Above the walkway was an enormous cone that stretched up more than ten meters to a glass-covered circle of sky that was visible at the top. Pasted to the inside surface of the cone were hundreds of photographs of Holocaust victims.

The symbolism suddenly struck her—the cone and the photographs represented the chimneys from concentration camp crematoriums up which the ashes of countless victims floated into the atmosphere more than seventy years ago.

She turned her gaze downward, where another enormous cone descended, inverted, from the walkway where she was standing like a well, complete with a pool of water in the bedrock at the bottom.

A few tears trickled down her cheeks. It took several moments before she noticed them.

It was no wonder the Mossad was so passionate about what it did. She thought of Eli Elazar, who had been buried the previous day in Jerusalem. Jayne would have liked to attend the funeral, but it had been primarily for family, close friends, and some of Eli's long-standing colleagues from the Mossad, such as Zahavi and Shiloah.

As Jayne exited the building, her phone vibrated in her pocket.

She took it out and examined the screen.

It was a message from Goldwasser.

Have found something of interest. Meet you at archives reception desk in 15 minutes.

* * *

Monday, April 18, 2016
Jerusalem

In the end, Jayne had to wait half an hour in the reception area before Goldwasser showed up. There were no seats so she had to remain standing.

The woman behind the reception desk, who seemed to spend most of her time fiddling with either her phone or her green hijab, kept throwing her sympathetic glances and attempted to engage her in conversation.

Jayne had noted the hijab the first time she checked in at the desk and was impressed that Yad Vashem employed Palestinians as well as Jews. But she was in no mood for conversation and, although she responded politely, didn't engage any further.

When Goldwasser eventually arrived he was carrying a

box similar to the ones she had seen on the archive's shelves and four other battered-looking files. "I'm sorry about the delay. I had another thought and that meant a further search," Goldwasser said. "I had to get into our secure vault."

They walked to the same meeting room they had used earlier, where Goldwasser dumped the box and files onto the table and, to Jayne's relief, disappeared to fetch two lattes.

"Right," he said on his return as he sat opposite Jayne and placed a coffee in front of her. He picked up one of the files and opened it.

"We have here what you might term a story. I assume you have heard of Klaus Barbie?"

Jayne nodded and sipped her coffee. She was well aware of Nikolaus Barbie, an SS intelligence officer who was dubbed the Butcher of Lyon after being appointed head of the Gestapo, the Nazis' secret police, in the French city in 1942. He acquired his nickname as a result of the extreme tortures he inflicted on Jews and members of the French Resistance.

"I know of him," Jayne said. "The CIA recruited him after the war—appalling as it seems. They squeezed him for intelligence about the Soviets and helped him escape to Bolivia in return."

"Correct," Goldwasser said, his furrowed brow clearly communicating his distaste. "Barbie was only convicted in 1987, after he had enjoyed more than forty years of freedom. Our historians estimate he was responsible for the deaths of about fourteen thousand people in Lyon."

Goldwasser leaned forward. "But have you heard of François Genoud?" He picked up another file and opened that one.

Jayne shook her head.

Goldwasser fingered a sheet of paper in the file. "He was a Swiss financier who funded the defense team at Barbie's trial. He was basically Hitler's finance manager in Switzerland. He handled much of the property and wealth plundered by the Nazis and deposited in Swiss banks. But he also acted for individual SS officers who enriched themselves and hid their stolen loot in Switzerland."

Goldwasser opened the box that lay on the desk and removed a thin sheaf of yellowing papers that were held together by a paper clip. He removed one of the sheets and held it out to Jayne.

"Take a look at that," Goldwasser said. "This is what I retrieved from our vault. It's classified. We keep it locked up securely."

It took Jayne less than a second to realize the sheet of paper was a copy of a CIA cable.

Headed "Top Secret, Eyes Only," and dated March 18, 1996, it had been sent to the director at Langley from the CIA's chief of Paris station. The subject line said "Pro-Nazi Swiss Banker François Genoud."

Jayne glanced up sharply at Goldwasser.

"Don't ask," he said. "We have sources everywhere. We often receive documents like this."

"*Really?* Top-secret, eyes-only documents?"

Goldwasser drained the remains of his coffee and lowered his voice. "I'm used to dealing with your brothers and sisters from various intelligence services, especially our own, of course. I'm what you might call the point man for that task. We often have a mutually beneficial relationship. We can help solve each other's problems."

Jayne said nothing but turned back to the cable, which went on to detail Genoud's background as a financial fixer for the Nazis and his relationship with Barbie. It also stated that from the 1960s onward he had arranged funding for pro-Palestinian causes, including the Palestine Liberation Organization, and had facilitated training for them by former Nazis.

"He was a Jew hater," Goldwasser said. "He was also

instrumental in facilitating war crimes in the financial sense. He was close to Joseph Goebbels and made a lot of money from publishing his diaries."

Jayne leaned back in her chair. Goebbels had been Hitler's minister of propaganda and one of his closest colleagues. This man Genoud sounded reprehensible. There had been many like him who profited from commercial links with the Nazis.

"Interesting," she said. "But what's your point in the context of Martin Zeller and Carl Steiner?"

"Wait," Goldwasser said. He passed another sheet of paper to Jayne.

It was a copy of another CIA cable from Paris, this time dated April 25, 1996, and also with Genoud in the subject line. The cable detailed a series of allegations against him that it said were based on information obtained by the CIA from two Swiss banking sources, code-named EIGER and MATTERHORN. According to the cable, the information was now being passed on to Swiss and US officials who were investigating Genoud's handling of the gold plundered by the Nazis from Jews and central banks across Europe.

The cable contained a list of eleven Swiss banks with which Genoud had dealt with on behalf of the Nazis and pro-Palestinian groups. The last name on the list was Zeller and Steiner.

A lightbulb clicked on in Jayne's mind. "These Swiss banking sources, EIGER and MATTERHORN, who provided the information to the CIA about Genoud. Do you know who they were?" she asked.

A hint of a smile flickered at the corners of Goldwasser's mouth. "You're smart."

"Zeller and Steiner, by any chance?"

"Steiner was MATTERHORN, Zeller was EIGER." He tapped one of the folders that lay on the table. "This is our file on Steiner. There are a significant number of Holocaust victims, and survivors, who had accounts at Zeller and Steiner before the war and who never saw their money and their jewelry and their artwork again afterward. As with many Swiss banks, many of the accounts opened by Jews before the war were dubbed dormant so heirs or survivors couldn't get into them. Either that or the banks demanded death certificates—which strangely enough weren't handed out by the Nazis."

"So what happened to the money and gold?"

"The banks kept it. Zeller and Steiner likely did extremely well out of it."

That sounded plausible to Jayne. She knew that while the larger Swiss banks, such as Union Bank of Switzerland and Credit Suisse, had taken all the heat because of their size, many smaller banks had also been equally guilty.

"What happened to Genoud?" Jayne asked.

"Very shortly after that cable was sent to Langley, the Swiss authorities and Jewish leaders set up a commission to search secret bank and government files for evidence of funds deposited in Swiss banks by Holocaust victims who never got their money back. Coincidentally, or perhaps not given the CIA interest, the commission was chaired by a former US Federal Reserve Bank chairman, Paul Volcker. At the same time, the US Senate Banking Committee chairman was investigating and campaigning for the release of billions of dollars of Holocaust victims' funds from Swiss banks."

"Right. So all of Genoud's activities were coming under the microscope for the first time. What happened to him?"

It crossed Jayne's mind that if Swiss bankers were leaking details about one of their own to the CIA, this wasn't going to end well. She needed to know.

"At the end of May 1996, Genoud committed suicide at his home near Lake Lausanne," Goldwasser said. "Poisoned himself after a dinner out with his friends. Two years later, following the various investigations, the Swiss banks agreed to pay $1.25 billion in compensation to the holders of all those accounts."

Jayne stared down at the two cables on the table in front of her.

This doesn't make sense.

She frowned and looked up at Goldwasser. "Why would Zeller and Steiner pass information to the CIA about Genoud? They were allied to anti-Jewish organizations like the Nazis and the PLO just like he was."

Goldwasser gave a short, sharp, sarcastic chuckle. "What's the usual motivation for bankers to do *anything*?"

Jayne tipped her head back. Now she understood.

Follow the money.

"You're saying the CIA paid Zeller and Steiner for the information?"

Goldwasser nodded slowly.

"How much?" Jayne asked.

"About forty million dollars."

"*Forty million bucks?*"

"They had to make it worth their while. They got twenty million each."

It was hardly surprising that Vic hadn't mentioned this to her, she thought. He probably didn't even know. It had likely been kept tightly compartmented at the CIA at the time.

"But given the suicide, the forty million was wasted," Jayne said.

"As it turned out. A nice payday for Zeller and Steiner, though."

A moment passed, then another alarm bell rang inside Jayne's head.

"Wait a minute," she said. "Under Swiss banking secrecy laws, it's a crime to disclose information about clients to someone else without consent."

This time, a broad grin spread across Goldwasser's face.

Jayne couldn't help grinning in response as she computed exactly how invaluable that information might be and how she could use it. This trip had just become absolutely worth the time and cost involved.

"I really do hope this meeting has been helpful to you," Goldwasser said.

"Very helpful."

She knew she needed to collect all the evidence she could before approaching Zeller and Steiner. "Do you mind if I photograph those cables?" she asked.

Goldwasser nodded, and she took out her phone and snapped pictures of the documents.

As she did so, Jayne realized there was a potential issue.

"Do you have any proof that the forty million payment was made?" Jayne asked. "That will be the essential ingredient. And also that it was them who passed information on their account holders, including Genoud, to the CIA?"

Goldwasser's smiled faded. "I don't have any documentary proof, no. But I wasn't the one making the payment. You will need to talk to the CIA about that."

Jayne frowned. "That's what I'm concerned about. They didn't exactly cover themselves with glory over this, did they. I'm not sure they'll want to admit to any of it."

CHAPTER SIXTEEN

Monday, April 18, 2016
Washington, DC

By quarter past eight, Cyrus Saba was sitting in the cab of the large green garbage truck in a parking spot next to a small park across the street from the embassy of Jordan.

Twenty yards behind him, hidden from view by a group of trees, were the bodies of the two garbagemen who had been operating the vehicle.

So far, Saba's plan had gone according to his script. He had arrived at the park on foot, having taken a public bus to a stop a half mile down the street.

Then he had watched from a distance as the garbagemen finished their collection from the embassy and, as usual, stopped at the park for coffee and a snack.

While they were sitting on their normal bench, Saba had approached from behind and, using his favorite SIG Sauer P229 9mm pistol with SRD9 silencer attached, had dropped both of them with double shots to the head before they could even turn around.

He had chosen his shooting position carefully and even marked it out on the ground several days in advance. The trees growing in the park shielded him completely from any potential observers and the surveillance cameras at the nearby embassy buildings, and now also neatly concealed the bodies from view.

Done.

Now Saba needed to move on to the second stage of the operation.

When he had first become involved in lethal operations of this type, twenty-five years earlier, it had been out of a furious passion that he felt for his home country, Iran, and anger toward its number one enemy.

Over the years, the motivation had changed significantly, but his expertise remained as razor sharp as it had ever been.

Here, there would be little margin for error. At eighteen minutes past the hour, he started the engine of the truck and waited, breathing deliberately slowly and relaxing to try and keep his heart rate down. He needed to be able to think clearly.

Less than a minute later, as Saba expected would happen, he saw through the side window of the cab a gleaming black Mercedes S55 AMG appear around the corner of International Drive NW.

He shifted the truck into gear and waited until the luxury sedan had passed in front of him, then he let out the clutch and followed about fifty yards behind it.

The Mercedes rounded the next bend and began to head down the slope, past the embassies of Bangladesh and Ghana, toward the Israeli embassy at the bottom.

As soon as the garbage truck negotiated the same bend, Saba began to accelerate.

Now he could see the Mercedes's brake lights flick on as it began to slow to turn left into the embassy gate.

That was when he stamped down hard on the gas pedal, and the truck's huge diesel engine roared as it gathered pace rapidly down the hill.

Saba swerved slightly left as he drew near the embassy gates, to ensure he struck the Mercedes exactly where he wanted.

The impact, when it came, was massive.

The truck smashed into the rear section of the car. Saba knew that the Israeli ambassador, Yosef Zeevi, would be sitting in the back seat.

The force of the collision shoved the Mercedes forward and sideways, causing it to spin and crash with a huge bang into the steel perimeter fence and concrete wall that formed the embassy frontage.

The rear of the Mercedes was destroyed and the front badly damaged.

Despite its mass and heavy steel bumpers, the garbage truck was thrown off course, and Saba had to fight the steering wheel to avoid slamming into another parked car. But he braked hard, brought the truck under control, and came to a halt at the side of the street, where he jumped out of the cab.

He drew his SIG Sauer from beneath his jacket and, before the guards in the security kiosk at the front of the Israeli embassy could react, bent double to reduce his profile and ran to the wreckage of the Mercedes.

Saba knew he needed to be careful. If the bodyguard, who would be armed, hadn't been badly injured in the collision, he might still be mobile and dangerous.

The rear window was broken and the door twisted into an unrecognizable mass of metal. Saba didn't need to try and open it; he could see quite clearly into the car.

Both the driver and the bodyguard appeared unconscious. Although Zeevi was injured, with blood streaming from a wound on his forehead, his head was moving and he was groaning.

Saba flicked off the safety and pumped three rounds in rapid succession into Zeevi's head.

Thwack, thwack, thwack.

Zeevi's head jerked back with the three impacts. Blood spurted out of the back of his skull as the rounds exited and splattered all over the unconscious bodyguard slumped next to him.

Saba then turned and sprinted to a BMW sedan with false license plates that he had parked in a spot across the street the previous afternoon.

Saba climbed in, turned on the engine and, with a screech of tires, accelerated onto Van Ness Street NW and away. In the mirror, he caught sight of the embassy guards emerging into the street.

CHAPTER SEVENTEEN

Monday, April 18, 2016
   Jerusalem

The cab driver who was ferrying Jayne from Yad Vashem along the twisting highway through the hills west of Jerusalem and down Route 1 to Tel Aviv soon gave up on his attempts to make conversation.

She was preoccupied with the need to communicate what she had learned from Leo Goldwasser to Joe and Vic, who she hoped would be able to corroborate the points about the CIA payment to Zeller and Steiner.

The more she thought about it, the more her worry mounted that the sheer embarrassment at having paid $40 million needlessly to two Swiss men whose bank supported the Nazis might have resulted in a cover-up.

It seemed a distinct possibility that all evidence of the payment would have been destroyed by Langley.

If so, Zeller and Steiner could simply deny everything.

There were a lot of uncertainties. But Jayne put them to the back of her mind for a few moments and made a call to the intensive care unit at the Sourasky Medical Center. She needed an update on how Mark Nicklin-Donovan was doing.

She got through to Nina Raslan, the head nurse whom she had seen on her visit to the hospital a couple of weeks earlier. To her delight, Nina informed her that Nicklin-Donovan had improved significantly in recent days and could be taken out of intensive care if that continued. There had been no further heart issues.

"That's incredible news. Is it possible to speak to him?" Jayne asked.

"Unfortunately not. He's still fragile and is undergoing treatment right now. I can give him a message, though. He's got his wife with him, so he's not short of support."

"Thank you. Just tell him to keep going and that I'm thinking of him and wishing him a speedy recovery, and I'll see him soon. That's all."

Jayne thanked Nina again and ended the call.

She immediately received an alert telling her that she had missed a call from Vic. There was no message. He would have to wait a short while until she was somewhere secure enough to return the call.

As soon as she arrived back at the Sheraton she headed toward the beach, where there was no danger of being picked up by hidden microphones, and sat on a concrete barrier next to the sand from where she could see in all directions. She took out her phone and decided to call Joe first, using her secure connection.

After a quick exchange of affections, Jayne immediately began to run through her account of the Yad Vashem revelations, and when she mentioned François Genoud, Joe interrupted.

"I remember that Genoud case—I worked on it for a while together with the CIA. That's why I'd said I recalled the name Steiner. We were certain we had Genoud nailed but then he committed suicide."

"So, forty million dollars of US taxpayers' money was wasted?"

"Yes, I know. But they were Swiss bankers. They wouldn't do it for five bucks, would they? And it opens the door to you now, doesn't it?"

Jayne gave a sarcastic half laugh. "Let's hope so. It sometimes seems the only way to get anywhere in this business is through bribery and blackmail."

"It's a means to an end," he said. Jayne could almost hear the shrug coming down the phone line from Portland. Joe was usually pragmatic about such things.

"Yes, I agree. Provided we have sufficient proof to make the blackmail actually work. Is there proof the payment was made, do you know?"

There was a brief silence at the other end of the line. "You had best call Vic and talk to him about this," Joe said. "He wasn't involved with Genoud, as far as I recall. He was still in Pakistan. But you'll need to involve him now."

"I'll do that."

After another few minutes of exchanging general updates, Jayne ended the call and called Vic's cell phone, again using a secure connection.

But this time, before she could open her mouth, Vic began to speak in his usual gravelly voice. He sounded distracted, his voice tense.

"Jayne, thanks for calling. I just need to update you on something before we start discussing other things. You probably haven't heard yet, but the Israeli ambassador here in DC has been assassinated. Happened about forty-five minutes ago. His car got hit by a garbage truck outside the embassy, and someone put three rounds into his head."

Jayne felt her stomach flip over. "A *garbage* truck?" she said. "What the hell? How did that happen? Did his bodyguard, the security team, not do anything?"

"Too quick. It was well planned. One man working alone. He stole the truck."

"Any idea who did it?" Jayne asked. This had to be linked somehow to the gas platform attack.

"Nobody's claimed responsibility."

"Just like the Samar. But presumably the Iranians, or Hezbollah? Anyone would think they were trying to provoke Israel and the White House into striking back at them."

"It does look like waving the proverbial red flag at the bull," Vic said.

Jayne frowned. "It's nonsense. Given that Iran has signed up for the nuclear agreement and doesn't have an actual nuclear weapon in place yet, it seems illogical that they would provoke a potentially devastating attack. Wouldn't they wait until the weapon was ready? It could trigger big protests in the streets and a resumption of sanctions. That was what Tehran was trying to avoid when they signed the nuke deal. It doesn't add up."

"I know. It doesn't make sense."

"How has the president reacted?" Jayne asked.

"We've only had a quick conversation with the White House, but they are furious. The Israelis are already going absolutely ballistic. There was no warning from the FBI, it came out of the blue, and we hadn't picked up anything, nor had the NSA. The president is going to be onto us again very quickly. He'll need to know who is doing this and why. Remember he's meant to be heading to Tel Aviv for the Cohen funeral on Thursday of next week. Though that is looking increasingly high-risk."

Jayne remained silent for a couple of seconds. "I called the hospital in Tel Aviv just earlier. Mark is improving. Any word on Paul Farrar?"

"Last I heard he was also improving but still in intensive care. I'll let you know if his condition changes."

"All right, thanks. Now, listen, I need to bring you up to date on what I learned at Yad Vashem."

"Ah, yes. Tell me."

Once more she ran through her account of her meeting with Leo Goldwasser, including details of the CIA cables.

"So, as you can see, it's a case of good news and bad news. This forty million dollar payment is the key. It could be the lever to get Zeller and Steiner to tell us what we need to know," Jayne said. "It's dynamite. They've broken every law in the Swiss bankers' bible as well as the Swiss national law. But we need the proof."

There was a pause.

"Genoud wasn't my case," Vic said, his voice now even more gravelly than normal. "But I became aware of it. It caused a lot of embarrassment internally. We somehow stopped it from leaking."

Vic paused and sighed. "I'm now deeply worried that Goldwasser has those details and the cables, frankly. No doubt we have our friends at the Mossad to thank for that."

"He wouldn't tell me how he got the copies of the cables, although you're probably right. But they were in his secure vault, if that's any comfort."

"Not really, no."

"Anyway, all that is irrelevant if Zeller and Steiner are able to claim they never passed information on their account holders to the CIA and never received any money."

"True. But I have no idea if we've got the proof you need."

"Come on, Vic. You must have files on those two. And I'd bet a large amount of money they contain what I need."

"We must have files on them, yes," Vic said. "But I'm also responsible these days for the Agency's reputation. So even if we do have proof, what if it leaks that we paid that money for nothing, especially to a couple of Nazi-sympathizing bankers? It's not going to look good on the front pages. The media and the White House will be on us like a ton of bricks over that, as well as the Samar disaster and now the ambassador. Ferguson will chew our balls off."

"Well," Jayne said, "you can't have it all ways. You're telling me that the Israeli ambassador has just been assassinated in DC. And that the president wants information urgently so he can decide whether to back a strike on Iran. If you want me to make any headway with this investigation and have a chance of getting what we need from Zeller and Steiner, you're going to have to make some tough choices, then."

"Maybe there's another way." Now Vic's voice sounded almost wistful. "I've got a teleconference with the internal team about this in half an hour. I'll break the good news and the bad news to them, and we'll discuss it."

Jayne glanced up at the azure sky above Tel Aviv and the Mediterranean to the west. She understood the potential for damage if there was a leak. But she was certain that Vic would realize he had no choice.

"If there's a better way than this to force two Swiss bankers to open their mouths, then I'll be very happy to consider it," she said.

Jayne ended the call.

She glanced at her watch. She sent a short secure message to Zahavi to let him know that she was on schedule to meet him at the airport early the following morning for their flight.

Progress made. Suggest we fly direct to Zürich not Munich. Will brief you later, she wrote. Zahavi would understand.

She then sent another to Rafael and Odeya to confirm she

would be heading directly to Zürich, where they were. She would brief them all on developments when she saw them in person.

Then she stood and walked back across the beach toward the Sheraton.

CHAPTER EIGHTEEN

Monday, April 18, 2016
  Jerusalem

As usual at the end of the day, Marian Khaldi cleared the reception area at Yad Vashem's archives and library building of the mess of papers, information leaflets, coffee cups, and other detritus left by the stream of visitors over the previous nine hours.

When she had finished, Marian adjusted her pale green hijab, which covered her shoulder-length black hair and neck, and checked the visitors file. She needed to ensure there were enough blank sheets to accommodate the details and signatures of guests who would arrive the following day. There were plenty.

Although a Yad Vashem employee, Marian wasn't Jewish, nor was her family. They were Arab Muslim, like most in the Central Galilee city of Nazareth, where they came from. Her grandparents on both sides had remained in Nazareth during and after the war that raged around them from 1947 to 1949 between Jewish forces and Palestinian Arabs.

The war was triggered by the United Nations decision in 1947 to create Israel within what had been Palestine. It ended in victory, of sorts, for the Jewish militias in 1948. Shortly after that came the withdrawal of the British, who had governed Palestine since 1917, and the separation of the country to allow the formation of Israel.

Of the Arabs who found themselves within the new Israel, about half, or seven hundred thousand, ended up either fleeing or being driven from their homes in a great exodus, known as the Nakba.

Although Nazareth had remained Arab-dominated after the war, across Israel as a whole, the Nakba left the Arabs in a small minority. That hadn't changed much since, and currently Arabs comprised only about a fifth of the country's 8.8 million people.

The war and the separation, though, all happened long before Marian's time. She had been born in Nazareth in 1988 and had moved to Jerusalem, about one hundred kilometers south, to study history at the city's Hebrew University after completing national military service at the age of twenty-two.

Unlike for Jewish youngsters, there was no obligation for Arab Israelis to serve in the Israel Defense Forces, but by the time Marian reached the eligibility age of eighteen, a growing number were doing so. Marian took the view that it would do her long-term career prospects no harm. Employers liked patriots.

Yad Vashem, despite its strongly Jewish core objectives, always tried to be an equal opportunity employer, and the senior management deliberately tried to avoid the kind of racial discrimination that had caused the Holocaust in the first place.

This approach had provided Marian with her first proper

job after leaving university. In fact, Yad Vashem was now handing her a promotion. After a two-year stint on the reception desk, she was due to start a new role the following month as a junior historian, with a particular focus on Israel's Arab history.

But her pay remained low, as did that of her boyfriend, Yusef Jabara, whom she had met at university. Unlike her, Yousef had declined to do military service and, by coincidence or not, had struggled to find a "proper" job. Instead, he worked three days a week as a delivery driver for a fruit and vegetable merchant and had to take potatoes, carrots, oranges, bananas, and other produce to the kitchens of two military bases outside Jerusalem.

Until six months earlier, Marian and Yusef had struggled every month to pay the rent and other bills at the one-bedroom flat they shared in West Jerusalem.

But then Yusef came home one day to announce that he had found a new source of income. He had fallen into conversation in a café with a man who had offered him money in return for any useful information he could elicit from the military bases on his delivery round. He was particularly interested in troop levels and planned movements of troops. The amount of money paid depended on the perceived value of the information given.

It took four days of fairly intense questioning on Marian's part before Yusef admitted that he was now a part-time agent for Hezbollah. It turned out that a couple of Yusef's friends had also been recruited. It left Marian feeling confused. She didn't like the secrecy and she didn't like that Yusef was doing something so obviously risky. If he were caught, there would be trouble, she knew that. But on the other hand, they were short of money.

At around the same time, Marian had become aware, after overhearing a conversation at Yad Vashem, that a man who she regularly saw in her building, the head of archives, Dr. Leo Goldwasser, was a key point of contact for the Mossad and other intelligence agencies. It seemed that Yad Vashem received more questions from such sources than Marian imagined.

One evening, after a relaxing Friday evening that involved pasta, red wine, and prolonged lovemaking, she had let this piece of information slip to Yusef.

In retrospect, that had been a serious error of judgment.

He had immediately seen the financial opportunity and, without first consulting Marian, had told his new Hezbollah paymaster.

It led to a furious argument, and she didn't speak to him for several days. But in the end, financial considerations took precedence, and she agreed to pass on any information that might have value.

Most of the information she provided comprised the names of visitors with whom Dr. Goldwasser had meetings.

For the past month, Marian had supplied a daily photograph of the visitors list at the archive, which included each visitor's name and the Yad Vashem person they were meeting. She added further brief details if any of the visitors seemed particularly interesting.

Yusef's contact clearly thought that some of it was worth paying for because cash was forthcoming. Before long, the pair of them were no longer struggling to pay their monthly bills.

So now, before she closed the visitors file and placed it in a drawer for safekeeping overnight, she took out her phone, and while appearing to do nothing more than check her messages, she surreptitiously photographed the list for that day.

The note she would later send to Yusef for onward distribution would include a list of the four files that Dr. Goldwasser had taken from the archive and, presumably, shared with his guest Jayne Robinson, from the United Kingdom.

Unfortunately, Marian was not able to obtain details of the box that Goldwasser had removed from the vault, as she didn't have security clearance for that.

She recognized only one of the four names she would pass on: Klaus Barbie, who she knew from her studies was a notorious Nazi war criminal.

The other names—Martin Zeller, Carl Steiner, and François Genoud—meant nothing to her. But perhaps taken together in the context of Dr. Goldwasser meeting Jayne Robinson, they would be worth something to Hezbollah.

CHAPTER NINETEEN

Tuesday, April 19, 2016
Zürich

The headquarters buildings of the two grand old gentlemen of Swiss banking, Union Bank of Switzerland and Credit Suisse, stood facing each other across Paradeplatz, one of the most upmarket and expensive pieces of real estate in the world, as they had done for more than a century.

Jayne, who had just disembarked from the number nine tram following a forty-five minute journey from the airport, checked once again that there was no sign of trailing surveillance.

Before leaving the airport following her arrival from Tel Aviv, she had put on a light disguise consisting of a headscarf and plain black-rimmed glasses.

Satisfied that she had no coverage, she stood for a moment, scrutinizing the elegant stone frontage of the Credit Suisse building, which ran almost seventy yards across the entire northern side of the square.

The headquarters of UBS, constructed from equally solid stone, dominated the western side. And in the center of the square was a tram stop, buzzing with tourists and office workers. Jayne had been here several times before, both on MI6 business and on vacations.

But although it was a financial institution that had brought her to Zürich, it wasn't UBS or Credit Suisse.

The object of her attention was rather in a six-story office building a few hundred yards to the southwest, on the more anonymous Dreikönigstrasse.

Jayne had studied photographs of the building that Odeya had sent her overnight, but despite that, she decided to walk past it en route to the Mossad safe house they were using, to ensure she had a feel for the lay of the land.

Zahavi had traveled separately to the safe house for security purposes. Although they were certain they had no surveillance, it was a sensible extra precaution. He had rented a black Peugeot 508 sedan at the airport.

After a five-minute walk, she passed the Zeller and Steiner building on the far side of Dreikönigstrasse, taking care to avoid staring at it.

The bank faced the street at the front, and at the rear it overlooked the stretch of waterway known as Schanzengraben, a canal originally built to help defend the old town center in the 1600s. A long row of small boats were moored next to a walkway that ran alongside the water.

Zeller and Steiner had a long history, dating back to the 1820s, and remained the third oldest of the fifteen family-owned private banks in the country.

Jayne continued over the road bridge that crossed Schanzengraben and made her way by a circuitous route toward the safe house in a shabby building in Tödistrasse, a long stone's throw from Lake Zürich. She deliberately passed through a small square that had only one way in and out, which gave her a good opportunity to check again for a tail. There was none.

She then went to the safe house door and pressed the buzzer and, after giving the agreed code word, was admitted by Odeya, who took her up to the third floor.

As she expected, Zahavi was already there after driving an extensive surveillance detection route around the outer suburbs of Zürich. He had parked the Peugeot two streets away, near to where Rafael had left the silver BMW, before walking to the safe house.

Jayne put her bags in the remaining vacant bedroom, took out her laptop, and walked to the dining room, where Rafael and Odeya had set up an office.

Like the Munich safe house, the apartment was spacious but sparsely furnished. However, it was already starting to look like an operational headquarters. Odeya had taped large-scale maps of the city center and an architect's internal drawing of the bank's floor plan to the walls. These were professionals, and if they were going into a building, they wanted to know as much about it as possible, including all potential escape routes in case things went wrong.

A series of photographs of Martin Zeller and Carl Steiner lay on the table. Rafael had taken them using a telephoto lens from a surveillance van with one-way glass windows that the Mossad kept in a garage behind the apartment building.

The other three were already sitting around the dining table, so Jayne took a seat and picked up a couple of the pictures.

Both men were dressed in dark suits and looked well groomed. But what was surprising was their appearance.

She knew from her research that they were both aged around sixty years old, and most successful bankers she had come across in that age bracket fell firmly into the fat-cat bracket. They were often flabby, overfed, and generally unfit.

These two, by contrast, looked barrel-chested and muscular.

Rafael noticed her looking at the photographs and must have guessed her thoughts.

"Fit guys," he said. "They both work out. I think they carry guns too. Hardly normal for bankers."

"Really?" Jayne said.

"Their suits are cut to hide them, but there's a hint of an outline beneath the armpit. Look." He pointed to one of the photos that had been enlarged.

Jayne looked carefully and indeed there was a suggestion of a bulge.

Zahavi leaned forward, his arms folded. "Let's talk business, then. We need to come up with a plan of attack." He looked around the table, eyeing each of them in turn. "Any ideas?"

Rafael glanced at Odeya. "There is a possibility. I talked to two investment bankers I know who specialize in the finance sector. I was just trying to get a feel for how Zeller and Steiner is viewed in the wider banking community, so I wasn't asking leading questions. But they both told me the same thing. Until now, this bank has been remarkable in that for the majority of its history, it has been run by family members. Mostly, the chairman has been either a Zeller or a Steiner, and often the chief executive too. As you can see, right now both positions are filled by the families. But these two guys are near to retirement age, and frankly, neither of them have any suitable heirs. Zeller and his wife have a son who works for an international charity in Paris, and Steiner's two daughters show no interest in the bank."

"Are you suggesting they're looking to sell?" Jayne asked.

"Precisely," Rafael said. "Zeller and Steiner is quietly up for sale. There has so far been nothing in the financial press, probably because business journalists are slow off the mark these days. And you won't exactly see a for sale sign outside, but discreet conversations have taken place with a couple of potentially interested parties, both Swiss."

Jayne leaned back in her seat, thinking. She had an idea.

"That's our way in, then," she said. "We're going to need an excuse to get these two men in a room alone where we can have a very confidential discussion. You've just come up with the excuse."

"What, we pose as buyers?" Zahavi asked.

"Yes, exactly." She turned to Rafael. "Can your investment banker friends facilitate such a discussion? Who do they work for?"

Rafael named a second-tier but nevertheless well-known investment bank, Altman Brothers, based in London and New York City but with offices in several European financial centers, including Zürich. Jayne had had some minor dealings with them years earlier, while at MI6, and she knew they were specialists in handling corporate merger and acquisitions activity.

"I've no idea if they would play ball," Rafael said. "It's a big thing to ask, and they have their reputations to think of. However, they are both Jewish. They understand. Perhaps we can make it attractive for them."

"Can you trust them?" Zahavi asked. "If Zeller and Steiner get even a hint that we're about to ambush them, we're finished."

"Completely. We go back a long way." Rafael's tone was emphatic.

"We would need coaching," Odeya said. "We would need to ask questions and use language that would entirely fit with how potential buyers of a Swiss private banking business would behave and speak."

That was for certain, Jayne thought, but she had done that before on operations involving dealings with banks and

investment companies. A key part of the armory for an intelligence operative was the ability to be a good actor.

But nevertheless, without the help of Rafael's banking
friends, she doubted it would be possible. They would also
need letters and documents that appeared convincing, again
something that could not be easily produced without expert
help.

"All right," Jayne said. "Rafael, sound out your friends. If
they're willing, let's get this moving."

Zahavi nodded. "As a Jew, I quite like the idea of buying a
Swiss bank that was implicated in financing the Holocaust."
He grinned broadly. "We may want to redistribute some of its
assets."

The development that gave their plan its final impetus,
however, came in a secure email that Jayne received from Vic
just as the team was about to break for some lunch.

The email contained two photographs and one document.

CHAPTER TWENTY

Tuesday, April 19, 2016
   Zürich

The two bankers from Altman Brothers listened carefully as Rafael outlined briefly what was required of them. Typical of their profession, they seemed to Jayne to be a skeptical pair, as she had half expected. There were more than a few raised eyebrows, pursed lips, and frowns.

Jayne was impressed that Rafael had managed to persuade the two doubtless extremely busy men to give the team from Tel Aviv a hearing at their offices on such short notice.

The two men, Joel Lindenstrauss, the younger of the two, in his mid-thirties, and Abe Shapiro, into his forties, sat on one side of a long, highly polished boardroom-style table that had seating for sixteen people. Jayne and her three companions sat on the other side.

The decor here was dramatically different than the generally basic level of furnishings found at Langley or Vauxhall Cross.

There were four large oil paintings hanging on the walls, and gold candlesticks stood on a sideboard together with polished silverware. At one end of the room were two floor-to-ceiling french windows, each with dark ruby satin curtains, that overlooked Zürich Yacht Club's pier on the lake. In fact, the entire premises, a heavily turreted red brick place, reeked of opulence.

Both men spoke fluent English and showed an immediate grasp of what was required. As Rafael had so eloquently outlined, their job was simply to get Zahavi, Rafael, and Odeya through the door of the bank without raising any suspicions.

"First question is, would these two men actually consider selling to foreign buyers?" Jayne asked.

"We understand that although their preference is to find a Swiss buyer, at the end of the day, it will come down to price," Shapiro said. "Of course, many Swiss banks do have foreign ownership. Safra Group in Brazil bought Sarasin not too long ago, for example."

Lindenstrauss leaned forward and ran a hand through his trendily coiffured blond hair. "Can you explain why you need this meeting?"

"It's Iran," Jayne said. She knew they had to be honest about their agenda. "We're trying to find out who's masterminding its nuclear supply chain. There are also potential links to the recent strikes on Israeli targets—the ambassador in Washington and the gas platform off Tel Aviv."

Lindenstrauss nodded. "Of course. I've seen the news. It's shocking. And presumably you think Zeller and Steiner are bankers for the Iran nuclear program?"

"We've been given reason to believe that's the case," Jayne said.

"And I assume you know about Swiss banking secrecy laws?"

"We do. But we think we have a way of getting around that difficulty."

She explained succinctly the detail they had about Genoud, the CIA, and their links to the Nazis and the PLO.

Lindenstrauss placed both hands behind his head and stared at the ceiling for a few seconds. "I see. At some point, probably quite early in the meeting, you are going to abandon your pretenses about buying the bank and explain the true purpose of your visit."

"Of course," Jayne said.

"If, at that stage, Zeller and Steiner deny passing information to the CIA and receiving money and say they have never had any dealings with François Genoud, and know nothing about acting as banker for the Nazis and the Palestinians, what do you do? These are powerful men, and you're asking us to put our necks on the line here—we've got a lot to lose."

"What are you saying?" Zahavi asked.

"I'm going to say no to your proposal."

"Wait a moment," Jayne said.

"No. I mean what I say," Lindenstrauss said. "They could badly damage our business—they could tell the financial community we're prepared to go around arranging meetings for clients under false pretenses and spreading highly libelous information that could ruin them."

Jayne had expected this pushback. It was time to play her trump card. She glanced to her right at Zahavi. He caught her eye and gave an almost imperceptible nod.

Jayne opened a folder containing printed copies of the photographs and the document that Vic had emailed to her earlier, and placed them on the table.

"What are these?" Shapiro asked as he tapped his gold-plated fountain pen on the desk.

"The proof," Jayne said.

The high-definition photographs were dated April

10,1996, and were taken through a telephoto lens at a quiet picnic spot in the hills south of Lake Geneva, on the French side of the border with Switzerland. They showed two chunky briefcases being handed to Carl Steiner and Martin Zeller by another man who Jayne now knew was the CIA's chief of Paris station.

The next photograph showed Steiner appearing to check one of the briefcases. The lid was only half open, at most, but nevertheless enough for wads of bank notes to be visible as he peered into it. The photographer had done well to capture what must have been a very fleeting but significant moment.

Another photo showed the two bankers climbing into a BMW sedan.

"Those photos recorded the transaction," Jayne said.

Next Jayne passed across a sheet of paper that contained a transcript of a short telephone conversation held two days prior to the meeting between Steiner and the chief of station during which the terms of the deal and the sum of money were agreed upon.

"We have a tape of the conversation from which that transcript was taken," Jayne said.

Vic had sent the materials after what he described as a heated debate with Director Veltman. Ultimately, they had decided there was no choice but to deploy the photos and the transcript if they wanted to give Jayne and the Mossad team the best chance of getting the information they wanted.

Shapiro pursed his lips. "This might change our view."

"You'll do it?" Zahavi asked.

Shapiro glanced at Lindenstrauss. "It might work. I see why you're keen to pursue this."

Lindenstrauss nodded slowly. "It's doable, I think."

"Have you dealt with Zeller and Steiner before?" Jayne asked.

"We have sold two businesses to clients of theirs, and

we've been in the same room at social functions," Linden-strauss said. "They know who we are. I think we'll get you through the door. We've got the credibility."

The two investment bankers agreed to spend some time preparing the team for the meeting, including a detailed briefing on what was known about Zeller and Steiner's operations and investments. Because the bank was privately owned, not a great deal of information was available, but Shapiro said that they had enough to provide an adequate amount of background data.

"When do you want to have this meeting?" Shapiro asked.

"Yesterday would have been ideal," Zahavi said, fingering his chin.

"There's some urgency, then?"

"You could say that," Jayne said.

Lindenstrauss and Shapiro looked at each other.

"I can make a phone call now, if you'd like," Shapiro said. "I have a cell number for Steiner. I will tell him I'm with a group of four financial investors who already own private banks in the US and the UK who are interested in expanding their portfolio. I won't need to go into too much detail—I'll play the confidentiality card. They won't expect anything at that stage, although they will want more information when you meet them."

"Yes. Let's get this moving," Jayne said. "Tell him we're in Zürich but only for a couple of days, so it's time sensitive."

Shapiro nodded. "I'll do it in my office." He rose and walked out of the room.

Lindenstrauss went to a side table on which stood a coffee thermos and cups. He poured out drinks for them all and passed around a plate of cookies. By that stage, Jayne was both hungry and in need of caffeine. It had been a tiring few days.

While they were waiting for Shapiro to return, they

sipped their coffee and looked out the window over Lake Zürich, its sparkling blue waters glinting in the spring sunshine. The city was at the northern end of the lake, a long, narrow stretch of water that ran as far as St. Gallen, some thirty-five kilometers to the southeast.

Out on the water, white yachts were moving slowly toward the eastern shore, lined with trees, hotels, and apartment blocks. Beyond the lake, the outline of distant mountains formed the horizon. This was not a bad place to work, Jayne reflected.

A few minutes later, the door of the meeting room swung open and Shapiro stepped back in, the corners of his mouth turned up a fraction. "You will be pleased to know our friends at Zeller and Steiner have agreed to meet us tomorrow afternoon, at four o'clock."

"Good," Zahavi said. "Where will we meet them?"

"I requested that they come here, but they refused. They also refused to meet at a neutral venue. So unfortunately we need to go to their offices. They refused to acquiesce on that point. Maybe they are less eager to sell their bank than I had heard."

That was a blow, Jayne thought. It meant that there would be no opportunity to install covert recording equipment or cameras, and it was almost certain that they would face airport-style security checks on the way in.

It would therefore also be impossible to take in weapons of any kind. If the bank directors carried guns, it seemed certain to Jayne that their security team would be even more heavily armed, and likely ex-military.

It was obvious they needed to do some very careful choreographing before embarking on this particular operation. Planning would be key. It was going to be a long evening back in the safe house.

* * *

Tuesday, April 19, 2016
    Zürich

Henri had never enjoyed operations in Zürich. It wasn't
because he didn't like the city, which he had to admit was
beautiful, albeit in a different way than Paris. It was more to
do with his main Hezbollah contact there, an arrogant
German-Lebanese man, Mo Issa, who admittedly had a good
network of contacts and safe houses but was a rude control
freak who had been less than helpful on previous operations.

When his instructions had come through from Beirut late
the previous night, Henri had immediately sent a request to
Mo for a safe house. He had stated his preferred location,
within two hundred meters of the address for the target
building he had been given, but based on past experience
thought the chances of Mo providing what he needed
were low.

Henri had therefore prepared his blue Volkswagen Transporter panel van for the trip, fully expecting to have to use it
as his sniper nest, his weapons and explosives storage cache,
possibly his sleeping quarters, and his getaway vehicle all in
one. He was accustomed to that and already had two sets of
false Swiss license plates ready to be screwed on after crossing
the Swiss border. The plates were stored in a compartment at
the rear of the van, along with similar plates for other countries, including the UK and Germany, and a variety of high-
quality magnetic branded signage.

The company signs could quickly be placed on the sides
of his plain blue van, turning it into a vehicle that looked
quite similar to the fleets operated by a French electricity
utility or a German water company or one of the ubiquitous

parcel delivery vans operated by Amazon, among other options.

However, to Henri's surprise, Mo had found him a fourth-floor apartment, located only 150 meters from the target building, a private Swiss bank named Zeller and Steiner.

The bank was due to be visited by the four people on his list. His task was to find a way to eliminate at least the two listed as priorities, Jayne Robinson and David Zahavi, and ideally the others as well, Rafael Levy and Odeya Leibovitch. Henri had downloaded photographs of all of them from the drive he shared with his paymaster in Beirut, Talal Hassan.

Henri had also asked Hassan for the address where the four were staying in Zürich as an alternative in case things went wrong at the bank, but Hassan was still trying to obtain that information.

Henri was familiar with the street on which the bank was located, Dreikönigstrasse. Indeed, he and Pierre had quite spectacularly blown up a car containing four Israeli diplomats around the corner from there, in Talstrasse, fifteen years ago. It was an operation that had become legendary among the Hezbollah old-timers across Europe as well as in Beirut.

From the fourth-floor apartment, Henri had an excellent line of sight across the canal to the main front door of the four-story bank building as well as several of its large arched windows.

That meant that his sniper rifle, the VSS Vintorez, would be his preferred weapon. However, he had also brought with him in the van a good supply of ammonium nitrate, which he had already mixed with fuel oil and packaged up with detonators inside the black plastic containers with their built-in magnets. They formed small but powerful bombs. The very last resort was his pistol, but he had no intention of coming within handgun range of his intended victims.

When the time came, Henri planned to move the van

from its current spot on a nearby side street to a row of parking spaces opposite the bank. Its disguised gunports would give him backup options as a shooting location, and most important, it meant that his means of escape was close at hand.

During Henri's most recent call with Hassan, he had asked if the Swiss bankers had been made aware that they were about to be approached by a group of Mossad intelligence operatives.

"Do my targets need to be taken out before they get into the building and speak to the bankers, or does it matter if I do it afterward?" Henri had asked.

"Tehran is informing the bankers," Hassan said in response. "We don't talk to the bankers—ever. However, Tehran thinks they are rock solid. They have come under scrutiny many times, but no intelligence agency has ever gotten anything out of them as far as we know. The Swiss just wave a copy of the Banking Act of 1934 in front of them—they know that giving away anything could put them straight in prison. So Tehran isn't worried."

What Hassan said made sense. If the bankers had let slip critical information, or if the intelligence community had found a way to hack into their computer systems, the Iranian nuclear weapons program would have been finished a long time ago.

The apartment, like many Hezbollah apartments he had used, badly needed cleaning and stank of cigarette smoke, take-out food, and stale sweat. The bed sheets and duvet looked as though they hadn't been changed in some time, but he would just have to make do.

Confirmation of the new target address in Zürich rather than Munich had come from two separate sources, each corroborating the other, according to Hassan.

One source was a Hezbollah informer in Tel Aviv. Apparently Robinson had been in Israel for a few days and had visited Yad Vashem, which Henri found interesting. He had been told nothing more, but presumably she had been in search of information, and it was undoubtedly no coincidence that on arriving back in Europe, she had headed directly to Zürich.

The other source, providing very similar information, was a mole inside Western intelligence, although Hassan, as usual, had not been specific about which service. He generally only shared a minimal amount of such detail. But given the Yad Vashem link and Robinson's visit to Israel, Henri guessed it was presumably the Mossad or the CIA, although he knew that Hezbollah also had strong contacts inside the French foreign intelligence service, the Direction Générale de la Sécurité Extérieure—the DGSE.

A further message that had arrived from Hassan a couple of hours earlier contained the precise time of the meeting, four o'clock the following afternoon.

Now Henri had enough information to begin putting a plan together.

He sat down at the dining table in the apartment, took out a notepad from his bag, and began to scribble down diagrams showing distances and timings for his main method of attack, together with a backup plan should that fail.

CHAPTER TWENTY-ONE

Wednesday, April 20, 2016
  Zürich

The tourist ambled absentmindedly northward up Beethovenstrasse and turned right when he came to a café on the corner. He paused, raised the small Canon camera that was hanging around his neck, and took two photographs of the street he was entering, Dreikönigstrasse.

After examining the photographs on the screen on the back of the camera, he pulled a pack of cigarettes from his pocket, lit one using a silver lighter, and took a deep drag as he resumed walking.

Rafael was dressed in a tatty pair of jeans with holes in the knees, a black round-neck sweater, and a brown leather jacket with a triangular tear on the right shoulder and scuff marks on the left sleeve. He also wore a pair of tinted glasses with nonprescription lenses and a cloth cap. A small navy backpack was casually slung over his left shoulder.

Any onlooker would have marked him down as just one of

the thousands of visitors who could be found walking the streets of Zürich on any given day. Many of them were either preparing to travel south to the Alps for skiing in winter or hiking in summer or returning from a few days there. Rafael himself usually spent at least a couple of weeks every winter in the Grindelwald-Wengen ski area, located about ninety kilometers south of Zürich. It was expensive in peak season, but worth every Swiss franc. There was nothing better than sitting with a hot chocolate after a morning's skiing, gazing at the 3,900-meter north face of the Eiger and the neighboring Jungfrau.

Now, though, Rafael's mind was rather focused on his role as countersurveillance backup to his three colleagues who would soon be heading to Zeller and Steiner Bank's premises a short distance away.

They all knew that the risks were considerable. If word got to Zeller and Steiner or the Iranians that the Mossad and CIA were on their tail, they could expect all hell to break loose. Thankfully, there was so far no sign that had happened.

Rafael continued to walk slowly along the south side of Dreikönigstrasse, lined on both sides with expensive-looking furniture and luxury goods shops. Above the shops were another four stories of apartment and office buildings.

Rafael paused at the next street junction with Claridenstrasse and stood beneath an expansive plane tree. There he pretended to make a phone call, using it as cover to ensure there was no surveillance either ahead of or behind him. There were no shadows ducking into doorways, no people who had taken a sudden interest in shop windows, nor others, like him, who had stopped to make phone calls. Rather, the only people in view were a couple of old ladies carrying shopping bags, two teenage girls chatting animatedly, and three businessmen in suits who appeared to be hurrying to their next meeting.

Satisfied that he had no coverage, he continued onward over the pedestrian crossing. The bank building, built from gray granite, stood on the other side of the street on the bend where the road bridge crossed the Schanzengraben canal.

Opposite the bank, on Rafael's side of the street and near a café, were a row of parking spaces where the team intended to park the Peugeot while visiting the bank. All the spaces were vacant except two. One of them contained a blue VW Transporter van and another a station wagon that belonged to a Mossad backup team who had been summoned by Zahavi from their normal base in Berne. They would remain in the parking space in order to ensure it remained available for Zahavi, Jayne, and Odeya when they arrived in the Peugeot. There was no need for Rafael to speak to them.

Beyond the bridge, a crew of workmen had just begun to dig a hole in the road using a noisy jackhammer. They had set up temporary traffic lights next to their Swisscom telecom company van to allow traffic to pass, but there were few vehicles, and it was causing drivers little inconvenience.

Rafael continued past the bank for more than a hundred meters, across the waterway, and eventually stopped just short of the junction with Talstrasse. There he turned, adjusted his backpack, which contained his Beretta 71, a silencer, and two spare magazines, and retraced his steps. He had seen nothing that caused him concern.

When he reached the bridge over Schanzengraben again, he paused. The canal, some five meters below street level, was lined with apartment and office buildings. Narrow concrete walkways ran along both sides of the water for pedestrians, and a row of small motor and rowing boats were moored on the western side, next to the bank.

Rafael paused, lit another cigarette, and took a long drag as he casually leaned over the metal fence that prevented pedestrians from falling into the water. Behind him, the jack-hammer clattered away.

From there, he carefully scrutinized the buildings on both sides of the canal. Some of the apartment buildings had balconies. On a couple of them people were sitting, enjoying the afternoon sunshine with a coffee.

There was nothing out of the ordinary.

After a few minutes, Rafael continued to the small café opposite the bank that had a handful of tables and chairs outside on the sidewalk, about twenty meters away from the parking spots. All the tables were empty, probably because of the noise from the workmen's drill, Rafael surmised. It would be better tradecraft to sit inside, but he had no option if he wanted to see what was happening in the street. He sat at the table nearest to the canal and ordered a latte.

He glanced at his watch. There was another half hour before his colleagues were due to arrive for the four o'clock meeting. A line of traffic was beginning to build up at the temporary lights, causing a strong smell of exhaust fumes to waft through the air. Coupled with the noise of the jackham-mer, the café's outdoor tables now seemed quite an unpleasant prospect.

Rafael took out a copy of a newspaper, the *Neue Zürcher Zeitung*, and opened it up on the table. However, he didn't intend to do much reading. His job during this period prior to the meeting was to ensure there was no sign of surveillance or potential threats of any kind. If anything aroused suspicion, he would immediately call the others and abort the operation.

* * *

Wednesday, April 20, 2016
    Zürich

· · ·

Henri was used to manufacturing his sniper's nests from whatever makeshift materials he could find in the various locations he operated from. However, this time, having driven from Paris, he had the advantage of being able to bring his own favorite cushions and soft foam mat from home.

He found that building the nest on top of the solid oak dining table in the safe house gave him the best angle to get a line of fire to the front door of the Zeller and Steiner building. It was long enough to lie on and at the perfect height to allow him to see over the top of the sill and through the balcony door that he had opened.

The Vintorez had a great advantage over many sniper rifles, particularly in busy places, where its lower noise level and easy portability could make the difference between discovery and a seamless getaway.

The long black bullets Henri preferred, with their hardened steel tips, were devastating: he had seen them go straight through a steel plate at over four hundred meters. He had one magazine containing ten rounds already inserted into the Vintorez and another spare magazine lying on the table next to him, not that it would be needed.

Henri lay flat on his stomach on the foam mat that he had rolled out across the dining table and squinted through the PSO-1-1 telescopic sight that was mounted on top of the rifle and was another favorite piece of his equipment.

The front door of the bank filled his scope in clear, bright detail.

But a few seconds later he frowned. A truck had come to a halt on the bridge over the canal, blocking his view. He swung the scope fractionally to the left to find a white delivery van at a standstill behind the truck.

Traffic.

When he had ventured out at lunchtime, he had noticed some workmen setting up their equipment, and over the past forty minutes or so there had been the persistent sound of a jackhammer. However, the workmen were out of his line of vision, so he couldn't see exactly what was going on. But presumably they were the cause of the jam.

Henri waited for a few minutes, and although the truck and van had moved on, they had been replaced by other vehicles, and he still couldn't see the bank or indeed much of the sidewalk on the far side of the street running in both directions from the bank. This wasn't good. He glanced at his watch. There were still another fifteen minutes until four o'clock.

He climbed off the table, put on a woolen hat and tortoiseshell glasses, slung a small backpack containing his Heckler & Koch P7 over his shoulder, and left the apartment to check what was happening.

A few minutes later, Henri emerged from a narrow alley and stood outside an upmarket wine shop about forty meters from the bank. Across the street, the workmen he had seen earlier were digging a large hole in the road with their jackhammer. Temporary traffic lights had caused lines of vehicles to build up in both directions.

He swore under his breath. The situation was unlikely to change for some time. A backup plan was going to be required.

Henri glanced along the street to where he had left his van. It might need to come into play, he thought.

It momentarily crossed his mind that the workmen might not be genuine and rather had been planted to provide cover for the meeting by the Mossad. It wouldn't be the first time that kind of device had been deployed. But after studying the Swisscom van that stood next to the sidewalk and the demeanor of the workmen, who wore Swisscom jackets, he came to the conclusion they were almost certainly genuine.

There had been no sign yet of his four targets. His guess was that if they were coming by car, they would likely park in one of the spots near his van, which were all currently vacant apart from one. That would at least put them on the side of the street nearest his apartment. Even if they arrived by cab, they would have to disembark on that side of the street too.

So either way, he figured he would have a chance of hitting them with the Vintorez before they entered the bank —which was by far the best outcome.

Despite Hassan's somewhat nonchalant view about whether the kill should happen before the targets entered the bank or after, Henri knew he would be far more relaxed if he could do it before. Once his quarry was in the building, there was always the risk of them exiting by another door. If they did by chance happen to get the information they were seeking, there was also the possibility they could transmit that information elsewhere before he had chance to take them down.

And if that happened, he would get the blame, not Hassan.

His primary fallback plan if the sniper rifle proved unworkable involved explosives, although that would require the four targets to arrive in their own car.

Before heading back to the apartment, Henri decided to make a check for any countersurveillance operatives in the area around the bank. In his experience, the Mossad sometimes deployed them ahead of operations.

He pulled his backpack tight against his shoulder, tugged his cap down a little, and strolled westward along Dreikönigstrasse over the canal bridge, the harsh and almost constant pounding of the jackhammer ringing in his ears.

Henri forced himself to concentrate on the other people

in the street, looking for anything that seemed out of the ordinary or unexpected. There was a man standing next to the safety fence that ran over the bridge and lighting a cigarette, a young girl checking her phone screen. One of the workmen was adjusting the temporary traffic light set on the far side of the bridge. That all looked normal.

He walked past his own van and a station wagon in which a couple were kissing and reached the far side of the bridge where there was a small café with a few tables outside, opposite the bank. An old man was entering the café, and there was a man wearing a brown leather jacket, tinted glasses and a cloth cap sitting alone at one of the tables outside, reading a newspaper and smoking a cigarette. A half-drunk cup of coffee sat on the table next to him. The other four tables were empty. A waitress was cleaning one of them with a cloth.

Henri continued past the café for another fifty meters, then stopped and pretended to check his phone.

The only person causing him concern was the guy sitting at the café table, in a brown leather jacket. He looked innocent enough, apparently engrossed in his paper, and was probably local.

But why would he choose to sit outside to drink his coffee with the workmen causing such a deafening racket nearby? And he *was* right opposite the bank.

Henri mentally put the man down on his risk list. Then he went into a tobacconist, bought some cigarettes, and walked back to the apartment the way he had come.

The man at the café table didn't look up as he passed.

However, if he *was* countersurveillance, then it could cause a complication if Henri needed to switch to his backup plan and deploy explosives.

Henri wasn't sure whether he had a clear line of fire from the apartment to the café tables where the man was seated, if needed. But when he got back he would check.

CHAPTER TWENTY-TWO

Wednesday, April 20, 2016
  Zürich

It was going to be touch and go whether they made it to the bank on time, Jayne realized. A message had come from Rafael reporting a sudden buildup of traffic along Dreikönigstrasse in both directions due to some roadwork and advising the rest of the team to leave immediately.

Jayne, Zahavi, and Odeya therefore left the safe house one by one ten minutes earlier than planned and walked to the Peugeot, parked two streets away. They decided to use that vehicle rather than the BMW because it was more anonymous.

Despite the rush, and as was her usual practice on operations, Jayne insisted on carefully checking beneath the car and the wheel wells, using a small makeup mirror and the flashlight on her phone, for any sign of tracking devices or explosives before climbing in. She found nothing.

Odeya had volunteered to drive as it had been decided

that it would look heavy-handed if five of them walked in for the meeting with Zeller and Steiner, and they couldn't exclude Shapiro and Lindenstrauss. Rather, she would wait with Rafael outside the building while Jayne took the spare set of car keys in case they were needed.

Zahavi, wearing a suit, sat in the front passenger seat, and Jayne, wearing a raincoat over her business-style navy skirt and jacket, sat in the back behind Odeya, who was also smartly dressed in a dark raincoat and suit.

As a precaution, they all wore the same light disguises they had deployed earlier, consisting primarily of glasses, which in Jayne's case were black-rimmed with no prescription. They decided against using wigs on the basis that in a long meeting in close proximity to the bankers they might be detectable.

Now, a few minutes later, they could see why Rafael had sent the alert. They were stuck in a long line of traffic that was crawling along Dreikönigstrasse in the direction of the bank. Ahead of them were trucks, cabs, vans, and cars. Other drivers were becoming increasingly impatient, judging by the number of horns being sounded.

Jayne glanced at her watch. It was five minutes to four.

Zahavi's phone pinged as a message arrived. He checked the screen and turned around to face Jayne. "That's from Lindenstrauss. He and Shapiro are already at the bank," he said.

"I think we'd better walk from here," Jayne said. "It will be quicker than waiting for this traffic to clear. Odeya can park after we've gone in."

"Fine by me," Odeya said.

Zahavi's phone pinged again. "Rafael's confirming the backup team's car is ready to leave its parking spot when Odeya gets there."

"Okay, let's walk," Jayne said. She picked up her attaché

case, which contained copies of the documents she needed to put in front of Zeller and Steiner, opened the door, and climbed out.

Zahavi did likewise and they walked briskly along Dreikönigstrasse, leaving the black Peugeot behind them, sandwiched between a laundry van and a builder's truck.

Just as Jayne's watch ticked over to four o'clock, they reached the bank and entered the vestibule, inside which was an airlock security entrance with two sets of doors and an airport-style metal detector at the far side.

A guard supervised Jayne and Zahavi as they passed through the detector, then searched them thoroughly.

A receptionist asked them to sign a visitor's register and gave them ID badges in a plastic holder. She then handed them over to a thin, tight-lipped woman who introduced herself as Carl Steiner's executive assistant. She escorted them along a corridor with deep-pile maroon carpets to a meeting room with heavy double entrance doors that were standing open.

Outside the room, two large security men stood guard, while inside, Lindenstrauss and Shapiro were already sitting at a conference table.

After they entered the room, the assistant asked if they would like coffee and poured four cups from a cafetière when they all nodded.

"Mr. Steiner and Mr. Zeller will be with you soon," she said as she exited the room.

"Ready for this?" Lindenstrauss asked.

Jayne patted the attaché case. "We are."

She took out her phone, switched on the voice recorder, and placed it face down on the table.

Two minutes later, the door handle clicked and in walked two men whom Jayne recognized from their photographs.

* * *

Wednesday, April 20, 2016
    Zürich

Henri cursed under his breath, his focus laser-like through his telescopic sight but his view partly obscured.

Through gaps in the line of traffic he had spotted a man and a woman walk along the far sidewalk and enter the bank. Although not 100 percent sure, he thought the woman was either Robinson or Leibovitch.

Then, a few minutes later, a station wagon that was parked two places in front of his van slid out and drove off, and immediately a black Peugeot took its place, directly across the street from the bank. A woman was driving. She got out, and Henri got only a brief view of her face before she turned her head. Short dark hair, glasses, slim build, dark raincoat. That was one of the two, he thought, although he wasn't certain which. Neither of the women had worn glasses in the photographs he had been sent, so they were likely a basic disguise.

He assumed that the station wagon had been keeping the parking space free for the Peugeot.

The woman walked toward the café and disappeared from his line of vision behind the building. Nobody else got out of the car. Was there anyone else in there? He couldn't see through the tinted windows.

Worse still, a cloud bank had moved over Zürich from the east, and it was starting to rain, further hampering visibility.

He glanced again at the photographs of Robinson and Leibovitch that he had downloaded on his phone. They were both quite similar in appearance.

"Shit," he murmured, and breathed in sharply. It actually

didn't matter which woman it was: he couldn't take out just one of the four targets anyway. That would set every alarm bell ringing, and his operation would be finished with a twenty-five percent completion rate. That wouldn't go down well in Beirut.

He would have to wait until he had the opportunity to take out at least three of them. And that now seemed to mean waiting until they emerged from the bank.

The other thing Henri immediately realized was that if he had spotted only a man and a woman entering the bank and another woman in the car, that meant the second man was also outside. It had to be the man reading the newspaper outside the café. He checked the photographs of the two men. It was more than likely Rafael Levy, which meant David Zahavi was inside the bank.

Henri swung his sight toward the café again. The man's head was just visible. He was still sitting at his table and it was possible to hit him. But the same problem applied: taking out just one member of the quartet would cause a stampede and ruin his chances of eliminating the others. There was no sign of the female driver.

Henri tried to think through his options. He became certain that he was going to have to deploy his backup solution, the IEDs, to the Peugeot.

He didn't have much time, however. The bank meeting might not last long, and his targets could be out and gone in a flash.

Quickly he devised a plan, a tactic that he had used before.

He went to his suitcase, took out a white lank-haired wig, and pulled it on. Over that he put on his woolen hat and slipped on the tortoiseshell glasses he had used earlier. Next he put on a tatty old full-length raincoat with a voluminous bottom section that stretched to his feet, and unfolded a collapsible walking stick.

Then he hunched his shoulders, stooped a little, and examined himself in a mirror that hung in the hallway.

An old man looked back at him.

That would do.

Before leaving the apartment he carefully put three of the IEDs into the large pockets at the front of his raincoat and picked up four paperback books from a bookshelf in the living room.

CHAPTER TWENTY-THREE

Wednesday, April 20, 2016
    Zürich

"So, you're interested in our bank, I understand." Carl Steiner folded his arms and eyed first Jayne, then Zahavi, from beneath well-groomed eyebrows. His gray suit looked expensive, his white shirt collar was crisply starched, and his deep tan had been cultivated in a warmer location than Switzerland.

His business partner, Martin Zeller, who sat next to him, wore a black suit and a pale blue shirt with a patterned pink silk tie. They both appeared to be in prime physical condition, but there was no sign of the telltale bulge beneath the armpits that had been evident in the photographs.

"We have acquired a number of privately owned financial assets over the past few years," Jayne said. "That has gone well, and we are now looking to expand our portfolio."

Jayne and Zahavi had agreed to ease their way into the meeting by continuing the pretense of being buyers for a short period, the object being to soften up the two bankers before dropping the bombshell on them.

"I must emphasize that we are at a very early stage in our thinking about Switzerland," Jayne continued. "So this will be a preliminary discussion. We won't be able to give you a great deal of detail about our plans."

Steiner nodded. "I understand. We too are at an early stage in our thinking about a potential sale."

Zahavi leaned forward. "Our objective at the moment is to begin preparing a risk-and-reward document—we need to do the usual strengths, weaknesses, opportunities, and threats analysis."

"Of course." Steiner glanced at Zahavi, then Jayne, clearly wondering where this conversation was headed.

"And it is probably easier for us as outsiders to assess opportunities in the Swiss banking sector than it is to identify the threats," Jayne said. "As we all know, in our world, threats tend to be reputational as well as related to competition. Negative coverage in either the traditional media or on social media can be highly damaging. We stand or fall by public perception and confidence in how we operate, and we are keen to build a business that appears ethical."

There was a faint trace of a smile on Steiner's lips. "We all like to appear ethical."

"And that's the issue we face in compiling our assessment prior to any potential offer for your bank," Jayne said. "We have no visibility of what the risks and threats are that you face."

"We don't tend to shout them from the rooftops," Zeller said, his tone as dry as the mahogany tanned skin around his neck. "This is Switzerland. And we're bankers."

Jayne leaned back in her seat and glanced sideways at Zahavi.

"We're quite interested in having a general discussion

about your approach to clients from, shall we say, less salubrious quarters of the world," Jayne said.

"Such as?" Steiner said. His voice had now taken on a distinctly cynical tone, and he took a sip from his coffee cup.

"Such as Iran," Jayne said.

Steiner raised both eyebrows. "Surely you don't seriously expect me to discuss our clients in a preliminary meeting such as this? We don't know you and you haven't even tabled an offer or anything."

"I was hoping you might discuss them, actually," Jayne said. "For example, do you have any involvement with providing financial services, payments, debt funding, credit, and so on to Iran's nuclear weapons program?"

Steiner leaned forward and folded his arms on the table, eyeballing Jayne with an expression on his face that required little interpretation. His cheeks had gone a distinctly pink color beneath his tan, and his eyebrows were gathering like storm clouds.

"I'm not sure I'm understanding you," Zeller said. "Do you know anything at all about Swiss banking secrecy laws?"

Jayne simply nodded.

Zeller turned to Lindenstrauss and Shapiro. The two investment bankers had stayed silent so far and remained inscrutable.

"Have you explained to these people what the Federal Act on Banks and Savings Banks is?" Zeller demanded.

"We have, indeed," Lindenstrauss said, his voice smooth as silk. "They know."

Zeller turned back to Jayne. "So you are aware that we would be breaking the law if we discussed our clients and such matters with you? We could go to prison. The bank would be finished. What is your agenda here?"

Jayne was now starting to enjoy herself.

"Yes, I know. But we need to find a way to discuss it," she said.

She tapped her fingers on the table for emphasis as she continued. "Our information is that you are operating as bankers to the Iranian nuclear program and funding payments to a supply chain that is illegal in terms of international law. There is a nuclear agreement in place, signed in Vienna very recently, that forbids Iran from carrying out most activities relating to the development of nuclear weapons, and yet you are facilitating the delivery of a wide variety of equipment to enable that to happen. That is illegal under international law."

Now Steiner's face had gone a shade of crimson.

He lowered his voice a couple of tones. "I think it's time to end this meeting. I doubt we are going to progress any further with our discussions."

Steiner stared alternately at Zahavi and Jayne. "We know exactly who you are."

He turned to Shapiro and Lindenstrauss. "I will remember this—I am surprised to see you two assholes involved in this circus, facilitating a meeting with us for these charlatans. But it won't happen again because I'll make sure your careers in Zürich end right here."

Steiner gathered his papers together and stood.

"Not so quickly," Jayne said, as she opened her attaché case. "I'm glad you know who we are, and I'm also glad you take the 1934 Act so seriously. I have something you need to see. Could you just sit down again while I explain."

She removed a small sheaf of papers and photographs from her attaché case, together with a notebook and pen, and placed them on the table.

Steiner ignored the request and remained standing, his gaze now fixed on the papers in front of Jayne. "What the hell are these?"

She picked up one of the photographs and pushed it across the table to Steiner. "Do you both recall this meeting? April 10, 1996. Near Lake Geneva."

Zeller leaned across and they both stared at the photograph. It was the first of Jayne's pictures, showing two briefcases being handed to Carl Steiner and Martin Zeller by the CIA's chief of Paris station.

"Where did you get this from?" Steiner asked, his voice now rising.

Jayne ignored the question. "What does the name François Genoud mean to you?"

"I really don't know what you're talking about," Steiner said, his voice continuing to rise. "This picture shows nothing and our business here is finished. Get out."

Steiner walked briskly to the door, flung it open, and called out. "Gerhard, get these people out of the building, now. They might need persuading. So persuade them."

One of the men who had been standing outside the room came quickly in. "Yes, sir. I'll do that."

He pulled a handgun from beneath his jacket and pointed it first at Jayne, then at Zahavi. "You heard. Get up and walk ahead of me. Now."

Jayne had been expecting a confrontation but had not anticipated guns being drawn inside a private Swiss bank.

She instinctively raised her hands above her head, as did Zahavi, and they both stood slowly, as did Lindenstrauss and Shapiro.

"There's no need for this," Zahavi said. "We're not armed. You know that. We were searched on the way in. You're being far too heavy-handed. We're trying to have a sensible discussion."

"This is *not* a sensible discussion," Steiner snapped. "You're threatening us and trying to blackmail us. You got in here under false pretenses." He turned to the guard. "Get them out, immediately."

The guard raised the barrel of his gun further and used it to indicate that they must move toward the door. "Go," he said.

Jayne decided in that moment to play her ace.

It was now or never.

"Before we leave," she said, "I'm going to give you something else."

Ignoring the potential threat from the security guard and his handgun, she reached down and picked up another photograph from the sheaf of documents she had put on the table.

"There," she said, as she pushed it across to Steiner. "Also from Lake Geneva." This time the picture showed the two men and a partly open briefcase with wads of dollars visible.

"You'll see from these photos that you were handed a very large amount of money that day," Jayne said. "I think you were checking it when these were taken. So you should know exactly how much was involved. Could you confirm the amount for us, please?"

"This is an outrage," Zeller said, his voice now low, flat, and menacing. "Gerhard, get them out now."

"You can do that if you like," Jayne said quickly. "Or you can shoot us now. But either way, if you do, I promise you that these pictures will go directly to Reuters, the Associated Press, and Bloomberg, as well as to the key Swiss newspapers, your Swiss president, and all the other six members of the Federal Council."

The Federal Council was the Swiss executive office, with the president seen as first among equals on the council.

"What's more," Jayne said, "I will make sure this third document is also sent. The final proof."

She picked up another piece of paper and pushed it across the table. "It's the transcript of a telephone call between you,

Mr. Steiner, and the CIA's chief of station in Paris during which the terms of the deal and the sum of money were agreed between you."

"We also have a tape of that conversation," Jayne continued. "We'll send that to radio and television stations too."

In her peripheral vision she could see that the security guard's mouth had dropped open.

Steiner put his hands on his hips. "The CIA has done this. Is that who sent you?"

Again Jayne ignored the question. "Tell me about the forty million dollars," she said, pointing toward the photograph of the open briefcase. "Because I know that is what you were paid that day for disclosing information about one of your clients. And that disclosure, as you have so carefully pointed out, was illegal under the terms of the 1934 Act."

Neither Zeller nor Steiner spoke.

"So, tell me," Jayne continued eventually. "Shall we stay and talk or shall we go?"

* * *

Wednesday, April 20, 2016
    Zürich

Grasping his collapsible walking stick, Henri shuffled slightly unsteadily along the narrow alley, around the corner into Dreikönigstrasse, past the wine shop, and toward the bridge over the canal. He tugged his woolen hat down a little and adjusted the bundle of paperback books he was carrying under his arm.

By that time, the rain had become heavier and was splattering into puddles on the sidewalk and in the gutters on both sides of the street.

Henri glanced up from beneath eyebrows that were considerably darker than his white hair and noted that despite the rain and the noise, the man who had been sitting outside the café was still there.

He was definitely Mossad countersurveillance. No matter. He wouldn't see what was about to take place.

When Henri drew near to the parking spaces where his VW van and the Peugeot stood, he made his way to the edge of the sidewalk, stepped off, and shuffled along in the gap between the parked car in the first spot and the slow-moving traffic that was edging its way toward him along the street.

When he drew level with the Peugeot, he suddenly stumbled a little, and the four books he was carrying beneath his arm fell to the ground, straight into a puddle next to the wheel well on the front passenger side.

Henri swore loudly, reached down, and tried to gather the books back together. As he did so, he appeared to lose his balance a little, requiring him to reach out with surprising speed for an old man to grasp the car's wheel well to steady himself.

The sleight of hand that enabled him to tuck a small, black, magnetic box out of sight beneath the top of the wheel well as he regained his balance was a well-practiced skill. The box immediately stuck to the metal surface with a slight clunking sound.

Henri then bent down once more to pick up the books. This time, he put his hand underneath the body of the car to retrieve the last one. As he did so, there came another clunk as he placed a second magnetic box on the underside of the chassis.

He then tucked the wet books back under his arm and resumed his shuffle until he reached his van, two spaces farther along.

None of the people on the sidewalks—including the

Mossad man—would have realized what he had just done, of that Henri was certain. Their view was blocked on one side by his van, the parked Peugeot, and other vehicles, and on the other side by the line of trucks and cars that was filing slowly along the street.

The only risk was that a driver or passenger in one of vehicles saw what he did. But there had been no vehicles coming to a halt, no windows wound down or questioning shouts in his direction.

He was certain he had gotten away with it.

Henri reached his van, keeping a constant check for any sign that the man at the café was taking an interest in him. That wasn't the case, as far as he could see. He unlocked the driver's door, climbed in, started the engine, and steered out into the traffic. When he reached the next junction, he turned right and parked safely in an empty space on Kurt Guggenheim Strasse.

That would neatly avoid damage to his van when he triggered the IEDs on the Peugeot. It also gave him an excellent position from which to make a rapid getaway once the operation was completed.

CHAPTER TWENTY-FOUR

Wednesday, April 20, 2016
  Zürich

Jayne braced herself for whatever might happen next as Carl Steiner stood rooted to the spot for what seemed like an eternity. Out of the corner of her eye she could see that Zahavi was likewise preparing himself for a potential confrontation. His hands were still raised, but he was flexing his knees, ready to propel himself in any direction if necessary. Farther down the table, the two investment bankers, Lindenstrauss and Shapiro, stood looking stunned.

Steiner's fleshy fists hung by his sides, both of them tightly clenched as if he was about to begin throwing punches, which Jayne guessed he was probably very tempted to do.

Zeller, still seated, was leaning forward, his face rigid with tension and drained of color.

Despite the presence of the armed guard, and despite appearing to have had some warning of a visit, the two men had been unequivocally ambushed. Jayne knew that this was a moment in which their investigation stood at a crossroads.

She decided it was time to lower the temperature of the situation, if she could, and dropped her voice a couple of notches.

"Listen, all we need is some information," she said. "Then we can all move on. You can continue your banking operations in peace, find yourself a buyer, and we can proceed with our investigation. Nobody needs to know where our information came from. It is actually quite simple, so let's not unnecessarily complicate matters."

Steiner turned to the guard, Gerhard. "Wait outside. I will call you if we need any more assistance," he snapped.

"Of course, sir." The guard nodded deferentially, put his pistol back into his jacket pocket, and withdrew.

When he had closed the door, Zeller eyeballed Jayne. "No, it's not simple, as you put it." His voice was quivering slightly with rage, his face visibly boiling. "I don't know who you bastards really are, but you're trying to blackmail us. There are Swiss laws against that, and our justice minister might be very interested to hear about your tactics. He's a friend of mine. I could add that carrying out an exercise of this kind—spying on our soil, as you appear to be doing—is also illegal."

Jayne took immediate encouragement from Zeller's use of the word "might." She doubted he would go to the justice minister, although he was correct that their current operation *was* illegal on Swiss soil.

"We're not blackmailing. We're talking," Jayne said. "There are no laws against that." She glanced up at Steiner. "Now, I suggest we all sit down and discuss this, because the only Swiss law I'm interested in is the 1934 Banking Act."

To Jayne's surprise, Steiner lowered himself back into his chair and exhaled loudly.

Jayne, taking her cue from the Swiss, also sat, followed by

Zahavi, Lindenstrauss, and Shapiro.

"Shit," Steiner muttered beneath his breath. He turned to Zeller and raised an inquiring eyebrow.

Zeller, his face pale, looked at Jayne, then Zahavi. "You're obviously from one of the intelligence agencies, aren't you?"

"We're carrying out an investigation," Jayne said. "That's all I can tell you."

"You people need to let us discuss this in a structured fashion," Steiner said. "You can't expect us to decide on a course of action on the spot. This is complicated, and it may require a complicated solution."

"A well-structured and complicated solution. I should expect nothing less from a Swiss banker," Zahavi said, his tone as dry as a chalkboard. "However, I am afraid we can't do that. We need the information before we leave this building. Otherwise the emails will go to the organizations my colleague mentioned earlier. You need to think of the implications of that for your hopes of selling this bank."

Unless Jayne was mistaken, Steiner now had a hint of resignation creeping across his face.

"I had a feeling this would come back to bite us," Zeller said, tapping his fingers on the photograph of money changing hands that was lying on the table. "I just didn't expect it after so long."

Steiner folded his arms and eyeballed Jayne. "Just explain what you are seeking." His voice was stiff and strained.

Jayne leaned forward and placed her palms on the table. "It is quite simple. We understand from a reliable source that there are five, or perhaps six, core black market suppliers to Iran of equipment to help them build nuclear weapons. I am referring primarily to centrifuges and their components, perhaps aluminum rotors, bellows, vacuum pumps, through to piping and electronic equipment. Everything. I am sure you know better than I do what is involved—these are your customers. Many hundreds of millions of dollars are changing hands. We need to know who those suppliers are."

She leaned back and waited. Surely these men could see they had no choice.

Steiner clasped the edge of the conference table and looked down at the floor. "All right." He looked up at Zeller, and this time Jayne could see there was a clear expression of surrender on his face.

Zeller leaned back in his chair, his lips pressed tight. "I suspect you will know some of the names already," he said.

"Possibly," Jayne said. "But give them to me anyway."

Steiner exhaled heavily. "Have you heard of a Pakistani group, AQ Khan?"

"Abdul Qadeer Khan, yes," Jayne said. "The man who supplied the centrifuge designs and construction technology."

"That is the one."

Jayne picked up her pen and notepad and scribbled down the name, not that she needed to.

"And the others?" she asked.

"There are four German and Swiss companies," Steiner said. He gave the names, pausing after each one while Jayne clarified the exact spellings and locations as she took notes. All the company names had been on the list that Müller had given her in Gundremmingen a few days earlier.

"How do you pay these companies?"

Steiner gave her a look. "How do you think? They all have bank accounts in Switzerland. Not with us, though."

Of course.

"Now, we were told that there may be a sixth major supplier," Jayne said. "Not a company but a middleman, a fixer, who coordinates arrangements with other suppliers. Is that correct?"

Steiner glanced at Zeller, who frowned.

There was another prolonged silence. Jayne just waited.

"What have you been told about such a supplier?" Zeller asked eventually.

"Very little. All we were given is a code name, or maybe it was a nickname," Jayne said.

"Which is?"

"The Dark Shah."

Zeller's eyebrows rose. He placed his palms flat on the table and stared at Jayne. "You were given that name?" There was a distinct note of skepticism in his voice.

Jayne nodded.

Zeller slowly shook his head but said nothing.

"Well?" Jayne pushed. "You're obviously aware of him. So, tell me, who is it, this Dark Shah?"

Steiner grimaced heavily. "He has been a central figure in delivering Iran's objectives."

"What does he supply?"

"Most items, through his network."

"So what is his name and where is he from?"

This time Steiner shook his head and folded his arms across his chest.

"Come on," Jayne said.

Steiner tipped his head back and gazed at the ceiling before answering in a flat monotone. "He has an address in England, although he is not from there."

"In *England?*" Jayne struggled to keep the surprise out of her voice. "And the name?"

"The name is Kourosh Navai."

"How do you spell that?"

Steiner spelled it out as Jayne wrote it down.

"Is the Dark Shah your code name for this Kourosh Navai?" Jayne asked.

Steiner shook his head. "No. I believe it is a nickname. Someone told me of it."

"Who?"

"I do not think I should tell you that."

"Do you have the address?" Jayne asked. "Or any other contact information?"

Steiner sighed, reached into his pocket, and removed his phone. He tapped on the screen a few times, then looked up.

"It is in a town called Henley-on-Thames, not far from London. A big house next to the River Thames. He showed me a photograph of it years ago, when I was checking his credentials." He read out the street address.

Jayne wrote it down, feeling somewhat stunned to learn that he had apparently been using the UK as his base, right under the noses of the British intelligence and security organizations who presumably knew nothing about him. How had that happened?

"I know Henley-on-Thames," Jayne said. "Does this Kourosh Navai live there permanently?"

"I have no idea."

Jayne chewed her pen for a few seconds. "Just a few more questions. Do you know why he is nicknamed the Dark Shah?"

"I think it is because he originally came from Iran."

"How has he managed to carry out this function and yet keep his name off the international radar?"

"You are asking the wrong person," Steiner said. "We like to know a little about our business connections, but knowing too much can sometimes be dangerous."

That was true. But Jayne couldn't help glancing down at the photograph that was still lying on the table of Steiner and Zeller collecting their $40 million. It crossed her mind that knowing too much about the right person could also sometimes be very profitable. But she said nothing.

"How long have you been acting as financier for Iran's nuclear operation?" Jayne asked. "And how long has Kourosh Navai been involved?"

Steiner narrowed his eyes. "More than fifteen years."

Jayne paused, assessing what they had learned. They probably had enough information for now. Having corroborated the names of the German and Swiss companies on the list provided by Müller, pressure to have them appropriately dealt with could be brought by the Israeli government on the IAEA and on the German and Swiss authorities.

But she had a different feeling about this Dark Shah, Kourosh Navai, clearly a lone maverick.

Jayne looked at Steiner and Zeller. "Thank you for the information. We have all we need at this time." She glanced at Zahavi, who nodded his agreement.

"You've got all we will give you," Steiner said in a level tone. He was visibly regaining his composure now. "As it is, this is likely to cost us a large amount of money."

Jayne found it impossible to resist rolling her eyes. "If your past became public, you would lose far more because your bank would not be sellable," she said, a dismissive note in her voice.

She and Zahavi both stood, as did Lindenstrauss and Shapiro.

Zeller walked to the door, opened it, and instructed Gerhard and his colleague to escort the visitors out of the building.

"I don't think you need me to accompany you," he said in a curt tone.

"Don't worry. We didn't expect you to," Zahavi responded as they moved toward the door.

"And don't even think about warning off Mr. Navai or anyone else," Jayne said. "Otherwise our information will go directly to the news organizations and authorities I have mentioned."

Neither of the Swiss bankers responded as the four of them filed out of the room.

CHAPTER TWENTY-FIVE

Wednesday, April 20, 2016
   Zürich

Henri lay motionless on top of the dining room table, where he had been since returning from his mission in the rain.

His right eye remained glued to the telescopic sight of his VSS Vintorez, and his right index finger rested on the rifle's matte-black trigger guard. The skeleton wooden stock, with its rubber end cushion, was tucked firmly into his shoulder. The fire selector switch, just behind the trigger, was set to semiautomatic.

On the table, placed slightly to his right so he could reach it without moving, was a cell phone that he could use to activate the two IEDs he had planted on the Peugeot. The number had been keyed in—all he had to do was press the green call button. The IEDs wouldn't be his first choice because of the certainty of widespread damage to other people, buildings, and vehicles nearby, but if need be, he would do it.

Despite the rain and gloom outside, the image through the scope remained surprisingly bright and clear. It was a high-quality piece of equipment.

However, the problem he had identified earlier remained unchanged. The line of traffic along Dreikönigstrasse was constant and slow-moving due to the roadwork, making Henri's view of the bank's front door more often blocked than not.

Nevertheless, he continued to concentrate, glancing occasionally at the clock on the cell phone next to him.

His patience was rewarded when finally, through a gap between a BMW SUV and a white van, he spotted four people filing out of the bank's door at ten minutes to five.

Henri stiffened slightly. Was that them?

Yes, he was sure it was.

The first person out of the door was a woman with short black hair and glasses, wearing a dark raincoat. That was Robinson—he was certain this time. The glasses were definitely a prop. Behind her were three men in suits. All were walking briskly.

He moved the crosshairs in his scope a fraction, trying to get a bead on the woman and to work out which of the men was his other priority target, Zahavi. But two pedestrians carrying umbrellas walked across his line of sight, and the white van began to move at the same time.

The next glimpse he got of the group, a few seconds later, he saw there were now six of them. Sure enough, the man who had been sitting outside the café had joined them, confirming his theory. With them was the second black-haired woman—Leibovitch. They were all looking for an opportunity to cross the street.

But immediately, a truck drove across in front of the group and came to a halt, blocking his view again.

Henri let out a Lebanese curse.

A few seconds later, the group emerged at the rear of the truck. They were now moving quickly across the street toward the Peugeot.

He moved the scope fractionally to his left onto the first woman, Robinson, as she neared the rear of the vehicle. But as he did so, she appeared to drop something behind the car and bent over, now out of sight again. The second woman was fully obscured behind one of the men.

This wasn't going to plan.

Nevertheless, he knew he had to strike now or else he would be out of opportunities.

He moved the crosshairs fractionally right onto the man who was obscuring the second woman. His head and chest were visible.

That was Zahavi.

He aimed for the head and squeezed the trigger gently.

But his round went right by the tiniest of fractions and zinged into the side of the truck that had blocked his line of sight earlier and was still stationary behind the group.

Zahavi appeared to jump slightly. Had he sensed the round as it passed him?

Concentrate.

Through his scope, he saw one of the two women in dark raincoats appear on the far side of the Peugeot, next to the driver's door.

It was Robinson.

She held up her key fob, clicked it to unlock the doors, and reached out for the door handle.

Henri got his crosshairs centered on her head, which was visible above the roof, and again pulled the trigger.

Thwack.

Robinson's head jerked back, and a plume of red was momentarily visible behind her. Her arms splayed out as her body fell backward into the street and she vanished from sight.

One.

Henri, very aware he now had only a second or two at best to finish the job, moved his scope to the other woman, who had reappeared.

But just as his scope reached her, she and the four men all suddenly broke into a sprint along Dreikönigstrasse in the direction of the café.

There was only one option.

Henri reacted instantaneously.

He grabbed the phone next to him and pressed the green button.

A second later, there were two massive explosions as the IEDs went off.

The Peugeot vanished in a gray-and-black blast cloud of debris, smoke, and flame. Through the scope, Henri could see pieces of car body and fragments of broken glass hurtling in all directions. Some of them splashed into the canal below, others collided with vehicles and pedestrians.

The Peugeot had been turned into a tangled mess of steel.

From his vantage point, Henri heard a series of piercing screams.

Then came another deafening bang, which Henri assumed had to be the Peugeot's fuel tank exploding.

Through the melee, the smoke, and the chaos, it was impossible to tell whether the blast had taken out his other three targets, but there was a good chance.

Henri jumped off the table and began dismantling his rifle.

He had to get out before the entire area was turned into a police stop-and-search zone and his van was seized.

CHAPTER TWENTY-SIX

Wednesday, April 20, 2016
    Tehran

It was deep into the evening in Tehran, and the mellow tones of a distant saxophone drifted through the half-open window of Nasser Khan's home office at the rear of his house. It was accompanied by the fragrant scent of *ghormeh sabzi*, Persian stew, that was being carried by the night air from one of the neighboring homes.

The dish, one of Khan's favorites, always reminded him of his youth and the sight of his mother serving up the tender meat and kidney beans accompanied by herb- and lemon-flavored gravy. His mouth began to water a little, despite having only finished his own dinner less than an hour earlier.

Khan finished reading the report in his hand and was about to place it back in his briefcase and join his wife in their living room when his phone rang. He glanced at the screen. It was Talal Hassan, leader of Unit 910.

Five minutes later, Khan stood at his window, staring out

into the darkness. The sax was still playing and the smell of the *ghormeh sabzi* was even stronger.

But Khan's mind was elsewhere.

The call had not brought good news.

Hassan had reported a failure. The operation run by JAFFA in Zürich to eliminate the Mossad and CIA team had not gone well.

The intention had been to assassinate the entire team on their way into the Zeller and Steiner building before they had a chance to speak to the financiers.

That had not proved possible, and then an attempt to kill them on the way out had also proved difficult.

JAFFA had killed the British woman, Robinson, with a sniper rifle, he reported, but the fate of the others was unclear. He had activated two IEDs that, according to news reports, had killed a number of people, but it was not yet known whether his targets were among them.

The situation had been further confused by the presence of two other men in the group, possibly bankers.

JAFFA's use of explosives to try and deliver his objective had been uncharacteristic. Normally he was precise and accurate with his rifle.

If innocent bystanders had been killed in the blast and buildings damaged, that would inevitably raise the profile of the entire operation and generate furious media speculation.

JAFFA had managed to flee Zürich without being caught and was now on his way back to Paris.

Khan shook his head. This was not good.

Moreover, he knew that Abbas Taeb had also made little progress in meeting the Supreme Leader's instruction to find out who had attacked the Israeli gas platform and why. Normally with such incidents, there was no shortage of leads to follow up and sources with information. But with this, Taeb had told him, it had been like whistling in the winds that blew off the Persian Gulf and across the arid plains of western Iran.

Well, Taeb and his team would now have to urgently try and speak with the bankers and determine what, if any, information had been divulged. That would not be easy. The Swiss financiers were notoriously elusive and determined to keep communications to an absolute minimum for reasons that Khan could fully understand.

Khan and Taeb were due at the Office of the Supreme Leader on Azarbayejan Street at nine o'clock the following morning to give a progress briefing.

Now he was facing a sleepless night.

The Supreme Leader had given him one last chance to eliminate the Israelis and British. That hadn't happened.

The consequences of reporting failure to the Supreme Leader were unpredictable, as Khan knew only too well from having closely observed the fate of several of his colleagues.

They could range from a verbal humiliation to instant execution, depending on his mood. One thing was certain: there would be no forgiveness.

* * *

Wednesday, April 20, 2016
Kaiserstuhl, Swiss-German border

It wasn't until the silver BMW passed over the low concrete road bridge that spanned the River Rhine at Kaiserstuhl, half an hour north of Zürich, and they were safely into Germany that Jayne and her companions felt able to stop and let out the emotion they had been feeling.

Rafael, at the wheel, pulled onto the side of the road just beyond the soaring ancient stonework of Rotwasserstelz

Castle, which stood guard over the bridge like some kind of medieval sentry.

As soon as he stopped, he put his head in his hands, closed his eyes, and remained silent for several minutes, his shoulders trembling.

Jayne, next to Rafael in the front passenger seat, placed a hand on his shoulder and turned to Zahavi, in the rear, whose face remained ashen.

For the second time in eight days, they had driven out of a major European city at speed after an operation that had gone unexpectedly wrong.

But this time, the impact was exponentially more devastating than it had been in Vienna.

They had lost one of their own, Odeya Leibovitch, who had been gunned down by a sniper outside the bank as she unlocked their car.

The rest of them had only just escaped the force of two bombs planted on their Peugeot that had exploded simultaneously and violently only a few seconds after they had begun to run for cover.

The left knee of Zahavi's trousers had a large rip where he had been sent sprawling by the force of the blasts behind them. Beneath the rip, Jayne could see congealed blood from a gash in his skin.

Jayne had also been sent flying and had bloody grazes on her palms and knees where she had instinctively thrust out her hands to avoid planting her face into the pavement.

One of the Swiss bankers, Shapiro, had come off worst. He had a badly broken collarbone, had ripped a large chunk of skin from his knee, which was pouring blood, and also appeared to have fractured an elbow.

In the confusion following the explosion, they had bundled him and Lindenstrauss, who was in shock, into a cab and sent them to the nearest hospital. They then fled back to the safe house, where they had packed their belongings and headed off in the BMW.

Jayne knew she had been fortunate to escape alive and relatively unscathed. Her guess was that quite apart from Odeya, other innocent bystanders who had taken the full force of the blast would not be so lucky.

Their survival was entirely due to her habit of checking beneath the car's wheel wells and chassis before getting into a car during such operations. Without that, none of them would have survived. She had seen the black box attached to the top of the wheel well and had realized immediately what it was.

"Another bloody leak," Jayne said.

Zahavi nodded. "How else?"

"It could have been all of us."

There was silence in the car for several moments as the reality sank in.

"I can't believe Odeya's gone," Rafael said eventually, a distant note in his voice. "Two decades we worked together. I feel we should have stayed after she got hit, but—"

"I know what you mean, but we couldn't," Jayne said, her voice faltering a little. "We would have been stuck there for weeks."

She felt awful as she said it and turned back to Zahavi for reassurance.

He nodded. "I agree, sad as it is to say. We will have to let Tel Aviv deal with the Swiss authorities over this—that's their job, not ours. We have other priorities now. Let's do this for Odeya."

They all left unspoken the task that now faced the Mossad's administrative department to resolve matters. Inevitably, the task would be pushed over to Israel's embassy in Bern, the Swiss capital.

Jayne knew that, as was usual in such cases, Odeya would

be portrayed by the embassy as some kind of low-grade government employee who had been caught up in an event that had absolutely nothing to do with her. They would do all they could to conceal her involvement with the Mossad. The Swiss were particularly opposed to foreign intelligence services operating on their soil.

Hopefully Shapiro and Lindenstrauss would remain silent. Jayne expected that the two men, well practiced as they were in discretion and subterfuge through their work, would do so.

Rafael reached over, took a bar of chocolate from the glove box, removed the wrapper, and shared it between the three of them. Jayne, who had been overtaken by a feeling of exhaustion, felt grateful for the intake of sugar.

"So what now?" Rafael said as he bit into his share of the chocolate. "Do we head to the UK? Do we go back to Tel Aviv, brief Avi on what's happened here, and regroup?"

"I think we go to London," Zahavi said. "We can't waste time. I'll speak to Avi, but I'm certain he'll agree with me. My gut tells me that this Kourosh Navai is more likely than the other suppliers to be responsible for the gas platform and some of the shit that's been going on. You saw how the bankers reacted to his name. For all we know, he might have arranged that little reception we just had in Zürich."

"More likely our Iranian friends," Rafael said. "They must know after Vienna that we're chasing the nuclear trail. But Navai is the best lead we have, so I agree we should head there. We can get Tel Aviv to chase up the other companies."

Jayne nodded her agreement. That felt logical.

"The reaction from Zeller and Steiner told us all we need to know," Jayne said. "They were far more reluctant to talk about Navai than the others. If he's the point man for other suppliers to Iran, then he's likely the source of the bulk of their profits from Iran."

Jayne realized she needed to brief Vic.

"You'll have to excuse me," she said. "I'm going to call Langley. They might have a file on Navai. Between them and your office, they must be able to turn up something."

Zahavi nodded. "I'll call Avi and do likewise."

They both climbed out of the car and walked farther up the street, where they found separate benches near the castle where they could sit and make the calls well away from any passersby.

Jayne dialed Vic's secure number. He listened in silence as she described what had happened in Zürich, then cleared his throat. "I'm sorry to hear about their girl Odeya, but you've been in this type of situation before. I know I have."

"Unfortunately, yes." It was true—Jayne had suffered similar losses on previous operations, most recently when a female CIA operative conducting countersurveillance was killed in Moscow after being hit by a security services pursuit car.

"You've got to use this in a positive way," Vic said. "There's nothing you can do, so take energy from it. Let it be a spur to you to finish the operation. You go to the UK, and I'll begin the checks on Navai, although it's not a name that rings any bells."

It was good advice from Vic. Jayne nodded, suddenly finding herself welling up after previously being too full of adrenaline and fury in the aftermath of the bomb blast and the escape from Zürich to feel much emotion.

"We'll do that, Vic, thanks," she said, glancing sideways at Zahavi, who was sitting a few meters away, deeply engrossed in his own phone conversation. "I'm sure Odeya would want us to finish the job."

Jayne was trying to hold it in but failed. "I'm sorry Vic, I need to go," she said as she ended the call. "I'll be in touch."

She sat there, fighting back the tears, until Zahavi had finished his call.

He turned and looked at her. "Are you okay?"

"Not really."

Zahavi got up from his bench, walked to Jayne, and placed a hand on her shoulder. "Me neither. It doesn't get any easier, does it."

She shook her head. It certainly didn't.

"What did Avi say?" she asked.

"He was shocked, but he's going to deal with what happened. He wants us to get moving and check out that address in the UK."

"Right." Jayne sat motionless.

Zahavi paused for a moment. "Come on. Let's carry on working. I've found over the years I forget quicker that way."

PART THREE

PART THREE

CHAPTER TWENTY-SEVEN

Thursday, April 21, 2016
  Henley-on-Thames, UK

The reflection of the early evening sunshine danced across the rippling expanse of the River Thames like an array of flickering Christmas tree lights. Two slimline, double-scull rowing boats knifed their way through the waters heading downstream, and a dog on the towpath barked incessantly.

Jayne paused and watched the rowers out on the river, which she estimated was at least seventy yards wide at this point.

She had found her thoughts drifting back to Odeya, replaying in slow motion a kind of internal movie of her last fatal seconds.

The oarsmen diverted her attention momentarily, and she then focused once more on the white painted house on the other side of a tall hedge that separated it from the towpath.

Carl Steiner had been correct when he said that Kourosh Navai's house was right next to the Thames. Indeed, it had a large brass nameplate on the gate that read Waterside House, and it stood no more than forty yards away from the river up a slight slope.

The two-story property was located on Mill Lane, on the south side of the town of Henley-on-Thames. The house was larger than Jayne had expected and comprised a central section with wings on either side. It was clearly owned by someone with significant wealth, given the stratospheric value of properties along this section of the river.

Jayne yawned. It had been a tiring thirteen-hour drive from southern Germany, which included passing through the Channel Tunnel between France and England.

The three of them had alternated at the wheel of the BMW, which they swapped for a rented Nissan Qashqai in Folkestone after arriving on British soil. Swiss license plates would have been far too distinctive in the UK. They had stopped only for a few hours at a French travelers' hotel for some essential sleep.

But despite sharing the driving burden, the fallout from the incident in Zürich had taken a toll on all of them.

Now, however, Jayne knew they needed to put that aside and concentrate on the next steps.

An hour or so of online research on her laptop earlier that afternoon had told her that Waterside House was not owned by Kourosh Navai but rather by Darius and Freema Navai. Presumably they were Kourosh's parents.

Interesting, she thought. Navai was a distinctly Persian name, as were Freema, Darius, and Kourosh.

A call to one of her old contacts, Alice Hocking, at the UK's Government Communication Headquarters—GCHQ —in Cheltenham yielded some basic information, including dates of birth for the Navais. Darius was aged eighty-two, his wife eighty-one. However, Alice, who was very busy assisting with an operation in Russia, could find nothing on Kourosh.

When Jayne was at the Secret Intelligence Service, she had worked with Alice on many occasions. She counted her as an old friend who, within reason, could still be relied upon to help out unofficially with requests for information, even though Jayne was no longer an SIS employee. GCHQ provided so-called signals intelligence to the UK, including monitoring internet, telephone, and email traffic for MI6 and performing other functions as required.

A check of the local voting roll showed that there was no indication that Kourosh Navai had ever registered to vote in national or local elections from Waterside House, or indeed from any other address, as far as Jayne could see.

That was consistent with findings at Langley, which had also drawn a blank on Navai. There was no file on him, and nothing had come up in the traces Vic's team had run. Perhaps he had changed his name.

Zahavi tasked the research team in Tel Aviv and also Unit 8200 with trying to find out what they could about the Navais. Meanwhile, he, Jayne, and Rafael carried out some surveillance of the property and its surrounds.

That proved reasonably straightforward, as the front and side of the house were partly visible from the lane that ran past it and also from the towpath that ran alongside the river. There were a number of hikers and tourists in the vicinity, and the three of them mingled with other visitors out for an evening stroll.

There were no signs of life at the house. Although a pair of white iron gates at the end of a gravel driveway stood open, there were no cars parked outside, all the windows were closed, and there were no humans or dogs in evidence.

Having gotten this far, Jayne was not alone in feeling doubly anxious about the possibility of discovery. If Hezbollah or another interested party had tracked them to Zürich, then it was quite possible they would turn up here.

All three of them took extensive measures to maintain strict security now, including the use of light disguise and surveillance detection measures. She again used her plain black-rimmed glasses and added a blue cap.

Upon arrival in Folkestone, before renting the Nissan, they had all separately bought British pay-as-you-go burner phones in an attempt to make their communications as difficult to trace as possible.

After a second reconnaissance stroll along the towpath and down the lane, the three of them headed to a bench near the river and waited for the light to fade. As dusk descended, there were still no lights showing at any of the windows.

Jayne glanced over her shoulder at the house, about three hundred meters away. "You know what I'm thinking?"

Zahavi grunted. "I can guess."

"We're not likely to get another chance very soon," Jayne said.

"So you're just going to break in?"

"I'm not planning to break anything," Jayne said. "I'd just take a look, see what I can find."

"Such as?" Zahavi asked. He turned to her, eyebrows raised.

Jayne shrugged. "I don't know. But there's surely going to be something in the house that tells us who he is, where he might be, and maybe what he's doing."

There was silence for several seconds.

"She's right," Rafael said eventually. "I say we take a look while we have the chance. Do you want me to go in there with you?"

Jayne nodded. "David can do surveillance outside."

"When?" Zahavi asked.

"We come back after midnight. If the place is still deserted, we go in."

"Right. How are you going to get in?" Zahavi asked.

Jayne patted her jacket pocket. "Pick the rear door lock."

She had many years earlier been taught by the techs at MI6 how to pick most types of common door locks using a small tension wrench and a set of pick rakes. They had given her a set that came in a cloth case and was smaller and slimmer than a wallet. She always carried it with her on operations, and it had often been useful.

"I learned that too," Zahavi said, with a thin smile. His phone beeped and he pulled it out of his pocket and studied the incoming message.

"It's the research team," Zahavi said. "The Navais are English. They were born here, but of Iranian descent. They were English-language teachers in Iran for more than a decade, based in Tehran. They returned here after the 1979 revolution."

"Understandable," Jayne said.

"Indeed. They have no biological children of their own, but they adopted while in Iran. And our so-called Dark Shah, Kourosh, is their adopted son."

Jayne sat up straight and looked at Zahavi. That *was* interesting. "In that case, even more reason to go into the house. They might have documentation for him or something. We'll find something, for sure. Let's go check into a hotel and grab something to eat and then return later."

＊ ＊ ＊

Thursday, April 21, 2016
Jerusalem

SOHRAB walked onto the balcony of his rented house, overlooking a green valley on the fringes of northeast Jerusalem, and tapped his private key into his phone. He then downloaded the secure briefing that was waiting on the server.

Headed "Top Secret," it contained a very brief update on the ongoing operation to locate the perpetrators of the drone attack on the offshore gas platform and elicit details of Iran's project to continue developing a nuclear warhead, despite the recent much-hailed international deal that specified they would not do so.

SOHRAB had watched the progress of the investigation with more than the usual interest. The consequences, if it succeeded, would be dire and extremely costly.

However, he doubted that would happen.

It seemed like a somewhat odd mixture of individuals who were heading the operation on the ground, consisting of three people from the Mossad—one of them very senior—and a woman who had a long track record at MI6 but was now working as a contractor for the CIA.

They had surprised him by extracting anything of value from the Swiss bankers, which was referenced in the briefing.

Useful leads have been obtained from bankers in Zürich, including UK address for Navai. These being pursued today in UK by the team. An internal investigation into the exact circumstances that led to the deeply regretful death of Odeya Leibovitch yesterday is already underway and further details will be circulated as soon as this is progressed.

Short and to the point.

However, SOHRAB's expectation was that ultimately, the investigation would founder when their leads ran out, as they would eventually. If they weren't eliminated before then, of course. In truth, he felt they had been lucky to get out of Zürich with just one casualty.

SOHRAB slid his phone back into his pocket, placed both hands on the railing that bordered his balcony, and gazed out across the stretch of land that was already beginning to look a little dry and brown. The scent of pine trees hung heavy in the air, and a cloud of dust swirled up from the street in a gust of wind.

The house was at the end of a residential cul-de-sac named Derech HaAlon, and SOHRAB had rented it partly because it was private and partly because it offered easy accessibility to both Jerusalem and the main highway to Tel Aviv, Highway 1. He liked to sit on the balcony and gaze out across the valley—the view always gave him a perspective that was often lost when he was sitting at his office desk under pressure.

The briefing he had received was enough to enable him to send a short update to his colleague ROSTAM.

His job was to send on anything that might be of help to either ROSTAM or to the Iranians. It was up to ROSTAM to decide whether to use it for his own purposes or send it on to Tehran. In some cases he did both.

SOHRAB would carry out that task in about ten minutes, after cycling to his usual spot next to Highway 1 that ran between Jerusalem and Tel Aviv and was little more than a kilometer away. There was so much cell phone traffic in that area that the use of a new burner phone was highly unlikely to be detected.

There was no doubt that Tehran would be concerned that the team of Mossad and British operatives who had visited the bankers in Zürich was now heading to the UK. They had obviously extracted a lead, including an address, although SOHRAB did not expect them to find the person they were looking for.

SOHRAB assumed that the Iranians would realize who that target was and would activate one of their agents in the UK or Europe, probably from Hezbollah, to nullify the threat accordingly. He guessed it would be the same agent who had narrowly failed to eliminate the chasing pack in Zürich.

It was like watching an intricate three-way game of chess going on. One move, or false move, by the Iranians, the Israelis, or the Americans, and the balance of the entire match could swing in a different direction.

And SOHRAB was in an almost unique position to influence the course of the game. He found it gave him quite a power rush, quite apart from the opportunity to fill his numbered bank account.

CHAPTER TWENTY-EIGHT

Friday, April 22, 2016
  Henley-on-Thames, UK

To Jayne's relief, there was only a thin sliver of a moon when they returned to Mill Lane. The darkness would definitely help for what they were about to undertake.

Zahavi parked the Nissan several hundred meters away from the Navais' house behind some trees in a deserted parking lot next to the Henley Town Football Club's ground. They then walked cautiously along the darkened lane, which was wide enough for only one car and was lined on both sides by tall fences and trees.

Finally they reached the house, which was partially illuminated by a streetlight at the end of the lane, near the river. It was approaching one o'clock in the morning.

A pair of redbrick gateposts marked the end of the gravel driveway that led to the property, but the white iron gates attached to them remained open, and there was still no car parked outside and no lights showing.

The owners clearly had no concerns about intruders. None of the neighboring properties appeared to have sophisticated security measures in place either. Perhaps crime wasn't a serious problem in this particular corner of southern England. Indeed, the manager at their hotel in the center of Henley, the Hotel du Vin, had said as much when they were chatting earlier in the evening.

Zahavi took up a position beneath some trees next to a wooden footbridge at the end of the lane, near the river, while Jayne and Rafael pulled on black woolen hats to match their dark clothing.

Rafael looked at her. "Let's get this done for Odeya."

She was trying to focus on the task at hand, but like Rafael, she continued to find herself unable to escape the image in her mind of the Mossad operative being gunned down in Zürich.

Jayne nodded. "For Odeya."

They all knew they should really have informed Britain's security services, MI6 and MI5, the minute they touched British soil. It was a normal courtesy between intelligence services to do so, and she had thought about it over the preceding few hours. But doing that would inevitably cause red tape, requests for information, briefings, and other delays and would also likely render impossible the illegal entry into the Navais' house that they were about to undertake. In the end, Jayne had taken the soft option and simply done nothing. She just hoped it didn't come back to bite her.

They walked carefully through the gate, stepping on the grass at the side of the driveway to avoid making a noise on the gravel. The area immediately around the house was paved with sandstone slabs, which made it far easier to walk around silently.

There was no sign of any burglar alarm system on the

front of the property. But that didn't necessarily mean the place wasn't alarmed.

There was a detached brick garage to the left of the house. Jayne decided to check it to make sure there was no car hidden away inside. But a quick glance through a side window told her it was empty.

Jayne and Rafael made their way to the rear of the property, where they found a wooden door into a single-story extension that jutted out at right angles to the main house.

The sandstone slabs extended from the rear of the house toward a lawn, forming a patio on which stood a wooden outdoor dining table and chairs. Beyond the lawn was a small copse of trees and bushes.

The door was old-fashioned, as, to Jayne's relief, was the lock, which was of the pin tumbler variety and appeared well worn.

There they stood still for a moment. Entering someone's property illegally was always something that gave Jayne pause. The thought of someone else entering her own home in similar fashion was not a pleasant one. But sometimes there were no alternatives.

There was almost complete silence around them, with only the occasional hoot of an owl from the nearby trees to break it.

Jayne pulled a pair of thin rubber gloves from her pocket and put them on, as did Rafael. Then she removed her set of rakes and tension wrench from her pocket and got to work.

It would have speeded things up if she had felt confident enough to ask Rafael to use his phone light to illuminate the lock, but she felt it was best not to. Instead she worked mainly by feel.

First, using her left hand, Jayne inserted the L-shaped tension wrench into the bottom of the keyhole and began applying a little pressure in a clockwise direction. Then she removed her favorite three-pin Bogota rake and used her right hand to slide it into the top of the hole, right to the back.

Suddenly, from behind them, came the sharp snap of a twig from the bushes, followed by a rustling of leaves.

What the hell?

Jayne spun around, as did Rafael, and she stood still, trying to focus on the trees through the darkness.

She could see nothing, but after a few seconds there came a further rustling of leaves.

A moment later, a small pair of reflective eyes emerged from beneath the bushes. It was a cat.

Jayne exhaled sharply and turned back to the lock.

She had to start the process all over again. After reapplying slight clockwise pressure with the wrench, she began to work the rake in and out of the lock, making sure to push it upward a little to prevent the lock pins from dropping.

It always surprised Jayne that people assumed a lock on a door was going to stop a burglar. But then, most people didn't know just how easy it was to pick a lock. Even the more sophisticated locks could be opened; it just took a little longer. Usually with those locks, the pins, generally five or six, required picking one at a time instead of by using the quicker back-and-forth motion of a rake to manipulate them.

Rafael watched in some fascination as she worked and let out a slight sigh when she got the tension wrench to turn fully and the door clicked open about thirty seconds later.

"Better job than I would do," he said.

Jayne looked up at him and gave a thin smile.

But that was just the start. Now they were faced with a search for a potential needle in a haystack. The house was large and old, and it was impossible to know where to look first for something that would help them. In Jayne's mind, that "something" was most likely to be documents.

"How about we look for a study first?" Rafael suggested.

Jayne nodded. "Then the main bedroom."

Once they were inside, Jayne covered her phone's flashlight with her thumb and turned it on. The faint glow that emanated was just enough to give them a sense of the property they had entered.

They were in a terracotta-tiled hallway that was being used as a depository for coats, shoes, boots, and other outdoor equipment. There were doors off it that led to a utility room, a toilet, and the kitchen, which was where they headed.

The kitchen smelled and looked old-fashioned, even in the extremely limited glow of the phone light. There was the distinct whiff in the air of vegetables that were well past their use-by date and food that had gone bad. Jayne could just about make out a huge square table that served as the centerpiece of the room and an ancient cast-iron oven.

They moved into a long, broad hallway with checkered tile flooring and a staircase to their left. Farther along the hallway, ahead of them, were several closed doors on the right and left.

"The study is likely one of these," Rafael murmured.

Jayne agreed. A glow from the streetlight, shining through a half-circle window above the front door, cast some illumination down the hallway. Jayne's eyes were also becoming more accustomed to the gloom, so she shut off her phone's flashlight.

They tried the doors in turn. The first opened to a living room with a large flat-screen television on the wall, the second a dining room, the third a library with bookshelves that ran from the floor to the ceiling.

It was the fourth room, at the front of the house, that turned out to be the study. The streetlight from outside again offered a little help here.

The study was dominated by a heavy wooden desk. On it was a large, old-fashioned desktop computer and a rectangular writing pad. It was completely clear of papers.

Jayne began going through the drawers beneath the desk, but there was little there either apart from boxes of staples, a reel of sticky tape, pens, and a few unused notebooks.

A filing cabinet that stood against the wall also drew a blank. Jayne briefly flicked her flashlight back on to take a look, but the cabinet held only household bills and bank statements.

Jayne stood up straight. This was not a well-used study.

She eyed the computer for a moment but decided it could wait. She could always try and hack into it if they drew a blank upstairs.

"Let's try the bedrooms," she murmured.

Rafael nodded and led the way across the hallway and up the stairs.

When they reached the U-shaped upper landing, Jayne had a quick look around. There were six bedrooms, two bathrooms, and a couple of large storage closets. Most of the doors were open.

Rafael agreed with her suggestion to separate to speed up the process. She would search the three bedrooms on the west side of the house, while Rafael tackled the other three on the east side.

Jayne began with a bedroom at the rear of the house, which turned out to be a guest room. It was tidy, with a king-size double bed and an en suite shower room, but there was nothing of interest.

The second one she tried was a smaller guest room, this time with just a single bed and no en suite. Obviously the Navais liked to have visitors.

The door to the third room was shut, and as soon as Jayne opened it, she noticed a faintly musty smell. This room faced the front of the house, giving her the benefit of a glow from the streetlight.

At first glance, the room appeared to be in use. A desk beneath the window had a few books scattered on it, together with a writing pad, some pens, a folded newspaper, a cordless phone, and a radio. There were a few posters on the walls, and a guitar stood in a corner. The bed was neatly made, and a jacket hung on the back of the chair behind the desk.

Jayne walked to the desk, turned her phone flashlight back on, and examined the writing pad.

There were a few scribbled notes on the pad in ragged handwriting that appeared to refer to air fares between London and Tehran. Then she noticed a date scribbled in the margin: 20 June 1994.

The radio, an old Roberts model that included a short-wave band, appeared to be from the same era, and when she examined the posters on the walls, she realized they were of pop stars from the 1980s and 1990s: Lionel Richie, Michael Jackson, Mariah Carey, and Whitney Houston.

A hi-fi system, with twin cassette decks and topped by a turntable but no CD player, stood on a low table in one corner, and there was a rack with several vinyl records in it.

Jayne checked the newspaper. Well, that was a little more recent—a copy of *The Guardian* from the previous year, but it appeared to be the only reasonably current item in the room.

She stood up straight. This room was like a museum, dating back at least two decades. But why had it been left like this?

Then she realized it. This must have been Kourosh Navai's childhood bedroom left intact. The room seemed quite tidy, with no signs of excessive dust, and appeared to have been cleaned. Perhaps he still used it occasionally, but not often, it appeared. She guessed it had to be her best chance of finding something useful.

She walked to a chest of four drawers that stood next to the hi-fi system and opened the top one. Inside were a few old sweaters and folded T-shirts. The other drawers also contained only items of clothing.

Next, she moved to a bedside table that contained three smaller drawers.

The top one contained two old dark blue British passports, each with a corner of their covers cut off where they had been cancelled following expiration in 1983 and 1993. Both were in the name of Kourosh Navai and carried photographs of a young, thin-faced man with a bony, slightly hooked nose and black, neatly cropped straight hair.

This was more like it.

Jayne had a moment of doubt about taking the expired passports but decided that given the room was unused, it was unlikely they would be missed anytime soon. They might have useful fingerprints too, she figured.

She slipped both into her pocket, then went through the other drawers. In one, there was a small clear plastic bag that contained half of a broken heart-shaped silver wrist locket. The chain was still intact, but Jayne could see where the hinge on the locket attached to the chain had been snapped. The half locket, which was badly scratched, had a small photograph inserted of Kourosh with a pretty young brunette, who looked as though she might well be Iranian. It was a close-up of their faces, both pressed together, looking forward toward the camera and smiling confidently. This was presumably his girlfriend. Jayne wondered whether they were still together.

She again hesitated, undecided whether to take the locket. However, it was a potentially highly valuable piece of evidence, particularly the photograph, and she couldn't resist. She stuffed it into her jacket pocket and turned her attention back to the drawer.

In there was also a birthday card, showing a picture of the Eiffel Tower in Paris. Jayne opened it. There was a date, December 28, 1993, and a message. It read, "To Kourosh, love of my life, Happy Birthday! Always with you. Yours forever, Zahra XXX."

Beneath the card was also another small framed photograph of the same girl seen in the locket, who was presumably Zahra, and an unframed photo of a man who, to Jayne's slight surprise, she recognized as the former shah of Iran, Mohammad Reza Pahlavi, who was overthrown in the Iranian revolution of February 1979 after nearly thirty-eight years in power. There was also a well-thumbed paperback biography of the shah there.

Obviously Kourosh Navai had a strong interest in his Iranian roots.

Jayne put the birthday card and the framed photo of the girl into her jacket pocket but left the picture of the shah and the book.

In the drawer below there was a collection of yellowing birthday cards, all of them handwritten and addressed to Kourosh. They all bore the same signature: "From your loving mother and father."

There was nothing much else of note in the bedside table, and she closed the drawers.

She had just stood and was about to leave the room when she heard a creaking floorboard out in the hallway.

Jayne stopped dead. For a couple of seconds, her stomach flipped over inside her, but then Rafael stuck his head around the door.

"I've been through the other rooms," he murmured. "Not much of interest apart from this." He held up a sheet of paper. "Looks like some kind of adoption document. I found it in a briefcase underneath the bed in the main bedroom. Written in Persian. Dated 1969."

"Great, but I'm not sure it's a good idea to take that. It's the sort of thing they might notice. Can you photograph it?"

"I already have."

"Okay, good. Best put it back. Then we can go," Jayne said.

"Yes, you're probably right. I'll do that." Rafael turned and headed back toward the main bedroom.

As Jayne walked back to the top of the stairs, her phone vibrated in her pocket.

She read the message, which was from Zahavi, sent to both her and Rafael.

Man approaching house. Black clothes.

Jayne knew immediately this was potential trouble.

She moved to the landing window that looked out over the front of the property just as another message arrived.

Now walking up drive. Get out.

A few seconds later she spotted a dark shadow cross the driveway and pause beneath a tree at the side of the gravel drive.

Jayne strode toward the main bedroom. Rafael was on all fours reaching beneath the bed.

"Quick, we need—"

"I've seen the messages," Rafael said. "Give me two seconds."

CHAPTER TWENTY-NINE

Friday, April 22, 2016
   Henley-on-Thames, UK

Jayne and Rafael reached the bottom of the staircase and without speaking moved swiftly through the kitchen to the rear door of the house.

The lock clicked shut behind them as they exited, and they stopped momentarily outside.

Jayne pointed toward the bushes at the far side of the lawn where they had earlier seen the cat. She knew it would be foolish to attempt to go around the front of the house.

Rafael nodded, and they both ran across the grass to the bushes and pushed through a gap in the foliage.

There they crouched. Jayne was confident they were hidden from view, given the darkness and their black clothing, but her biggest concern was stepping on a twig and causing the same kind of snapping and rustling sounds that the cat had done earlier. She therefore remained absolutely still and knew that Rafael would do likewise.

No more than ten seconds later, a tall, dark figure, a shadow in the gloom, emerged from the left side of the house. Jayne could tell from the body movement that it was a man. She caught a slight glint from his head and a smooth outline against a window that told her he was bald.

The man was walking swiftly and stopped at every ground-floor window before moving on. When he reached the rear door he tried the handle.

He then took something from his pocket and bent down, and a faint, repetitive metallic sound was just about audible on the night air.

Less than half a minute later the man opened the door and disappeared inside, closing it behind him.

Jayne swore to herself and heard a faint grunt from Rafael. The guy had picked the lock a lot faster than she had.

Neither of them moved.

Within a couple of minutes, the man reemerged from the door and closed it behind him.

As he did so, another loud, distinctive owl call sounded from behind Jayne. It was one of those calls that sounded almost as if it had been made by humans signaling to each other, and it carried clearly on the night air.

The man whirled around and stared in their direction. He put his hands on his hips and stood there for several seconds.

Jayne felt herself tensing up. Surely he wasn't going to come and take a look?

But to her relief, the man turned again, walked briskly along the rear of the house, and disappeared out of sight around the right side.

This could not be a coincidence, she felt. The man had to be linked to the Iranians, and Jayne assumed he was under instructions to ensure that she, Zahavi, and Rafael made no further progress with their investigation, or any others.

Just as well the old couple wasn't at home.

There must have been yet another leak.

This was becoming a joke, except it wasn't, because it was costing lives. What the hell was counterintelligence at Glilot Interchange and Langley doing?

The mental video of Odeya's body being thrown back into the street by the force of the sniper's round played itself yet again in her mind.

They squatted there for what seemed an eternity although it was no more than ten minutes. By that time, Jayne's thigh and bum muscles were burning and her knees were groaning.

Then finally, her phone vibrated in her pocket. She took it out, taking care to shield the screen, despite it being on its dimmest setting.

It was a message from Zahavi.

He's gone.

A little later, as they drove back the short distance to the hotel, Jayne, sitting in the front passenger seat next to Zahavi, described to the others what she had found in the bedroom.

"Interesting," Zahavi said. "The room sounds like some kind of shrine to the guy. It's the kind of thing you'd do if your child had died or something."

She realized he was spot on. It was true, it was like a shrine.

"What do you think we should do next, then?" Zahavi asked.

"This might sound counterintuitive given we've just broken into the house," Jayne said, "but I think we should go and visit the old couple. I just have a feeling they might talk if there's been some kind of estrangement. The room was untouched, and there were old birthday cards in a drawer. I don't think they've seen him for a long time."

Zahavi slowly nodded his head. "We'll give it a try. I'm just worried that the Iranians will be thinking the same thing, though."

Sensibly, and despite the late hour, Zahavi had taken a circuitous route around the town center just to make certain they had no coverage before proceeding to the hotel.

Jayne turned around to Rafael. "What was on the adoption document you found?"

Rafael tapped a couple of times on his phone and passed it to Jayne. "Take a look. That's the document. A little odd."

She looked at the photograph Rafael had taken. Her Persian was just about good enough to read it.

It actually wasn't an official government adoption paper. Rather, it was on headed notepaper from the Tehran School of Social Work and was in the form of a memo from the director, Dr. Mahdi Gharavi, dated July 9, 1969, and addressed to "whomever it may concern."

This is to certify that Kourosh Navai was deposited at the Women's Hospital, Pich-e Shemiran, Tehran, soon after birth, believed to be December 28, 1968, according to a paper left with him. Officials from the Tehran School of Social Work conducted an extensive search for the baby's true parents, but this failed to produce a result. The boy remained at the hospital unclaimed for six months. After that time, the baby boy was officially declared an orphan and was given up for adoption. After lengthy discussions with Darius and Freema Navai, British citizens but of Iranian families, it was agreed that they should adopt Kourosh.

The document was signed in ink by Gharavi and both of the Navais.

"As an adoption document, it seems just about as informal as you could get," Jayne said. "I wonder if there's a story there."

Zahavi, finally confident they had no tail, pulled into the Hotel du Vin's small underground parking lot, out of sight from the street. "We'll need to talk to the old couple before we can move any further forward, I feel," he said.

She paused, an image of the bald man picking the back door lock of the house on Mill Lane in her mind. "But I don't want to put them in danger too—I don't want them to end up like Odeya. They'd be sitting ducks."

"So what then?"

"I'm going to make use of my MI6 contacts."

* * *

Friday, April 22, 2016
    Henley-on-Thames, UK

Henri swore quietly to himself as he climbed from the cab into the rear compartment of his Volkswagen van, which he had parked at a deserted picnic spot outside Windsor.

It should have been the easiest of jobs. They would have been helpless.

But if the old couple he had been sent to deal with were not at home asleep, where were they?

That was something for Hassan and his team at Unit 910 to work out.

Henri felt exhausted after the long drive from Paris, no sleep, and now yet another failure to report.

He had been informed the previous evening that the woman he had shot dead in Zürich was not the primary target, Robinson, but the Israeli Leibovitch.

So another complication here was not what he had been hoping for.

It wasn't his fault, he knew, but he was a man who always struggled to come to terms with plans not working out. And his suspicion was that Talal Hassan's patience, never a plentiful commodity, would now have run out.

If there was another opportunity, Henri would be expected to make sure he delivered.

Maybe he was getting too old for this game. Perhaps it was time to retire and stick to his business.

Twenty years ago, he would have been energized by the challenge.

But now?

He decided he would sleep in the back of the van for a few hours and then reassess things in the morning.

CHAPTER THIRTY

Friday, April 22, 2016
London

After what happened at the Navais house, Jayne decided to finally involve Britain's security services in their operation rather than try to work behind their backs.

In the absence of Mark Nicklin-Donovan, still in the hospital in Tel Aviv, she had earlier that day gone directly to the office of C, the overall boss of Britain's Secret Intelligence Service, Richard Durman. She knew Durman reasonably well, having worked with him on a number of operations during her long career at the SIS. But because he was busy preparing for a meeting with his boss, the British foreign secretary, Tim Pontefract, he delegated responsibility for Jayne to his number three, a fearsomely bright woman whom Jayne also knew, Stella Hambledon.

Jayne had been bracing herself for being told off for not notifying her old service of her operational plans in the UK earlier and had mentally prepared a list of excuses, mostly involving the incapacity of Nicklin-Donovan, invariably her first port of call.

During her initial call with Hambledon, there was a silence that Jayne could have cut with a knife when she described the lead she had and what she was seeking. Of course, she neatly omitted to add that she had already been inside the Navais' property in Henley.

"So good of you to tell us at such an early stage," Hambledon said. "You don't change, Jayne, do you? Team-work's not your thing."

She's probably not wrong.

Jayne decided to sidestep the barb. "Well, given that my former boss and your current one is in an Israeli hospital bed and lucky to still be alive, there's a certain urgency. Teamwork isn't top of my list of priorities. I might be a little late with the request, and I apologize for that, but I really could do with your help."

Thankfully, Hambledon quickly cooled down, and also being close to Nicklin-Donovan, she too wanted to get to the bottom of who was behind the Samar attack.

Hambledon had immediately called her best contact at Britain's domestic Security Service, commonly known as MI5. Harry Buck had been deputy director general for the past couple of years and was seen as a likely candidate for the top job in time.

As a result, Jayne, Zahavi, and Rafael were now, a few hours later, sitting on a sofa in the living room of an MI5 safe house in Hounslow, a short distance from Heathrow Airport.

Opposite them in two armchairs were the elderly couple, Darius and Freema Navai, who peered at her through similar pairs of brown plastic glasses. They were sipping cups of tea, and even after a lengthy period of being put at their ease, they were understandably still looking shocked.

Not long ago, they had been whisked in the back of an

anonymous MI5 car from Freema's sister's house in Oxford, where they had been staying for a few days, to the quiet detached house on the western fringe of London.

The living room was formed of one long open space that stretched from the front of the house to the back, with folding doors in the center that were open but could be closed to make two separate rooms.

The sofa and chairs where Jayne, Zahavi, Rafael, and the Navais were sitting were at the rear end of the room. At the other end, sitting at a dining table near the front window, were Hambledon and Buck.

In the narrow hallway outside the room were two armed MI5 officers, a woman with blonde hair and a man with a silver crewcut. They both had walkie-talkies strapped to their belts, which occasionally emitted quiet but annoying squelch breaks and crackles of static.

Jayne had to admit, there was no way she and the Israelis would have been able to locate, persuade, and transport the Navais in such a short amount of time.

But finding and transporting them to a safe location was one thing. Getting them to talk about Kourosh was proving quite another.

They seemed reluctant to speak about him, despite being told that they had been brought to the safe house because it was suspected that he was involved in activities related to Iran's nuclear program that might pose a global security threat.

Darius, a bony-faced man with leathery skin, had a habit of fiddling with his glasses and glancing suspiciously through a pair of black eyes at his interrogators every time a question was asked. He then spoke hesitantly, continually looking at his wife for reassurance. It took more than three quarters of an hour, more tea, and a plate of cookies before he began to loosen up a little.

"We haven't had much contact with Kourosh for years, apart from an occasional brief phone call," Darius said eventually. He closed his eyes momentarily. "So it's difficult to answer your questions about what he's doing now."

Jayne's hunch about the estrangement had proved correct. The pain was written over Darius's face. "Why do you have little contact?" she asked.

Darius shrugged. "After he left university he began to mix with people who we thought influenced him in a negative way."

His wife nodded in agreement. "He was involved in groups and activities we didn't really like," Freema said. "Then he went to work in the US. So we drifted apart."

Jayne leaned forward. "What groups and activities?"

Darius ran a hand through his full head of short white hair. "Oh, he decided he was going to be a patriotic Iranian, loyal to Islamic Shia theology and loyal to Ayatollah Khomeini. So the usual people."

"You mean activist groups?" Rafael asked.

It crossed Jayne's mind that loyalty to Khomeini didn't correlate to the photograph in Kourosh's bedside drawer of the man Khomeini had ousted as the Iranian leader, the shah of Iran, Mohammad Reza Pahlavi.

There was a slow nod from Darius. "Yes, you could say that."

"Or do you mean more than just activists?" Rafael persisted.

Now Jayne was getting a feeling that finally, Darius was inching his way toward disclosing something meaningful.

His wife interrupted. "He started working for Hezbollah," she said, unexpectedly candidly. "We love Iran, and we supported the shah until he was kicked out, despite all his many faults. But we didn't agree at all with what Kourosh was doing. We don't like the current Iranian regime or Hezbollah with their violent agenda."

This major disclosure surprised Jayne.

"What was he doing for Hezbollah?" asked Buck, who had sat in silence until then.

Freema shook her head. "I think there were a lot of bad things going on."

"In the UK?" Buck asked.

"He wouldn't talk about it. I only know of it because I overhead a conversation he had with his girlfriend. That was when relations with him started to worsen. I questioned him, and he thought we were spying on him."

"That was Zahra, right?" Jayne asked.

Freema looked up sharply at Jayne. "Yes. How did you know that? Zahra Moin was his girlfriend in the nineties."

"But they split up?" Jayne asked.

"When Kourosh went to the States, yes," Freema said. Her face was almost as thin and angular as her husband's.

"Why did he go?" Jayne asked.

"He'd studied nuclear physics at Manchester University, then he worked in research and completed a PhD at the same university, and then he got a job at one of the nuclear power plants in the US, Three Mile Island. He worked there for a few years, then moved on."

"Where to?"

"No idea, but I think somewhere else in the States."

Jayne made the connection to the late deputy director of the Atomic Energy Organization of Iran, Jafar Farsad, dead after falling from his Vienna hotel balcony, who had also studied nuclear physics at Manchester at around the same time. Had the two known each other? It had to be a possibility.

She knew of Three Mile Island, near Harrisburg in Pennsylvania, not least because of the accident there in 1979 involving a partial meltdown and radiation leak from one of its two reactors. She would get Vic to check employment records at the plant.

She also made a mental note of Zahra's surname. It would be possible to run a trace on the name and photograph. If there was nothing on Kourosh, maybe there was something on his former girlfriend.

It was that last thought that prompted Jayne's next question.

"Do you know if Kourosh ever used a different name to his own? For example, did he change it when he moved to the US?"

There was a pause, and Freema opened her mouth as if she was about to say something, but her husband jumped in first.

"I did overhear part of a phone conversation once," Darius said. "He introduced himself as . . . well, he used another version of his name."

"Which is?"

"Koresh. I don't know why he was doing that. I didn't speak to him about it. Maybe I should have."

"Did he adopt any other last name?" Jayne asked. "Is there another version of Navai?"

Darius shook his head. "I never heard him use anything other than Navai."

"And how did he qualify to move to the United States?" Jayne asked.

"The job he was offered. The nuclear power company arranged it and sponsored him. I think he obtained a specialty occupation visa. Then he got his green card."

It was a well-trodden path, so it sounded perfectly normal to Jayne. She hesitated, deciding what to focus on next. Her mind went back to the somewhat strange adoption document that Rafael had photographed, but obviously she couldn't mention that directly. Instead, she settled for a more general line of questioning.

"All right," Jayne said. "Tell me how you came to adopt this boy. Was he an orphan?"

Again the old couple looked at each other, but neither said anything.

"I mean, I know this is difficult, but were you not able to have children?" Jayne asked as gently as she could. It felt like a deeply intrusive question, but she knew she had to get to the details of the adoption somehow. It was possible that Kourosh had ongoing contact with people in Iran.

Freema averted her eyes from Jayne and slowly shook her head. "No, I was not able to. And there are a lot of orphans in Tehran. We saw it, working there as English teachers."

"Was he one of them?"

"Actually, he wasn't an orphan. But his family didn't want him, so it was the same."

"You knew his family?" This sounded intriguing.

"We didn't know them but we knew of them."

"How was that?"

Freema shook her head slowly and looked at her husband.

"We've not talked about this to people before," Darius said. He shifted in his chair. "It is quite private."

"I can understand that, but we need to trace him given the potential threat that we believe he poses, so we need to know his background, particularly relating to Iran. It may yield important clues. Did you adopt him through an agency, through social workers, through a hospital?" Jayne felt she had come as close as she could to using the information in the adoption document without giving her hand away.

Darius pressed his lips together. "We taught English to a physician, a gynecologist who ran the Women's Hospital in Tehran, as well as to his family. He looked after us. This man was also the gynecologist to a number of well-known families in Tehran. The father of one of those families had a baby he could not keep."

"A father couldn't keep his baby?" Jayne asked. "Was the baby, was Kourosh, illegitimate? From a mistress or something?"

Darius nodded slowly. "That was exactly the situation."

"You say well-known families. How well known was this one?"

This time Darius didn't speak. Instead, he raised his right hand as far as he could, stretching upward.

Jayne's mind was now whirring. "Government?"

"The top."

Realization dawned on Jayne.

"Not the shah?"

Darius remained impassive, but his wife nodded, wiping her face with her sleeve.

Surely not. If true, that explained the photo and the biography in the drawer.

For once, Jayne was rendered momentarily speechless, and her astonishment must have been written across her face, because Freema continued with an explanation.

"Mohammed Reza, the shah, did not behave like a king. He was a playboy. He treated his wife, Fawzia, appallingly and was constantly unfaithful to her for much of his long reign," Freema said, distaste written all over her face. "They only had one official child, a girl, and he had girlfriends everywhere. I am sure he had unwanted children everywhere too. Kourosh was just one of them, and we managed to rescue him."

In many ways, what Freema was saying had plausibility. Jayne had read about the shah's notorious infidelity. The couple's body language, combined with the document in their house, indicated to her that they were telling the truth. And yet it still seemed odd, even a little fantastical.

If true, though, the story might also account for his nickname: the Dark Shah.

"How did the adoption affect Kourosh?" Jayne asked instead. "Did he know who his true father was?"

"We told him, eventually," Darius said. "He had a lot of anger toward his true father because of that and read everything he could find about him. I believe that was why he became so supportive of Ayatollah Khomeini."

"You think that is what drove him to sign up for Hezbollah and to get involved with the Iranian nuclear program?"

"I believe it was partly that."

"What else, then?" Jayne asked.

Darius gave a short, sarcastic laugh. "Money. That is the driving force he has. He realized that if he had remained in the Iranian royal family, as the shah's son, he would have been wealthy beyond his dreams. And so he wanted to achieve that wealth by other means instead."

Jayne caught Zahavi's eye. Her mind went straight back to Müller's advice.

Follow the money.

If Kourosh Navai was now orchestrating the supply of black market nuclear equipment to Iran, he was likely making a massive amount of money, which was doubtless being funneled into a numbered bank account somewhere.

Jayne turned back to the Navais. "So do you have any idea at all where Kourosh might be now? In the US?"

Darius shrugged.

"He could be anywhere," Freema said. "He's got his own plane, I believe."

"His own *plane*?" Zahavi asked. He was stroking his chin with his thumb and forefinger.

Freema nodded. "The last time I spoke to him, about four years ago, he said he might come to visit us again. I asked if he had bought a ticket, and he said he didn't need to buy tickets anymore as he had a plane and had a pilot's license too."

Jayne caught another glance from Zahavi, who had an inscrutable expression on his face.

She sat up straight. The meeting with the Navais had yielded more information than she had anticipated. Much of that was due to the obviously strained relationship they had with their adopted son.

"Thank you," Jayne said. "I think we will let you have some rest now, unless anyone else has questions." She glanced around at the others in the room.

Buck leaned forward. "Unfortunately, we have reasons to believe that you both might be in some considerable danger," he said to the Navais. "The Iranian nuclear supply business is a big money maker for some, and there are people who would like to stop you speaking to us. Our advice is that you should stay in this house until that situation is resolved. The facilities here are basic, and I know it's not home, but it is safer. Do you agree with that?"

The Navais looked at each other again. To Jayne's relief, Darius nodded slowly. "If you advise that, we will accept it."

On the wall behind Darius was a large digital clock that showed the time and the date: April 22. Jayne needed no reminding that it meant she had only six days left to find his adopted son before President Ferguson touched down in Tel Aviv for the funeral of Moshe Cohen and talks with the Israeli prime minister, Yitzhak Katz.

Time was running out.

CHAPTER THIRTY-ONE

Friday, April 22, 2016
   London

The secure video conference briefings for Avi Shiloah, who had now decided to get directly involved, his team in Tel Aviv, and Vic and his colleagues at Langley, went on late into the evening.

Jayne felt exhausted, but they needed to move quickly to follow up on all the leads that had emerged from the visit to the Navais' house and the interviews with them.

She was encouraged by the cooperation between the two intelligence services, who had agreed on joint briefings given the urgency and the commonality of interest. That hadn't always been the case in the past, and in her view they were both missing a trick by maintaining rivalries that seemed more grounded in embedded culture than in any true justification.

One thing that made her uncomfortable, however, was the location for the briefings. She had to accompany Zahavi and Rafael to the Mossad offices on the top floor of the elegant redbrick three-story Israeli embassy building at number two, Palace Green, off Kensington Palace Gardens.

The sight of the property, originally occupied in the 1860s by author William Thackeray, always caused strong emotions in Jayne, given the fate of her father outside that very same building nearly twenty-two years earlier. She had been there a few times over the years, and it was always the same. She found herself choking up a little as she entered.

The thought of him being injured so badly that he passed away two months later after multiple operations left her reliving once again the endless hospital visits and the pain of watching him suffer.

"Are you all right, Jayne?" Rafael asked. He had clearly noticed she was distracted.

"Just a few bad memories," she said. She told Rafael and Zahavi how she was feeling and described how she had watched helplessly as her father's Catholic priest friend Michael Gray, now a cardinal at the Vatican, had given him the last rites at his hospital bed.

They were sympathetic, but nevertheless, Jayne initially found it difficult to concentrate on the conference call. The Tel Aviv end of the call was conducted from a secure sound-proof communications room deep in the basement of the Mossad building at Glilot Interchange. The comms room, together with an adjacent larger operations room, had been set up on Avi Shiloah's instructions. They were to be used as the hub for all activities connected to the gas platform attack and the related investigations that were ongoing.

Despite the fact it was past midnight in Tel Aviv, Shiloah himself was now sitting in the comms room, staring at them via a video camera. He was accompanied by Mossad's assistant head of operations, Zahavi's deputy, Jacob Shaked,

known to everyone as Jake, and Mossad's director of counterintelligence, Martin Mavashev.

At Langley, Vic was accompanied by the CIA's head of
counterintelligence, Ricardo Miller, a notoriously dour character who had always taken a dim view of Jayne's involvement
with the Agency as a contractor on security grounds, no
matter how good the end results were.

Jayne was pleased on the one hand that both agencies
were involving their heads of counterintelligence and were
taking seriously the threat posed by the ongoing leaks, given
the mounting death toll.

On the other hand, the sight of Miller's scowling counte-
nance never failed to dampen her spirits. She suspected he
was some kind of closet misogynist.

Zahavi led the briefings in London, with Jayne and Rafael
contributing at frequent intervals.

After the interview with the Navais, Jayne had rapidly
prepared her list of items that needed to be tackled, in order
of priority. She now ran through them.

There was the need to determine Kourosh Navai's current
identity and whether he was using the name Koresh, as his
adoptive father had suggested. Jayne also outlined what
Freema Navai had said about Kourosh owning a plane and
requested that checks be made on that.

"We'll get on this," Vic said, as he scribbled notes. As
soon as Jayne mentioned the plane and the pilot's license, he
frowned and went into a short rant about how easy it was for
"terrorists, drug dealers, and arms traders" to register and
operate aircraft in the US, often under false identities, and
the failings of the Federal Aviation Administration to tighten
up its systems. "We'll do what we can," Vic said. "But the
FAA is useless."

Jayne also showed the broken wrist locket, the birthday

card with the picture of the Eiffel Tower, and the photograph of Kourosh's former girlfriend Zahra Moin. She had removed the smaller photograph from the locket and had found Zahra's name scribbled on the back. She had then carefully scanned the photos and taken close-up photographs of the locket from all angles, then sent the images securely to Langley and Tel Aviv.

"Avi and Vic, can you both run facial-recognition searches on these photographs and see if there are files on Zahra," Jayne asked. "She may well have connections to Hezbollah too and could still be active."

Both men nodded their agreement and Shaked also added his confirmation. "I'll take care of that," he said. "We'll run it all through our databases."

Jayne also asked for the Navais' story about the adoption to be checked out thoroughly, although it sounded credible.

"So what's the latest on tracing our mole?" Jayne asked. "Any progress?"

She intended it more as a rhetorical question designed to emphasize the need for urgency, with no real expectation of an answer. Counterintelligence chiefs by nature were suspicious, obsessive people who tended to operate by the rules of the night, in her experience. They worked underground and struck after they found evidence. It would be naive to expect them to talk about it before they had run down their spies and moles.

There was silence from all on the call for several seconds. It was broken only by Ricardo Miller. "As you can imagine, there are a few potential avenues we are exploring in multiple countries."

Mavashev was similarly reluctant to go into detail. "We are all over this issue, believe me," he said.

Shiloah had a somewhat haunted look about him, with bags visible beneath his eyes, and his voice was a little croaky and strained, although Jayne guessed that may have been partly due to the volume of Camels he was undoubtedly smoking.

With only limited progress so far, and the pressures of unexpectedly being handed the top job thrown in, was the stress beginning to tell on Shiloah? It was difficult to say.

"Where are the Navais now?" Miller asked. "I'm concerned about their security, given the leaks."

Jayne was about to answer, then hesitated. There had been too many leaks.

"They're staying with some friends in London," she said. It seemed prudent to keep it vague on such a call involving people from multiple services.

"I hope they're in good hands," Miller said. "How many security people on-site?"

That had crossed Jayne's mind too. She wondered if MI5 was planning to draft in more than just the two officers who had been at the property. It was a difficult balance, though, because the more there were, the more likely they were to attract attention.

Again she kept her answer vague. "Not sure. MI5 is handling that."

"Avi, go and get some sleep," Zahavi advised his longtime colleague and friend as they completed the call. "You've got an intelligence agency to run now. Stand back a little and let Jake take care of the ops side at that end."

"Old habits and all that," Shiloah growled. "It's like trying to give up smoking." He tapped his pack of Camels, which was lying open on the desk in front of him.

By the time they terminated the connection, it was quarter to midnight in London.

Jayne decided it was too late to drive all the way back to the hotel in Henley. Rather, the idea of sleeping in her own bed in her own apartment in Whitechapel, just a few miles away near Tower Bridge, was proving irresistible. She had kept the apartment despite her relocation to Portland, and given her frequent trips back to London, it had been very useful. She found herself wishing that Joe were with her to share the bed—and perhaps make his own contribution to their investigation, which currently seemed long on leads but short on actual progress.

Instead, she offered her spare bedroom and her sofa bed to Zahavi and Rafael. They too were visibly exhausted and gratefully accepted the invitation.

CHAPTER THIRTY-TWO

Friday, April 22, 2016
  Langley

After the video call with Jayne and the Mossad teams had finished, Vic turned off the monitor, leaned back in his chair, and glanced at Ricardo Miller, who was sitting a few feet away, his expression grim.

"So, Ricardo?" Vic asked. "Where are you laying your chips? Is this traitor in our service or in theirs?"

There had already been a number of conversations about the likely identity of the mole over the previous two weeks, ever since it had become clear that classified information was leaking. But Vic had growing doubts that Miller had made any progress with his inquiries.

The counterintelligence chief always hid behind a veil of confidentiality, but Vic usually got a sense of whether his investigations were bearing fruit or not.

Miller pushed his thick black-rimmed glasses up his nose

and ran a hand through his receding curly ginger hair, which gave him the air of an eccentric academic.

"Money may be the motivation here," Miller said. "But I've found it's never a good idea to make assumptions. If it's not money, then I struggle to see why anyone on our side might be doing this. On the other hand, there are plenty of hawkish Israelis who might be quite happy to push their country toward an assault on their biggest enemy."

Vic stood and raised himself to his full six feet. "True, but let's be honest. How many moles have you found who dealt in politics?" he asked. "They don't bank votes, they bank money. Isn't this more likely to revolve around dollars?"

He picked up his papers and made for the door. As he reached for the handle, he turned and eyeballed Miller. "The retired nuclear inspector who Jayne went to see in Germany gave her some good advice. Follow the money. I suggest you do the same."

Miller shrugged. "Maybe that's good advice, Vic. But there is, of course, one person involved on our side who seems to have a foot in all camps and is therefore well placed to know exactly what's going on across Langley, the Mossad, and MI6 as well. Someone who's in all the camps but not accountable to any of them."

Vic stared at Miller, who raised both hands in mock surrender.

"I'm not making accusations, Vic," Miller said. "I'm just highlighting an elephant in the room. Someone needs to mention it. I'm aware Jayne is someone you've known for decades, and you'll doubtless defend her to the hilt, but in this game you can't rule anything out."

Vic shook his head, his face reddening a little. "You're barking up the wrong tree, buddy. Jayne's a hundred percent committed to her work. I know she's not staff here and she's a Brit, but that makes no difference. I use her because she delivers great results for us, and I can use her in ways that would be difficult for a staff member. That's the whole point. She goes the extra mile and puts herself through all kinds of crap without any kind of corporate safety net if the shit hits the fan."

With that, Vic walked out of the room and headed for the elevator en route back to his seventh-floor office.

He felt suddenly angry. In some ways, he knew Miller was only doing his job by questioning the position of everyone involved in the operation, but he'd gone too far. Vic felt it personally, and he knew Jayne would be mortified if she ever heard about it.

He had no doubt that Miller's team was putting Jayne under the microscope behind the scenes. They were likely checking her phone records, emails, maybe even her bank accounts.

As the elevator car made its way upward, Vic calmed down—he would be stunned if Miller found anything from his inquiries in Jayne's quarter.

But if Miller was going to waste valuable time that way, Vic resolved to find a way to try and flush out the mole himself. Until then, he would cut back on the briefings he had been carrying out with other people involved in the Iran nuclear operation, even at the risk of provoking furious back-lash from those left out of the loop.

The elevator arrived at the seventh floor and the doors opened. He walked to his office, sat at his new oak desk, and picked up the Starbucks latte that his secretary, Helen, had left for him. It was only lukewarm but was nonetheless welcome.

Vic knew that Helen would have departed for home twenty minutes earlier but had still made the effort to pop down to the Starbucks café on the ground floor, grab the coffee, and bring it all the way back to his office before putting on her coat and heading to her car. It was not some-thing to take for granted, he reminded himself.

He wasn't even sure that his wife, Eleanor, would have done that for him.

The desk was a replacement for an old glass and chrome model behind which he had never felt comfortable. There was something reassuring about solid, high-quality wood that relaxed him and took him back to his younger days when he had fewer responsibilities. Modern furniture simply made him feel more corporate and more pressured—the last thing he needed.

On the opposite wall, above a couch, was a row of red-and-green digital clocks that covered five key time zones. He had thought about having them replaced with proper analog clocks with hands but had done nothing about it so far. In his current location, Washington, DC, it was now seven in the evening. In London it was midnight. In Tel Aviv it was two in the morning.

He shook his head and pushed his new rimless glasses up his nose.

What the hell was Avi Shiloah doing working at this time of night? Vic was the first to admit that he had found it hard to delegate as he climbed the career ladder, but Avi was clearly finding it even more of a struggle.

Vic took a sip of the latte and picked up his phone. His first call was going to be to the FBI's director, Robert Bonfield, who he knew would still be in his office at the J. Edgar Hoover Building nine miles away in downtown DC. He wanted the feds to find out what alias, if any, Kourosh Navai had been using in the US while working for the Three Mile Island nuclear plant and afterward.

Once he had the name, he could ask Bonfield and his own teams to discover the details and current whereabouts of whatever aircraft Kourosh owned or leased—assuming he actually did have one. Based on past experience, though, Vic knew that tracing an aircraft in the US wasn't always as easy a task as it sounded.

Twenty minutes later, as he finished the call with Bonfield, he had an idea about how he might be able to identify the mole. It involved deploying one of the oldest counterintelligence tricks in the book and would require the assistance of Jayne and her contacts at MI5, possibly MI6 too.

* * *

Friday, April 22, 2016
London

Jayne pulled her pink cotton robe tight around her and was about to head for the bathroom to brush her teeth before bed when her phone vibrated on her bedside table.

She glanced at the screen. It was Vic again, calling on their secure connection.

What now?

Jayne hesitated, then decided she had best answer the call.

"Apologies for calling so late," Vic said. "I'll be quick. It's about the mole. There's something I want to ask you."

"Has Miller got a lead or something?" she asked.

"He hasn't. That's the issue. And it's how we go about getting one that's bugging me. I'm thinking of feeding barium meals to certain people and wondered what you thought about that."

"A James Jesus?"

"Yes."

Over the years, Jayne hadn't just been an intelligence officer, she had also been a keen student of her craft and the operations and characters that made it what it was on both sides of the Atlantic.

James Jesus Angleton was the legendary and deeply paranoid CIA counterintelligence chief from the mid-1950s to the mid-1970s. The barium meal, sometimes known as the canary trap or the marked card, was one of his favorite techniques for flushing out those who he believed—often erroneously as it turned out—were betraying the United States' deepest secrets to Moscow.

It involved feeding specifically crafted pieces of false information to certain individuals, tailored to that person. If that specific piece of information subsequently leaked, that person would have incriminated themselves. It got its nickname from the barium meals fed to patients by radiographers in hospitals, who then use X-rays to reveal abnormalities in their stomachs and bowels.

"What's your thinking, Vic?"

"The Navais are at a safe house, right? Location unknown and hopefully secure?"

"Correct."

"How about if we let slip a few other addresses where they might, for instance, be staying with friends for a few days."

Jayne sat on the bed. This was not the worst idea.

"We could double up," she said. "We could perhaps catch both predator and mole at the same time."

"That's my thinking."

"We'll need MI5 to play ball," she said. "They'll need to involve Special Branch. I can talk to Stella Hambledon and Harry Buck. Who are you going to feed the barium meals to?"

Vic paused. "There are five on my shortlist. You don't need to know."

"Come on, Vic. I do need to know. All at Langley?"

Jayne was fully aware she was asking a question that she had no right to ask. But she felt very deeply invested in the operation, given the damage done to Nicklin-Donovan and Odeya, and knew its success depended on locating whoever was betraying them.

"No, not all at Langley," Vic said, dropping his already gravelly voice another couple of tones.

"Who?"

"I'm sorry, Jayne, I can't tell you who."

Surely he's not suspecting me?

"All right. Just be careful you don't upset somebody," Jayne said. She felt like saying that if it turned out she was on the list, Vic could go screw himself, but held herself back.

"Frankly, Jayne, I don't give a shit. All I care about is catching whoever's leaking our operational details, and if that means upsetting a few people, then so be it. I shouldn't be doing this—it's Miller's job. But he's making no progress, and the egg timer is running out."

Vic was correct about that, Jayne thought.

"Sooner you than me," she said. "So you want five dummy addresses in London, apart from the real one, and we'll need undercover armed officers well skilled at discreet surveillance staking out all of them. If the bastard who's been chasing us spots them before we spot him, we're wasting our time."

"Yep."

"That is asking a lot of our friends here in London." *Maybe too much.*

"Sell it to them."

Jayne momentarily closed her eyes. That would be the tricky part. "I'll give it a try in the morning. You're right. It's probably the best option we've got."

CHAPTER THIRTY-THREE

Saturday, April 23, 2016
  Los Angeles

Cyrus Saba stood at the window of his second-floor office and stared out over the loading docks at the rear of his industrial manufacturing business, LA Pumps Inc. The sun was about to set and the yard was bathed in a golden glow, typical of a spring evening in the San Fernando Valley, a few miles north of Los Angeles.

A short line of trucks was waiting to be loaded, after which they would head out to all corners of the United States. One would be driven the short distance to the nearby Van Nuys Airport, where the cargo would be put onto one of Saba's private jets that was due to fly across the Atlantic to Riyadh and Qatar the following morning.

Saba had run the business for nearly two decades from this location and another in Mexico. The one he was at now stood amid a group of other heavy industrial businesses on Haskell Avenue, east of Van Nuys Airport. It had a solid niche in the business of pumps and valves for international oil and gas businesses and generated a decent profit every year.

The other, no more than a kilometer from Toluca International Airport and only half an hour west of Mexico City, manufactured high-precision measuring gauges for the same industry. The two airports were less than four hours flying time apart, which made it easy for Saba to travel between them as needed.

But more to the point, the operations provided perfect cover for Saba's far more lucrative business as a middleman for black market nuclear warhead manufacturing equipment, as well as a convenient explanation for the wealth he had accumulated over the years.

The pumps business also offered a convenient excuse to travel globally, and especially around the oil- and gas-production territories of the Middle East, without awkward questions being asked.

Saba had long ago installed a highly capable managing director at LA Pumps, leaving him free to focus on his nuclear equipment business, whose only customer was the land of his birth and of his abandonment: Iran.

Iran was the country that had effectively left him an orphan and yet from which he had made a fortune. The one with which he had a love-hate relationship that continually pulled him in different directions and that sometimes seemed to have stolen his very identity so that he could never escape.

Having been given away as a baby, he had been forced to leave his home country a few years later—two traumas suffered through no fault of his own. Although there was no doubt his adoptive parents loved him, he nonetheless felt that what he was now doing provided a stronger identity and anchor point than he had through his family life.

Saba turned and walked through his office to a specially constructed soundproof and triple-glazed room at the back, where he often conducted his most confidential calls. He wheeled a filing cabinet from its position, lifted a square of carpet, and unlocked the underfloor safe that lay beneath. He removed a cell phone, inserted the battery and SIM, and switched it on.

After he had checked the current market prices of crude oil on his Bloomberg screen, he dialed a number. When it was answered, without preamble, Saba spoke in a low tone. "The spot price of West Texas Intermediate today is forty-three dollars eighteen cents."

The answer was immediate. "Brent Crude is trading at forty-two dollars twenty-five cents."

"Hello," Saba said.

The person on the other end of the line, who Saba knew was sitting in an apartment in Houston, was one of two men who had partnered with him for many years. Both had rewarded him handsomely for his work, which had in turn made them a huge amount of money. Now they were worried it was about to come to an end.

"Greetings. Listen, I have concerns. I don't think we have done enough—it's not working. The Samar and the job you did on the ambassador were good, but it's not enough."

"We don't know that yet," Saba said. "Don't we want to wait until after Cohen's funeral and the Tel Aviv meetings and see what they do then? They might decide on some major operation against Tehran and southern Lebanon. Katz is in a rage. Ferguson must be furious."

There was a pause and a sigh at the other end of the line. "As the days tick by, and the smoke signals come out of Jerusalem, it's looking increasingly unlikely. His advisers are urging caution. I'm worried they decide not to strike and not to provoke Iran further. Then our opportunity is gone."

"What are you suggesting?" Saba asked.

"If we want to make sure this works, the funeral is our

opportunity to up the ante and make it impossible for Israel not to react."

"How? We can't hit the Knesset," Saba said. "There's no chance. It will be locked down and watertight. We can't do what we did to the platform."

"We don't need to hit the Knesset. Not based on what I've heard this afternoon. There's going to be a separate memorial ceremony after the funeral at Moshe Cohen's family winery, their farm down in the Negev. Near to Sderot. They're going to bury him there."

"They're going to have a ceremony near Sderot?" Saba couldn't keep the surprise out of his voice. The small city, no more than a town really, had come under regular rocket attack from the Gaza Strip, only a short distance away, and anywhere near there would be a high-risk location.

"Yes."

"But Ferguson and Katz won't go there," Saba said.

"That's where you're wrong. I've heard they are both going."

Saba exhaled sharply. "Really?"

"I've heard it from my source."

Saba knew who the source, code-named SOHRAB, was. He also knew that some of the information received from SOHRAB by the man on the other end of the line—code-named ROSTAM by the Iranians—was passed on to Tehran. Both he and Saba needed to keep them happy too.

But the Iranians certainly did not know that some of that information was being used by ROSTAM and Saba to engineer attacks on Israeli targets, nor why.

"Have you shared this information with the Iranians?" Saba asked.

"No, Tehran doesn't know."

"Keep it that way," Saba said. "And rockets won't work out of Gaza. But you know that."

Israel's defense systems, in the shape of its Iron Dome, meant rockets fired from Gaza could now be intercepted easily enough.

"Yes, I know. I'm not talking about rockets. We would need to use a drone again. I'm thinking we deploy your contractor who carried out the Samar operation again. He did a fine job."

Saba leaned back in his chair, thinking.

"Maybe. But time is short. It's now Saturday. The funeral is on Thursday."

"That's enough time. You told me he has drones and missiles in the Sinai. He can get them into Gaza, no problem, can't he?"

"Yes, probably," Saba said. "The weapons are there. But unfortunately my contractor is not."

"Well, get him there."

"Do you know his price is double for doing jobs on short notice, for anything less than a month?" Saba asked. "He will want a million bucks. Speaking of which, you and your partner still owe me for the platform operation. I'm not doing any more until I get paid. I'm sure you understand."

There was a long silence. "I know. Look, me and my partner can both fly separately to Toluca on Wednesday and bring you what you need in cash to pay your contractor. We'll bring half each. And we'll pay you for both jobs by bank transfer before then."

"Wednesday? Can't you get there before then?" Saba asked. "We need to move quickly."

"Impossible. I'm tied up here until then."

"Can I come to Houston, then? I could fly into Hobby."

William P. Hobby Airport, located only seven miles or so from downtown Houston, where ROSTAM was based, was the main private jet airport for the city and was Saba's normal port of call when visiting.

"I'm not going to risk meeting for this type of transaction on US soil. In any case, I'm busy until Tuesday night. Sorry."

"All right, Wednesday at Toluca it must be," Saba said. "I need to send the coordinates for the Sderot target site and a couple detailed maps to my drone friend."

"Wednesday, okay. We'll bring the million in cash. Hundred-dollar bills."

"All right. We can both confirm on Tuesday night," Saba said.

"Will you put the usual security process in place for Toluca?" the caller asked.

"Of course," Saba said. "I'm the last one to take any risks. You should know that."

The security process he was referring to was a complex one, but in Saba's view, it added a comforting level of security to a potentially risky meeting. Ideally, he wouldn't meet up at all, but given the need to transfer very large amounts of physical cash and the impossibility of trusting anyone else with the transaction, there was no alternative.

Saba ended the call.

There was one other call he needed to make with the phone before removing the battery and SIM again. That was to his contractor Emad Madani—the man who had carried out the gas platform drone attack with such deadly precision nearly three weeks earlier.

He tapped in the number.

* * *

Saturday, April 23, 2016
Henley-on-Thames

. . .

Henri's burner phone rang just after he had climbed back into his van to leave Henley following a walk along the River Thames towpath near the Navais' house.

Henri checked the screen. It was an encrypted call from Talal Hassan. He had been expecting the call requesting an update and giving him further instructions.

"Hello," he said.

"Hello, my friend. The market price of Super 180's twelve-ounce, superfine cloth is rising. I have an order for you."

After giving the required response to identify himself, Henri continued, "If you're looking for an update, I have just checked the property. Still no sign of targets. No movement, no car, no evidence of surveillance."

"No, there wouldn't be any sign there. We have received information that they are staying with friends in west London —I have the address."

"Do you know what type of property?"

"Research has checked it. It's a semidetached house, busy residential street, unfortunately. Large garden at the rear, small one at the front. A bit run-down. A typical British safe house."

Henri frowned. That meant plenty of potential witnesses and possible interference. The British weren't stupid.

"So what do you want me to do?" he asked.

"Continue. If you can't hit the intelligence team, then get the people they're trying to talk to. If they give away leads to the main man, it will screw the entire supply chain."

Henri paused, his forehead now creased. "It's quite likely they have protection now if they've moved out of their own home and are staying with friends. The risks have increased sharply. I suspect we're too late."

"We aren't. Check out the property first. I'm sure you can create a cover for that—I don't need to tell you what to do," Hassan said. "Didn't you have a similar situation in

Marseille a few years ago? You solved that one, I seem to recall."

Henri could detect a note of desperation in Hassan's voice now. He was clearly being put under a lot of pressure from above.

"This is a top priority for the Supreme Leader—maybe *the* top priority," Hassan continued, confirming Henri's suspicions. "We can't afford to give up on this. If the supply chain gets taken down, I can tell you he will take both of us down with it. Understand?"

"I will do some surveillance and see what is possible. If it is not, I will inform you."

"If it is not, it will probably be the last job you do for us."

And there it was.

It was obvious to Henri that the Supreme Leader had given orders to his top men, most probably Nasser Khan in the Quds Force and Abbas Taeb in the Ministry of Intelligence, and threatened them with the ultimate penalty if they failed. They in turn had likely done the same to Hassan. And so it went on down the line.

Henri, unfortunately, was the last one in that line, with nobody to pass the parcel on to.

He sat in his car thinking for a while. This didn't smell good.

However, Hassan did have a point about the operation in Marseille just over a decade earlier, in which Henri and Pierre had eliminated an infiltrator into Hezbollah's ranks in southern France together with his Israeli handler. It had been one of Pierre's last operations in France before moving to Los Angeles.

In that case, the infiltrator had realized he had been blown and had been taken by the handler to a Mossad safe house on a residential street, there they awaited a boat to safety from the port.

After a tip-off, Henri and Pierre had managed to flush both men out of the house into a rear yard, where they had gunned them down and escaped over a fence.

However, it had been a high-risk strategy and could have gone wrong. It certainly wasn't his usual surgical, long-distance method of dealing with such issues.

Henri decided that before deciding what to do, he would call and discuss it with the one man in the world he felt he could trust—his twin, Pierre.

CHAPTER THIRTY-FOUR

Sunday, April 24, 2016
London

Jayne made her way up the communal staircase to her second-floor apartment, carefully clutching a carrier containing three take-out coffees and a paper bag full of croissants from her favorite baker across the street.

She had bought the apartment, on the corner of Port-soken Street and Minories, following a long posting in the Balkans with MI6. Despite being based in Portland now, she still loved coming back to it.

In spite of her fatigue, Jayne had woken early that morning and had decided to go out for a run along the Thames. She had gone over Tower Bridge, then along the south side of the river as far as Waterloo Bridge and back, a total of about five miles. She now felt better for the exercise, and it had given her a chance to think about what the next steps should be in their operation.

Jayne let herself in to find Rafael and Zahavi had gotten

up while she had been out. She could hear Zahavi in her spare room, talking on the phone, and Rafael was sitting at her small circular wooden dining table, tapping away on his laptop.

She had spent most of the previous day communicating via phone calls and emails with Stella Hambledon and Harry Buck to put in place the necessary arrangements for the barium meal exercise that she had discussed with Vic.

After lengthy debate with his internal teams over the practical difficulties—which were significant—Buck had agreed to the proposals. They included the provision of four properties, none of them real safe houses, plus surveillance teams, in addition to the actual site already being covered in Hounslow where the Navais were accommodated.

Jayne had originally asked for five new addresses in order to avoid including the real one on the list, but Buck was forced to rule that out because there simply weren't enough surveillance teams available.

It was annoying that the real one was going to be included, but surveillance and security at the house was good, and she trusted the MI5 teams.

The surveillance teams would be in place from seven o'clock Sunday morning onward, Buck promised, and each would include at least one armed officer from the Metropolitan Police's Special Branch.

MI5, whose officers did not have arrest powers and generally weren't armed, worked hand in glove with Special Branch on such operations.

"I'll look after the details at my end," Buck had said. "You take care of yours. I'll send the addresses within the hour."

"Thanks," Jayne said. "Vic will be extremely grateful."

"We might need a favor from Langley one day," Buck said. "You never know."

In Jayne's view, it was smart of Buck to think that way. She knew that Vic was the sort of guy who would remember an important favor of that kind, and given his current stratospheric level of seniority at Langley, he was in a position to repay it if he was so inclined.

Buck had immediately risen in her estimation, and she had told Vic so when she called him to let him know he could begin feeding his barium meals. His plan was to build the different safe house addresses into individual variants of a top-secret update briefing document that would go to those on the circulation list. The address would be buried toward the end of the document, and only a person specifically looking for it would likely see and make use of it.

Jayne closed the door of her apartment behind her and put the bag of coffee and croissants down on the table. "Got some breakfast," she said.

"It smells good," Rafael said. He paused, then added quietly, "Odeya loved croissants and coffee."

Jayne nodded. She could see he was battling with his emotions. "You worked with her a long time. I do feel for you. It's so difficult when it's someone you've been that close to."

"Sure is. We worked as a team for a lot of that time." Rafael shrugged. "I know it's an occupational hazard in this business, but that doesn't help."

There was a pause as Jayne unpacked the bag.

"Did you sleep okay on the sofa bed?" she asked. It was Rafael's second night on the improvised sleeping facility after they decided to remain in central London rather than return to Henley.

"I sleep anywhere," he said. "Wherever I lay my hat, that's my home."

Jayne smiled at the reference to the old Marvin Gaye song. She could see he meant it, and without a doubt, it was one reason why he thrived on the constantly itinerant lifestyle that was a requirement of his role. She had always been the same, but it wasn't for everyone.

She handed Rafael one of the coffees and put the croissants on a large plate, laid out smaller plates for all of them, and then sat down.

The sun was glinting in from the east onto a small balcony that led off the living room. The apartment, which looked out toward Tower Bridge, had a galley-style kitchen and a small dining area. The black leather sofa bed that Rafael had been using and two matching armchairs stood in the living room.

The bookcase held various souvenirs and tomes that she had acquired on her overseas postings and holidays. There was a variety of novels, most of which were spy and political thrillers, along with a number of travel books, political biographies, and military histories from all over the world. Some were in foreign languages—Jayne was fluent in French, Russian, Spanish, and other tongues, and she tried to maintain that fluency by reading.

Rafael pointed to a photograph on the wall of a smiling man sitting in a restaurant holding a glass of wine, graying hair neatly coiffured, wearing an open-neck shirt. "Is that your father?"

Jayne nodded. "That's him. It was taken on his fiftieth birthday. We went to Claridges. Happy times."

The door to the spare bedroom opened and Zahavi emerged, unshaven and wearing a well-worn white T-shirt with a hole on the shoulder. He had a serious expression on his face.

"There's some breakfast here for you," Jayne said. She pushed the third coffee over the table in his direction and indicated toward the food.

"Thanks. This is very welcome," Zahavi walked over and sat across from Jayne. He removed the plastic lid from his coffee and took a sip.

"I was speaking to Avi and Jake," Zahavi said. "They've just had a briefing from the research team."

Jayne looked at him. They had waited all day yesterday for the call. "Good. Anything useful?"

"There is some news," Zahavi said. "It concerns one of the items you found at the Navais' house. The wrist locket."

Jayne grasped her coffee cup and took a sip. Now what was coming? "Go on," she said.

"The photograph inside the locket you found showed the girl, Zahra. They drew a blank on her—there was nothing on Zahra Moin in the files in Tel Aviv."

"Right."

"But when they ran images of the actual half locket through the system, they did find a match."

Now Jayne felt confused. "A match for what?"

"The other half of the same silver locket. It was identical to photographs of another half of a silver locket in a much older file, which dated back to 1994."

Jayne put her coffee down on the table and stared at Zahavi. "What did the other file relate to?"

Zahavi shifted in his seat. "It related to the 1994 Israeli embassy bombing in London."

Jayne suddenly felt slightly faint and gripped the edge of the dining table with both hands. "The bomb blast that killed my father, you mean?"

Zahavi nodded and he ran the back of his hand across his mouth. "The other half of that locket was found, along with a few other items, by a Mossad officer outside the embassy after the attack."

She suddenly had a flashback to what Kourosh's adoptive parents had said.

He was involved in groups and activities we didn't really like . . . He started working for Hezbollah . . . there were a lot of bad things going on.

"Are you suggesting . . . Are you saying these two carried out the bombing?"

All Jayne could focus on were Zahavi's lips as she waited for him to speak again. Everything else went into slow motion.

"It seems very possible." Zahavi took a long drink from his coffee and put the cup down. "Jake's been through the files. He says that according to what's in there, just before the bomb went off, a woman who had a Mediterranean appearance left an Audi in the parking area of the apartment building next to the embassy. She walked off carrying a Harrods shopping bag and disappeared around the corner. A few seconds later, the Audi exploded, and—"

"Yes, I know all this. It was well reported at the time," Jayne interrupted. "I've got all the news reports in a box in my bedroom over there." She pointed toward the main bedroom door. She could remember the reports almost word for word, she had read through them so many times.

"Yes, of course. I'll get to the point. What was not reported was that immediately afterward, a couple of Mossad officers who were on duty had the presence of mind to go out and photograph everything they could see and find before the British police could get to it and move it. It was a precaution, just in case something was missed. Among the items they found was the broken half locket. A policeman nearby described how he saw the woman with the Harrods bag being knocked off her feet by the blast. She picked herself up, walked off, and was seen climbing into a car farther down the street. That was the last anyone saw of her—the woman was never found. The car license plates were noted by the officer but were false. But the half locket was found where she fell by our officers. It seems her wrist locket broke when she fell over, and half was left behind."

Zahavi tapped on his phone screen and held it out toward

Jayne. It showed a close-up photograph of half a locket, clearly a match for the one Jayne had found.

"What happened to the actual half of the locket?" Jayne asked.

Zahavi shrugged. "It must have gone into the British police evidence bag, I assume. I don't know if it surfaced during trials."

Jayne leaned back in her chair and gripped the edge of the dining table harder. She couldn't recall any mention of a locket in the news reports she had read.

She knew that two Palestinians, a man and a woman, had been subsequently convicted in December 1996 of conspiring to cause the explosion and were given twenty-year sentences. But they had consistently denied any involvement, and the convictions had been seen by many as rushed and likely incorrect, despite the failure of an appeal in 2001. The man and woman were eventually released in 2008 and 2009.

"Why the hell didn't all this come out earlier?" Jayne asked. "Why wasn't the photograph of the locket highlighted by the embassy? Or by the Mossad, for that matter?"

Zahavi shook his head. "Jake says there is a note in the file stating that the photo was offered to police, but they declined. Presumably because they had the real thing. But at the time, there were no clues on it linking it to anyone—no marks, no name, no photo inside, nothing. CCTV outside the embassy wasn't working, so there were no images of the woman who left the Audi or of the car she got into afterward. So it was next to useless. And it remained useless and meaningless until you found the other half of it."

Jayne exhaled. She felt she could apply a few other somewhat more colorful adjectives to what had happened, in addition to *useless*. But she decided to let it go. There was no point now.

"So the bottom line is that the man who might have

blown up the gas platform off Tel Aviv is possibly the same man who, with his girlfriend, organized the bombing that killed my father," Jayne said. "Is that what you're saying?"

Zahavi slowly nodded his head. "It looks that way. It all fits together."

It certainly did all fit together like a jigsaw puzzle, even through the slightly dizzy feeling that Jayne was experiencing.

All these years, she had felt a deep sense of unease at the conviction that had been handed down by the courts in 1996 but without being able to quite put her finger on why. Many commentators and observers inside the justice and political system had argued the same thing, to no effect.

But now? Could that all change?

The thought sent a jolt of adrenaline through Jayne. She was now feeling an overpowering urge to get this investigation moving.

"Right," she said, almost to herself. She grabbed her phone.

Instinctively she wanted to tell Joe—the man she had talked to most about her father and about the pain she had felt over his death. He, more than anyone, would understand. He was a war crimes investigator who loved nothing more than digging out the truth about evil deeds done far in the past and more than once had told her he would like to investigate her father's death when she shared her concerns over the convictions.

She tapped out a secure message on her phone outlining what she had learned and sent it to Joe.

The simple act of letting him know calmed Jayne's racing thoughts and made it easier for her to think in a more operationally focused way. There were people whom she needed to brief, and she tried to mentally prioritize them.

The first two were Stella Hambledon at MI6 and Harry Buck at MI5, with whom she knew she would need to keep on good terms if what she had learned was proven correct. She would likely need their help to pave the way at the political level if Kourosh and his girl Zahra were shown to be the true perpetrators of the embassy bombing in 1994.

It wouldn't be easy for the UK's Home Office, in charge of policing and security, as well as the Crown Prosecution Service and the Ministry of Justice to admit they gotten it wrong all those years ago.

But that was jumping the gun.

She also needed to tell Vic her news and work out a way to find Kourosh Navai, or whatever he was calling himself. She wondered if Vic had made any headway on that front.

Jayne picked up her coffee. "I just need to make a couple of calls," she said.

She left the two Israelis to their croissants, walked out onto her balcony, and sat on one of her old oak patio chairs looking out toward the River Thames, a few hundred yards to the south.

There she placed an encrypted call to Vic, who, it turned out, was on the way to meet his grown-up daughter, Francine, for a very rare Sunday morning walk together along the banks of the Potomac. He was stunned into a rare state of silence as she told him what the Mossad had unearthed.

"That original conviction never looked right," Vic said, his voice low and serious. "I was working in the Islamabad station at the time, and I remember reading the news reports. Now we know—this looks very personal for you now."

Jayne remembered receiving a telegram from Vic at the time offering his condolences.

"Very personal," she said. "Have you heard anything from the FBI about tracking down Kourosh?"

"We have. I was going to call you after I'd finished seeing Francine." He told Jayne the FBI had determined that Kourosh had worked for the Three Mile Island nuclear plant under his true name for five years. After that the trail had run cold.

"The feds are investigating what he did after Three Mile Island, whether he's using the name Kourosh, Koresh, or something else, and whether he's still in the US now, and whether he owns a plane," Vic said.

"To my mind, Kourosh has to be the one responsible for the gas platform," Jayne said. "But we need to check out the Swiss and German companies on the supply chain list Müller gave us, just to be sure."

"Already done," Vic said. "Our checks show they're likely involved in illegal supplies, though we'll need proof. But there's nothing to indicate any of the people linked to those companies might be capable of or interested in taking out a gas platform."

"Good," Jayne said. She always liked to see other people making sure they were a step ahead of the game.

"If he is in the US, you need to be ready to travel here at short notice. We'll need you—given all the leaks, and the additional risk of the president flying to Israel, I'm now trying to keep the size of the team working on this to an absolute minimum, which is difficult. But if you're here, it means I can avoid bringing someone else into the loop unnecessarily."

"That makes sense," Jayne said. "I'll get ready to fly back. I suggest you speak with Avi and work out a plan and decide whether Zahavi and Rafael should join me."

She left unspoken her thought that heading back to the US would enable her to see Joe again sooner rather than later.

But the mention of plane ownership triggered a vague memory of a conversation with Joe about a difficult investigation he had worked on a few years back. She was certain he had an inside man at the Federal Aviation Administration.

"I know someone who can help with that," Jayne said.

"Maybe you could use him to bypass the feds and speed things up."

"Who?" Vic asked.

"Joe. He's got someone at the FAA in his back pocket, I think. I'm unsure of the details but I can talk to him about it."

"Yes, sure."

Jayne ended the call.

The new disclosures had left her feeling a little overwhelmed, especially on top of the other events from the previous couple of days. There had been so little time to distance herself from events and to see things from the wider perspective.

Was there anything she had missed, some clue that might prove vital?

It was only as she stood to go back indoors that she realized there was something, a loose end that she had meant to follow up on with Darius and Freema Navai but hadn't.

Jayne sat down again and called Harry Buck.

First she updated him on the situation relating to the Israeli embassy bombing, which brought a reaction similar to that from Vic: shocked silence. He was only too aware that it raised the likelihood of renewed criticism over MI5's part in the original conviction.

After that, Jayne moved on to inform Buck about the loose end she wanted to close off with the Navais.

"I understand," Buck said. He gave Jayne details of the surveillance teams that were watching the safe house.

"I'll inform the teams and get you on the visitors list for today, so they'll be expecting you. If we need you to abort the visit, we'll message you."

After finishing the call, Jayne went back inside, polished off her share of the croissants, and helped Zahavi and Rafael clear up the mess of flaky crumbs, coffee cups, and plates.

Then she explained what she had in mind, put on her jacket and shoes and, as an afterthought, took her Walther PPS and a spare magazine from the safe inside her wardrobe and put them in the inside pocket of the jacket.

Then she headed out the door and toward the underground station at Tower Hill, just down the street and opposite the Tower of London.

* * *

Sunday, April 24, 2016
    London

A sweeper truck was working its way down the street, which lay just off the much busier traffic-laden Bath Road.

Jayne, who had walked a somewhat circuitous route from Hounslow West tube station to ensure she had no coverage, paused as she passed an Indian restaurant and a men's barbershop. Overhead, a jumbo jet, engines throttled back and landing lights glaring, passed low on its approach to Heathrow, a couple of miles farther west.

She continued until she reached the safe house, number thirty-two, which was absolutely typical of those on the street. It was detached with a cracked and fragmented concrete driveway that had seen much better days.

One of the wooden gateposts was leaning over at a drunken angle, half rotted through at its base. The fence was battered, the straggly grass on a tiny patch of lawn was several inches long, and a six-foot privet hedge required trimming.

Nobody would give it a second glance. But that was the whole point. It had been carefully selected.

There had been no abort message from Buck, so Jayne

assumed it was safe to proceed. She bent down and retied her shoelace, which enabled her to make one last check in both directions. There was only an old man walking a collie, which had its leg cocked against a hedge. Farther down the street was a Tesco supermarket van on one side of the street and an Amazon delivery van on the other. Two boys were walking along, kicking a football. Nothing out of the ordinary, and she was certain she had not been tailed.

She checked her watch. It was eight minutes before midday, as agreed with Buck, so she walked up to the front door, which opened before she could knock. The same blonde MI5 woman who had been there two days ago opened it, nodded a greeting, and stood to one side to allow her in.

"They're in the living room again," the woman said. "They're expecting you."

Jayne walked through, past the other officer with the silver crewcut, who nodded a polite greeting. As she passed the man, his radio emitted a soft squelch break. Presumably it had come from the surveillance team outside the property.

The old couple, Darius and Freema, were sitting on the same two armchairs. This time, the large folding doors positioned between the front and rear parts of the living room were closed.

"You're back again," Darius said, his black eyes flicking between Jayne and the blonde woman.

"I do apologize," Jayne said. "You've no doubt had enough of answering questions. I know it's exhausting. Are you coping with it?"

Freema gave a slight shake of her head. "We're finding it difficult and we didn't sleep well. You know, a strange bed."

"I hope it won't be for long," Jayne said. "I'm sure it's a sensible precaution."

She sat on the sofa and accepted an offer of coffee from the female officer, who poured three cups from a glass pot.

"As I said before, we're trying to locate Kourosh, and there is something I would like to ask." She turned to Freema. "There was a question I asked, about whether your son had ever used any other name. Your husband spoke about Koresh, but when I was thinking back this morning, I realized that you opened your mouth as if to say something but never did, and it's been bothering me."

Freema picked up her coffee cup and took a sip.

"Yes, I *was* going to say something, then we got distracted. I was going to mention Koresh, too, like my husband, but also something else."

"What was that?"

"Years ago, Kourosh had a perverse interest in the madman who killed several police officers, an event that began a siege in the States. His name was David Koresh. I think that may be why he used the name Koresh, not just because it's just a variant of Kourosh. It's a common Persian name."

Jayne recalled the episode at Waco, Texas, involving David Koresh and his sect, which had happened the year before her father's murder and had ended in tragedy with upward of eighty deaths. "I remember the Waco siege, yes. Go on," she said.

"But I also remember seeing a newspaper story he had cut out about that crazy man. David Koresh had done some interview in which he said that—" Freema paused suddenly. "You probably don't know much about Persian history, Persian kings, I assume?"

Jayne shook her head, feeling a little confused about where this was going. "I've read a few bits and pieces, that's all."

"Well, who was the most famous Persian king, to your knowledge?"

Jayne could recall only one. "Cyrus the Great?"

"Yes, that's it." Freema gazed at Jayne. "You see, the article Kourosh had cut out, in that interview David Koresh had said he was a modern-day Cyrus the Great. Kourosh had highlighted that bit with a pen."

She turned to her husband. "Do you remember all that?"

Darius pushed his glasses up his nose. "Yes, he was a little obsessed with reading about that man."

"Quite. Well, he'd circled this name, but also Cyrus is the Western variant of Kourosh, or Koresh too. And I thought that if my son was going by Koresh, then perhaps—"

"He might go by Cyrus," Jayne said completing her sentence. "I see what you're saying. That could make sense."

Freema shrugged. "It crossed my mind when you asked if he'd changed his name. I'm pleased I've got the chance to mention it now. It had been bothering me too."

Jayne drained her coffee. She had no idea how important this additional piece of information would prove, but it was worth adding to the collection.

"There's one other thing," Darius said. "I remembered this morning that when I spoke to Kourosh a few years ago, must be four or five years, I asked him if he was still in the United States, and he said he was in Los Angeles."

"Five years ago?"

"Yes."

"Thanks, that's also useful to know," Jayne said.

She felt an increasing sympathy for the elderly couple, who had clearly cared a lot for a son who was estranged from them.

"There is one other thing," Jayne said. "Do you recall the bombing of the Israeli embassy in London in 1994, by any chance? It was well covered in the media at the time."

"Very vaguely," Darius said. "Why?"

"Do you recall Kourosh ever mentioning it? Or do you recall how he reacted to news about it?"

Darius shook his head and looked at his wife.

"No, I don't recall him reacting especially to it," Freema said. "Why, do you think he was involved?"

"It's possible," Jayne said. She decided not to mention her father, as she knew she would get emotional. Instead, she sat for a few moments, trying to think if there was anything else she should discuss with them, but couldn't pinpoint anything.

She stood and stepped forward to shake hands with the couple, who remained seated in their chairs.

As she did so, the doorbell rang with a loud melodic chime that made her jump slightly.

"Who's that?" Jayne called out to the armed officers in the hallway.

"Don't know," the blonde MI5 officer replied tersely. "I'll check."

Jayne stepped toward a small gap in the folding doors and peered out through the front window toward the street. Through gaps in the hedge she could see a blue van with an Amazon logo on the side. It looked like the same one she had seen farther down the street when she arrived.

"There's an Amazon van outside," Jayne called out.

"Amazon? There's nothing expected here," the MI5 woman replied.

Jayne felt her stomach turn over. She walked to the living room door and stood in the entrance to the hallway. The two MI5 officers were looking tense. Through the frosted pane of glass in the top half of the front door, the dark outline of the visitor could be seen.

"We had no alert call from the surveillance team," the MI5 woman said.

Perhaps just a mistake then.

"Maybe a wrong address," Jayne suggested.

"Must be," the officer said. "I'll get rid of them." She took a step toward the door, then called loudly, "Can I help you?"

"Got an Amazon delivery for this address," came a deep voice with an accent that sounded vaguely French.

"We haven't ordered anything," the blonde woman said. "You have the wrong address. I'm sorry."

There's something wrong here, Jayne instinctively thought. A red light flashed inside her brain.

"Number thirty-two?" came the voice from outside.

"Yes, but—"

But the blonde woman got no further.

There was a rattle as a slim, rectangular cardboard box was pushed through the plastic mail slot flap halfway up the door. It fell to the tiled hallway floor with a heavy thud.

Even before the brown cardboard package had landed, Jayne had reacted instinctively.

"Don't touch it. Move!" she screamed. "Get out!"

Jayne flung herself back into the living room, dived to the floor, and rolled sideways toward the Navais in their armchairs, her old MI6 instincts kicking in—better safe than sorry.

Get something, anything, between them and the door. Get down low and flat.

If this was what she feared, Jayne knew she had only a couple of seconds at best, and getting as low as possible to protect against the inevitable fragmentation as the device went off was all she could do. Behind the armchairs was the only option she had.

"On the floor," she yelled at the couple. "Quick!"

Neither of them moved.

Without hesitating, Jayne reached up and in one motion grabbed Freema's left wrist and Darius's right hand and yanked them both simultaneously to the floor next to her.

Darius's chin hit the carpet with a thud and Freema shrieked, "What are you doing?"

"Face on the floor, now!" Jayne yelled at them.

She flattened herself on the floor next to the couple between the armchairs and a TV cabinet, folded both arms over her head protectively, and closed her eyes.

It was now too late to do anything more.

In that moment there was a massive explosion from out in the hall, the force of which somehow shoved Jayne's body forward so that her head struck the corner of the TV cabinet.

Her eyes opened on impact, and from behind her came a crunching, splattering noise.

As if in slow motion, the wall and ceiling near the door collapsed into the room amid a huge cloud of brickwork, plaster, dust, and debris that showered down all over Jayne like a rainstorm.

Then a second or two later she heard the intermittent rat-tat-tat of semiautomatic gunfire.

CHAPTER THIRTY-FIVE

Sunday, April 24, 2016
London

When the gunfire stopped, Jayne turned her head, brushed pieces of plaster, brick, and dust from her face and hair, and tried to sit up.

She felt a stinging pain near her right ear where she had hit the TV cabinet and put her hand to the spot. It came away smeared with blood.

There was a loud ringing sound in her ears that wouldn't stop, and the air in the room was thick with a fog of dust.

Jayne turned to check the old couple who were lying next to her, motionless.

Are they still alive? What about the MI5 pair?

Freema, facedown on the floor, was covered with debris and dust.

Then Jayne heard her moan gently. Darius was lying silent, but his hand began to move. A trickle of blood coursed its way down the side of his face through the layer of dust that covered it, and a piece of wood with a sharp jagged end that looked as though it was from the door frame lay next to him.

"Are you okay?" Jayne asked, her voice croaky.

No response.

She hauled herself up and placed a hand on Freema's head, then repeated the question.

"I don't know," the old woman whispered. "Is Darius all right? What happened?"

Jayne reached over and took Darius's hand. "Are you okay, Darius?" she asked.

The old man groaned and turned over. "My head. My chin hurts."

"Yes, you've got a cut. We'll fix it. You'll be all right."

Thank God.

The cut didn't look too serious, although the white and pink dust that was covering his face and scalp made it difficult to discern his pallor.

What had happened to the two MI5 officers? They hadn't made it into the living room. Jayne had a sinking feeling in the bottom of her stomach.

Then the realization hit her: whoever had pushed the explosive through the door would likely be coming in the front to finish the job.

Jayne looked at the Navais. She knew she had to get them out the back of the house somehow. But that was going to be difficult in their condition.

Jayne hauled herself to her feet, ignoring her own head wound, which she could feel was still trickling blood.

She reached inside her jacket, took out the Walther, flicked off the safety, and rapidly pulled back the slide, chambering a round. Then she stepped carefully over the debris that lay all over the floor and moved toward the remains of the living room doorway.

The door itself was hanging by the top hinge only. The

bottom two hinges had been blown away, as had a large portion of the frame, leaving plasterwork and bare brick exposed.

Jayne ducked beneath a piece of ceiling plasterboard that was hanging down and peered cautiously with her right eye around the edge of the remains of the doorway.

She immediately retched and sank to a squatting position.

There was no sign of the man who had delivered the package bomb.

But the gory remains of the two MI5 officers were lying next to each other, covered in debris.

Both were within a few feet of the door to the living room.

They had obviously tried to make it to safety.

The blonde woman's face was unrecognizable. Half of her head had been blown away, and the shredded remnants of her left arm lay on the floor a couple of feet away from her body.

The silver-haired officer's throat had a huge gaping wound, and his left leg was hanging by a sliver of flesh above the knee and stuck out at right angles to the rest of his body. A large splintered femur bone was jutting out, and blood was pouring from the massive wound.

The hallway had been completely destroyed. Pieces of flesh and bone were littered everywhere among the debris, and splatters of blood were visible on the few segments of white wall surface that remained.

Beyond the bodies, the front door and most of its frame had been blown outward, so Jayne could see the garden and street beyond.

Jayne stepped over the wreckage, flattened herself against the wrecked hallway wall, and edged forward, gun at the ready, until she could just see out the door.

At the corner of the house to her right, on a concrete path that led to the rear garden, lay the body of a tall, muscular, olive-skinned bald man with a stubbly beard. He was lying faceup and his legs were splayed at a strange angle. He had two large bullet wounds in his chest and another on the left side of his head that were oozing blood. In his right hand he was holding a pistol.

"Bastard," Jayne muttered to herself.

Out on the street, three members of the surveillance team were approaching the house, one of them carrying a rifle—this had to be the marksman who had shot dead the bomber.

Despite her state of shock, Jayne could feel a rising tide of anger inside her.

As the men drew near, Jayne stood and stepped toward the door. In the distance, she could hear sirens wailing.

"Are you okay?" the man with the rifle asked.

"Does it look like I'm bloody well okay? Does it look like these two are okay?" Jayne said. She brushed another cloud of dust from her hair and indicated toward the mess of bodies and plasterwork behind her.

The man shook his head. "I'm sorry, I didn't mean it like that. I don't know what happened—how the hell did this guy know . . ." His voice trailed off.

Jayne forced herself back into operational mode. "Have you called for paramedics? Too late for these two, but I've got the old couple in the living room who will need attention."

"They're coming, yes," one of the unarmed officers said. "There's a police unit on the way too."

Jayne stared into the distance, past the two men.

It had happened again.

Another leak. Another attack. More lives lost.

"I don't understand it," the officer with the rifle said. "That was the third time the Amazon van had been in the street today. The previous two times he delivered parcels to other houses. He seemed genuine. Never thought he'd come to thirty-two. We thought it was a mistake, that he'd walk away. Then he pushed the parcel through the letterbox, and before it went off he pulled his gun out and began running toward the back of the house. That was when we took him out."

"But you were too late."

The officer shook his head. "It was an impossible situation. He really looked like an innocent delivery guy, and he was out of the van and up to the front door in a flash. But then we realized the explosive was to try and flush you out the back of the house. So we shot him. We couldn't—"

"I understand. It doesn't matter, I just—" Jayne stopped. She looked the guy in the eye. "Let's have the postmortem later—not now."

It was at that point that it dawned on her that Vic would now know who his mole was.

* * *

Sunday, April 24, 2016
London

Within ten minutes, the street had been sealed off and was swarming with police cars, two ambulances, and other unmarked vehicles from the security services.

A gaggle of residents from the street that had gathered near the blue Amazon van had now been pushed back behind a cordon that police set up farther down the street. Some were taking photographs and videos using their phones. Other neighbors could be seen staring from upstairs windows.

Officers had already put up a tall white screen to prevent onlookers from viewing the body of the bomber outside number thirty-two and the even greater bloodbath inside the hallway. But Jayne had little doubt that the images taken after the incident were already going viral on social media and would be plastered over television news and the next day's newspapers.

After speaking with the surveillance team, she returned to the living room and, not daring to move the Navais, sat with them amid the wreckage until paramedics arrived. The paramedics checked the old couple over thoroughly and then took them to the kitchen, which was relatively unaffected by the blast, to clean them up.

To Jayne's immense relief, the Navais had suffered only cuts and bruises, including some caused when she had yanked them off the sofa. However, they were deeply shocked and initially struggled to answer even the simplest of questions from the paramedics.

Jayne opened the secure message app on her phone and sent Vic a brief missive.

All going to shit here. Will call asap. Have a pilot/plane owner name suggestion. Try Cyrus. Los Angeles.

He would know what it meant.

After tending to the Navais, a paramedic cleaned the cut on Jayne's head, applied antiseptic, and stuck on a small bandage. He also wiped Jayne's face.

Eventually, the paramedics helped the elderly couple out through the rear door of the house, avoiding the carnage at the front, and toward an ambulance. While they were doing that, Jayne walked over to the Amazon van and took a quick look inside the cab.

What she saw explained how the deliveryman had managed to get out of his van and up to the front door so quickly. The van was not a right-hand-drive British model but a left-hand-drive variant from Europe. The driver's door opened closest to the house, not into the street. He had been able to climb out and walk straight up the path to the house before they could move to stop him.

She returned to the ambulance, where the paramedics were helping Freema in.

It gave Jayne a moment alone with Darius.

She put a hand on his shoulder. "I am so sorry that this happened," Jayne said. "I know saying that isn't going to be enough, but I really apologize that you have been put through this."

Darius nodded and looked Jayne in the eye. "Do you know who did this?"

"Not yet. But we believe it was done by someone trying to stop us from finding Kourosh."

"Hezbollah?" he asked.

"Possibly. It is quite likely."

"Thought so."

The old man looked down at the ground for a few seconds, then straightened himself and eyed Jayne once more.

"He's really up to no good, is he, Kourosh?"

"We think not," Jayne said.

He indicated toward the house. "I thought this was meant to protect us."

Jayne opened her mouth to reply but he held up a hand. "I won't ask what went wrong," he said. "There was a screwup, though. I can see that."

The old man slowly extended his right hand to Jayne. She noticed it was shaking. She took it and held it for several seconds.

"I hope you don't mind if I keep in touch," Jayne said. "I would like to be certain that you and Freema are both okay, and I hope you're able to go home again safely soon."

The paramedic emerged from the rear of the ambulance and headed in their direction. Farther up the street, a black

BMW pulled up next to a police car. Buck climbed out of the front passenger seat and began striding toward Jayne.

Darius suddenly grasped her forearm in a surprisingly tight grip.

"If you are to continue chasing after Kourosh," he said, "I would give you one piece of advice. Be more careful than you were today. He knows some dangerous people, as you can see."

"I will be careful. Thank you. And I apologize again."

Darius nodded and plodded beside the paramedic toward the ambulance.

Jayne stood there as Buck approached, his lips pressed tight together.

Zip up, she told herself. This wasn't the time to vent her feelings.

"Are you all right, Jayne?" Buck said.

She nodded. "I will be."

"Bloody disaster. I just spoke to my Special Branch colleague. He tells me the Amazon van—"

"Had already visited the street twice," Jayne interrupted. "I know. Maybe it had. But I'm sure it's carrying false plates. I guess the number wasn't checked. And if you go and look, you'll see it's a left-hand-drive vehicle. It's probably been driven over by some Hezbollah fanatic from the Continent. The surveillance team presumably didn't pick that up, even after two visits?"

Buck shook his head.

She paused, then added, "It's a pity we had to use the real address."

The color had drained from Buck's face. He shook his head. "I know," he muttered. "Not my choice. There was no other option, unfortunately."

There's always another option.

She should have insisted on doing it differently. Insisted

on Buck either finding another surveillance team so they could use a fifth house elsewhere or on Vic feeding just four barium meals instead of five. She should have thought it through better, been more risk-averse, been more insistent. It now seemed unprofessional.

Should have, should have, should have . . .

"We should have done it differently," Jayne said. "But as I said to your officer, let's have the postmortem later."

However, that proved to be wishful thinking on Jayne's part.

She spent the following three hours with Buck and the head of the Metropolitan Police, Commissioner Sir Richard Blackthorn, ensconced in another MI5 safe house nearby as they thrashed out internal statements and also a brief public one that Blackthorn's head of communications could use with the media.

To Jayne's relief, given the highly sensitive ongoing investigation, there was a consensus that no material details should be disclosed. The entire episode would be hidden behind the smoke screen of a security incident with implications solely for the United Kingdom for the time being. There would be no public reference to Iran, Israel, the United States, MI5, or any other intelligence service.

Work across all services was continuing to identify the dead man who had pushed the explosive through the door, but the only documents found on him were a false French passport and matching driving license, both containing a false address. The Amazon van was registered in the same name in France but was carrying false British license plates that actually belonged to a genuine Amazon van that operated in south London. An array of other false license plates had been discovered in an underfloor compartment, together with handguns, a sniper rifle, IEDs, and fake signage for a number of European utility and retail brands in addition to Amazon.

The whole time, Jayne was itching to call Vic to find out who the barium meal had been fed to. But she dared not do so while on MI5 premises that were undoubtedly full of hidden microphones and cameras.

There were a few breaks in the discussions as Buck and Blackthorn made calls. During one of them, remembering Freema's reference, Jayne took out her phone and looked up Cyrus the Great and his Persian Empire. From 559 to 530 BC he ran a series of bloody campaigns to forge the largest empire yet seen, stretching more than 2,500 miles from modern western Turkey, across Iran and Afghanistan, to the Indus River in modern Pakistan in the east.

It crossed her mind that if Kourosh was indeed fueling Iran's nuclear weapons capability, he might have a different and significantly more deadly kind of domination as his objective.

During another break, Jayne made a brief and difficult call to Zahavi and Rafael, who struggled to comprehend how their operation had almost been torpedoed by a lethal cocktail of incompetence and misfortune. Once again, Jayne felt unable to give a full explanation from the MI5 safe house, which she knew would cause frustration.

As Jayne watched Buck and Blackthorn work the phones, she knew there was no doubt that more questions would follow. Indeed, Buck had mentioned he would need to schedule a call with Vic for later in the day to discuss the affair.

But finally, they let Jayne go in the back of an unmarked police car that dropped her at her apartment.

As Jayne climbed the stairs to her apartment, she mentally prepared herself to spend some time explaining to Zahavi and Rafael exactly what had occurred. She also needed to call Vic.

But even before she began, the two Mossad veterans

seemed to have an instinctive grasp of what had happened in Hounslow. They had seen it all before.

Years of covert meetings in dubious safe houses in some of the darkest corners of Europe, betrayals, treachery, double dealings, and operations that had gone right and wrong meant there was little left to their imagination.

Nevertheless, they both jumped in periodically with questions.

"This has screwed our operation," Rafael said, a cynically resigned note to his voice. "If this was some Hezbollah operative dispatched to stop us getting to Kourosh—which I'm guessing was the case—then, of course, word will get back to Kourosh. There's no doubt about it."

Zahavi folded his arms. "Not necessarily immediately, depending on what goes out in the media in the next day or so."

Jayne nodded. "I agree. MI5 is going to say little externally. So assuming it is Tehran behind this, it might take them a little while to piece everything together."

"But not too long," Rafael said.

"Agreed," Jayne said. "That means we have to now move doubly fast."

"There is one thing, though," Zahavi said. "You should now know the identity of the mole."

Jayne grimaced. "Yes—at the cost of two dead MI5 officers. Was it worth it?"

Silence.

"Anyway," Jayne said, "that's what I'm going to find out now. I'm going to call Vic."

She walked to her bedroom and shut the door behind her.

* * *

Sunday, April 24, 2016

London

"Jayne, I'm glad you're safe and the Navais are safe," Vic said. "I'm taking responsibility for what happened. It's not your fault. Don't blame yourself. I could say it's an occupational hazard of war—and make no mistake, we are in a war. But I should have done it differently, should have foreseen this."

Jayne, who had just described events at the Hounslow safe house to Vic, was sitting in a chair in the corner of her bedroom.

She uncharacteristically found herself welling up a little as she listened to his response.

Should have.

Those words again.

But she knew she couldn't simply blame Vic. After a few seconds, she forced herself to focus on the task in hand. "Yes, we're in a war. But we have to do better."

"I know. But it sounds like your quick actions saved the Navais."

"That's little consolation for the others." She paused. "All right, Vic. Now you can tell me. Who got the doctored meal?"

She heard Vic exhale hard.

"Come on, spit it out."

"Garfield Wattley."

Jayne let out a long breath. "Wattley?"

"Yes, unfortunately," Vic said. "It's not going to look good on me. I had already told Arthur I was going to promote him to Paris."

"Bloody hell. How long have you known him?"

"I've worked with him for more than twenty years. It's bizarre. What I can't work out is why he's doing it. He's always been so anti everything that Ayatollah Hashemi has stood for, so precisely what's driven him to betray us to Tehran is something I've been struggling to figure out."

Jayne snorted. "Money?"

"I guess so. You know what CIA staffers earn. It's decent but nothing great. His father was a businessman but I don't think particularly successful, so I doubt Wattley would have inherited a fortune."

Of course. It's always money, 99 percent of the time.

"So, out of interest, who else did you serve the meals up to?"

Jayne still had it in the back of her mind that Vic was suspicious of her since he hadn't shared his list of suspects earlier.

"I'm not telling you this, but I had Jodie Geary on the list, together with Miller, and—"

"Miller?" Jayne couldn't help herself. "Counterintelligence Miller?"

There was a two-second silence. "You heard me correctly. Miller, Garfield Wattley, Jodie Geary, someone at the Mossad, and someone at the White House."

"White House? You mean Charles?"

"Uh huh. I couldn't afford to make assumptions about this, Jayne. I didn't want to close off avenues prematurely. Charles has his fingers in an enormous number of pies. It's impossible to know who he talks to. I assumed he was clear, but stranger things have happened."

Jayne felt slightly stunned. Had Vic really thought that the president's bespectacled adviser might be leaking material to Iran or Hezbollah? He knew the man far better than she did, so she wasn't going to pass judgment. After all, it wasn't that long since the president's previous national security advisor, Francis Wade, had been caught leaking secrets to the Russians.

"Who at the Mossad?" Jayne asked.

There was another long silence. "Avi. But don't tell David or Rafael."

"Really, Vic? Avi's only just taken over that role in an acting capacity. I hope you were careful." Again, she could have almost guaranteed that Avi Shiloah wouldn't be leaking material, but then again, who knew anything for certain in this game.

"And me?" Jayne ventured. "I hope you never doubted me?"

"No. Although your name was mentioned, I have to be honest."

"By whom? That bastard Miller, I bet." Jayne could feel a well of anger building inside her.

Vic said nothing.

"Come on, it was Miller, wasn't it?"

"I was as angry as you are, but remember, he has a job to do," Vic said. "Whether we like it or not. And it's a tough job."

"Bloody unbelievable." Jayne seethed in silence for a few seconds.

"Sorry, Jayne."

"All right," she eventually said. "So now what do you do about Wattley?"

"I've quietly removed him from the circulation list for this operation. He'll still get a few documents so he doesn't get suspicious, but not sensitive ones. That's the first step. Next step is to talk to the FBI. My thinking is to bring Wattley to Langley to talk with me and Arthur about his proposed role in Paris. When he lands, Bonfield's boys will arrest the bastard, and we'll also get the feds' Jerusalem office to search the house he's been renting over there."

Vic paused. "I also need to discuss the name and location you sent me, Cyrus in Los Angeles. My team is trawling data-bases, but we'll need to get into the FAA's register to check pilots' and plane owners' names, and that's a nonstarter on a Sunday."

"That name came from Freema Navai," Jayne said. "I got it from her just before the guy with the IED turned up. I only went back to see her after getting a feeling she had something she was going to say the other day but never did."

"Good call. Gut instinct."

"Yes."

"Interesting. All arrows are pointing to the United States, it seems," Vic said.

"It does look that way."

"Just confirms we're right to get you back over here. You've done a superb job, getting all this information. But I think your task in the UK is complete. Look, you've had a tough past couple weeks. If you want to take a break, you can. Go back to Portland, see Joe. Do you want to hand this over? My team here can pick it up."

Jayne had to agree with him. She had run out of leads in Europe. It was time to change the focus.

But there was no way she was going to hand over anything.

Her voice hardened. "Vic, this Kourosh is likely the man who, with his girlfriend, killed my father. He's also likely the guy who's responsible for leaving Mark fighting for his life in Tel Aviv, and if it wasn't for him, a Mossad operative and two MI5 officers would now still be alive. So, no, I'm not giving this up until it's finished one way or another."

"I thought you'd say that. I'm just giving you the option."

"Thanks anyway. I'll get a flight to DC tonight."

"I'm thinking the Israelis should come with you," Vic said.

"I'll suggest it," Jayne said. She guessed it was another case of Vic getting someone else to do his work for him, especially if it was happening on US soil, where the CIA was not meant to be operating.

After they had finished the call, Jayne walked through to the living room and explained the situation to the two Mossad men.

"We'd best come," Zahavi said. "If this all goes downhill, Israel's going to be on the wrong end of it. Better if we're there, where at least we have some input into what's happening."

The three of them booked a flight to Washington, DC, leaving that evening.

Jayne then sent a short message to Joe, informing him of her travel plans.

PART FOUR

CHAPTER THIRTY-SIX

Sunday, April 24, 2016
   Van Nuys Airport, Los Angeles

The man code-named VALENCIA tapped his fingers lightly on the aircraft seat armrest. "What did the message say, exactly?"

"Let me find it." There had been no room for ambiguity in the encrypted message. Cyrus Saba scrolled down his phone screen and found it.

Strong evidence of Mossad/CIA team on your tail. We know of recent visits to Zürich bankers and your parents house in UK. Concern growing about compromise of supply chain. Strongly suggest precautions and an exit from US asap. Recommend you seek help from VALENCIA. Please advise.

Saba read it out to the man sitting opposite him, whose real name was Pierre Fekkai, whom he had last seen along with his twin brother, Henri, more than twenty years earlier in London. He still looked similar, like a mirror image of his sibling: about six feet two, strongly built, and largely bald apart from a gray semicircle of short hair.

"That neatly summarizes the problem," Saba said. "What I need to know is, can you give me the backup I need, here and in Mexico, for the next few days until I'm through this? I would like a safeguard in place."

Pierre folded his arms. "Yes, I can do that." He glanced around the cabin of the Bombardier Global 6000 aircraft, which was standing silently in a hangar at Van Nuys Airport. "Nasser must be worried, to have sent that message. He rarely gets in touch."

Saba had to agree. Indeed, he very rarely received any communications from Nasser Khan, head of Iran's Quds Force special operations group, unless there was a serious security issue. Until recently, the majority of his dealings with the regime in Iran had been through Jafar Farsad, his old friend from university in the UK who until his demise in Vienna had been deputy head of the Atomic Energy Organization. Indeed, it had been Farsad who had given him the nickname the Dark Shah while they were both still students, and it had stuck. He never told people why.

So this message, short and to the point, had sent a slight jolt through him when it arrived late the previous evening. He had agreed to the suggestion in it after Khan had mentioned in a follow-up message that Henri had already been involved in a partly unsuccessful Hezbollah operation against a Mossad and CIA unit in Zürich.

Saba guessed that the lead to his adoptive parents' address in Henley-on-Thames had somehow been extracted from the bankers in Zürich.

"Nasser mentioned Zürich. Have you spoken to your brother about what happened there?" Saba asked. "Something went badly wrong."

Pierre leaned forward. "Not in detail. It appears to have

been a rare failure by him. However, I did have a short conversation with him about a follow-up operation to Zürich that he was planning in London—possibly for today—to nullify this same threat you are referring to. Indeed, I encouraged him to implement his plan. It sounded well designed. I may speak to him later to get an update. Don't worry, we always use secure communications."

That sounded in line with Henri's character, Saba reflected. He knew his reputation for persistence in the face of obstacles.

"This may be a stupid question," Pierre asked, "but if you are worried, are you not in a position simply to run for cover, to go underground somewhere, until this is resolved?"

"I will be," Saba said, "but not for another three days, unfortunately. I have a crucial meeting at Toluca Airport, then I'll be heading farther south. But until then I need some backup, which is where you come in."

It was indeed unfortunate that Saba's paymaster could not get to Toluca before Wednesday, but there was no way around that.

Saba watched as Pierre cast an appraising glance around the cabin. Until Khan had suggested using Pierre's services, Saba hadn't even known that he now lived in the United States. He thought he still operated in Europe.

"Can you show me around the aircraft?" Pierre asked.

Saba rose from the white leather seat in which he had been sitting. "Come."

He led the way from what he termed the club lounge area of the cabin, which had four well-spaced seats facing each other, through the narrow galley, with its crystal glassware in elegant rosewood storage cabinets, to the bedroom suite.

They were the only two people on the hundred-foot-long twin-engine private jet. Nor was there anyone else in the vicinity of the hangar—he had made sure of that.

Saba knew he needed to tread carefully. He felt as though he was trying to keep several plates spinning in the air at once, given his different objectives.

The overriding one, as always, was to earn as many dollars as he could by whatever means available. At the back of his mind he felt he was entitled to wealth, given the overwhelmingly unfair hand he had been dealt at the start of his life. How many kids were forced to leave not just their natural parents but the land of their birth in the way he had been? And not just that—if circumstances had been different, he would have grown up rich beyond all imagination.

He felt robbed. He was entitled to compensation. If Iran could pay, as it had done for most of his career, then so be it.

But alongside that, Saba also felt a deep love for his home country, a longing to one day be a big part of its success, to help it return to its former glory—to make it a new Persian Empire. And the only way he could see that happening was by ensuring it became a nuclear power. The current leadership, the Supreme Leader Ali Hashemi and his inner circle, were far too soft. The nuclear agreement Hashemi had signed with the West was a joke in Saba's view, so anything he could do to ensure it failed would be a positive step forward.

He was confident that Tehran had no idea of the part he had played in engineering the attack on the offshore gas platform or the assassination of the Israeli ambassador, and he intended to keep it that way. They wouldn't be happy, given the likelihood of Israeli reprisals against Iran, which was inevitably being blamed. It didn't suit the Supreme Leader's timing, that was certain.

Saba was equally confident that he had left no paper trail that would enable Western intelligence to link him to those attacks either. In fact, through being obsessive about his own security and by keeping his profile very low, he had so far managed to stay completely off the radars of any intelligence organization for more than two decades.

So where had this threat come from?

Saba had had virtually no contact with his parents for the past couple of years and prior to that only infrequent and brief calls for a long time. They didn't know his current identity or what he did. They'd never understand, and he'd never trusted them enough to share that information. So even if intelligence organizations had latched onto his parents, he didn't think they would have much to reveal.

However, given that all their phone and email communications would inevitably be tightly monitored now, he couldn't call them and ask what they might have disclosed.

It seemed that either someone in his tight-knit circle was feeding secrets about him to Western intelligence, which seemed unlikely, or the Mossad and CIA had someone very smart on his tail who was somehow finding ways to dig out information.

Either way, his acute sense of self-preservation told him that his time in Los Angeles had run out. It was time to leave.

If he were caught, it would put at risk the wider black market nuclear weapons supply chain to Iran. That would be a financial disaster for him and for others.

Moreover, if he was going to be backed into a corner, he didn't intend allowing it to happen in the United States, where he was likely to find himself at a natural disadvantage in a tight situation given the firepower that law enforcement and security forces could draw on.

Mexico should be a little safer than LA, given the greater level of control he had built up over a number of corrupt officials during the preceding decade. He would fly to Toluca, near Mexico City, in a couple of days, collect the funds he needed to pay the drone guru Emad Madani, and then head farther south.

"Is this the aircraft you will use to fly to Toluca?" Pierre asked.

Saba nodded. "And after that meeting I will leave Mexico for Caracas."

The Venezuelan capital was something of a safe haven for those with dubious links to Iran, and Saba had a number of highly placed friends there with whom he could take refuge.

Saba watched as Pierre made his way around the cabin. He paused in front of the emergency exit on the starboard side of the plane.

"Always have a second escape route," Pierre said, when he noticed Saba's glance.

Pierre rattled through a series of questions about the nature of the meeting at Toluca and what the choreography would be at the airport.

"You've had similar meetings with these two men previously, I assume?" Pierre asked.

Saba nodded.

"What are your security protocols for that?"

Saba ran through the usual process.

"All right. That's a good basis. I suggest we adapt it a little. What weapons do you keep on the aircraft?"

Saba always kept a well-stocked armory on his plane, hidden in a large subfloor compartment in the bedroom suite. He listed the items stored there, consisting of several handguns, a Remington semiautomatic rifle, and an old AK-47 assault rifle, together with ammunition. There was also a box of hand grenades.

"We'll need to add a few items to that, just in case," Pierre said. "But I'm certain we can put a robust plan in place."

The two men then sat down at the four-seater dining table in the main cabin, which doubled as a conference table, and Pierre outlined his thoughts.

As they began sketching out a slightly revised plan, Saba

relaxed a little. Like his twin brother, this guy knew his business.

A few minutes later, Saba's phone vibrated in his pocket. He took it out and checked it.

It was a one-word message from Emad Madani, sent using an encrypted secure app, replying to his query about the Moshe Cohen funeral.

Confirmed.

CHAPTER THIRTY-SEVEN

Monday, April 25, 2016
Washington, DC

"I need help," Jayne said, trying her hardest to sound like a flirtatious damsel in distress. It was an act she always struggled to pull off convincingly, but it conjured a sympathetic grin from Joe, whose unshaven face was staring at her from her laptop screen.

"Is it the kind of help I could supply from Portland?" he asked. "Or does it require, let's say, a more physical approach?"

"The latter is the kind of help I'm most in need of right now, yes," she murmured, dropping her voice to the whisky-low level she knew he found most alluring.

It was true too. She did feel an urgent physical need to have Joe right there, right now.

She was lying on an immaculate, sprawling king-size bed on the third floor of her favorite hotel in DC: the elegant redbrick Georgetown Inn. It was located amid a quaint collection of cafés, restaurants, and fashion boutiques on Wisconsin Avenue NW, where a cab from Dulles International Airport had deposited her an hour earlier.

"It seems a waste of a good bed," she said, turning the laptop around so he could see it properly.

"I see exactly what you mean. Soon, soon," he said, leaving unspoken the reason why he couldn't be anywhere other than Portland this week. Jayne knew his son Peter's senior-year exams were due to start the next day.

"All right. Perhaps you can give me some other kind of assistance, then?"

"I will try."

Jayne switched to business mode and described how she had extracted possible false identities for Kourosh Navai from his adoptive parents.

"The alternative names are Cyrus or Koresh," she said. "I don't have a last name. And he's a pilot, possibly with his own plane, or a leased one. Vic's team is on the case, but they've come up with nothing so far. He warned it might be difficult to get what we need. It's irritating."

In fact, Jayne was feeling something more than irritation at what she perceived as a lack of urgency by Langley. Maybe she was getting impatient as she got older, but she had somehow expected the CIA to have tracked down both Kourosh and his aircraft by the time her flight from London touched down in DC.

Jayne shifted position on the bed and propped the laptop on her stomach. "I seem to recall a case where you tracked down a pilot and a plane via a contact at the FAA. Wasn't it a hunt for some war criminal several years ago?"

"Yes. The Axel Meindl case. Another old Nazi," Joe said. "The Federal Aviation Administration is your starting point. But I'm warning you, the FAA is a nightmare to deal with— Vic was correct about that. It's like winding the clock back fifty years. Might be a little easier to check for the pilot's name than to find any aircraft."

Jayne hesitated. "What do you mean?"

"The FAA has a basic pilot records database, so carriers can check any pilot's records before hiring them or not. It's likely there won't be too many with the names Cyrus, Kourosh, or Koresh. If your man is on there, we should be able to find him."

"Right. What about the plane?"

"Different story."

"Why?"

There was a prolonged sigh from Joe. "How long have you got? Look, registering planes with the FAA in the US and keeping their true owners' identities anonymous is an industry in itself. There are front companies that do it on behalf of all kinds of crooks for a living. It costs five bucks to register a plane and there's virtually no vetting. So it's a honeypot for drug dealers, corrupt businessmen, and officials from all over the world—and of course people with links to terrorism. It's a joke—about two-thirds of all business jets worldwide are registered in the US. It's so quick and easy, and anonymous."

"Foreigners register their planes here? I guess at five bucks it's a no-brainer."

"It's not just the cost," Joe said. "It's mainly that letter N at the beginning of the tail number that you get if the plane's registered in the States. An N-number on the tail gives an aircraft a stamp of legitimacy. Right or wrong, a US-registered plane is less likely to be searched by police or customs or impounded than one with a B registration for China or AP for Pakistan." He shrugged.

What Joe was saying made sense, Jayne thought. She'd heard similar tales about crooks registering their planes in the

US from others. "Doesn't the FAA keep a tight grip on that kind of thing?"

Joe shook his head slowly. "When I was searching for Axel the Nazi, I spent two months trying to locate the plane we knew he had. The address listed on the registration documents turned out to be a small strip mall in Texas. No checks had been made by the FAA. About one in six of the three hundred thousand or so planes in the FAA's system are registered using some sort of device designed to disguise the true owner. If your man is linked to the Iranian nuclear supply chain, you can bet your life savings he'll be among them."

"So what do we do?" Jayne could hear the slightly weary note in her own voice as she leaned back on the bed. "Are you still in contact with the guy at the FAA?"

A slow smile crossed Joe's face. "That's where my contact can help," he said. "When I was hunting for Axel, I spent a lot of time drinking with this guy who works in the bowels of the FAA's aircraft registration branch in Oklahoma City. In fact I bought him a lot of drinks."

"And?" Jayne asked. "Was it worth the bar tab?"

"I'll come to that. Let's call the guy Bill, though that's not his real name. He feels strongly about terrorist activity, and so he started keeping a private notebook with extra details about aircraft owners that aren't always in the official system. Since 9/11, there's been a few like him at the FAA, apparently. They didn't like the system, so they developed their own, thinking the additional information might come in handy one day. They like to ask questions as aircraft registration applications come in, and some of them are better at it than others. It was Bill who led me to Axel—eventually."

"You got this information for the cost of a few beers?" Jayne asked.

Joe gave a short, sarcastic laugh. "I wish. It wasn't just the bar tab—there was another grand in bribes. And a lot of gentle persuasion needed."

"So what's it going to cost us?" Jayne asked.

"Since then, he and the others have come to realize the information they collected has very significant value to certain parties. Now they monetize the hell out of what they've got. A grand might be just an opening shot."

"Is this guy Bill still working at the FAA?"

"As far as I know," Joe said. "It's been a while since I've had contact. He doesn't talk about any of this over the phone for obvious reasons."

"So you'd have to go to Oklahoma City?"

"Yes."

"That's a long trek." Jayne tried to work it out mentally. "You can't even get a direct flight from Portland, can you? It'll take hours."

"No. I'd probably have to get there and back in a single day too, because of Peter. But I'll see what I can do."

This was typical of Joe. He knew she was desperate to close the case, and he knew it was because of her father.

"Joe, you don't have to do that."

"Sure, but I'd like to try."

Jayne blew him a kiss. In fact, she had a deep-down desire right then to do much more than blow kisses at him, but that would have to wait.

"All right," she said. "Yes, please, then. If he has what we need in his notebook, I'll owe you hugely. You know the president is flying to Tel Aviv on Wednesday, and he's due at Moshe Cohen's funeral and memorial on Thursday. We need that information ASAP."

"You'll owe me? I'll hold you to that," Joe said. He winked at her. "I'm on it. But what about the need to oil the machinery?"

"If you absolutely can't avoid greasing the guy's palm, then

Vic can damn well pay. I'll work it into my expenses. It's the president who's demanding we get a result, so it shouldn't be a problem."Joe nodded. "Although it might be a problem if we don't get a result."

"You'd better make sure your guy delivers, then. And don't tell him the president wants the information; otherwise it'll cost you a fortune."

CHAPTER THIRTY-EIGHT

Tuesday, April 26, 2016
Oklahoma City

High-tech skylights and concealed fluorescent strip lights made the Federal Aviation Administration's airmen and aircraft registry building look brighter than would have been expected for a windowless structure. However, although the building was futuristic in design, Joe couldn't help thinking about the antiquated systems and work practices within it, which he knew wouldn't have improved since his previous visit.

He strode through the lobby across the elegant tiled cream floor, past the potted plants and the security guard, and through a set of double doors into the expansive public access room. There he stood beneath a large wall clock, which read three minutes until two o'clock.

Joe put his hand over his mouth to stifle a yawn. He had risen at four thirty that morning to start his seven-hour journey from Portland to Oklahoma City via Charlotte,

North Carolina. But he felt he was making a contribution to Jayne's investigation. Given the link to her father's death, which he knew had been nagging away at her for years, as well as the Iranian nuclear elements, he felt it was the least he could do.

He glanced around. The public access room, white walled, open plan, and bland, contained rows of computer workstations—almost fifty, by Joe's quick calculation.

There were three ancient terminals at the rear of the room that were designed for public use and which looked seldom used. Joe knew they all ran off a mainframe computer that was long past its sell-by date.

The rest were more modern terminals, some with two monitors, and were occupied by mainly middle-aged men and women, mostly casually dressed and equipped with flasks of coffee, packed lunches, and newspapers, novels, and magazines that were spread on the desks next to them. There was a gentle but persistent hum of conversation and the tapping of fingers on keyboards.

These people, Joe knew from previous visits, worked for the glut of third-party aircraft title and law firms whose clients employed them to navigate the labyrinthine FAA system on their behalf, to locate information about aircraft registrations and owners, and to carry out aircraft registrations for them.

Some in the room were carrying out the function he had described to Jayne the previous day: the business of creating anonymous trusts through which aircraft could be registered without disclosing the actual names of the true owners. The fee of five bucks to register an aircraft at the cashier's window in the corner applied no matter how valuable the plane.

These third-party organizations had paid to reserve the terminals for their long-term use, and users had marked out their territories by sticking family photos and other personal items to the monitors and leaving coffee mugs and other belongings on the desks.

It reminded Joe of a cottage industry—which it was.

The FAA had no real-time online capability to offer those who needed to know the fine details of plane ownership with up-to-the-minute data, as lawyers and bankers always did in order to complete multi-million dollar aircraft sale and purchase transactions. Instead they were required to visit the FAA's offices in Oklahoma City in person. Or, alternatively they could employ the services of those go-betweens who occupied the terminals in front of Joe.

He knew from previous investigations that the FAA often failed to ensure registrations were completed properly. But the thing that was bothering him most was the looming deadline given the president's imminent departure for Tel Aviv. In his experience, the FAA's cogs turned extremely slowly, even if the information was there to find.

He checked his watch and walked toward the cashier's window and waited, as instructed. Two o'clock was the time arranged.

The FAA's headquarters was known as the Mike Monroney Aeronautical Center. It extended across a sprawling campus of low-rise buildings and parking lots next to Will Rogers World Airport, the main airport serving Oklahoma City a few miles to the northeast. The civil aviation registry building was nestled in the center of the complex next to a gym.

Joe tugged anxiously at a nick at the top of his right ear, the legacy of a sniper's bullet in Afghanistan in the late 1980s when he was working for the CIA.

A couple of minutes later, a door next to the cashier opened and a stocky man with a navy jacket buttoned over his paunch and a mop of unruly gray hair appeared. He sauntered up to Joe, waddling rather than walking.

Jerry Swatton shook hands. "Another Nazi hunt?"

Joe gave a thin smile. "Not quite."

Swatton glanced around him. "You can tell me in the office."

He beckoned Joe to follow and led the way back through the door from which he had emerged. They walked along a corridor and into a small office piled high with a clutter of documents, files, and boxes. The only clear space was around the computer terminal. A typical civil servant's office. It hadn't changed since Joe's previous visit.

Swatton sat in the black swivel chair behind his terminal and indicated to a plywood seat in front of it. "Sit down."

Joe did as requested.

An ID badge pinned to the breast pocket of Swatton's jacket stated his title: Acting Deputy Director, Office of Foundational Business.

"Been promoted?" Joe asked. He had been a manager last time.

"Acting, so far. But yes. Big promotion, actually. More stress, of course. We need to modernize this place."

"I'd agree with that."

Swatton sighed. "What can I do for you?" he asked, glancing at Joe from beneath a spiky set of eyebrows. "Not a Nazi, so who this time?"

Joe glanced around him, looked up at the ceiling, and scrutinized the light fittings.

"You don't need to worry," Swatton said. "There are no cameras or mikes in here."

"Thought not. Just looking. No, not a Nazi, but it's someone who may have similar objectives," Joe said.

"Hamas?"

"No. Close."

"Hezbollah?"

Joe inclined his head by an inch or two. "Are you still keeping that special notebook of yours?"

"I've modernized. My notebook is now a spreadsheet," Swatton said, tapping a USB memory stick that was inserted in one of the sockets in the computer box on his desk. "So what are you looking for?"

"There's three things I need," Joe said. "The first is to find details of a pilot for whom I only have a first name."

"That should be easy enough," Swatton said, his voice dripping with sarcasm. "We only have 650,000 on the airman registry."

"The names I need to check are Kourosh, Koresh, and Cyrus. Not very common," Joe said.

"All good Persian names. I can see where you're coming from." He paused. "Before I start, my fee."

"I'll pay you the same as last time."

Swatton shook his head. "That was years ago. Scrutiny is greater, the risks are higher. I charge $2,500 now."

Joe doubted the scrutiny was greater, knowing the FAA. "I'll pay $1,500. No more."

Swatton didn't argue. He turned on his computer terminal and entered a username and password. He then tapped away for a minute or two and finally typed the name *Kourosh* into a search box.

"The airman registry is all on the mainframe," Swatton said. "Don't need my spreadsheet for this. Normally you need to provide a last name, and the first name is optional. But I have a way around that." He looked up at Joe, his mouth turned up slightly at the corners.

Joe moved his chair so he could see the screen.

"Twelve years old, this system," Swatton said. "Uses some computer language I'd never even heard of before. Natural, or something, it's called. Give it a minute or five."

Joe glanced at his watch. He had just over an hour before

he needed to be back at the airport to catch his flight back to Portland. That meant forty-five minutes to extract what he needed from Swatton.

The screen gradually loaded with data.

"There's nobody named Kourosh on the system," Swatton said. "I'll try Koresh."

He repeated the process. Another long wait.

"Nope. Nothing. Let's try Cyrus . . . Cyrus the Great."

"Nothing great about the one I'm chasing," Joe said.

"There are six Cyruses," Swatton said a minute later, pointing at the screen. "Take your pick."

Joe looked. None of the last names meant anything. "Go through them all."

There was minimal information stored for all six. Just a name, date of their first medical exam and current medical status, the pilot's certificates they held, and dates of issue. All were qualified commercial pilots for single-engine aircraft, and two of them had certificates for multiengine planes.

In the data section for four of the six, there was a bland statement: "Airman opted out of releasing address."

That triggered a wry smile from Joe. "We'll focus on those four to start with," he said.

The two qualified to fly multiengine aircraft were among those who hadn't supplied an address. On the assumption that the Cyrus they were targeting was flying internationally and was therefore qualified for multiengine planes, the men left on the list were Cyrus Saba and Cyrus Handing.

"What can we tell from the medical information?" Joe asked.

Swatton explained that pilots on commercial scheduled passenger planes were required to hold a first-class medical certificate, renewed every six months for those aged over forty, while second class was required for other commercial pilots. Third class was for private and recreational pilots.

He pointed to the monitor screen. "Handing has a first-class certificate, Saba's is third-class." He spread his hands wide. "Unless your man is flying scheduled airlines, he wouldn't have a first-class med."

Joe nodded slowly. "Give me the dates their certificates were issued."

Saba's commercial pilot's certificate was dated July 2001 and Handing's December 1992.

"Cyrus Saba has to be our man," Joe said. He remembered that Jayne had told him Kourosh Navai had only moved to the United States sometime after the Israeli embassy bomb attack of 1994. A shot of adrenaline ran through him, as it usually did when he made a breakthrough of this kind in his investigations.

"The second thing I need is to know whether Saba owns a plane," Joe said.

That drew an intake of breath from Swatton. "That might be trickier."

Joe glanced at his watch. Half an hour to go.

"Let's get moving, then," Joe said. "Your spreadsheet?"

"I'll try the main database first. You never know. Are you sure your guy has a plane?"

"We're fairly certain."

Swatton turned back to his terminal and logged into a different database, this time the FAA registry. Joe watched as he typed "Cyrus Saba" into the search box.

He scanned down the results. There was a list of seventeen aircraft owners with *Saba* included in their names or titles. But none of them were Cyrus Saba.

"I'll try my special spreadsheet," Swatton said. "I exported the data from the main system and added my own additional columns."

He toggled over to the Excel sheet that was stored on his USB drive and again typed *Cyrus Saba* into the search box.

The cursor immediately jumped to an entry far down the sheet.

Swatton hunched forward, scrutinizing the monitor screen.

"Here we go," he said. "A Bombardier Global 6000 aircraft. Decent-sized private twin-engine business jet. It'll cross the Atlantic no problem. It's been registered by a trust company. I thought that might be the case."

Swatton stabbed at the screen with a fat, hairy, index finger and reeled off a five-digit number prefixed by N, which Joe tapped into his phone.

"This is a classic disclosure-avoidance case," Swatton said. "I do remember this one. Registered to Plane and Simple. I know the outfit very well. They're in Oklahoma City, actually, based in a three-bedroom family house. The guy has about two hundred and fifty planes registered to his address— including this one."

"But Saba is the one who actually owns it?" Joe asked, tapping in the added details.

"Correct. Plane and Simple just registered it on his behalf."

"How do you know?"

"Let's say I'm good at reading documents upside down and I'm good at asking oblique questions in a way that doesn't arouse suspicion. It also helps to have a photographic memory. I read, remember, and then insert the information into my spreadsheet. I deal with a lot of registrations and a lot of trust companies and their lawyers. I see a lot of useful things in documents that have value." He tapped the side of his temple in a knowing manner.

"And that's how criminals keep their aircraft below the radar, so to speak, no pun intended?"

"Indeed. You'd be amazed at who has planes registered here through these trust companies. Cocaine traffickers, corrupt South American government officials and politicians. You name it."

"But you're not doing anything about it?"

"That's above my pay grade, Joe. I've told them the system stinks and needs changing. They know that and say they're working on plans. It'll probably take a big newspaper front-page exposé and questions asked in the House and the Senate before things speed up."

"But you're still happy to take money off me and others who want the information?"

Swatton shrugged and leaned back in his chair. "It serves all parties well, for the time being. You, me, my wife's retirement plans." He gave a short laugh and scrolled a little farther down his spreadsheet.

"Ah, I have an address here for Saba," Swatton said. "I remember getting that—it was on one of his attorney's letters. In the San Fernando Valley, near LA. You'd never normally get that on the FAA database, but if I can get one, I take it."

He read out the street address, which Joe wrote down. That was in line with what Jayne had said about Kourosh Navai's adoptive father reporting him as being in Los Angeles. Now he was making headway.

"You said there was a third piece of information you needed," Swatton said.

"Yes. I need to know precisely where this Bombardier Global 6000 is right now." Joe glanced at his watch. He had about ten minutes.

"Anyone can track a plane," Swatton said. "There's any number of apps you can put on your phone to do that. The difficulty is if the owner makes a blocking request to us, the FAA. Then it goes on the ASDI list and the apps can't track it."

"I know that. And I'm assuming Saba has had his plane blocked. I'd like you to bypass that, if you can."

Joe knew that plane owners could apply to the FAA to have their tail numbers removed from the Aircraft Situation Display to Industry list, which meant their aircraft could not be followed by the public or listed on tracking apps or websites.

Swatton whistled through his teeth. "You can add another five hundred bucks to the fee, then. I'm really not supposed to be doing this."

"Go ahead. Quick as you can. I need to be out of here in a few minutes."

Swatton went through two log-on processes and arrived at a screen that had a search box, into which he typed the tail number for Cyrus Saba's Bombardier.

A couple of seconds later a grid appeared on screen. Swatton again hunched forward, studying the information.

"It's at TLC. That's Toluca International Airport. The plane flew there this morning from Van Nuys Airport in LA."

"It's in Mexico right now?"

"Yup."

"Shit," Joe said.

"Problem?"

"It looks like the bird has flown the nest already."

Joe took an envelope from his inside jacket pocket and removed a sheaf of $50 bills from it. He counted out $2,000 and pushed them across the desk to Swatton. "That's for services provided."

Swatton nodded. "Thanks."

"However, I may need more information at short notice. If that bird who's flown the nest moves again, I'll need to know where it's migrated to. What can I do to persuade you to keep your phone switched on at all times?"

Swatton shrugged. "Make it another thousand."

Joe was in no position to argue. He counted out another thousand dollars and handed it over.

Joe stood. "Nice work if you can get it. Thank you. I need to go now. And remember—phone on."

* * *

Tuesday, April 26, 2016
   Washington, DC

"Are you sure you want to make this trip, Mr. President?" Arthur Veltman asked, as he stroked his chin and surveyed President Ferguson from his seat at the conference table in the White House Situation Room. "It's your call, but our assessment is that the level of risk remains just as high now as when Cohen and Paul visited the Samar platform three weeks ago."

Jayne immediately could see that the president was feeling somewhat irked by the question. Ferguson's forehead was creased, and there was a faint tinge of red at the bottom of his cheeks.

"Yes, I am sure," the president said. He tapped his fingers on the highly polished table, the presidential seal mounted on a plinth on the wall behind his head. "Cohen was a good friend to me and to the United States. He did a huge amount of good work for Israeli-US relations, and he had my back. Paul's still in the hospital there, so it's the least I can do to turn up. I'm not bowing down in the face of terrorists."

He paused. "I'm certain the Israelis wouldn't be inviting me if they didn't have this covered properly from a security point of view, especially now, after what happened."

Nobody said a word in response. The president looked at

Veltman, who was sitting nearest to him. "How close are you to finding out who carried out that attack?"

Jayne realized as he spoke that at that moment, more than 1,100 miles to the west, Joe was in a critical meeting to try and get that information from his contact in Oklahoma City.

Veltman gave Ferguson a brief summary of the work that Jayne had done with the Mossad team. "We're getting close, sir. We think we know who probably orchestrated it. We're hoping to get the full false ID the guy's using today, and the aircraft he's using."

The president nodded. "Just keep going, flank speed if possible."

Ferguson was known for using submarine terminology, stemming from his time spent on submarines during the Cold War, and Jayne knew that *flank speed*—an exclusively US Navy term—meant the equivalent of flooring the gas pedal.

She could see the president's aide, Charles Deacon, suppressing a smile, despite the tension in the room. She had been somewhat relieved to discover that Deacon wasn't the mole leaking information to Tehran. It really would have been quite a betrayal, if so.

As if reading her mind, Ferguson turned to Veltman. "What is the latest situation with that traitor in your Tel Aviv station?"

"Wattley?" Veltman said. "We're recalling him here for meetings, sir. When he lands, the FBI will arrest and charge him. So far we've just cut him out of some communications, but not all, so he doesn't get suspicious and run."

Ferguson nodded. He had called Veltman and Vic to the Situation Room for a briefing prior to his flight to Tel Aviv, which was due to depart that evening. Veltman had asked Jayne to attend too in order not to be caught out if the president had any of his famously detailed questions about the operation to track down Kourosh Navai in Europe and the UK.

Ferguson caught Jayne's eye. "I hear that you have been instrumental in the pursuit of this Navai?"

Jayne pressed her palms together. "I've been fully occupied, yes, you could say that. With the assistance of our cousins from Tel Aviv, as well as Vic's team, I should add. But we haven't got to him yet, sir, so don't jump the gun."

"Don't be too modest, Jayne," Ferguson said. "You Brits are all the same."

"Jayne's discovered it's likely this guy was responsible for murdering her father in London, sir," Vic said. "During the bombing of the Israeli embassy in London, 1994."

Ferguson looked slightly stunned. "I'm very sorry to hear that. I remember that incident. And in that case, you've got full license from me to do whatever's needed to reel him in. Don't quote me on that, though."

That was typical of politicians, Jayne thought. Trying to appear generous, but always covering their own ass first. However, it was extremely useful to have Ferguson's private endorsement in case things got messy.

"Thank you, sir," she said. "That's very helpful to know."

Veltman leaned forward. "Sir, just one question, if I may. It would be useful to hear your latest thinking on the Iran nuclear deal and what you're planning to say to Prime Minister Katz."

The president eyeballed him. "Nothing's changed, Arthur. That deal is going to play a big part in preserving Middle East peace. We just need the atomic energy people in Vienna to properly monitor what those damned Iranians are doing."

"That is the challenge, sir. Does the criticism you've been getting concern you?" Veltman asked.

It's a good question.

"No. I know McAllister and his acolytes on Capitol Hill

and his business cronies are arguing the opposite, but they can go to hell. I'm not going back to sanctions, which the Iranians would take as a green light to go ahead even faster with their nuclear weapons underground. It'll encourage the black marketeers."

Ferguson glanced at the clock on the wall and stood. "I need to go. I've got things to do before leaving for Tel Aviv."

He headed toward the door, followed by Deacon. Just before he reached it, he swiveled and fixed a stare on Veltman, Vic, and Jayne in turn.

"Thanks for the briefing," Ferguson said. "Wish me luck. And whatever you do, don't screw this up. I'd prefer that Navai is brought back here for trial, but frankly I don't care if another solution is necessary. Anything's better than him escaping and continuing what he's been doing."

The president turned and walked out.

Twenty minutes later, having retrieved their phones from the security locker at the Situation Room reception desk, Jayne, Vic, and Veltman were climbing into a CIA car for the short journey back to Langley.

Jayne turned her device back on to find two messages from Joe. Both said the same thing.

Urgent. Call me.

CHAPTER THIRTY-NINE

Wednesday, April 27, 2016
Toluca International Airport, Mexico

The towering mountains to the east and west of Toluca International Airport were covered with low-hanging cloud as the unmarked Gulfstream V jet touched down on Runway 15 and rolled toward the end of the long stretch of asphalt.

Jayne had tried to sleep during the five-hour flight from Camp Peary, the US military base that was 110 miles south of Langley and home of the covert CIA training base known as the Farm. But she had managed no more than the occasional few minutes. On each occasion, she had been woken with a start by the same shallow dream, in which she was holding her father's hand in London as a bomb went off, catapulting both of them backward into a brick wall.

She looked around the compact cabin. The twin-engine Gulfstream contained only fourteen seats, and although it wasn't exactly configured to the specifications of the billion-aire businessmen who normally owned this kind of jet, it was definitely more business class than economy. The seats were wide, made of gray leather, and flattened into reasonably comfortable beds. There was a large television, high-speed Wi-Fi, and sleeping quarters at the rear with two divan beds.

Next to Jayne was Neal Scales, Vic's number two at the Directorate of Operations, who had not wasted the opportunity to get his hands dirty on an operation that took him out of Langley for a change.

He let slip that the aircraft had previously been used for rendition flights—the controversial seizure, or abduction, of terrorism suspects for prosecution and questioning.

"This could be another rendition, then," Jayne said. Because that was exactly what they were planning: kidnapping a terrorist suspect and executing a cross-border transfer to deliver him to the FBI in Washington.

Across the aisle, the two Israelis, Zahavi and Rafael, sat in quiet conversation, as they had done for much of the journey. The pair were defying convention by hitching a lift on a CIA jet from a high-security air base rather than making their own way, thanks only to Vic's insistence.

Behind them were two special agents from the FBI's Special Weapons and Tactics operations unit who had been attached to the team at short notice and were fluent in Spanish. Federico Gonzalez, a barrel-chested six-footer with a bone-crushing handshake, was a skilled sniper who had brought his heavy-duty Barrett M107 rifle. His colleague Denis Cotton, by contrast a compact but wiry figure, was an explosives expert. Their instructions were to bring back Kourosh Navai to the United States for questioning, not to kill him.

In fact, Vic and Neal had moved with great speed once the information had been received from Joe about the false identity that Kourosh Navai was almost certainly using: Cyrus Saba.

The Langley team had worked through the night to prepare for the operation, devising plans that could be used and adapted depending on circumstances. They had cross-checked the address for Saba in Los Angeles that had been provided by Joe's FAA contact. Traces run by the analysis directorate revealed that Saba owned an industrial oil and gas pumps and gauges manufacturing business with operations near Van Nuys and Toluca airports.

It occurred to Jayne that such a business would not only provide excellent cover for Saba to travel between the two locations but also form an instant explanation for trips to various shady parts of the Middle East.

Now they had to hope that the Bombardier aircraft with the tail number linked to Saba was still at Toluca.

All the operatives, including Jayne and Neal, were wearing dark blue coveralls, yellow reflective vests, and ID badges that were branded with the insignia and name of AXOS Services, one of several fixed-base operators, as they were called, at Toluca airport. The FBOs provided ground handling, hangar parking space, hospitality, and other services to aircraft owners.

The AXOS identities, all under assumed names, were to be their cover and should allow them to move around the complex. However, Jayne knew the false photo ID card on a ribbon around her neck wouldn't stand up to much close scrutiny and her knowledge of ground-handling processes even less so.

The CIA Gulfstream, having braked to a crawl, turned right at the southeastern end of the main and only runway and began to taxi toward the terminal. Jayne peered out the cabin window, looking for the Bombardier among the rows of aprons, hangars, and ancillary buildings that lined most of the western side of the airport. She checked each of the landmarks against a detailed paper map of the airport that Langley had provided.

There were a large number of aircraft parked on the various aprons near the hangars, but the Bombardier wasn't among them.

Once the CIA aircraft had left US airspace, Neal had left his seat and returned with four Beretta M9 pistols, all with silencers and spare magazines from a weapons locker at the rear of the cabin. He handed one set to Jayne, which she now had in her coveralls pocket, kept a set for himself, and gave the others to Rafael and Zahavi.

During the briefings prior to takeoff at Camp Peary, Neal had dismissed Jayne's concerns that the weapons would cause an issue with Mexican customs and immigration.

Now she raised the issue again.

"We won't get searched," Neal said. "In fact there'll be no customs or immigration process. The airport manager is one of us."

"He's on the payroll?" Jayne asked.

Neal nodded and ran a hand through his mop of deliberately unkempt blond hair. "He is, although he's not exactly happy about us running an operation at his airport. We won't be speaking to him directly this trip, unless things go badly wrong, though I will be communicating with him." He held up his cell phone.

"How was he recruited?" Jayne asked.

"Drugs. A huge amount of cocaine was coming into the US from here. He's helping us identify the supply routes, and we're giving him quite a lot of help in return—don't ask."

Sure enough, the captain of the Gulfstream turned off the main taxiway before they reached the customs and immigration building and headed down one of several minor taxiways, labeled with a large number seven. The jet continued toward two corrugated steel hangars at the end of taxiway seven, next to the perimeter fence, that were leased by the airport to AXOS Services.

The captain nudged the Gulfstream inside the hangar on the right side of the taxiway.

As soon as the jet had come to a complete standstill, all members of the team were on their feet and moving toward the integrated airstairs at the front of the plane. As the stairs descended to the hangar floor with a hydraulic whine, Jayne thought she could almost smell the adrenaline wafting off each of them. It gave her pause; she preferred everyone to be calm and clearheaded.

Despite the cavernous space inside, which Jayne guessed could hold perhaps six aircraft, the CIA jet was the only one there. Although it was almost one hundred feet long, the aircraft was dwarfed by the structure around it.

Neal saw her scanning the hangar space and read her thoughts. "Don't worry, we won't have company. We've procured the entire hangar, including the office and lounge building."

He pointed toward a two-story internal building in one corner of the hangar that housed offices, a luxury lounge, a bar and restaurant, and sleeping accommodation for aircrew members.

Despite the overcast conditions and the 8,400-foot altitude, the temperature already felt warm.

Parked near the hangar wall were three vehicles: an aviation refueling truck, a white Toyota 4x4, and a low-slung aircraft towing tractor that looked like a flat white box on wheels.

Jayne eyed the vehicles, which Neal had mentioned in the briefing prior to departure and which had been arranged by the airport manager.

Neal's phone beeped and he took it from his pocket and read the incoming message.

"Right," Neal said. "According to the airport manager, the Bombardier we're looking for is in a hangar off taxiway five. That's two taxiways farther down from where we are now toward the customs building."

"But is Saba on the plane? Or is he off-site somewhere, at his business, or whatever accommodation he's got here?" Jayne asked.

"On the jet, apparently, the last time they saw him, which was half an hour ago. He's got one security guard posted next to the plane steps."

It would certainly make things a lot easier if they were able to tackle Navai within the airport, Jayne thought.

"Any other aircraft or people in the hangar?" she asked. Her concern was that there might be an audience who could witness the operation they were planning.

"Three other planes. All private. The manager knows little about them or the people on them. There are people in the lounge and office building there, he says. It's a similar setup to our hangar. There are another three jets in the hangar opposite it too."

"We need the tail numbers so we can get Joe's FAA contact to find out who they belong to, then, just in case."

Neal nodded. His phone beeped again, and he reached for it inside his pocket, then studied the screen.

"Looks like we don't have much time to figure this out," Neal said. "Navai, or Saba, if we're calling him that, has apparently just filed a flight plan to leave here in an hour."

"Back to LA?"

"No. To Caracas."

"*Venezuela*? Shit. Looks like he's running."

Neal pursed his lips. "He could be. We'd best get moving."

CHAPTER FORTY

Wednesday, April 27, 2016
  Toluca International Airport, Mexico

The white Toyota 4x4 trundled at a steady twenty-five kilometers per hour along the main taxiway and then turned left onto the side taxiway number seven. Jayne, at the wheel, steered toward the pair of enormous hangars three hundred meters away at the far end of the taxiway, next to the airport's perimeter fence.

Neal, sitting next to her, spoke into his cell phone, on which he had a secure connection to the FBI pair, Federico and Denis, who had five minutes earlier driven the aircraft towing tractor to the hangar to the right of the taxiway. Jayne could see it parked outside the main doors.

"What's the scene inside the hangar?" Neal asked. He flicked on the speaker so Jayne could hear.

"All quiet," came Federico's voice. "One guard at the bottom of the aircraft stairs."

"Okay, we'll drive into the hangar, then proceed as arranged."

The core plan, devised at Langley and refined on the journey to Toluca, was for Federico and Denis to provide cover for Jayne and Neal, who would make the initial approach to Kourosh's aircraft. Coming two minutes behind them in the fuel truck would be Zahavi and Rafael, who would also park outside the hangar and be ready to act as required.

The two Israelis were also responsible for gathering the tail numbers of the other aircraft in the hangar, plus those in the hangar on the opposite side, and feeding them back to Joe for cross-checking with the FAA. It was essential for security purposes to know who else was in the vicinity.

A minute later, Jayne drove through the hangar doors and pulled to a halt on the concrete surface on the right side of the building, near the entrance to the lounge and restaurant quarters.

Twenty meters away stood the white Bombardier Global 6000 aircraft with its telltale tail number that belonged to Cyrus Saba. There were several orange cones placed in a ring around the aircraft, forming a makeshift no-go area, and sure enough, a uniformed security guard sat on a chair at the bottom of the aircraft's stairs, which were lowered. Jayne could see a light on inside the cabin.

"Let's go," she said.

They had all agreed on the need to move decisively and confidently to minimize suspicion from any onlookers, including those who were doubtless watching via the security cameras around the hangar. Jayne could see red LEDs winking on the front of all the cameras.

Neal and Jayne climbed out of the Toyota and walked up to the security guard, who stood and blocked the way to the stairs.

Jayne held up her security ID badge, smiled at the guard, and said in fluent Spanish, "Hello, sir, we need to speak to Mr. Saba or his pilot about the departure flight plan they have filed. There are a couple of additional questions we have."

The guard still didn't move. "They are not seeing anyone right now. Very busy," he said.

At least that tacitly confirmed Saba's current identity and the fact he owned the aircraft, Jayne thought to herself.

"Yes, but they want to leave in forty-five minutes," Jayne said. "Unless we resolve these outstanding points, they won't be able to go."

The guard shook his head. "I have my instructions."

"I do not think Mr. Saba will be happy if he knows you have unnecessarily delayed his departure," Neal said, also in Spanish. "If you value your job, I would let us speak to him. It will take two minutes, maximum. Otherwise he is likely to be extremely angry."

The guard looked doubtful and blinked a couple of times. "Hmm. All right, I will take you in. You will need to be quick. You can just speak to the captain. He's in the cockpit."

Jayne nodded. "Thank you. Is Mr. Saba not there?"

"I am not permitted to say anything about Mr. Saba's whereabouts."

Jayne glanced at Neal, who gave a slight nod. Even if Saba wasn't in the aircraft, they needed to get inside and obtain whatever information they could.

"Okay, then. Let's go," Jayne said.

The guard began to climb the eight steps to the aircraft door.

As he did so, from outside the hangar came the low vibrating growl of the refueling tanker's diesel engine. The vehicle, driven by Rafael, came into view and pulled to a halt on the apron to the left of the hangar doors.

The guard ignored the tanker, presumably because it was

just one of many around the airport. He continued through the cabin door, turned right, and stood inside the main cabin waiting until Jayne and Neal had joined him. Saba wasn't there.

"Wait here. I'll fetch the captain," the guard said. He walked toward the cockpit.

Jayne glanced around the front area of the main cabin, which had been set up as an office with two monitors and a printer on a desk. However, there were no PCs or laptops in sight. Farther back there was a dining table for four and a television, and beyond that a galley.

She caught Neal's eye. "You hold the guard and pilots. I'll have a look around, see if I can spot a computer."

Neal nodded. He slipped his Beretta out of his overalls pocket, flicked off the safety, quietly pulled back the slide to chamber a round, and held the gun in his pocket so it wasn't visible. Jayne did likewise.

Almost immediately, the security guard reappeared, followed by the pilot, an older man in uniform and a peaked cap.

"You have an issue with our flight plan?" the pilot asked, an irritated note in his voice. "There's no problem with it. I checked it myself."

Neal pulled out his Beretta and pointed it at the captain, whose eyes widened as he reflexively raised his hands in the air. Jayne also pulled out her gun, covering the guard, who also raised his hands.

"What is this . . . what the hell are you doing?" the captain said. "Who are you?"

"Both of you, lie facedown on the floor," Neal said. "Then put your hands together behind your backs. Now! I would suggest you don't try anything stupid."

After pausing for a second, both men did as they were instructed. Once they were on the floor, Neal removed some long plastic cable ties from his pocket, lashed both men's hands behind their backs, and tied their ankles together.

"We need some information," Jayne said. "Where is Cyrus Saba?"

Neither man said a word.

"Come on, where is he? Talk—otherwise I'll start by putting a round through your ankles. After that it'll be your knees and elbows."

Silence.

Jayne picked up a dirty coffee cup from the desk, tossed it to the floor between the two men, and took aim with her Beretta.

Thwack.

The shot shattered the ceramic cup, sending pieces and splinters flying across the cabin floor.

"Okay, okay, cool it," the guard said, his voice now sounding panicky. "He's gone to the other hangar."

"What other hangar?" Jayne asked. "There's dozens of them."

"The one opposite this one, across the taxiway."

"Is he on a plane?"

"I don't know," the guard wailed.

"Who is he meeting?" Jayne asked.

"I don't know."

Thwack. Jayne fired another round into the largest remaining piece of coffee mug, which sent more fragments flying.

The captain turned his head. "I think he's meeting someone on a Gulfstream G600," he said, his voice high-pitched and strained. "There's only one there. I don't know who he's meeting—that's the truth. You can shoot me dead. It won't make any difference."

"Fine. Now tell me, where is the laptop that's used with those monitors?"

"I don't know," the captain said. "Umm . . . maybe in the rear of the plane. The sleeping quarters."

"Where in the sleeping quarters?" Jayne demanded.

The captain swore. "I really don't know. Maybe in a cupboard."

Jayne turned toward Neal. "I'll go check."

She walked through the galley, past another lounge area, and into a section at the back that had cupboards and a divan bed on either side and a suitcase on the floor.

First she tried the cupboards, which contained clothing, shoes, phone chargers, and a toilet bag. There only clothing inside the suitcase.

She looked around. There was a long sliding drawer beneath each bed. She tried the one on the right first, which contained only a duvet and two pillows. She pulled them to one side and checked underneath, but there was nothing there.

The drawer on the left also had a duvet and pillows but nothing else.

Jayne swore. There seemed to be no other obvious hiding places. She was about to walk back through to the main cabin when she noticed the mattress on the right side bed was slightly raised at the head end.

She lifted the mattress. Beneath it was a pillowcase, which she pulled out to discover that it contained a slim black leather laptop case and a small cloth bag. She removed the case and unzipped it. Inside was an Apple laptop computer.

"Bingo," she said out loud.

She reached into the cloth bag and found a phone, a battery, and a SIM card.

"Burner," she murmured to herself.

She shoved the phone, battery, and SIM into her jacket pocket and walked to the front of the plane to find that Neal had gagged both men using rags and a reel of duct tape.

"Got a laptop," she said, holding up the case. "Found a burner phone too. Nothing else there. We can go."

The two of them walked out of the cabin and descended the aircraft stairs at a relaxed pace, not wanting to attract unnecessary attention.

Jayne walked to the Toyota and placed the laptop beneath the driver's seat, then locked the doors and pocketed the key. It was better to leave it there safely until they had successfully tracked down Kourosh, she figured.

They then continued out of the hangar to the refueling tanker, where Rafael and Zahavi were waiting, cab window down.

From the hangar opposite, about eighty meters away, there came the continuous whine of jet engines.

Jayne inclined her head toward the hangar. "He's over there in a Gulfstream G600," Jayne said to the two Israelis. "Did you get the tail numbers of the jets in there?"

"Yes, got the Gulfstream," Zahavi said, holding up a pair of binoculars by way of explanation. He read out an N-number.

"We need to know whose plane it is," Jayne said. "There's one with its engines running right now, not sure which."

"They're all US-registered. I've sent them to Joe. He said give him two minutes. He's getting the IDs."

"We haven't got two minutes," Jayne said. "We'd better—"

But she was interrupted by a beep as a message pinged on Zahavi's phone. He scrutinized the screen.

"It's Joe," Zahavi said. "That G600 is registered through a trust. But actual owner is a Leslie Crowther, a US businessman, he says. He's sending details of the other planes in a few minutes."

"Bloody hell," Jayne said. "Leslie Crowther? He's one of the businessmen who's been funding Nicholas McAllister."

"Unbelievable," Neal said. "What's he doing here?"

"He's been all over the news recently, talking about Iran and slamming the nuclear deal," Jayne said. "So Saba's meeting him on his jet—in Mexico. Why?"

Jayne had a huge surge of adrenaline of the type that she only got when she realized she was onto something significant. It sent butterflies tumbling around in her stomach.

But exactly *what* was she onto?

"Let's get over there, quick," she said.

The bench seat in the front of the fuel tanker was only designed for two people, plus the driver. But Jayne and Neal climbed up and squashed in alongside Zahavi.

"Go," Jayne said, a note of real urgency in her voice. "Park outside the hangar."

Next to her, Neal was on his phone, calling Federico.

As Rafael let out the clutch, Neal told Federico the bare bones of what was happening.

"Get ready in case it turns into a shit show," Neal snapped. "We'll need backup."

No more than fifteen seconds later, the fuel truck pulled up outside the second hangar.

Now Jayne could clearly see the tail numbers of the three aircraft in the hangar. The Gulfstream G600 was nearest to them, its airstairs down and a ring of orange cones around it.

As they climbed out of the truck's cabin, the roar of jet engines got louder. But the noise wasn't coming from the Gulfstream but rather from a smaller Cessna Citation parked at the far end of the hangar.

Jayne stared at the Citation, which also had an N-number on its tail and twin engines on the rear of the fuselage, like the Gulfstream. It began to move out of the hangar and across the apron toward the taxiway.

Because Jayne had been focused on the Cessna, she didn't notice a man who had emerged from the cabin door of the

Gulfstream until he was halfway down the airstairs. He strode vigorously toward them, wagging his finger.

"Go, leave, all of you. Get away from here," the man called out in Spanish, his black leather jacket flapping. "We have ordered no fuel. There are private meetings going on. Move, now."

Jayne stepped forward. "We need to speak to Cyrus Saba. I understand he is on this aircraft with Leslie Crowther." She pointed at the Gulfstream.

The man shook his head. "No. They are not on this aircraft. You have missed them. Now just leave."

"*Missed* them?" Jayne asked. A sense of foreboding overtook her, and she suddenly realized what had just happened.

"Is he on that other plane?" Jayne asked, pointing at the Cessna, which had turned off the apron onto taxiway five and was beginning to speed up as it headed toward the main taxiway.

"That's none of your business," the man said. "Did you not hear me? Leave now!"

Jayne knew what had just happened.

She turned to Zahavi behind her, who was reading a message on his phone.

"We've got to stop that Cessna. He's on it," Jayne said.

"That Cessna. It belongs to Ian Nettles, another American businessman," Zahavi said.

"*Nettles?*" Jayne asked. "Is he certain?"

"Yes."

"Shit. There must be some huge deal between all these guys." Jayne turned to Neal, who was doing a double take at the news. "Did you hear that?" she asked.

"Yes. What the hell's going on?"

Several pieces of a jigsaw puzzle clicked together.

"He's another McAllister supporter," Jayne said. "We've got to stop this."

"Federico," Rafael said. "He's got the rifle. He can shoot out the tires."

Jayne knew in that instant it was probably their last chance. "Tell him to do it, Neal. If he can get a few rounds into the engines, that would do it too. And get Denis to block the plane with the tow tractor."

Neal pressed a speed dial on his phone and rapped out instructions to Federico, whom she could see eighty yards away standing next to the cab of the aircraft tow tractor, holding his phone to his ear.

She watched, squinting a little, as Federico opened the cab door and took out his long sniper rifle with its inverted V-shape bipod attached to the barrel.

He dropped flat to the floor, got into position, and put his eye to the telescopic sight.

Meanwhile, Denis jumped into the driver's seat of the tow tractor. A few seconds later, the big box-shaped vehicle began to move.

At that moment, the man who had approached them from the Gulfstream began to sprint across the concrete apron toward Federico, waving his arms and yelling something unintelligible in Spanish, but clearly consisting of orders to step away from the gun.

Instead, the FBI agent began methodically squeezing off a series of rounds.

After about twenty meters, the man took a handgun from his pocket and, while still running at full speed, started firing toward Federico, albeit completely ineffectively.

Jayne didn't hesitate.

She took out her Beretta, dropped to one knee, took careful aim at the back of the man's legs, and began firing.

The first round missed, but the second struck the guy somewhere in the thigh region, and he went down full length, flat on his face. His gun flew from his hand and skittered across the concrete apron.

Meanwhile, the crack of high-powered, unsuppressed semiautomatic rifle shots echoed from Federico's position near the other hangar.

The tow tractor, driven by Denis, was moving swiftly along taxiway five in pursuit of the Cessna.

The Cessna was within fifty meters of the main taxiway when it suddenly lurched to the left. A second later there was a bang, and an orange flash of flame emerged from the exhaust of the port-side engine.

"He's hit it," Rafael said.

"Let's get down there after them," Neal said.

Jayne paused. "Wait a minute," she said.

There was one thing worrying her.

She turned, sprinted into the hangar and up the airstairs to the Gulfstream G600 with her Beretta in front of her, and flattened herself against the fuselage outside the aircraft door.

Jayne put her head cautiously around the door opening, checked in both directions and, on seeing nobody in the forward segment of the main cabin, stepped in, gun held at the ready.

The last thing she wanted was to chase after the Cessna in the belief that Cyrus Saba was on it when in fact he was hiding inside the Gulfstream.

Like the Bombardier, a table in the main cabin had been fitted out as an office, but there were no computers in sight.

Jayne moved carefully through to the rear cabin, checking the toilet as she passed.

The plane appeared empty.

She moved swiftly back to the front of the plane and checked the cockpit, also empty.

Jayne then headed down the steps, sprinted back to the refueling tanker, and climbed in with the others.

"Nobody there," she said. "Had to check."

Neal was on the phone, speaking animatedly in fluent Spanish. It immediately became clear he was talking to the airport manager, explaining briefly what had happened and requesting backup from the airport police and other emergency services.

"Just tell them make sure they don't fire on us by mistake," Neal said into his phone, his voice sounding tense. "And tell them it's urgent."

He ended the call and glanced at Jayne. "He's instructing the emergency services to get here as quickly as possible. Apparently they're on a shift change. Hopefully that won't delay them."

Rafael gunned the engine and set off across the apron, past the man in the black jacket who was now lying on his back on the concrete, clutching his thigh and visibly in agony. He would have to wait.

Three hundred meters away, Jayne watched the tow tractor swerve off taxiway five onto the grass and cut around to the front of the Cessna, which had come to a halt. It braked sharply and stopped sideways in front of the aircraft.

There were now steady orange flames visible from the Cessna's portside engine. Jayne could see Federico had hit both of the two twin tires on the rear port side of the Cessna, as they were deflated. That accounted for the plane's lurch to the left.

Rafael brought the fuel truck to a halt forty meters behind the Cessna. "That's close enough—this truck's full of fuel."

"They're going to have to come out of that plane," Neal said. "The whole thing could blow up any minute."

"Let's give them a welcome, then," Jayne said. They all

climbed out of the refueling truck and stood on the asphalt. She turned to check on Federico, but he was already jogging across the grass toward them, rifle in hand, now only a couple of hundred yards away. He would provide high-powered cover that must surely exceed anything on the Cessna, Jayne assumed.

As she turned back toward the Cessna, the plane's hydraulic airstairs began to open.

"I suggest we give ourselves some cover behind the fuel truck," Jayne said. "Federico can back us up while we try and negotiate."

"Agreed," said Zahavi. "The best would be if—"

But Zahavi was interrupted by the rat-tat-tat of semiautomatic gunfire from the direction of the Cessna.

Jayne's instinct was to duck down behind the refueling tanker until she realized that the series of metallic thuds she could hear were coming from the other side of the vehicle. A stream of liquid appeared beneath the tanker and began to flow across the asphalt.

"Move. They're trying to blow up the tanker," Rafael said.

The four of them turned, ducked low, and sprinted away from the tanker, which was giving them some cover from the gunman in the Cessna. They reached the shoulder of the taxiway thirty meters away and flattened themselves on the grass.

It proved a smart move.

A couple seconds later, there came a loud whoosh as the leaking aviation fuel ignited, including the fuel on the taxiway, creating a wall of flame. It was followed by a much louder explosion that sent flames more than thirty feet into the air, accompanied by a spiral of black smoke that became rapidly thicker.

The gunfire from the Cessna continued, and Jayne could feel the heat on her face from the blazing fuel.

This was a seriously dangerous situation.

The leaking fuel had caught light, but the tanker itself had not exploded yet and remained intact. If it did explode, as seemed highly likely, it was certain to engulf her and the others, given the short distance.

It seemed that Neal, next to her, was thinking the same.

"If it goes up, we're goners," he said. "Maybe run for it. We need to be much farther away."

Jayne hesitated. "I know. But if we break cover we'll be sitting ducks for the gunman."

CHAPTER FORTY-ONE

Wednesday, April 27, 2016
  Toluca International Airport, Mexico

Jayne cursed to herself as she tried to think through their options. The four of them were in a bind, that was for sure.

In their current position, the burning tanker was creating a blind spot for the gunman. If they moved, that advantage would go away.

But staying where they were seemed increasingly foolish.

At the same time, she felt certain the group on the Cessna would have to evacuate the burning aircraft very soon. The fire appeared to have engulfed the tail unit. To remain on board much longer would surely be fatal. The smoke and fumes inside the cabin would eventually drive them out.

Jayne glanced behind her. Federico was now lying on the ground behind a small grassy mound about thirty meters away. He had his right eye up against his powerful telescopic sight, and Jayne realized that if he could get a shot in, perhaps he could flush them out of the aircraft.

Above the loud crackling noise from the blazing refueling tanker, Jayne heard three explosive cracks as Federico fired the Barrett.

She guessed that he was aiming at the plane's open door, where the gunman must be firing from. Federico's .50-caliber rounds would cause enormous damage if they were on target.

Sure enough, the gunfire from the Cessna stopped.

Jayne glanced sideways at Neal. "Time to move?" she asked.

He nodded. "Let's join Federico."

Jayne checked with Zahavi and Rafael, and together they stood, bent double, and sprinted across the grass toward Federico, who was still lying prone, glued to his sight. They too flattened themselves on the turf.

"They're surrendering," Federico said, still looking through his scope. "Waving a white towel out the door."

"Really?" Zahavi asked, a note of incredulity in his voice.

"Looks genuine," Federico said. "First man's coming out the door, arms above his head. Want me to take him down?"

"No," Jayne said, an alarmed tone in her voice. "Don't do that. I want them alive if possible. Is it Saba?"

"Not sure. Another one's coming, and another. And the pilot."

This was it.

"Let's go get them," Jayne said. "If they run, you *will* have to take them down. But otherwise just give us cover."

"Agreed," said Federico. "Denis is also covering. I can see him behind his tow tractor. Got his gun out. He's got a line of sight to the aircraft steps."

"Where the hell are those airport police?" Jayne said. "We need them right now."

"Useless," Neal said. "But we can't wait."

Federico stood, picked up his rifle, and folded the bipod legs beneath the barrel. "Let's go."

Fuel leaking from multiple holes in the refueling tanker was now ablaze across an ever-widening area of the taxiway and had engulfed the vehicle. The group, all carrying weapons, gave it a wide berth as they moved toward the Cessna.

By that stage, the occupants of the jet had descended the aircraft steps. There were five, including the pilot and copilot in uniforms and peaked caps. All kept their hands in the air and were under the control of Denis, who had emerged from his position behind the tow tractor and was walking toward them, handgun pointing.

Jayne saw him immediately.

The short, dark hair was now flecked with gray, compared with the passport and other photographs she had seen, and the face was a little more fleshed out. But the slightly hooked nose was unchanged, and the black eyes flicked between members of the group that was now apprehending him.

It was Kourosh Navai, also known as Cyrus Saba.

Next to him were two men in well-cut suits whom Jayne recognized from TV interviews she had seen: Ian Nettles, a stocky silver-haired man, and Les Crowther, who wore glasses and was taller, with coiffured steel-gray hair.

Nettles had a bulky black laptop bag slung over his shoulder.

Jayne stared at Kourosh and suddenly felt a surge of emotion run through her.

The man who, together with his girlfriend, had killed her father was standing in front of her.

A part of her wanted to simply lift her handgun and drill multiple rounds through his head.

Another part wanted an explanation for what he had done.

Federico's mind was on more practical matters. "Cover me while I search them," he said.

Denis covered his colleague, who placed his rifle on the asphalt next to Jayne and systematically carried out a body search of all five men. He removed wallets, phones, passports, keys, and the bag that Nettles was carrying.

"Where are your guns and who was doing the shooting?" he asked.

"I don't have one," Nettles replied.

"Neither do I," added Crowther.

"Okay. I was obviously badly mistaken in thinking you were firing a semiautomatic rifle at the fuel tanker," Federico said, his voice taking on a hard edge. "Now let's try again, you assholes. Where are your guns?"

There was silence for a couple of seconds, then Kourosh finally answered in slightly accented English. "On the plane."

"So it was you firing the rifle?" Denis asked.

Kourosh shook his head. "No."

"Bullshit," Denis said. "What's in that bag?" He pointed at the black bag that Nettles had been carrying.

"Cash."

"Cash? Open it. Show me."

Federico drew his handgun and pointed it at Nettles while the businessman unzipped it and held it open. Inside were bundles of hundred-dollar bills.

Federico whistled. "How much is in there?"

Nettles paused for a second before answering. "A million."

"Whose is it?"

"You don't need to know that."

Federico raised the barrel of his Glock a little. "I do need to know."

Nettles cleared his throat. "It is funds I am transferring to this man." He indicated toward Kourosh.

"For what reason?"

Silence.

Federico was visibly running out of patience. "We'll get that information from you later. Give it to me."

Federico reached across and took the bag.

A thought crossed Jayne's mind. Which of them had been firing the rifle from the Cessna? She doubted the two businessmen had done so, and Kourosh had denied it.

Maybe he was lying, but on the other hand, was there someone left on the burning plane?

"Is anyone else on that plane?" Jayne demanded.

Kourosh, Nettles, and Crowther all shook their heads.

There was still no sign of the airport police. Jayne's immediate thought was that they should be responsible for checking the plane was empty, but that clearly wasn't going to happen.

"I'm just going to check," Jayne said.

She looked at the blazing tail section of the Cessna and hesitated for a moment. Surely nobody would have stayed on board? But then she ran over to the plane's airstairs and up to the door.

Immediately she saw the damage wreaked by the 0.50-caliber rounds Federico had pumped through the door with his rifle. The galley and countertop opposite the door had been destroyed, with large holes in the fascia, and cupboards left in a splintered mess. There were pieces of wood and broken glass scattered all over the cockpit to her left. The men on board had been fortunate not to have been badly injured or killed.

She looked right. The interior was thick with smoke, but there was still enough visibility. She sucked in as much oxygen as she could and took a few steps into the main cabin. There was no sign of anyone and the heat was intense.

It was then that she felt a breeze blowing toward her. She took a couple more steps and saw that the small emergency exit on the opposite side of the aircraft to the main door, out of sight of the group outside, was wide open. It led out onto the starboard wing.

Shit.

By now her lungs were bursting.

A rifle was lying on the floor near the emergency exit. She picked it up, coughed violently, and ran back out the main door just as a burst of gunshots rang out.

CHAPTER FORTY-TWO

Wednesday, April 27, 2016
   Toluca International Airport, Mexico

Federico was on one knee, aiming his rifle at the aircraft tow tractor, which was speeding away from them toward the main taxiway.

Jayne clattered down the aircraft steps toward him, holding the rifle, a Remington, and coughing uncontrollably.

"Someone was on the plane," Jayne spluttered when she eventually got her breath. "Emergency door was open." She erupted into another bout of coughing.

Federico was continuing to fire shots at the fleeing aircraft towing tractor and swearing violently as he did so.

The tow tractor, now traveling at surprising speed, swerved briefly onto the main taxiway, cut across a swath of grass, and disappeared behind an aircraft hangar.

"Bastard," Federico said as he stood up.

"Who the hell was that?" Jayne asked.

"No idea. First I knew was when I heard the tow vehicle engine revving up. Then it was gone."

"Whoever it was must have gone out the emergency door, jumped off the wing, and run around to the tractor."

"That's my fault," Denis said, a grimace on his face. "I left the damned keys in the ignition."

Jayne turned to Kourosh, who stood expressionless. "Who was that on the plane?" she asked.

"Some fish you catch, but this one, he got away," he said.

"Who was it?" Now Jayne raised her voice.

Kourosh just stared at her.

"He dropped this rifle," Jayne said, holding up the gun she had found on the Cessna.

"Forget it," Federico said. "We can't chase after him now, whoever he is. Hopefully airport security will trap him."

Jayne's instinct was not to simply let the man go, but she knew Federico was correct. They already had their hands full dealing with the other men, and the priority now was to get them on the CIA jet and out of Mexico.

Federico took the rifle from Jayne and examined it. He removed the magazine, pulled back the slide a couple of times, and a round dropped out. "It was jammed. That's probably why he stopped firing and ditched it in the plane. A lucky break for us."

"Hopefully not for him."

Federico inclined his head. "We need to get this bunch away from the plane and the fuel truck. It could blow up any minute."

He turned to the five men to his right. "Walk along the taxiway. Go."

Federico indicated with his gun in the direction they should take. Jayne and the others followed until they were even farther away from the burning plane and onto the grass shoulder, out of the danger zone and at least fifty meters away from the blazing refueling tanker. Even there she could feel the heat.

Jayne stopped just a couple of meters from Kourosh and eyeballed him.

"Kourosh Navai. That's you, isn't it?" she asked. "Cyrus Saba is the alias."

Kourosh's head didn't move but his eyes followed Jayne. He didn't respond.

"The gas platform attack off Tel Aviv," Jayne continued. "You arranged that, didn't you? And the Israeli ambassador. You've been trying to trigger some kind of war between Iran and its enemies—Israel, the US."

She still didn't know for sure, but her gut instinct was that the Swiss bankers and nuclear inspector Müller had pointed her in the correct direction. She glanced at the bag full of dollars that Federico was holding.

Follow the money.

Silence. Kourosh's eyes bored into Jayne's but he said nothing.

"You might as well tell me now, because it's all going to come out. You can tell me about your links to these two," she said, indicating toward Nettles and Crowther. "What's that all about? And let's go back a few years, to 1994, and the bombing of the Israeli embassy in London. That was you and your girlfriend, Zahra Moin, wasn't it?"

This time Kourosh's eyes widened involuntarily and his mouth half opened, as if to say something, but he checked himself again. "I don't know what you're talking about," he said.

"Yes, you do. That day in London, several people were injured. One of them was a senior police officer. He died sometime later from his injuries. Two people were convicted of the bombing, but they got the wrong people, didn't they? It was you and Zahra."

She held back from disclosing her father had died, not wanting to give Kourosh any emotional leverage.

"No, not me," Kourosh said.

"Unfortunately Zahra fell over and lost half of her locket that day. The other half of it was found at your parents' house in the UK."

"*What?*"

"Yes. Security services found half of it at the scene of the bombing. The other half was in your old bedroom, in a drawer, with a photo of you and Zahra inside it. Don't worry, we've got the evidence."

Now Kourosh couldn't prevent his face from betraying the shock he was feeling. It was frozen like a mask, his eyes were wide, and he seemed to be struggling a little for breath.

Jayne knew she had hit the target.

This was the man, without any doubt. And he knew that she knew.

"There are many collateral casualties in war," Kourosh said, appearing to gather himself. "I could tell you about a friend of mine whose aunt was a Palestinian refugee in 1948. She and her family were forced out of their homeland by the Jews and fled to Lebanon, only to have her legs blown off many years later in an Israeli bombing raid in 1996 during Operation Grapes of Wrath. She died of shock and blood loss. Have you heard of that operation?"

Jayne said nothing, although she did know something about it. Kourosh's story about his friends aunt touched a raw nerve somewhere inside her. It felt uncomfortable, perhaps because it was absolutely true—there were many collateral casualties of war. There seemed to be some kind of human tragedy on both sides behind everything linked to the Arab-Israeli conflict.

"I can see you don't like what I'm saying," Kourosh said. "I'll tell you something else. The guy who just escaped from the Cessna, the one whose rifle jammed, it was his aunt that was murdered."

Jayne pursed her lips. "What's his name?" she asked, as casually as she could. It was worth the question, but she didn't expect an answer.

Kourosh gave a flicker of a smile. "Nice try," he said in a level tone. "What I will tell you is this: if he gets out of the airport and away, it definitely won't be the last you'll hear of him."

"Sure," Jayne said dismissively.

"I'll tell you about another collateral casualty of war," Kourosh said. "And that's Zahra."

Jayne had been about to ask what had happened to Zahra, of whom there seemed to be no trace.

"What became of her?" she asked.

"She died in southern Lebanon in 2006—the house she was staying in was hit by an Israeli missile. One of many houses and many people to die during that particular conflict."

Jayne paused, wondering whether he was telling the truth or covering up for Zahra, protecting her. "How do you know she was killed?"

"Her friends told me the following day."

"Were you still a couple at that time?" Jayne asked.

Kourosh shook his head. "We split up after I moved to the United States. We kept in touch, though."

To Jayne, given what Zahra had done to her father, it seemed like some kind of cosmic justice that she too had been killed, although it wasn't satisfactory. Hopefully a better version of justice would be handed down to Kourosh.

In that moment, Jayne knew she was getting sidetracked. She needed to stay focused and get to the bottom of the links between Kourosh and the two businessmen.

"Now tell me about the arrangement you have with these

two men," Jayne continued. Logic told her the relationship had to be business-related. "You all like making money, lots of it. Just explain to me what you've been doing. It will be better for you to be frank. Otherwise we can make life very difficult for you."

Kourosh folded his arms and looked at her defiantly.

Finally, there came the wailing sound of sirens from somewhere over near the main airport buildings. Jayne found it hugely irritating that the airport police had taken so long to appear following Neal's call.

"The police are coming," Jayne said. "We can arrange for you all to spend some time in a Mexican prison if you like, or you can cooperate."

She turned and looked in the direction of the sirens just in time to see three police cars appear around the side of a hangar off the main taxiway and speed in their direction, followed by two fire trucks.

Nettles was shaking his head. "We have a purely business arrangement," he said. "I supply industrial equipment to this man, Cyrus. What he does with it, I have no idea. I believe he exports it to the Middle East. We were here to discuss an updated supply contract. Nothing more."

Jayne scrutinized Nettles. He kept rubbing his right index finger and thumb together in a nervous tic and looked deeply stressed.

"We have a similar situation," Crowther said, folding his arms defensively across his chest. "My business supplies his with a variety of industrial items. He sells them to his contacts."

"Bullshit," Jayne said. "You're not helping yourselves by lying. Don't worry, we'll work it out in time now that we know you're all connected."

The police vehicles turned off the main taxiway and headed in their direction.

Jayne beckoned Neal and Federico to one side and lowered her voice. "How will it work with the police?"

She knew Mexican officers technically would have to carry out the arrests since they were on Mexican soil and then make a handover to the two FBI agents. Federico had previously given them updates on negotiations between the FBI's legal attaché office in Mexico City and the Mexican attorney general's office and senior Mexican police officers.

"They will make the arrests," Federico said, also keeping his voice low. "But don't worry, these three will be on the plane home with us. It'll be fine."

"Yes, it's under control," Neal said with a nod in Jayne's direction.

"There's also the laptop," Jayne said, taking care that Kourosh could not hear her. "We'll need to go through it and get the files uploaded to Vic before those police think about confiscating it or something. It's urgent."

"Yes, I've already contacted Langley about that," Neal said. "We'll upload the entire hard drive to the analysis guys, and they can go through it much quicker than we can. They'll put a team on it. If it's password-protected they'll get around that."

"Good," Jayne said.

The police cars pulled up and three officers got out. The two fire trucks following them continued on and were about to skirt around the Cessna when, from behind Jayne, there came a loud bang from the fuel tanker.

Jayne turned just as there came a second, far greater explosion with an enormous orange fireball that sent flaming aviation fuel spitting in a huge circle around the fuel tanker.

Some of the blazing fuel reached the rear half of the already-burning Cessna, and a massive mushroom cloud of black smoke was blasted outward to within twenty meters of where they were standing, causing them to jump backward.

"We need to get out of here quickly," Jayne said. "This is going to attract attention. They'll see the smoke in Mexico City. People are going to ask questions. We don't want to be detained. I hear what you said about an arrangement, but if the politicians get involved, the operation could get taken out of our hands by the Mexicans."

Neal nodded. "You're right. I'll tell you what—you go get the Toyota, upload the data right there, and then drive it back here while Federico, Denis, and I work things out with the police."

He reached in his pocket, took out a USB stick, and handed it to Jayne. "Here. Plug this into the laptop, switch the machine on, and it'll do the job automatically for you as long as it gets a connection to a cell phone network. It's got a high-speed data connection built in. Should only take a few minutes. Quick as you can. Then we'll use the Toyota to take these guys back to our plane."

"I'll do that. But what about the contents of their phones as well?" Jayne asked.

"We'll do those from the plane once we're back on it," Neal said.

Jayne pocketed the USB stick. "And tell those cops to get an ambulance to the guy I took down outside the hangar, or else he'll bleed out. There's also the pilot and security guard tied up on Saba's plane who might need attention."

She set off at a run across the grass, giving the blazing tanker a wide berth, then continued along the taxiway toward the hangar where the Toyota was parked.

CHAPTER FORTY-THREE

Wednesday, April 27, 2016
  Toluca International Airport, Mexico

Pierre Fekkai dodged around the forklift, stepped over a pile of scaffolding poles, and made his way past two pallets loaded with building bricks.

He coughed heavily. The back of his throat felt as though it were on fire, and his lungs were sore. The smoke in the burning Cessna had been horrendous.

To his right, a construction crew was busy building a new hangar. He had noticed it while doing a reconnaissance tour after arrival, as was his usual habit. He had very quickly spotted that workers were coming in and out through a narrow gate in the fence past a hut manned by a security guard. The guard was checking ID documents for those coming onto the site, but Pierre saw there were no checks for those exiting.

It was a perfect escape route, and it meant he wasn't even going to need the false passport that he had brought.

Pierre had found a yellow plastic safety helmet in the cab of the aircraft tow tractor he had used as a getaway vehicle. It was similar to those being worn by the construction workers and gave him good cover.

Now, he pulled the helmet down over his forehead, walked confidently past the hut without looking at the guard, and made his way out into the parking lot. He continued past the parked cars toward two buses that were waiting to take workers to Toluca city center.

A few minutes later, Pierre climbed into the first bus, paid his fare, and took a seat next to the emergency exit at the rear, as he always did.

As he sank into the seat, the reality hit him.

It had been the worst of days. Things had gone as wrong as they possibly could have done.

That morning he had received a message from Beirut telling him that his beloved twin brother, Henri, had been shot dead a few days earlier when his operation in the UK had gone wrong. There were no further details, just a request to call his contact, Talal Hassan, for more information—something he had not yet been able to do.

The news had struck him like a hammer. He had always thought his brother invincible, and although they had been living physically far apart for some time, they remained in almost daily contact.

Pierre knew what the fatal operation in the UK had involved, because Henri had called him to discuss it. When he received the bad news, he had put two and two together and had realized it involved the same group of CIA and Mossad operatives who had then come here for Cyrus Saba and from whom he had just fled.

And now they had succeeded.

He had lost his client, something that hadn't happened for a very long time. Hassan and his superiors in Beirut and

Tehran would be furious—they were likely to take a large amount of flak over it too, he knew that. He was dreading reporting back with the news.

Everything had gone wrong.

Even his rifle had jammed, and although he'd used it to set the refueling tanker on fire, it hadn't exploded immediately as he had hoped.

The only things in his favor had been that the emergency exit in the Cessna had opened easily, allowing him to climb out onto the wing, and that someone had left the ignition keys in the nearby tow tractor.

Pierre glanced out the window. Several hundred meters away, a huge plume of black smoke was rising above the airport from the blazing refueling tanker and the Cessna.

He coughed again, triggering an agonizing burning sensation deep in his throat, and took out a handkerchief to try and stifle it.

Once he was safely out of Mexico, he was going to find out exactly who these operatives were, and there was going to be payback, no matter how long it took.

In the meantime, he had to decide whether to return to the United States or not. It might not be a wise idea, given they would be squeezing Saba for information. In some ways, France seemed more appealing. Maybe he should go back to the tailor's shop on Rue de Saint-Simon and pick up where Henri had left off.

But in the end, it would probably depend on whether Talal Hassan needed to involve him in any more operations inside the US.

* * *

Wednesday, April 27, 2016
  Toluca International Airport, Mexico

· · ·

After successfully uploading the entire contents of Kourosh's hard drive to Langley, Jayne drove the Toyota back along taxiway five, where there were now four fire crews trying to control the blaze that had engulfed the Cessna and refueling tanker.

She cut across the grass and discovered, to her relief, that Federico, Denis, and Neal were concluding their negotiations with the Mexican police inspector. The deal appeared to be sealed by the offer of a brown envelope from Federico's pocket, which the Mexican officer swiftly pocketed.

Ten minutes later, Kourosh Navai, Ian Nettles, and Leslie Crowther were sitting on board the CIA's Gulfstream in the hangar at the end of taxiway seven, hands in cuffs in front of them, their ankles secured with plastic cable ties, and their seat belts fastened. The decision had been made to leave the pilots and co-pilots in the hands of the police inspector. There was no point in taking them, as they were clearly simply hired hands. They would have to make their own way back home.

While the aircraft crew prepared for takeoff, Kourosh sat in silence, while Nettles and Crowther loudly continued to protest their innocence and threatened legal action for unlawful arrest.

As the Gulfstream climbed into the skies heading north out of Toluca, Jayne watched the spiral of black smoke from the still-burning tanker slip out of sight behind them on the port side of the aircraft.

Soon after, the seat belt lights went off, and Neal took the confiscated phones from the three men and disappeared to the rear of the aircraft to upload their contents to Langley for analysis.

Jayne, meanwhile, decided to have a look at the laptop

hard drive herself rather than simply wait for Langley to go through its contents. There was no way of knowing how long that would take, and she felt anxious to make a start.

The captives were confined in a group of four seats at the front of the cabin, forward from the four-seater dining table where Jayne and the others were. However, although the background engine noise meant they were out of earshot of Jayne's table, they could see what was going on. When she removed the laptop from her bag, Kourosh, who was facing her, exploded in a volley of curses in both English and Persian. The swearing grew exponentially louder when she walked forward and asked for the passwords for the device.

Federico turned out to be the key to solving that problem. He disappeared into the rear of the plane and came back with a black case, from which he removed a black device that was about eight inches long and resembled a handgun, but instead of a barrel had a blunt rectangular opening with silver steel nodes at top and bottom.

He showed it to Kourosh. "Do you know what this is?" Federico asked.

Kourosh evidently did. "You bastard," he spat. "Keep your Taser for your Guantanamo prisoners and your FBI torture chambers."

"We might put you in one of those if you're not careful. You know what it's like to have one fired at you, then?"

"No."

"Would you like to try it?" Federico asked, a wolfish grin spreading across his face. "If so, I'm happy to oblige."

Jayne watched with interest. Part of her felt she would quite like to see Kourosh suffer the extreme pain of being Tasered.

She knew what it was like—she had once had one fired at her as part of a training exercise while working with MI6, and it had been easily the most agonizing experience of her life.

She had been instantly thrown on her ass, her body had gone rigid, and she'd completely lost control. At the time it had felt as though her brain were on fire, and she had shaken like a jelly.

Jayne didn't believe in taking an eye for an eye, but since finally coming face-to-face with the man who had killed her father, she had struggled to contain a rising tide of anger and a whole lot of other emotions she was struggling to put a name to.

Right then, some form of torture felt completely justified.

"I'll fire it," Jayne said, almost involuntarily. She stared at Kourosh.

"You bitch," he said. "I'd rather give you the passwords than let you have the satisfaction of that."

Jayne mentally counted to ten. It was the only way she could find to stop herself from lunging at him.

But somewhat to her surprise, after a further blast of insults, Kourosh did indeed give up the passwords, just as Neal returned. He joined Jayne at the dining table opposite Zahavi and Federico, who had the bag containing the $1 million taken from Nettles at his feet.

Jayne started up the laptop, logged on, and spent the first ten minutes in a fruitless search for anything useful in Kourosh's email inbox and the myriad of folders and subfolders he had created on his main drive. She then switched to doing keyword searches across all files in the machine.

After typing in "Sinai," Jayne found a folder titled "EM" that contained a number of PDF maps of the southeast Mediterranean area. Two of them covered the northern Sinai area around El Arish and the Gaza Strip. Another showed the locations of the gas platforms and production wells off the Israeli coast, including the Samar gas platform hit by the drone. There were also three detailed large-scale maps of El

Arish city, the northern part of Gaza, and the area around Sderot in the southern Negev Desert, east of Gaza.

She turned the laptop so the others could see it.

Zahavi scrutinized the maps. "So these show the gas platform and the El Arish area where, presumably, the drone was launched from."

Neal nodded. "All for ops planning purposes."

Jayne toggled to the next two maps and hunched forward, studying them. "This is the Sderot area—where the president's heading. It shows the Cohen family's winery. And here's Gaza—if they're going to attack Sderot, that could be the launch site. It's only a short distance away." She leaned back and folded her arms. "What's the betting it'll be another drone?"

"I agree—our Iron Dome will stop missiles but not drones," Zahavi said. "It'll likely be the same drone operator as for the Samar."

Jayne nodded. "It's not difficult to get into Gaza from the Sinai. But who the hell is it?"

She stared at Nettles's bag on the table. "And is that million bucks the cash payment for the job?"

"Must be," Neal said.

Jayne nodded toward Kourosh, who was still sitting motionless facing them. "We could threaten him with the Taser again and find out that way," she said. "He obviously doesn't like the idea of it."

"Wait," Neal said. "Just do more searches for Sderot and Gaza and El Arish and see if anything else comes up."

Jayne tapped "Sderot" into the file search window.

But there was nothing apart from the map. Jayne tried "Gaza," but again there was nothing.

Finally, she tapped in "El Arish." The only item was in Kourosh's contacts folder and was for someone named Emad Madani. There was a cell phone number with a +20 prefix, for

Egypt. The reference to El Arish was in the address section of the contact file, but there was no street or house number, nor was there an email address.

"That's an Egyptian number," Jayne said. "Emad Madani. Those initials fit with the label he's put on the folder that contains the maps—EM. Check his phone. See if he's got that number on his call register."

Neal picked up Kourosh's phone and began going through the register.

"Nothing there," he said eventually.

It was at that point that Jayne remembered the small burner phone she had removed from Kourosh's plane.

"Wait," she said. She took the phone from her jacket pocket, inserted the SIM, which was from a US telecoms provider, and the battery and powered it up. Then she clicked onto the recent calls register.

There were only two calls listed, both of them made four days earlier. One was to a US cell phone number, the other to the Egyptian number for Emad Madani.

She then checked the messages folder on the burner phone. There was only one, and it was from Madani. It had been received the day after the call between them and consisted of one word: *Confirmed*.

Jayne leaned back in her chair and glanced sideways at Neal. "This Madani has to be our drone man. Let's get Langley to do some traces on him and on his cell phone. If these people are plotting an attack on Sderot, we need to move fast."

"I'll call Vic on the satphone now," Neal said. The CIA aircraft was fitted with a variety of secure encrypted satellite communications links.

"I can get my guys to check our files too," Zahavi said. "If Madani has been active in the Middle East, we may well have something on him."

Neal nodded. "You can use our network. Come with me." He stood and headed toward the rear of the aircraft to make the call, followed by Zahavi.

Jayne smiled inwardly at the sight of CIA and Mossad officers cooperating with such energy. It hadn't always been the case, in her experience. In fact, quite the opposite on many occasions. But throughout this operation, with their respective president and prime minister and other senior government officials potentially under threat, their interests had been aligned for once—and their careers were all at stake.

She refocused on the task at hand. The other material she needed to trawl the laptop and phones for was evidence of linkages between Kourosh and the two businessmen, Nettles and Crowther, and also between Kourosh and Garfield Wattley.

Although Wattley's guilt had been proven by Vic's barium meal sting, they still needed evidence of exactly what classified, top-secret information he had passed on, how long he had been doing it, and why.

First, she checked the US cell phone number recorded on Kourosh's burner phone against Nettles's and Crowther's phones. It took her less than thirty seconds to establish that the number was for Nettles.

Jayne then returned to the laptop. In the search box she typed in "Nettles Food Group," which she recalled from news reports was the name of Ian Nettles's business. Nothing came up. She then tried simply "Nettles," but again found nothing.

She logged her phone on to the plane's satellite broadband network and found Nettles Food Group's website, which listed six subsidiary companies under different industry sector headings. There were four under food, all in the US, one under drinks, also in the US, and one under engineering in Hamburg, Germany.

She decided to try the latter first and typed in the name, Optimal Mechanics GmbH, into the laptop's search bar.

It threw up a long list of items. Jayne scrolled down the list. There were several spreadsheets, a number of emails, and other assorted PDF and presentation sheets.

She began clicking on them. The first tab of the first spreadsheet she tried contained a list of twelve companies that included Optimal Mechanics. Among them were four of the Ring of Five names obtained from Heinz Müller and confirmed by Zeller and Steiner. The only one missing was AQ Khan.

Each company then had its own tab on the sheet. Jayne clicked on the one labeled "Optimal Mechanics" and studied the data that popped up.

It had a list of what looked like different items and materials running down the left side of the sheet. Across the top was a series of dates, beneath which were listed quantities, prices, and values for the various items. It was effectively an order book. The first date listed was in August 2002, and Jayne scrolled across multiple columns before arriving at the final one, dated only three months ago.

Jayne studied the equipment items, which were listed in some detail and quite precisely. They included high-strength aluminum, maraging steel, electron beam welders, balancing machines, vacuum pumps, computer-controlled machine tools, and flow-forming machines for both aluminum and maraging steel.

She was no engineer, but her sketchy knowledge of the nuclear industry had improved over recent weeks in the light of what she had been exposed to.

It was very clear to Jayne that these were all items essential to the production of centrifuges that could enrich uranium to the levels of purity required to develop nuclear warheads. The orders added up to more than $2.1 billion over many years. She assumed profit on that must have run into hundreds of millions, if not more.

She then repeated the exercise for Crowther's business, called Badminton International Holdings. Again, she found that although most of his business activities were in Silicon Valley in the US, he had another subsidiary company, Alan Technologies, a high-tech manufacturing operation based near Basel, in Switzerland. That was also listed on Kourosh's spreadsheet, where she found multiple components that she also had little difficulty linking to the uranium enrichment process. Crowther's order total was more than $1.3 billion.

These were all black market, illegal deals—and were against the terms of the Nuclear Non-Proliferation Treaty that Iran had signed in 1970 barring it from developing nuclear weapons, quite apart from the newer, much more recent nuclear deal.

And Kourosh Navai was acting as the coordinator through whom any number of companies were illegally channeling their components to Iran, including the firms owned by two American businessmen now sitting a few yards away.

Just then, Neal and Zahavi returned from the rear of the plane, having completed their calls to Langley and Tel Aviv.

It must have been the grim look on Jayne's face, but Neal realized immediately she had found something significant. "What is it?" he asked.

"It's those two duplicitous bastards, Nettles and Crowther," Jayne said. "Take a look at Kourosh's spreadsheets. They'll tell you all you need to know about exactly why these murderous scum have been arguing against a nuclear deal with Iran."

Jayne turned the laptop so they could see and explained what she had found.

"These tell you precisely why they're supporting McAllister's bid for the presidency," Jayne continued. "It tells you why they're giving him fistfuls of dollars and encouraging him to rip up the nuclear deal if he makes it to the White House —they don't want a deal when the alternative of sanctions leads to a thriving black market where they can make a fortune."

Neal nodded as he scrutinized the spreadsheet. "You've found the smoking gun here. No wonder they can afford to pay vast sums of cash to some drone operator in the Sinai. They're making billions out of Iran—it's blood money."

"Yes, it is," Jayne said. "The gas platform attack has already cost twenty-seven innocent lives and dozens of casualties—it could have been a lot more. And now they're trying to double down on it by ordering an attack on the memorial service for Moshe Cohen."

CHAPTER FORTY-FOUR

Wednesday, April 27, 2016
  Washington, DC

The atmosphere in the concrete, monolithic J. Edgar Hoover
FBI building at 935 Pennsylvania Avenue always reminded
Jayne of a slightly run-down public hospital. The decor was
basic, there was paint peeling off the walls in places, the corridors stretched forever and had a faint smell of disinfectant,
and the strip fluorescent lighting was harsh.

She glanced around the fourth-floor conference room in
the counterintelligence department, where a debriefing was
underway on events in Toluca and the wider operation to
track down the terrorists who had wreaked such havoc.

In truth, the cascade of revelations had initially sent the
FBI into something of a tailspin.

Once the CIA's Gulfstream had crossed the Mexican
border and was in US airspace, there had been a number of
conference calls between the teams at Langley and the FBI
building to prepare for the arrival of the three men appre-

hended by Federico and Denis. Jayne's impression at that stage was of an organization in some disarray.

However, the FBI team, led by director Robert Bonfield and counterintelligence deputy director Iain Shepard, now seemed to have a strategy in place to deal with the situation.

The wiry figure of Shepard and the somewhat more portly Bonfield were at the head of the table. With them were Federico Gonzalez, Denis Cotton, Vic, and Neal. Protocols meant that the two Israelis, Zahavi and Rafael, had not been invited—instead they were at the Israeli embassy, carrying out briefings and conferences with their own teams by secure video link.

The first element in the FBI plan, the arrest of the unsuspecting Garfield Wattley, had already happened earlier that afternoon. He had flown back from Tel Aviv on the instructions of Vic and Arthur Veltman, ostensibly for strategic discussions at Langley prior to taking up his role as the CIA's Paris chief of station.

But he had been arrested by Bonfield's agents the minute he stepped off the plane at Dulles International Airport.

"What's the latest with Wattley?" Vic asked Bonfield.

"Still locked up downstairs," Bonfield said, pointing with his fleshy thumb to indicate somewhere farther down the building. "But my Jerusalem team carried out an interesting search of his rented house over there—they found a burner phone and have cross-checked the calls with the help of Shin Bet."

The Shin Bet was Israel's notorious internal security service, the equivalent of the FBI or Britain's MI5, often better known in their home country as the Shabak, an acronym for their full name.

"Calls to Nettles, Crowther, or Navai, by any chance?" Jayne asked.

Bonfield nodded. "Apparently Wattley was cycling a kilometer or so from his house to make the burner calls at a spot near the main highway between Jerusalem and Tel Aviv, according to Shin Bet. Probably thought he could get away with it there. There were calls made to Nettles in the days before the Samar attack, before the Vienna Hotel Imperial shootout, the debacle in Zürich, and the attempt to wipe out the Navais in London."

There was silence in the room.

Jayne was not surprised at the disclosures, but nonetheless a feeling of deep disgust rose inside her that someone in a position of such trust could have carried out such betrayals that had cost so many lives and had put others in jeopardy— including Nicklin-Donovan.

What was puzzling her, however, was how Wattley, Nettles, Crowther, and Kourosh had joined forces in this international money-making conspiracy to try and provoke war between Israel and Iran and to have the nuclear agreement with the latter scrapped.

"Just one thing," Jayne said. "How did these guys all get together?"

"That's the other interesting thing," Bonfield said. He eyed Vic as he spoke. "We've done a lot of checking. It seems that Ian Nettles is Wattley's stepmother's brother. Did you know that, Vic?"

A slight tinge of red rose up Vic's cheeks. Jayne wasn't sure if it was anger or embarrassment. Maybe both.

"We knew that Wattley's parents had separated," Vic said. "And we carried out all the usual due diligence on him prior to his various promotions, but when he went to Tel Aviv, his father hadn't remarried at that stage." Vic leaned forward, his arms folded, and stared at Bonfield. "Anyway, Wattley was a high-class operator. None of us had reason to suspect him. I believe I'm right in saying that the FBI didn't have cause to suspect Nettles, until now. Is that correct?"

Bonfield, who had clearly been trying to have a somewhat clumsy interagency dig at Vic, inclined his head. He couldn't disagree.

"Anyway," Bonfield said, "that's where it all apparently started, together with the fact that Kourosh got to know Nettles because of his sideline business in Germany making these dual-use components that just happened to be vital for centrifuge manufacture."

"What was in it for Wattley?" Jayne asked.

"It seems some kind of profit share arrangement. Whatever the businesses owned by Nettles and Crowther made, Wattley got a cut—a sizeable one. Many millions. This was all down to money at the end of the day."

"So what's on the charge sheet?" Jayne asked.

"Apart from the charges under the Espionage Act, we're still in discussions with Brian to work out what else should go on the sheet. Probably corruption. I'll keep you all informed."

Brian Parker was the fresh-faced attorney general, who Jayne had met a couple of times. Nettles and Crowther were both facing charges that would almost certainly include conspiracy against the United States.

"Any update on the pilots and co-pilots of the planes?" Jayne asked.

"Mexican police confirmed they knew little," Bonfield said. "Just hired hands. They'll be on a plane back to Houston later."

Bonfield folded his chunky arms on the table and hunched forward, looking at Jayne from beneath iron-gray eyebrows that matched his hair, his double chin hanging down a little and his face serious. "I just want to commend Jayne on the work she's done, together with my team and those from Langley, and our Israeli friends. A first-class piece of work—great persistence and ingenuity, I have to say."

Jayne nodded her thanks. "Much appreciated, thanks."

Bonfield looked at Vic. "Do you want to update us on Kourosh Navai, or Cyrus Saba, whatever you want to call him?"

Vic nodded in agreement. "Yes, the Dark Shah, as he's been dubbed. We're agreed he will face charges of murder and conspiracy to murder in the United States relating to the attack on the gas platform and the killing of the Israeli ambassador here in DC. The Israelis are likely to charge him too, but I need to inform you we're also in discussions with the UK regarding a bombing and murder he appears to have committed with his girlfriend in London in 1994—that of the Israeli embassy and Jayne's father, respectively. We don't know how the logistics of such a prosecution will work as of yet, but we will inform you when we do. We're certain he's been involved in other killings over the years. Whether it will be possible to pin down evidence on those remains to be seen, of course."

It was with more than just a little relief that Jayne had heard about the British Home Office's interest in pursuing the Israeli embassy bombing aspect. Perhaps at long last there would be justice for her father. She just hoped that some kind of extradition agreement could be reached between the two countries to allow a trial to take place in London.

Veltman and Vic had briefed the White House and had been immediately patched onto a call with President Ferguson, who was at the US embassy in Tel Aviv and now fully up to speed on the fast-moving situation.

Meanwhile, Bonfield was preparing to make a call to Nicholas McAllister to inform him that his biggest financial backers were about to be charged and would face public disgrace. A press conference would be called as soon as the charges had been finalized. He wanted to underline the seriousness of the situation to McAllister.

Jayne wondered whether the news would come as a bomb-shell to McAllister or if he knew what was going on. Had the presidential candidate cranked up his opposition to the Iran nuclear deal in the knowledge that his financial backers would make an even greater fortune if it was scrapped?

If he didn't know, he should have—in Jayne's view, politicians shouldn't just blindly accept large sums of money without doing some due diligence and asking a few awkward questions about why it was being given and where it had come from.

Even if it proved that McAllister hadn't been a conspirator, surely his chances in the upcoming presidential election would be significantly damaged by the association, Jayne assumed. There would without any doubt be uproar among the wider political community and the US and international media, all of whom were certain to throw large amounts of mud at him.

Bonfield had promised that McAllister would need to go through some intense questioning on the issue.

"What about the funeral?" Bonfield asked, directing the question at Vic.

Vic detailed his discussions with Avi Shiloah in Tel Aviv ahead of both the funeral service for Moshe Cohen scheduled for the next morning in Jerusalem and the memorial service and burial due to take place in the afternoon at the winery near Sderot.

"Shiloah's assured me that action will be taken to ensure the security of the memorial service against any possibility of a drone attack from either Gaza or the Sinai Peninsula," Vic said. "If there's no certainty over that, the service will be postponed."

Shiloah had made clear to Vic that the key lay in cooperation with the Mukhabarat, the Egyptian intelligence service, to trace the cell phone used by Kourosh Navai's contact in

Egypt, Emad Madani. Relations between the two services had improved in recent times, helped by the assistance Israel had given to the Egyptians as the security situation in the Sinai deteriorated in recent years.

"The next few hours will determine whether this memorial service takes place," Vic continued. "But whatever happens, I'd like to conclude here by saying that we have taken massive steps to damage Iran's illegal nuclear supply chain—it is an outstanding effort. I would like to add my thanks to those of Robert. And I know the president is hugely thankful. We all know the Iranians won't stop trying to build nuclear warheads—they never have. This battle will continue—it's never-ending. But we have certainly caused a couple of wheels to fall off their wagon."

He added that all the German and Swiss companies that had been illicitly supplying equipment and components to the Iranian nuclear program would now face prosecution and potentially huge fines. The same applied to Zeller and Steiner.

Vic paused. "I'm also pleased to report that Paul Farrar is doing well and will return to the US in two days. It's a relief to all of us—he could so easily have gone the same way as Moshe."

He caught Jayne's eye. "I also understand that Mark Nicklin-Donovan, for those of you who know him, is also progressing well, and the hope is he can also return home to the UK before long."

"Good news," Jayne said. "That's also a relief."

Vic nodded. "By the way, Jayne, Avi sends his thanks and congratulations on the work you've done. He's very pleased and is hoping the developments of the past few days will confirm his position as *ramsad*. If that happens, I for one will be delighted. Despite our occasional differences, he will be an ally of ours in Tel Aviv."

"Let's hope so," Jayne said.

Vic let slip a thin smile in Jayne's direction. "We'll need you for a couple more days here. What next for you after that?"

Jayne shrugged. "Back to Portland, I guess. I need to spend a bit of time with Joe." She smiled. "We've got a couple of bottles of very decent Israeli red, recommended by Avi, that we need to drink."

CHAPTER FORTY-FIVE

Thursday, April 28, 2016
  El Arish, Sinai, Egypt

Normally, Emad Madani spent the hour before sunrise in prayer and contemplation, asking Allah for forgiveness and reciting from or reading from the Koran. It was usually followed by a breakfast of avocados, eggs, and lentils.

Today had been different, and his routine had been trimmed short because he and his men had a long day ahead of them.

Instead of prayer and breakfast, he had already left the basic apartment in central El Arish he used when in the Sinai and was behind the wheel of his Toyota pickup, heading along a steeply winding hillside track toward his warehouse just outside the city.

In the back of the truck were the same three men who had assisted him in the destruction of the offshore gas platform three and a half weeks earlier.

Following a series of phone conversations with his

contacts in Hamas over the previous few days, he had been given clearance to take his launcher frame, two Ababil drones, and a couple of booster rockets through one of the remaining tunnels that led from the Sinai Peninsula into the Gaza Strip.

Traveling into Gaza through the tunnels had become increasingly problematic in recent years. There used to be more than 1,500 tunnels beneath the fourteen-kilometer border between Egypt and Gaza, used primarily for smuggling food, fuel, weapons, and other goods after Egypt and Israel closed the official borders with the strip, and also for launching attacks on Israeli targets.

But Egyptian and Israeli intelligence and security forces had uncovered and destroyed the vast majority of them. Most recently, the Egyptian Army had pumped seawater into many of the tunnels to make them impassable. However, a few remained open, and a handful of new ones were being dug at various places.

The one Emad had been given clearance to use later today was small and narrow, unlike the larger ones that were easier to detect and were now mostly gone.

He knew the tunnel allocated for his use started from the basement of a house in the Egyptian part of the city of Rafah, which straddled the border with Gaza and was located a short distance from the Mediterranean Sea. It then ran about two kilometers north and emerged in the basement of another house in the Gazan sector of the city. It would be a difficult, nerve-racking journey on foot, but he had been promised helpers to assist with carrying the equipment.

Once through the tunnel, the plan was to head to the northern part of Gaza and launch the drone from a secluded spot behind a disused factory.

The mission was a dangerous one given the levels of Egyptian security in and around the border, but like the previous one, it would earn him and his colleagues so much money he couldn't afford to turn the job down.

The planned operation against the United States president and the Israeli prime minister and his colleagues—all attending a memorial service for Moshe Cohen—would also make such a devastating impact that it would never be forgotten. The international shock waves would be huge.

The orange glow in the sky to the east told Emad that sunrise was now very near. He rounded a clump of trees on a corner and arrived at a vantage point on the hillside from where he could see the warehouse that contained his drones and other equipment about half a kilometer away at the bottom of the steep track.

But instead of accelerating down the hill toward the warehouse as he normally did, he braked sharply to a halt, threw up his hands, and cursed long and hard.

The scene in front of him was one of complete devastation.

The flat-roofed concrete building that he used as his base in the Sinai and which housed his drones and other equipment was a smoking ruin. The roof and three of its four walls had vanished, reduced to rubble, and a fire was blazing in the center of the pile of smashed building blocks.

There came yells from the back of the truck as his men also saw the wreckage.

Emad knew immediately what had happened.

Even from this distance, he could see the building had either been hit by a rocket or a drone, or someone had rigged the building with explosives and triggered it. He suspected it was the latter. The damage was too precise and had left surrounding buildings untouched. That meant they had sent in a specialist small unit overnight to carry out the attack.

The three men in the back jumped out and stood next to his open driver's window.

"It's the Israelis, or their slimy Mukhabarat friends," Emad said. "That's the end of today's operation. How the hell did they know?"

That was the mystery.

How did they know?

Then he remembered. Amid the rush to prepare for today, he had left his burner cell phone inside the warehouse overnight by mistake—he had simply put it on a bench the previous evening and had forgotten it. That mistake wouldn't normally be an issue—but had he compounded his error by leaving it switched on? Normally he was very careful to turn it off and remove the battery and SIM card when it wasn't being used, and to keep it with him. Again he cursed himself.

Had they somehow gotten the number and tracked it?

That was the only possibility he could think of. But how would they get the number?

Stupid idiot.

He would have liked to go examine the wreckage and try to determine whether whoever had destroyed the warehouse had also found his weapons cache, including three highly valuable drones.

But that would be extremely foolish. He would likely be walking into an ambush or a booby trap.

"It could have been worse—we could have been inside," one of his colleagues said. "Praise Allah we weren't."

"Yes, praise Allah for that, at least," Emad said, his mouth set in a grim line. "We live to fight another day—and that's exactly what we'll do. Get back in the truck, quick. We need to get out of here, fast."

As soon as the men had climbed in, he rammed the stick shift into reverse, turned the pickup, and accelerated hard back in the direction of El Arish.

CHAPTER FORTY-SIX

Thursday, April 28, 2016
   Tehran

This time, Nasser Khan, the head of Iran's Quds Force special operations group, knew it was the end. He hadn't slept for two nights running. His head felt as though it had a fire burning somewhere inside it, and the primeval feeling of pure terror that had taken control of him just wouldn't go away, no matter how much he tried to rationalize that it was Allah's will what happened to him.

It was the third time that month that he had found himself sitting in the meeting room at the Office of the Supreme Leader, Ali Hashemi, with bad news to impart.

On the last occasion, just over a week earlier, he had been here to discuss with Ayatollah Hashemi the failure of an operation in Zürich against the Mossad and CIA team that was trying to destroy Iran's nuclear supply chain. The time before that, it had been the death in Vienna of the deputy director of the Atomic Energy Organization of Iran, Jafar Farsad.

He had expected the worst on each occasion but had been spared, as had his colleague, the minister of intelligence, Abbas Taeb. Their fates seemed to hang on no more than a whim, the mood Hashemi happened to be in. On those occasions, he was feeling merciful.

The Supreme Leader gives and the Supreme Leader takes away.

Now he knew it would be different.

Unit 910 leader Talal Hassan had informed him a few hours earlier that the linchpin of Iran's nuclear equipment supply chain, Kourosh Navai, had been seized by the FBI in Mexico.

Also, the two key nuclear equipment suppliers from the United States whom he was meeting with had been apprehended as well, including ROSTAM—Ian Nettles—a key intelligence source who was close to the front-runner for the US presidency. It seemed certain that ROSTAM's nephew Garfield Wattley, code-named SOHRAB, a mole inside the CIA and arguably an even more important intelligence source, would be taken down with him.

News of the disaster had come the previous evening to Hassan directly from a distraught VALENCIA, who had failed in his task of protecting the three men during their meeting at Toluca International Airport. The only upside was that VALENCIA had evaded capture himself and was now trying to extricate himself from Mexico.

Khan had gone into a spiral of despair when he heard the news.

It was one thing to lose the deputy director, Farsad, who could be replaced.

But the supply chain, the manufacture and flow of critical components, could not so quickly be substituted.

Khan knew it was the biggest single setback that Iran's nuclear weapons program had suffered since the Israelis and the Americans had deployed a computer virus, Stuxnet, that had destroyed more than a thousand centrifuges at Iran's main uranium enrichment facility at Natanz six years earlier.

Although he knew it would make no difference to his fate, Khan had at least succeeded in one task set by the Supreme Leader.

He had found out who was responsible for the gas platform attack.

This answer had also come from VALENCIA via Hassan.

VALENCIA had learned that Kourosh, ROSTAM, and the other US nuclear supplier had been secretly and cynically plotting to provoke a potentially devastating attack by Israel and the United States on Iran. They were apparently angry about the drastic slowdown in Iran's nuclear warhead development work since the nuclear deal was signed because it meant a big cut in their income, and they wanted to reverse that.

Their objective, VALENCIA reported, was to cause the nuclear agreement to be abandoned and sanctions to be reimposed. This would inevitably accelerate work on the illegal nuclear program once again and restore their revenues.

It was *they* who were behind the attack on the gas platform three and a half weeks earlier, with the objective of making it look as though Iran had carried out the operation.

And they were now plotting an even greater and more dramatic massacre—a drone attack that very day on the memorial service for Moshe Cohen, due to be attended by the United States president and the Israeli prime minister. The objective was to guarantee war.

Khan had been stunned by what he had heard.

Of course, in many respects, the idea of the US president and Israeli prime minister being wiped out was music to his ears.

But he knew the consequences, coming so soon after the

Samar bloodbath, would likely be enormous—the Americans and the Israelis could cause all hell to rain down on Tehran.

After sitting on the information and thinking about it for an hour, Khan had finally felt compelled to pass on this information to Taeb and to the Supreme Leader's office.

He had also made the decision to slip the information about the planned attack on the Cohen memorial service to an old friend of his in the Egyptian intelligence service, the Mukhabarat.

Not entirely to his surprise, the Egyptians knew about it already. They had been informed by the Israelis only a few hours earlier and were jointly dealing with it.

It was as a result of all these events that Khan and Taeb had been summoned to the Supreme Leader's offices on Azarbayejan Street that morning.

The two men had been sitting in silence for half an hour, awaiting the Supreme Leader. He liked to keep people waiting, sometimes for hours. The only thing in the room to look at was a portrait of Hashemi that hung on the wall.

It was unnerving.

The quiet was suddenly broken by the shuffling of feet on the stone surface of the corridor outside the room.

Then the unmistakable figure of Hashemi appeared in the door. His gray-and-white beard and the checkered black-and-white Palestinian kaffiyeh beneath his black robe were flecked with spots of brown, probably where he had spilt his tea.

He shuffled to his plain wooden chair, four meters away from the sofa where Khan and Taeb were seated.

"I hear you are delivering disappointment to me," the Supreme Leader said, his voice completely free of emotion, as he took his seat. His black eyes swiveled alternately between his two visitors.

He knows everything already.

"I am afraid the news is disappointing, sir," Khan said.

"Explain."

Khan did his best, frequently stumbling over his words, to describe what he knew of events in Toluca.

There was silence for some considerable time once he had finished his account.

"It is a story of incompetence," Hashemi said eventually. "The failures, it seems to me, are partly operational ones."

He paused and pointed a crooked, bony finger at Khan. "That is your responsibility."

"I accept the responsibility, sir." Khan lowered his head subserviently. "Sir, I humbly apologize and beg for your forgiveness."

When Khan looked up again, Hashemi had switched his gaze to Taeb.

"However, the failures are partly of intelligence too," Hashemi said. "We knew nothing of this plot by the infidels, the Americans, to seize our nuclear suppliers in Mexico."

"Sir, I can only offer my most heartfelt apologies for what happened," Taeb said. "We are working around the clock, every day, to prevent these things from occurring. Prior to that, we did have several successes thanks to our connection with SOHRAB."

The Supreme Leader folded his hands neatly in his lap. "Some things you knew; many you didn't."

He paused for several seconds.

"There is something else," Hashemi continued. "I have told you both before, many times, that despite the nuclear accord I have signed, I want to continue to develop our warhead capability so that in time, when we are ready, we can destroy the Small Satan and the Great Satan. Yes?"

Both men nodded in agreement.

"But I have also stressed time and time again—it will only happen when we are ready," Hashemi continued. "I have emphasized I wanted nothing to cause sanctions to be reimposed. So I was very concerned to hear the news that came to me from you, Nasser, that the same group of men in our supply chain who have now been seized by the FBI were cynically plotting to provoke Israel and the United States into attacking us. They wanted to trigger a war for their own financial gain at a time that does not suit me."

"It is shocking, sir," Khan said.

"Yes, more than shocking. These are people we trusted. Thankfully that threat has now been dealt with at the final hour. Yet I remain furious. Our failure to be aware of this devious plotting, committed by people who are close to us, people who are at the center of our nuclear supply chain, is seriously unprofessional—it is deeply worrying to me."

He reached over and pressed a buzzer on the wall behind him. A few seconds later, two of his private bodyguards, both of whom Khan recognized, came swiftly into the room.

Khan's stomach flipped over. He stared unblinkingly at the guards, now paralyzed with fear, unable to move. He had heard about this scenario from others. The buzzer. The guards.

This was it.

The Supreme Leader eyeballed Khan, then Taeb. "But it is above all a failure of intelligence."

Hashemi then pointed at Taeb. "Him. In the name of Allah."

Taeb's eyes widened.

One of the guards removed a pistol from a holster at his hip, flicked off the safety, and swiftly racked the slide.

Taeb instinctively raised his hands.

He opened his mouth as if to speak, but before he could do so, the guard pointed his gun at Taeb's head and pulled the trigger twice in quick succession.

The rounds splattered Taeb's brains and blood over the

beige-colored wall and sofa behind him. His body was flung back over the sofa, where his head fell sideways, revealing a huge exit wound at the back of his scalp, with white skull and brain tissue exposed.

Khan had felt something hit the side of his face and instinctively put a hand to the spot. He found a piece of bloody flesh stuck to his cheek, which he reactively flicked off onto the floor.

"Clean this mess up," Hashemi said to the guards.

He stood and looked down at Khan. "We will improve our intelligence network under a new director. I expect you to improve our operational capabilities in support of that. I want to move stealthily below the radar—not raise our heads to be shot at. Understood?"

"Yes, sir," Khan said, his mind now operating on autopilot.

"I expect you to avenge what has happened to our people," Hashemi said. "If you are unable to do that, consider what has happened to your friend here. Go. Get out."

With that, Hashemi walked out of the room.

EPILOGUE

Sunday, May 1, 2016
  Portland, Maine

Joe picked up the bottle of Yarden cabernet sauvignon from his silver wine coaster and examined the classy white label, written in both Hebrew and English. He had uncorked it an hour earlier, and Jayne could see he was now desperate to try it.

They were sitting next to each other at the oak outdoor table on the deck in Joe's garden. The spring sunshine felt warm and inviting, and for the first time in almost a month, Jayne could feel herself beginning to relax.

Cocoa, who was Joe's chocolate-colored Labrador, lay on the grass, seemingly asleep, although Jayne knew from experience that peaceful state likely wouldn't last long.

Jayne had been out for a long, eight-mile run that morning, her first since her run along the Thames when Zahavi and Rafael had stayed at her apartment. The exercise had cleared her head and removed much of the tension she had been feeling.

Just before she had set off, she had received two messages. The first, to her surprise, had been from her father's old archbishop friend, Michael Gray in the Vatican, congratulating her.

Well done, Jayne. Your father would be proud. Justice coming at last. It's been a long 22 years.

It certainly had been—he was correct about that.

The second message was from Vic, confirming that President Ferguson and the Israeli prime minister, Yitzhak Katz, had agreed there would be no retaliatory air strikes against Iran and Hezbollah in relation to the gas platform attack, thanks to the investigation Jayne had carried out.

However, there had been no such commitment by Katz regarding strikes on the Iranian uranium enrichment sites at the military bases identified by Farsad—Parchin, Bandar, and Lavizan. The president suspected that action would be taken at some point over the coming few months, and Vic thought it might be much sooner than that.

Jayne guessed he was correct. Based on their past record, the Israelis wouldn't waste time.

All of that had put a distinct spring in Jayne's step as she ran, and it gave her something to ruminate on, as she often did while out running. Today her thoughts had dwelt on the fine line between success and failure in this business, and even between death and life. A strike by Israel and the US on Iran or southern Lebanon would cost countless lives, as would the successful development of nuclear warheads by Iran.

The life-death distinction was also true at the individual level. The short email she had received that morning from Mark Nicklin-Donovan, telling her that doctors had advised him to wait another two weeks before flying back to the UK from Tel Aviv, had given her a sobering reminder that she should take nothing for granted in her line of work. Mark's recuperation would take some time once he had returned home, but at least he was well enough to write emails on his phone, which was many steps forward from when she had seen him in the ICU unit.

I got away with it this time it seems but have used up yet another of my nine lives, Mark wrote. *Which means that, as my wife has repeatedly reminded me, I probably have one or two left at most. Make sure you keep a few lives in reserve for your old age. Joe will need you. And remember, take nothing for granted.*

Jayne thought of Mark's note again now as she watched Joe holding the bottle. Sometimes it was the simple pleasures in life that made it worthwhile, not so much the great triumphs. And sharing a bottle of good wine with someone she loved was one of them.

"Go on, pour it," she said. "We've waited long enough to drink this—it's been a long month."

Joe turned. "A month? You don't say?"

"You're so amusing." Jayne leaned over and kissed him. "Time might have been flying for you, but not for me at times." She smiled.

"Sorry, you're right. You must be desperate for this. Give this a try."

He poured some wine into a glass until it was about a third full and passed it over to her. She held it close and looked down into the liquid, which was a deep purple-black color, then held it up to the light.

"Looks good, brilliantly clear," Jayne said. She didn't claim to be a wine expert, but she thoroughly enjoyed a good bottle and knew a little about what to look for. There was no sign of any sediment in this one.

She gave it a slight swirl and sniffed. The aroma reminded her of fresh herbs, although she would have struggled to pin it down to a particular variety.

Jayne took a sip and circulated it around her mouth. "This is superb. Worth the wait. Cheers, Avi! Well-deserved promotion."

She and Joe had received short text messages the previous night from Shiloah.

Use the Yarden to toast the new ramsad. Official. Just been confirmed. Thanks to Jayne—and my guys.

Joe poured himself a glass and sipped it. "Very good. Here's to Avi, excellent at his job and at knowing his wine."

Jayne took another drink. "We also need to remember those lost on this operation."

She knew from Shiloah that Odeya's funeral was the following day in Tel Aviv. There were also the two MI5 officers in London. She would have liked to attend Odeya's funeral, but the prospect of another trans-Atlantic journey was too much at that stage.

Joe nodded. "To those lost. And also here's to your father, and to justice." He raised his glass. "Let's hope we get it. A bit like this wine—it's been a long wait but hopefully worth it."

"Yes, here's to my dad." She looked up to the clear blue sky for a moment, picturing her father vividly as she did so.

Jayne felt a sudden strong bond with Joe. He had been in a similar position himself. A few years earlier she had helped Joe trace the old Nazi commander who once viciously tortured his Jewish mother in a concentration camp in southwestern Poland. He knew what it was like.

Jayne was still finding it difficult to get a proper perspective on the deeply complex, intense investigation she had just been through, with its tragedies and triumphs all mixed together. She knew that perspective would come with time, once the fog had cleared and she could view events from a distance. The run earlier had helped a little.

"How are you feeling now about the investigation?" Joe asked, as if reading her mind.

She gave a short, abrupt laugh. "Good question. Better than Kourosh, Nettles and Crowther, that's for sure. But in truth, I'm finding it difficult to put it into perspective. You know, although I mentioned the Israeli embassy bombing to Kourosh, I didn't actually tell him it was my father who died. I didn't want to give him the satisfaction, although of course he'll find out in due course when he gets charged. He then said something about collateral casualties of war, implying my father was one of those, and told a story about a Palestinian refugee who died in an Israeli bombing raid, and his girlfriend who went the same way."

"Well, maybe there is some truth in that—collateral casualties of war happen all the time, unfortunately," Joe said.

Jayne nodded slowly. "Yes, but what is a collateral casualty to one person is another person's war crimes victim. Saying my father was a collateral casualty implies his death was just incidental. But Kourosh and his girlfriend deliberately targeted that embassy and the people in and around it, just as he deliberately targeted the gas platform. Dad wasn't a collateral casualty, and neither was Moshe Cohen or Eli Elazar. They were all victims of targeted bombings. War crimes. It's bullshit. It's really been getting to me."

Joe shrugged. "It's impossible to put these things into neat categories."

"True. It's not worth trying, I know," Jayne said.

"Instead, focus on what you've achieved."

"Well, Kourosh is no longer free. When he's convicted, that will bring closure, which is important to me. That's enough in itself."

But she knew she had achieved a lot more besides. The investigation had yielded a combination of high-level rewards of huge political and deeply personal significance.

By contrast, the three coconspirators faced the loss of their fortunes and their freedom. The episode had put a big dent into Nicholas McAllister's presidential campaign too. It would be interesting to see if the Republican governor from Maryland could somehow ride it out.

Bonfield's team and the people at MI5 under Harry Buck had wasted no time in quickly cooperating and digging into Kourosh's background, including his bank accounts. Earlier that morning, Jayne had received an email from Buck containing two screenshots taken from an old statement for one of Kourosh's UK accounts, which had been opened in the 1980s.

I thought you might be interested to see these, Buck wrote in his email. *No explanation required. They will be added to the pile of evidence*.

The first screenshot showed an international transfer from an unknown payer into Kourosh's account in early August 1994, just over a week after the bombing of the Israeli embassy, for £800,000. The second, dated five months later, showed a payment going out for £452,000 to a firm of solicitors, with the reference being the address of the property in Henley-on-Thames that his adoptive parents were still living in.

The disclosure of evidence that Kourosh, the Dark Shah, had apparently used the payment for carrying out the bombing to buy a house certainly improved the chances of a successful extradition so he could face trial in the UK. But it would take a long time for that process to be completed, Jayne knew.

She took another sip of the Yarden. It really was excellent.

The door from the living room behind them creaked open.

Jayne turned to see Peter standing in the doorway. He stretched his slim six-foot frame and yawned.

"How's the studying going?" Jayne asked. Peter had hardly emerged from his room while preparing for his ongoing senior-year exams, and his face was uncharacteristically pale.

Cocoa jumped up, his ears pricked, ran over to Peter, and shoved his nose into his crotch, one of the dog's less endearing habits.

"Rough," Peter said, as he ran a hand through his unruly mop of curly dark hair. "Looking forward to finishing so I can party and get to the beach." He nodded toward the bottle of wine on the table and smiled.

"Wish I could offer you some of that," she said. "All the way from Tel Aviv."

He grinned again. "It might help. But I'd better get back to it." He turned and disappeared again.

Joe reached over and put his arm around Jayne. "I'm glad to have you back safely. I was worried about you working with the Israelis. They seem to spend their whole time with the needle on red in the danger zone."

It was true. She could see exactly what he meant. All the energy that Zahavi, Rafael, and Avi Shiloah possessed was focused on dealing with existential threats to their homeland. That was the entire raison d'être for the Mossad and stemmed from the circumstances surrounding Israel's creation after World War II. They were surrounded by enemies out to destroy them, and that wasn't going to change.

"They do," Jayne said. "But having that intense purpose to their work gives them a real meaning to daily life that sometimes we lack. Working for the CIA or SIS is similar, but it doesn't have quite the same edge."

"Probably doesn't help their life expectancy," Joe said. "Look at Odeya."

"No, but I can understand why those guys somehow seem addicted to what they do."

"You just need to tread carefully if you're involved with

them, though," Joe said, pursing his lips. "My guess is the Iranians aren't going to take the demolition of their nuclear supply chain lying down."

Jayne shrugged. "Maybe not. We'll see. They'll try and rebuild it. And if they come for us, we'll deal with it."

Joe glanced sideways at her. "Us? Sounds like you quite enjoyed working for them."

"They're good people."

"Avi will be reeling you in for more work now that he's got the top job. Then you'll have your fingers in every pie."

Jayne shook her head. "Fingertips, I'd say."

After two and a half decades working for the Secret Intelligence Service, the variety of high-level contacts she had forged across a number of other intelligence services and the reputation she had built was offering her opportunities she had never considered prior to going freelance in 2012 to help Joe on his investigations. She now had an indefinite US visa, engineered by Vic, and strong connections across arguably the three most powerful intelligence services in the West.

"I feel like an outsider with all of them," she said.

"But that's the whole point. It's why they need you."

"Hmm, maybe. I probably prefer it that way, to be honest —plenty of action, none of the internal politics." She paused. "But who'd have thought I'd end up working as some sort of disposable, deniable laborer for the CIA and the Mossad as well as the Brits? The invisible woman."

Joe grinned. "Jayne *who*?"

"But it feels meaningful, work with a purpose," she said. "That's important to me."

Jayne drained her glass and held it out toward Joe for a refill. He obliged.

Purpose was important. But it *was* the simple pleasures that were the best, Jayne thought as she watched the rich ruby liquid splash into her glass.

* * *

THE NEXT BOOK:
Book 3 in the **Jayne Robinson** series

The Confessor

If you enjoyed **The Dark Shah**, you will probably like book 3 in the **Jayne Robinson** series, entitled **The Confessor**.

To order **The Confessor** just type "Andrew Turpin The Confessor" in the search box at the top of the Amazon page.

I should mention here that if you like **paperbacks**, you can buy copies of all of my books at my website shop. I can deliver to anywhere in the US and UK, although not currently other countries. That may change in future. You will find generous discounts if you are buying multiple books or series bundles, which makes them significantly cheaper than using Amazon. Buying this way also means I do not have to give Amazon their usual large portion of the sale price—so it helps me as well as you. Go to:

https://www.andrewturpin.com/shop/

To give you a flavor of **The Confessor**, here's the blurb:

The horrific killing of four cardinals on a quiet street in Washington, DC. Deadly threats and intrigue at the Vatican. And Jayne Robinson battling against an unknown enemy to find out the truth for a desperate pope.
Intelligence operative Robinson is deployed by the CIA to discover why the American cardinals were murdered on their way to a top-level meeting at the White House—with a mysterious message to deliver.

At the same time, a British cardinal and key ally of the pope asks Jayne to help with his own line of inquiry—before it's too late.

The case becomes increasingly complicated as the Israeli intelligence agency, the Mossad, is sucked into the drama in a most unexpected way as the international political stakes rise.

And tension mounts rapidly as Jayne fights for her life in the West Bank city of Ramallah against plotters ruthlessly determined to prevent the facts emerging.

The Confessor, book number three in the Jayne Robinson series, is a gripping modern spy thriller with sharp twists that will stun the reader.

* * *

ANDREW'S READERS GROUP

If you enjoyed this book, I would like to keep in touch. This is not always easy, as I usually only publish a couple of books a year and there are many authors and books out there. So the best way is for you to be on my Readers Group email list. I can then send you updates on the next book, plus occasional special offers. There's no spam and you can unsubscribe at any time.

If you would like to join my Readers Group and receive the email updates, I will send you, **FREE**, the ebook version of another thriller, ***The Afghan***, which forms a prequel to both the **Jayne Robinson** series and my **Joe Johnson** series and normally sells at $4.99/£3.99 (paperback $11.99/£9.99).

The Afghan is set in 1988 when Jayne was with Britain's Secret Intelligence Service and Joe Johnson was with the CIA —both of them based in Pakistan and Afghanistan. Most of the action takes place in Afghanistan, then occupied by the Soviet Union, and in Washington, DC. Some of the characters and story lines that emerge in my other books have their roots in this period. I think you will enjoy it!

The Afghan can be downloaded **FREE** from the following link:

https://bookhip.com/RJGFPAW

The **Jayne Robinson** thriller series so far comprises the following:

1. The Kremlin's Vote
2. The Dark Shah
3. The Confessor
4. The Queen's Pawn (due to be published late 2022)

If you have enjoyed the Robinson series, you will probably also like the **Joe Johnson series**, if you haven't read them yet. In order, they are as follows:

Prequel: *The Afghan*
1. The Last Nazi
2. The Old Bridge
3. Bandit Country
4. Stalin's Final Sting
5. The Nazi's Son
6. The Black Sea

To find my books on Amazon just type "Andrew Turpin" in the search box at the top of the Amazon page — you can't miss them!

* * *

IF YOU ENJOYED THIS BOOK PLEASE WRITE A REVIEW

As an independently published author, through my own imprint The Write Direction Publishing, I find that honest reviews of my books are the most powerful way for me to bring them to the attention of other potential readers.

As you'll appreciate, unlike the big international publishers, I can't take out full-page advertisements in the newspapers.

So I am committed to producing books of the best quality I can in order to attract a loyal group of readers who are happy to recommend my work to others.

Therefore, if you enjoyed reading this novel, then I would very much appreciate it if you would spend five minutes and leave a review—which can be as short as you like—preferably on the page or website where you bought it.

You can find the book on the Amazon website by clicking on the following links:

Amazon US
Amazon UK
Amazon Australia
Amazon Canada

Or, you can go to the Amazon website and type "Andrew Turpin The Dark Shah" in the search box.

Once you have clicked on the page, scroll down to "Customer Reviews," then click on "Leave a Review."

Reviews are also a great encouragement to me to write more!

Many thanks.

THANKS AND ACKNOWLEDGEMENTS

Thank you to everyone who reads my books. You are the reason I began to write in the first place, and I hope I can provide you with entertainment and interest for a long time into the future.

Every time I get an encouraging email from a reader, or a positive comment on my Facebook page, or a nice review on Amazon, it spurs me on to press ahead with my research and writing for the next book. So keep them coming!

Specifically with regard to *The Dark Shah*, there are several people who have helped me during the long process of research, writing, and editing.

I have two editors who consistently provide helpful advice, food for thought, great ideas, and constructive criticism, and between them have enabled me to considerably improve the initial draft. Katrina Diaz Arnold, owner of Refine Editing, again gave me a lot of valuable feedback at the structural and line levels, and Jon Ford, as ever, helped me to maintain the authenticity of the story in many areas through his great eye for detail. I would like to thank both of them—the responsibility for any remaining mistakes lies solely with me.

As always, my brother, Adrian Turpin, was a very helpful reader of my early drafts and highlighted areas where I need to improve. I also had very valuable input from my small but dedicated Advance Readers Group team, who went through the final version prior to proofreading and also highlighted a number of issues that required changes and improvements—a big thank-you to them all.

I would also like to thank the team at Damonza for what I think is a great cover design.

AUTHOR'S NOTE

As an author, I really enjoy taking real-world global events and situations and building fictional stories around them. For me, this adds a layer of realism and immediacy to the plots, and also gives me a chance to dig into topics that are of great relevance to all of us.

Of course, these books are fictional, designed for entertainment, so the characters and the plots are all either from my imagination or used in a fictional sense. You should not read anything more into them, particularly when it comes to domestic political figures. I'm definitely not aiming to take sides.

However, in situations where the Western world is facing a threat of one kind or another, whether it's from Russia, Iran, China or whoever else, you should expect to find certain characters from those countries portrayed accordingly.

In the case of **The Dark Shah**, my protagonist Jayne Robinson moves in a new direction and gets involved with Israel and its arch-enemy Iran for the first time.

Almost inevitably, therefore, the overarching threat that forms the theme and backbone of the book is an existential one. As most people know, Iran has for a long time been trying to build nuclear warheads and has been clear about how it might use them—Israel and the United States are the prime potential targets.

In December 1979, immediately after the start of the Iran hostage crisis, Ayatollah Khomeini made a speech in which he dubbed the United States as the "Great Satan." In the same year, he also labeled Israel as the "Little Satan," partly because of its backing for the Shah, whom Khomeini replaced as the Iranian leader, and its close relationship to the US.

The labels have stuck and have often been invoked by other Iranian political and military leaders, as well as Hezbollah, the Lebanese-based political and terrorist organization which acts as a proxy for Iran, from whom it receives weapons, military training and financial support.

The nuclear threat from Iran is one that preoccupies Israel in particular, hardly surprisingly given the two countries' geographical proximity and Israel's small size. If a nuclear weapon was detonated in Jerusalem or Tel Aviv—only 650 miles from the Iranian border—a very sizable proportion of the Israeli population would be wiped out.

Therefore, the Israeli security and intelligence services, particularly the Mossad, are intensely focused on nullifying that threat. Over the years, we have seen a string of attacks on Iranian nuclear facilities and on key individuals, particularly the nuclear scientists and engineers who are leading the development of Iran's capacity to enrich uranium to the point where it can be used to construct nuclear warheads.

But although such attacks might temporarily hamper the Iranian effort, they have not so far stopped it. Neither have international sanctions prevented the Iranians from obtaining the equipment and technology they require. A healthy black market has ensured that Tehran has been able to get what it wants and gradually, its capability has grown.

These themes are the glue that binds this particular thriller together.

The action that seemed to carry most promise in slowing or stopping the nuclear program was the 2015 agreement between Iran on one side and the United States, United Kingdom, Russia, France, China, and Germany on the other. Under this, Iran undertook to cut or reduce its stockpiles of uranium and its gas centrifuges, vital for enrichment. It also undertook not to enrich uranium beyond 3.6 percent purity, sufficient for power generation but a fraction of the 90 percent required to manufacture a nuclear warhead.

The International Atomic Energy Agency said in 2018 that Iran was implementing its obligations, amid skepticism by the US and Israel. Then the US president Donald Trump, with the backing of Israel, unilaterally pulled the US out of the agreement and instead reimposed sanctions against Iran, the key objective being to force a change of regime from within.

Since then, Iran has resumed development of its enrichment capability, and indeed appears to have accelerated the process during 2021 with the recent election of new hardline Iranian president Ebrahim Raisi. It has recently increased the purity to which it is refining uranium to about 60 percent, according to the IAEA.

It is obvious that although the sanctions imposed by the US have hit ordinary Iranians hard by damaging their livelihoods and the wider economy, they have not impacted the enrichment process and the international black market has filled the gap. Iran has also made use of the black market to sell its crude oil to international purchasers, again defying sanctions, and by so doing, has earned revenues that can be used to help fund its nuclear program.

Despite the efforts of the new US president Joe Biden to persuade Iran to revive the nuclear agreement, which is one of his top foreign policy objectives, and to lift sanctions in return, this is currently looking increasingly unlikely.

There have been covert strikes against the Iranian nuclear enrichment process by the Mossad, including sabotage of its centrifuge assembly facility at Natanz and the assassination of its top nuclear scientist, Mohsen Fakhrizadeh, in Tehran. However these attacks appear to have only delayed the process, not terminated it.

In summary, the Iran nuclear threat is therefore likely to

remain a live topic for news reporters and thriller writers alike as the stakes increase on all sides. You can expect more threats against Israel and the West from the direction of Tehran, more covert strikes from the Mossad against Iranian nuclear facilities in both real life and in fiction—and possibly more investigations for Jayne Robinson!

In terms of the locations and buildings featured in **The Dark Shah**, some of them are real but are used in a completely fictional sense. Others are fictional, but may resemble real-life places.

For example, readers will search in vain for any evidence of an Israeli offshore gas platform named Samar, but they will find one called Tamar.

Finally, I should also mention that readers who are athletics enthusiasts will fail to find any record of an Israeli Olympic runner who later worked for the Mossad named Rafael Levy, as he is completely fictional. I thought it best to keep it that way!

All the best,
    Andrew

RESEARCH AND BIBLIOGRAPHY

A new topic for *The Dark Shah* in the shape of Israel and Iran has brought fresh challenges and required a lot of research, which has been interesting and enjoyable, but it has also meant dusting off some of my previous knowledge.

Traveling over the past year or two has been pretty much impossible, but I have been able to draw on a previous visit to Israel while writing this book. The trip gave me a good feel for the geography, the people, and the politics, and I've thankfully been able to supplement that with a lot of online reading too.

Although some of the chapters of *The Dark Shah* are set in Israel, the majority of the story takes place in Western Europe, the United States, and Mexico, and again, my frequent visits in the past to some of these places have proved very useful. For example, Zürich is one of my favorite cities and I've spent a number of happy hours wandering alongside the lake there, stopping off at a selection of the bars and cafés en route. I happen to know a couple of Swiss bankers, whose advice came in useful for the scenes set in the city.

For those of you who are minded to follow up this book with a little background reading of your own, I can thoroughly recommend as a starting point Barry Rubin's excellent guide to Israel, entitled Israel: An Introduction. You can find it at Amazon here: https://www.amazon.com/dp/B007Q27VNO

The Mossad is one of the world's most fascinating intelligence agencies. It is also regarded by many as among the most ruthless, and given the existential threats posed to their country, that may in some ways be unsurprising. For those who would like to learn more about the Mossad, I would recommend a book entitled Gideon's Spies: Mossad's Secret Warriors, by Gordon Thomas: https://www.amazon.com/dp/B017M4AA38

An interesting profile of a recent director of the Mossad, Yossi Cohen, can be found here: https://www.jpost.com/jerusalem-report/mr-charming-566680

Another profile of the Mossad and Yossi Cohen: https://www.haaretz.com/israel-news/.premium.MAGAZINE-more-ops-more-secrets-more-money-mossad-s-supercharged-makeover-1.6410934

I mentioned in my Author's Note that my fictional offshore Israeli gas platform, named Samar, does not exist. But there is a real one called Tamar and it forms part of a growing and hugely important Israeli offshore gas production industry that is giving the country self-sufficiency in energy. Those keen to learn more about this can find multiple articles online, including this article about the Tamar asset, which began life in 2013: https://www.offshore-mag.com/subsea/article/16761306/tamar-a-triumph-for-both-noble-and-israel

For those who think a rocket or drone attack on the gas platform is far-fetched, the Israeli government has a different view. It has more than once shut down the platform at times when a threat has been perceived. See for example: https://www.timesofisrael.com/amid-rocket-fire-israel-shuts-tamar-offshore-gas-field-as-precaution/

The Israel Navy has robust plans in place to protect the country's offshore production platforms, which are seen as prime candidates for attacks by both Hamas and Hezbollah. https://www.jpost.com/arab-israeli-conflict/navy-readies-defenses-around-strategically-vital-gas-drilling-rigs-off-israels-coastline-415006

The fictional drone attack on the Tamar platform was carried out using an Ababil drone, manufactured by Iran. More information about this type of drone can be found here: https://www.fpri.org/article/2019/01/low-tech-high-reward-the-houthi-drone-attack/

For those who are keen to learn more about the international black market in nuclear weapons technology and components, there are a number of articles I would recommend.

This article, 'Understanding Clandestine Nuclear Procurement Networks,' by Mark Fitzpatrick at the International Institute for Strategic Studies, London, is a few years old now but gives a good overview of how Iran got its nuclear industry moving in the early years of this century: https://www-pub.iaea.org/mtcd/meetings/PDFplus/2007/cn159/cn159_Fitzpatrick2.pdf

And this one, "The Centrifuge Connection," by David Albright, also gives a fascinating insight into the history of Iran's complex procurement network: https://journals.sagepub.com/doi/full/10.2968/060002017

A good analysis of how Iran ramped up its uranium enrichment program after the US withdrew from the 2015 nuclear deal can be found in this article from the Washington Institute for Near East Policy: https://www.washingtoninstitute.org/policy-analysis/moving-goal-posts-irans-uranium-enrichment-program

The Quds Force, Iran's foreign policy enforcement unit, similar to the CIA, is the source of much fascination, not least because of the lethal operations it has conducted on foreign soil. A good portrait of the organization can be found in the New Yorker here: https://www.newyorker.com/magazine/2013/09/30/the-shadow-commander

Some readers will doubtless recall the real-life bombing of the Israeli embassy in London in 1994. I have added significant fictional elements to my account of this incident, not least the death of Jayne's father Ken from injuries sustained during the attack and the part played by my fictional bombers Kourosh Navai and his girlfriend. However, it is worth noting that two Palestinian students, a man and a woman, were indeed jailed for the bombing in 1996, receiving twenty year sentences. It is also true that those convictions were widely seen as unsafe, with a large number of organizations and individuals campaigning on their behalf, and they were released in 2008-2009. No other suspects have since been identified. For those who would like to read more, I would recommend the following: https://www.theguardian. com/theguardian/2000/oct/21/weekend7.weekend1 and also this one in Wikipedia gives a good overview with links to more articles: https://en.wikipedia.org/ wiki/1994_London_Israeli_Embassy_bombing

The blackmailing of my two fictional Swiss bankers, Zeller and Steiner, forms a key point in the story as it gives Jayne a critical lead. For those who would like to read more about the real-life Swiss Nazi financier François Genoud—a big supporter of Hitler—I would point you toward the following highly damning article in the Philadelphia Inquirer by David Lee Preston: http://www.writing.upenn.edu/-afil-reis/Holocaust/swiss-and-hitler.html

This article, about the trial of Klaus Barbie, also details some of the work that Genoud did on behalf of the Nazis: https://www.jewishvirtuallibrary.org/trial-of-nazi-criminal-klaus-barbie

I enjoyed writing and researching the short cameo that Joe Johnson plays in this story, involving the Federal Aviation Administration headquarters in Oklahoma City. Johnson was eventually able to track down an aircraft and its owner, Kourosh Navai, who had taken advantage of the flaws in the FAA's systems to try and disguise the identity, ownership, and location of his plane. For more detail of how the FAA's systems make it difficult for investigators to trace criminals, read the following well-researched series in The Boston

Globe: https://apps.bostonglobe.com/spotlight/secrets-in-the-sky/series/part-one/

The above gives you at least a flavor of some of the sources and locations I have used in this book. There are of course many more, too numerous to mention. I hope it is helpful—I am quite willing to exchange emails if readers have questions about any others not detailed here.

ABOUT THE AUTHOR AND CONTACT DETAILS

I have always had a love of writing and a passion for reading good thrillers. I also had a long-standing dream of writing my own novels, and eventually, I got around to achieving that objective.

The Dark Shah is the second in the **Jayne Robinson** series of thrillers, which follows on from my **Joe Johnson** series (currently comprising six books plus a prequel). These books pull together some of my other interests, particularly history, world news, and travel.

I studied history at Loughborough University and worked for many years as a business and financial journalist before becoming a corporate and financial communications adviser with several large energy companies, specializing in media relations. I am now a full-time writer.

Originally I came from Grantham, Lincolnshire, and I now live with my family in St. Albans, Hertfordshire, UK.

You can connect with me via these routes:

E-mail: andrew@andrewturpin.com

Website: www.andrewturpin.com.

Facebook: @AndrewTurpinAuthor

Facebook Readers Group: https://www.facebook.com/groups/1202837536552219

Twitter: @AndrewTurpin

Instagram: @andrewturpin.author

Please also follow me on Bookbub and Amazon!

https://www.bookbub.com/authors/andrew-turpin

https://www.amazon.com/Andrew-Turpin/e/B074V87WWL/

Do get in touch with your comments and views on the books, or anything else for that matter. I enjoy hearing from readers and promise to reply.

Ingram Content Group UK Ltd.
Milton Keynes UK
UKHW022040190723
425463UK00020B/224/J

9 781788 750387